THE UNDINE'S TEAR

THE UNDINE'S TEAR

RISE OF THE GRIGORI BOOK 1

TALENA WINTERS

MY SECRET WISH PUBLISHING

Published by My Secret Wish Publishing
www.mysecretwishpublishing.com

The Undine's Tear
Copyright © 2019 by Talena Winters. All rights reserved.
Contact the author at www.talenawinters.com.

Summary: Calandra is the most powerful undine healer in three thousand years—her people's last hope for salvation. In order to save them from the humans they fear, she must choose between enslaving the man she loves or trusting a cryptic, seditious message left behind by the mother who abandoned her as a baby. But if she can't find the brother she's never met, she doesn't have a hope in Tartarus—and all the powerful healers go mad eventually. Can she save everyone before she goes crazy and kills them all?

ISBN (hardcover, new cover): 978-1-989800-07-2
ISBN (paperback, new cover): 978-1-989800-06-5
ISBN (ebook): 978-0-9947364-6-8

Cover design by Patrick Knowles www.patrickknowlesdesign.com
Edited by Ellen Michelle www.ellenmichelle.com; Denise Willson beop.ca
Author Photo © Amanda Monette. Used by permission.
Printed in the United States of America, or the country of purchase.

To my boys.
You make my life an adventure.

NOTE:

For those who like that sort of thing, there is a glossary in the back of this book to interpret unfamiliar words and world-specific concepts. Characters are also included.

Okay, I like that sort of thing. I hope you find it useful, too.

T. Winters
March 2019

Sirenia
Trinity
Silkie Lake
Pearl Bay
Perrynea Ridge
Shield of Atargatis
Margaret House
Dragontooth Mountains
Elpida
Perrynea
Light Lake
Mermaid Rock
Light River
Opal Palace

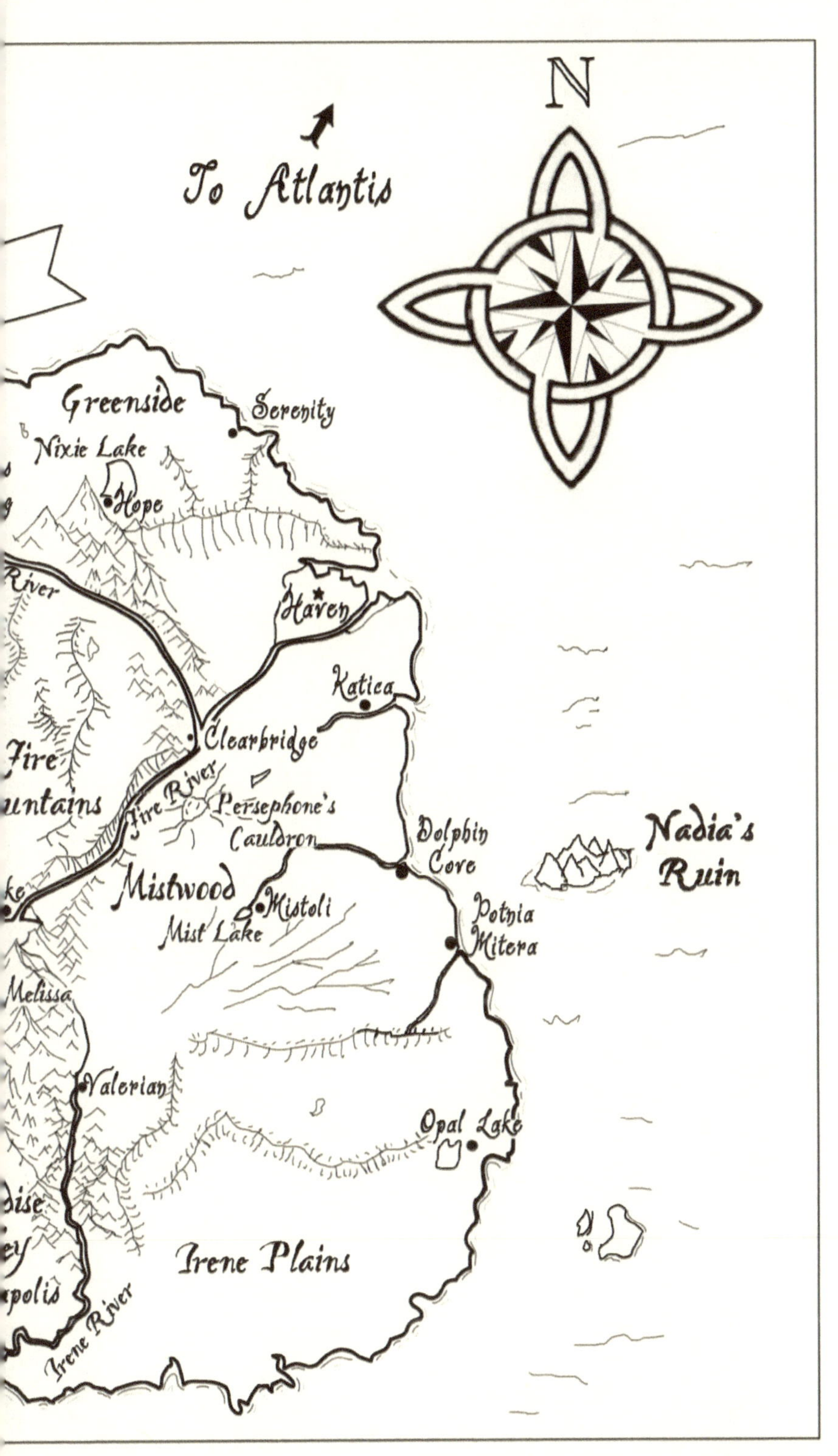

To Atlantis
N
Greenside
Serenity
Nixie Lake
Hope
Haven
Katica
River
Clearbridge
Fire
Fire River
Mountains
Persephone's
Cauldron
Dolphin
Cove
Nadia's
Ruin
Mistwood
Mistoli
Potnia
Mist Lake
Mitera
Melissa
Valerian
Opal Lake
dise
ey
Irene Plains
polis
Irene River

PROLOGUE

FOR AS LONG AS SHE could remember, Calandra had been running from the Madness.

She could hear it taunting her in the laughter of the other girls, see it lurking at the edges of her vision as she completed her lessons, sense it in the wondering eyes and hearts of her aunt and teachers when they thought she wasn't looking.

All the powerful healers went Mad. Even her mother had gone Mad and abandoned her.

I am the most powerful healer in three thousand years.

That's what Thea, the headmistress of the Royal Academy, said. And it was up to Calandra to heal the Heartstone and save her people.

If I don't go insane and kill us all first.

1

NIGHTMARES

The Opal Palace, Island of Sirenia
Summer AD 1794/4150 EK

CALANDRA HUNG SUSPENDED IN A black ocean. Empty water surrounded her in every direction, crushing her, rushing through her gills. The void pulled at her, diluting her sense of self. Not a mote of light intruded into the perfect, horrifying dark, and no matter how wide she opened her heart, she could not discern a single spark of life.

She had failed. She had destroyed them all. There was no one left but her. She would always, always be alone.

Panicking, she thrashed her powerful undine tail, its broad fins only thrusting her into more darkness. Her sensitive eyes strained to find any variation in this unnatural nightmare ocean.

That's when she saw it.

Light. Not the green of sunlight filtering through water or the blue of a bioluminescent creature. A speck of golden light bloomed before her in the blackness, swirling and expanding until it took the form of a man.

No, not a man. All the men she knew were human. Below this being's tightly muscled torso, instead of human legs there was a powerful, scaled, fish-like tail—golden where hers was a banded blue-green. Where feet should be were broad fins, flat like whale flukes—or an undine's tail. *Impossible.* A cloud of long dark hair surrounded a face with strong features, a sensual mouth, and a brawny complexion. As his form coalesced, the golden light flowed into his eyes until he floated before her, as solid as she was. Only, instead of the green irises of her kind, his eyes swirled with molten gold.

"Calandra," he said, and smiled. His voice was sweet liquid caramel, and the moment he spoke, the fear and defeat that imbued the darkness dissolved into a feeling of safety, security, and longing. "I have been looking for you, little lark. My name is Damon."

"Damon," she said, even though she shouldn't be able to speak underwater. "What do you want?"

"Why, I want to help you, my child." His eyes and inviting smile mesmerized her, drawing her in. The fear of the void could not touch her, not while he was here. His undine form, so disconcerting at first, now seemed completely natural.

She reached out a hand to touch him, ignoring the sense that something was not as it should be, yearning to let this feeling envelop her. "Will you stay? I've been alone for so long."

He held up his hand, still smiling.

"You need never be alone again."

Their fingers connected in a shower of golden sparks.

*

Thirteen-year-old Calandra kor'Delphine lay on her bed, legs tangled in the sheet, trying to determine what had awakened her. She blinked to let her eyes adjust to the dim light. Nothing seemed out of place in her bedchamber.

She smacked at her side table, and her hand wrapped around the broken Tear pendant and chain she had placed there before she went to sleep. She breathed a sigh of relief and sat up, reassured by seeing the broken dark green opal with its slanting, jagged corner still sitting where she'd left it.

Her mother's Tear—what remained of it—was safe. So why was her heart filled with a creeping dread?

She worked the silver chain of her most precious possession over her head, gently pulling her waist-length wavy golden hair free, then checked the rest of her room.

The small sliver of moonlight leaking onto the floor through the arched window had moved only a short distance since she'd fallen asleep, which meant it was probably still first watch. To her keen eyes, the silvery light easily illuminated her wardrobe on the far wall, her washstand and basin, her tidy desk filled with stoneworking tools and geodes, and her small trunk of belongings. A banana palm near the window was the only seeming sign of luxury in the otherwise spartan room—besides the room itself. Vaulted ceilings in pink marble and intricate copper lattices on the windows conveyed a certain amount of luxury on their own.

Then she remembered the nightmare and a shot of adrenaline brought her fully awake. The strange part was, that was usually how she woke from that nightmare—bolt upright, her nightdress dripping with moisture. But this time when she'd awoken, she'd felt unsettled, but not afraid.

What had been different?

Then she remembered the undine man. Damon. The first male of her kind she had ever seen.

She scowled. He'd called her by name, which no man should ever do. But he'd stopped the nightmare.

She shook her head at herself. It had only been a dream. A foolish dream. Still, it left her too unsettled for sleep. She thought about continuing work on the aquamarine she'd been shaping and imprinting before bed, but decided that what she needed to calm her nerves tonight was a swim. And she didn't want to do it alone.

Rolling out of bed, she padded on bare feet toward her rosewood wardrobe with its door overlaid in elegant brass filigree, not turning on the lightstone on the wall. The palace was on forced blackout to conserve energy, but she didn't mind. She didn't fear the darkness when she was awake. The darkness in her recurring nightmare was a vacuum, a void of chaos yearning to be filled, but the darkness of the real world felt more like a warm blanket she could wrap herself in. Darkness was security.

The blackout was more of a problem for the humans with their limited night vision, anyway. The only time she felt the need to light her oil lamp was when she couldn't sleep and decided to do some stone healing work at her desk to pass the time until morning.

The cool marble under her bare feet was refreshing in the steamy mid-summer tropical night. Still, sweat trickled down her temples and dampened her hair, collecting in the hollow of her back. A swim would be welcome, for more reasons than one.

With deft movements, she slipped out of her linen nightdress. She partially pulled her bone-handled diving knife from the woven sheath on her hemp swimming belt to check it. Satisfied that it was clean and sharp, she tied the belt around her waist and wrapped the ends of the cords around a brass button so they wouldn't catch on anything in the water. A sleeveless, natural hemp bodice and white linen sarong completed her swimming outfit. She combed her thick hair with a tortoise-shell comb, then braided it, tying it off with a cotton cord.

Holding her breath, she slowly opened her folding brass-worked chamber door, breathing a silent sigh of relief when she managed to avoid the click. Closing it again behind her, she crept down the hallway on naked feet, past her cousin Narcissa's door, keeping to the shadows to avoid notice by the guards that would be waiting for her at the entrance to the royal wing.

Calandra never used to have to worry about getting around guards here. At the entrance to the Heartstone chamber? Yes, but even that post was more of a tradition than an actual precaution. But recently her aunt, Queen Adonia, had increased security measures, posting guards in all the major palace hallways, such as the one hosting the bedrooms of Calandra and her two cousins. The queen had probably been trying to prevent exactly what she was doing—midnight gallivanting by novices and apprentices from the Academy, or anyone poking around where they shouldn't be.

This had been a great inconvenience for Calandra, who found walking the halls at night a good way to pass the time after her frequent nightmares. Fortunately, in a place where crime was practically unheard of, the sirens were somewhat less than vigilant. And, thanks to her special talents, she had a whole arsenal of tricks for getting around undetected, not least of which was that her mother's Tear shielded her from being detected by others who could use spirit. Like sirens.

Calandra stood in the shadows behind one of the enormous potted palms that lined the hallway, deciding on a distraction. She'd seen these two guards before—singers, judging by the silver three-pointed triquetra pins of rank, each with a single pearl, mounted on the left shoulders of their linen bodices above their communication stones. She eyed Calliope with her close-cropped black hair and Sandra with her regulation chestnut-brown braided ponytail trailing down the back of her turquoise-blue siren's bodice and repressed a sigh. She would have to get creative if she wanted to sneak past. Why were the lowest-ranking sirens always the biggest sticklers for the rules?

The two women crouched in the middle of the hallway playing a game of stones, their bamboo *deiktis* staves laid across their knees. Calandra couldn't blame them. She knew very well how long the night could be. Momentarily, she considered joining their game instead of pursuing her original goal, then changed her mind. She very badly wanted a swim in the canal, and these two would never even allow her into the courtyard at this hour, let alone outside the palace grounds. Not that she blamed them for that either—Adonia's wrath was not a thing to be desired. Which was why

Calandra would have to be careful.

Just then, Sandra stood, her *deiktis* casually balanced in one hand. Calandra caught her breath. Had the Tear failed her? But the singer only tilted her head to each side, stretching her stiff muscles.

"I need to use the lav, then I should do the rounds," she said.

Calliope stood, too, nodding and stretching. "I'll be here."

Calandra held her breath, waiting for Sandra to move out of sight down the curve of the vaulted hallway. Then she crouched and laid her hand on the marble floor tiles. Gathering earth energy into her gut, she focused it on a large terracotta pot containing a fronded tree a short distance down the corridor. Channelling her power over that distance pushed her limits, but the pot moved, giving a satisfying screech as it scraped on the marble floor.

Calandra grinned. Thea had been pushing her to explore her stone healing ability lately. Calandra was sure her mentor would be less than impressed at how she was applying her expanding power, but she couldn't help but be proud of herself—most stone healers had to touch the object they were affecting directly. What Calandra could do, transferring power through another medium, was rare. For her to do so at only thirteen years old was astonishing.

Fortunately, the palace guards didn't know about that particular ability yet.

Calliope snapped her staff into a defensive position and cautiously moved toward the sound. While the singer had her back turned, Calandra slipped around the corner and down the hall in the opposite direction. At the end, she hid behind a beam and dared a quick peek back. Calliope poked her staff into the fronds of the plant a few times, peering at it in suspicion. Calandra chuckled to herself and continued on her mission.

When Calandra had begun her novice training at age six, she had moved into the dormitory wing of the Opal Palace with all the other new girls who had been brought to the Royal Academy that year. But when she had turned eleven and been raised apprentice two years ago, her aunt had decided it was time for her to move back to her own apartment. Adonia said it was so the other girls wouldn't become too familiar with her, something about keeping a distance from the common folk. Calandra was certain the only distance her aunt wanted was between her and her best friend, Tanni.

Tanni had arrived at the Academy eight years ago, the granddaughter of a weaver from Haven who showed promise with Song. Novices were not yet differentiated by their specific gifts, so she and Calandra had been bunkmates.

On the surface, theirs was the least likely of friendships—Tanni was a year older and, with spirit as her only element, fated to become a siren cadet, whereas Calandra was already showing her magnificent potential as a healer in all three disciplines. One had been raised in a hut, one in a palace. Tanni was level-headed, Calandra was impetuous. They even looked opposite each other—Tanni was tall, wiry, and dark, sailing confidently into every room, while Calandra's petite frame and fair features made her easy to underestimate, or so the evidence would suggest. But they connected because of one simple fact—they were both orphans.

And Tanni had never once made her feel childish.

Calandra's mother had abandoned her when Calandra had been only one year old, taking her father with her. Tanni's mother, a siren piper, had died squelching a rebellion led by human women, of all people. And Tanni's father—well, Redeemed men made good guards, but terrible guardians. That's why Tanni had been raised by her grandmother.

Being sent to train as a siren had been the first step toward Tanni's dream—to honour her mother's memory by following in her footsteps and becoming a guardian of the island. Now, at age fourteen, Tanni was top of her class.

"I'm going to be the *despoina* someday, you wait and see," she'd told Calandra.

"You want to be Narcissa's Mistress at Arms?" Calandra wrinkled her nose. "Each to their own."

Tanni had shrugged. "'If you're going to aim, aim high,' my grandmother always says." She glanced down. "I'm doing it for Mother."

Calandra had no counter for that. She understood well the burden of fulfilling the unmet duties of one's parent.

As she carefully placed one bare foot ahead of the other on the carpeted hallway floor, she shook her head at the memory of the rebellion that took Tanni's mother. She couldn't understand what the humans could have been rebelling against. In a society as peaceful as Sirenia's, what could be the cause of discontent?

She reached the stairwell that descended to the siren cadet level and crept forward. Another guard at the lower end of the stairs was nearly as easy to fool as the others had been. This time, Calandra rattled the brass handle on a door at one end of the hallway, then, when the guard went to investigate, scurried in the opposite direction through the third-year dorm room door. Moments later, she crept between rows of bunk beds to where her friend slept, her curly black hair framing her burnt-umber face on the pillow. Calandra laid a gentle hand across Tanni's mouth.

Tanni's dark green eyes flew open but she didn't move. Calandra gestured toward the window with her head. Tanni shook her head and mouthed "No," her eyes widening in silent protest. Calandra gave her a pleading look. Resigned, Tanni nodded. She slipped off her bed and into her clothes, gathered her hair into a ponytail at the nape of her neck, and secured her own diving knife to her hemp belt.

The windows were unguarded, probably because no one considered that any student would be foolhardy enough to use them—they opened over a seventy-foot drop to the Atlantic Ocean far below. However, few students approached Calandra's talents. Or determination.

A small granite ledge below the window extended around the gently curving wall. Pushing open the well-oiled scrolled-iron lattices, Calandra led the way. Their toes gripped the ledge as they shimmied several spans along the wall, then carefully worked their way around the abrupt point that terminated this wing of the triquetra-shaped palace. At this elevation, they were too high for the salt spray from the pounding surf to reach them, but the dull roar from below was enough to muffle any whispers made by their bare toes on the granite. Air was not Calandra's strongest element, but she had long ago discovered the trick for thickening it when the situation called for it. She created an air cushion behind their backs as extra security in case they slipped.

At last, they reached a window on the opposite side of the pointed palace wing that led to an empty dormitory. Calandra laid her hand on the lattice and concentrated on the sliding bolts on the inside, then smiled as they slid open to her mental prompting. She pulled the grate open and clambered through the arched window with Tanni right behind her.

Once inside, they moved stealthily through the abandoned room to the door and waited. Calandra closed her eyes, focusing her empathic energy into the broken Tear hanging over her heart, then extended it into the hallway. Sensing the siren guard coming down the corridor on her rounds, Calandra put a warning finger to her lips and held out her hand for Tanni to grasp, bringing her friend into the protective field of the Tear. Once the singer had passed, they slid open the folding door and crept down the corridor—away from the guard and toward freedom.

Minutes later, flushed and giggling, the girls burst into the moonlight-flooded atrium garden known as the Grotto. The name was used ironically. While the stone walls shimmered with multi-coloured tiled depictions of undines among peaceful underwater landscapes, the only water in the courtyard sprayed in graceful arcs into the white marble basin around the statue of Atargatis, the First Mother, in *ichthys* state. Her effigy balanced impossibly on her tail fins inside a giant open cockleshell at the centre of the fountain, hands cupped around a polished crystal sphere the size of a child's head that represented the Heartstone—the Light of Atargatis.

The Grotto's real name was the Garden of the Mother's Delight, and it was the most intricately designed garden on the entire island—a masterpiece of the Gardener's House. It was also an ideal place for two young apprentices to find a quiet corner to confer, with direct access to the palace courtyard and, from there, freedom.

They had not taken more than five steps down the flagstone path when a voice behind them nearly made Calandra's heart stop.

"What are you doing here?"

As one, Calandra and Tanni turned to face the emotionless voice's owner—a human boy with obsidian skin and short, tightly curled black hair. He wore the leather baldric and short sword of a *taps* cadet over a fitted sleeveless coarse-linen tunic and dark breeches, and held a *deiktis* staff only slightly shorter than he was in front of him like a shepherd's crook—ready, but not in defensive position.

Calandra hadn't sensed him. She should have, but she'd been so caught up in their victory, she had forgotten to remain aware of other people's presence in proximity.

"O—Osaze!" Calandra stammered. "H—how nice to see you."

Dumb. Osaze wouldn't be allowed to have a conversation. Nor would he even be able to carry one on that wasn't strictly about facts. He was incapable of pleasantries like greetings—which, unfortunately, made him difficult to distract.

This particular boy had been their friend and playmate until he had reached the age of twelve last summer. At the age of Redemption, Daskala Lida, head of the Siren House, had determined that he was an ideal candidate for a *tapeinos* guard—the rank for human members of law enforcement—and he'd been sent to the barracks to begin his training.

Standing before them now, there was no flicker of warmth in Osaze's up-slanted coal-black eyes. A twinge of sadness pinched her. She understood why men needed to be Redeemed to the Mother. She had been told from birth how the *sklavia* bond protected men from their natural state of rage, ambition, greed, and all sorts of other evils that infected their minds once they reached a certain age. But still, Calandra missed her mischievous friend, the one who would save his coconut pudding for her because he knew it was her favourite, or who used to trick the koi in the Pool of Atargatis by throwing small brass coins into the water while they were feeding. The fish would blink stupidly at the shiny objects, probably wondering if they could eat them. Or they would have, if fish could blink. Somehow, with his quick smile and imaginative stories, Osaze had made her *see* them blinking, whether they did or not.

Since he'd been Redeemed, she had never once seen Osaze smile.

Tanni recovered first.

"Hello, Osaze," she said as though she had expected to see him there all along. "We are doing an errand for Daskala Thea. She asked us to retrieve a set of datastones from the Archive. Please excuse us so we may continue."

Tanni crossed her arms and stretched to her full height, which still meant she had to tip her chin up to look the tall teenage boy in the face. The lie was a bit of a stretch. The Grotto was nowhere near the route between the Archive and the headmistress's rooms. Calandra hoped the mention of Thea's name would be enough for Osaze to let them go. Why was he even on duty, anyway? Wasn't he a little young for that?

Then again, it was only First Watch, and the Redeemed boy would be considered much more reliable than any undine girl that age—as evidenced by the situation Calandra and Tanni were now in. She blushed as she made the mental comparison.

Osaze's brow furrowed slightly and he shifted his hands on his *deiktis*.

"Daskala Thea is in the Archive. I just saw her there. Why would she send for you to retrieve something she could easily find herself?" He reached for the small conch shell whistle attached to his baldric, probably to alert whichever siren he was reporting to that night.

Calandra's gut clenched in alarm and she froze. This was their third infraction in as many months. She shuddered to think what the punishment would be if they were caught again. Her brain scrambled for a solution, but she came up blank.

Calandra was about to put up a hand to snatch the conch shell from Osaze, for lack of a better plan, when Tanni once again came to the rescue. She placed her forefinger on his forehead and sang a short sequence of notes. Osaze froze with his arm in mid-air, blinking rapidly.

"What did you do?" Calandra watched as Osaze's blank expression transformed into one of confusion.

"Something I read in one of Mother's old datastone texts. It makes someone forget what they just saw."

Osaze looked around him, then at the girls. "What did you do to me?"

Calandra's chest constricted. "And if that's not what you did, what might it be?" She glanced from the frowning Osaze to her friend.

Tanni stared at the boy, her face pale. "I'm not sure. Maybe I Released him?"

The words hit Calandra like a glass of cold water. That Song wasn't even taught until sixth year.

"Chains of Prometheus! You did *what*?"

"I'm sorry," Tanni whispered. "I can't afford another demerit. I was only trying to give us a chance to get away."

"You and your books. Do you know how to Redeem him again?"

Tanni shook her head. "No. I'm not even sure how I did *this*." She indicated Osaze with splayed hands, then bit her lip. "Oh, this is so bad."

Calandra sighed. "You know we'll get more than a demerit for this, right?"

Tanni's face was pure misery. She glanced at Osaze and took a step back. Calandra knew why—a Redeemed male was safe. An Unredeemed male was unpredictable and volatile.

Osaze looked around as though trying to figure out where he was. Calandra could sense distress welling up in him like a volcano about to erupt. A siren guard—her calm, bored presence gave her away—made her way toward them down the colonnade that edged the Grotto, obscured only by the thick vegetation.

Calandra snatched Osaze's hand and looked him in the eyes.

"Osaze, it's me, Calandra. You know me, right?"

She infused the words with warmth and calmness, tamping down her own anxiety so she could also project calm through their physical connection.

Osaze's clouded expression cleared slightly, and his inner turmoil—which had nearly overwhelmed Calandra on contact—dissipated somewhat.

"Calandra? What's happening?"

"A . . ." How could she explain that he'd been separated from his emotions and will for a year, and had accidentally been reunited with them by a moment of panic? "A mistake. But we'll fix it. Can you trust me and come with me?"

Osaze's emotions still roiled slowly, and Calandra thought he might be on the verge of tears. But he nodded. So did Calandra.

"Good."

She didn't let go of his hand—it was easier to project calm when they were touching, and frankly, it was easier to *be* calm. She pulled him back into the shadows of the banana palm, then turned to Tanni. "I might be able to figure out how to fix this, but I need a safe place to work it out. I know where we can go. Someplace they'll never think to look. And we might still be able to go swimming."

Tanni huddled under the tree beside them. She looked worried. She could probably hear, or at least sense, the approaching guard by now.

"Where?"

Calandra took her friend's hand in her free one. "The Mother's Heart."

Tanni shook her head in disbelief, glancing toward the statue as though praying for patience. She turned to Calandra.

"You're insane. But you're probably right. Once we're in there, no one will bother us. It's the getting in that concerns me."

Calandra smiled. "Leave that to me."

2

THE MOTHER'S HEART

THE OPAL PALACE WAS BUILT in the shape of the Holy Triquetra, representative of Atargatis herself—each of the three wings were in the shape of an *ichthys* fish conjoined in an infinite path. A ring of indoor and outdoor terraces and gardens replicated the circle that bound the symbol in unity.

At the core of the structure was the Mother's Heart, a vast tricorn-shaped marble chamber tiled in rock crystal that was founded in the bedrock below sea level. The room housed the Heartstone—the gift of Atargatis and power source for everything on the island, the most important of which was the barrier that protected Sirenia from unwanted eyes.

Access to the chamber was well guarded at the upper levels. But once you got past the entry point to the staircase that led you down six storeys—where one could access the pool of water that perpetually filled the bottom of the chamber—not so much.

Calandra had sneaked down to the chamber so many times that getting past the guards at the top of the stairs with two extra people hardly even required her to be creative. So far, no one had discovered her solo nighttime forays into the depths of the palace. It was only when she was with Tanni that trouble seemed to find her. Or rather, she found it, and dragged Tanni into it with her. No wonder Tanni hadn't wanted to come.

By the time Calandra, Tanni, and Osaze reached the antechamber that opened into the Mother's Heart, Calandra was seriously beginning to regret her impetuous decision to sneak out of bed tonight.

All she'd wanted was a swim to clear her head and help her forget the unsettling undine man in her dream. But now she had a major problem, and his hand was growing sweaty in her own. She could think of no quieter place to solve it than the tunnels that serviced the base of the Mother's

13

Heart chamber—not even the servants went there unless they were assigned to clean the Mother's Pool. The few people allowed to go there rarely felt that admiring the beauty of the Stone without a glass barrier in the way was worth the effort of the multiple flights of stairs required to enter the chamber. It was one of Calandra's favourite escapes.

Tanni leaned against the wall of the small room and caught her breath. Her normally placid expression was pinched in frustration and flushed with exertion. She looked at their male companion, who bore the expression of someone determined not to panic—or perhaps determined not to throw up.

"I hope whatever you wanted to talk about was worth this, Calandra kor'Delphine."

Calandra gave her friend a sharp look. "I'm not the one who Released a *taps*."

"Well, I'm not the one who dragged me out of bed in the middle of the night," Tanni snapped back, crossing her arms.

Calandra bit her lip on her retort and glanced at Osaze, who stood looking around the small chamber, clenching and unclenching his fists. Releasing a human without authorization was a capital crime for adults. She wondered what their punishment would be.

"I know. I, uh, I . . . oh, the whole thing seems so stupid now. All I've done is make it worse. This isn't going to solve *anything*."

When she saw the distress on Calandra's face, Tanni stepped forward, uncrossing her arms.

"Solve what, Cali? What are you talking about?" Her expression softened. "Did you have another nightmare?"

Calandra dipped her chin. Tanni was the only one she'd told about the nightmares. Her friend understood the fear as well as Calandra did. She thought about telling Tanni about the man, but decided that now was not the time. The man hadn't been part of the nightmare—he'd helped it go away.

"Yes, but that's not what this is about."

Tanni's brow furrowed. "What, then?"

Calandra took a deep breath, then beckoned for her friend to follow her. She led the way to the small arch that connected the access chamber to the Mother's Heart. Warm, moist air met them as they stepped onto the small platform suspended about a storey above the water below. The thousands of crystals lining the walls of the tricorn chamber gathered the silvery light coming in through the glass ceiling and amplified it, reflecting it in a symphony of luminescence. On a sunny day, the sun's rays would set the entire column on fire. On Summer Solstice, when the sun stood directly above the chamber, the light became an entity you could almost feel.

Suspended by golden spokes at about three-quarters of the chamber's impressive height and encased in a transparent crystal orb several fingers thick was the pulsing Heartstone, an enormous spherical fire opal. Over half the surface of the crystal was marred with cracks and blackened areas, and the light of the opal within was subdued, like a fire that has burned to red-hot coals. It was still fairly bright, but only a shadow in comparison with its former glory.

Tanni stepped up beside her and drew in a soft gasp, the light of the Heartstone reflecting in her dark green eyes.

"The Stone—it's getting worse."

There was a painting in the Great Hall of how it used to look, blinding at any time of the day. Now, her people's most enduring symbol of hope and longevity was scarred and broken from millennia of use.

"Aunt Adonia means for me to heal it."

She turned back to the stone and blinked at it, overwhelmed by the enormity of the task.

"What?" Tanni's voice was filled with disbelief. "Our strongest stone healers and panaceas for three thousand years have not been able to heal this, and she expects you can?"

Calandra nodded. "She thinks I might be strong enough to heal the stone on my own, or at least lead the circle that finally does it. She intends to bond a consort to me as soon as I come of age."

Tanni shook her head. "With all due respect to the queen, I think she's cracked. I mean, I know you're powerful, but no one is that powerful. Not even after being bonded."

Calandra faced Tanni. "Thea thinks I am."

"Oh." Tanni bit her lip at the mention of the Academy's headmistress. "But aren't they worried you might bear a child?"

The unspoken question hung between them, as always when the subject of her inevitable bonding came up. *Aren't they worried you'll go Mad like your mother did?*

No one was exactly sure what caused the Madness, but most of the healers who succumbed had two things in common—they were extremely powerful, usually panaceas like Calandra, able to work with stones, plants, and animals. And they had often recently had children.

That didn't explain the case of Lydia, a siren who had gone Mad over a millennia ago and had drowned half of the island's humans before being confined to the Abyss. Sirens affected by the Madness were extremely rare, though. Calandra had never heard of another.

It also didn't explain Thea, a powerful panacea with three adult daughters and full possession of her wits. But she was the exception, not the rule.

Calandra shrugged. She knew that Tanni was as worried about her potential future as she was. But every healer designated to heal the Heartstone had to be bonded. She didn't know why.

"Perhaps Adonia isn't crazy, just desperate."

She glanced at Osaze, who had slumped against the far wall and was watching them intently with fever-bright eyes, his jaw clenched. She leaned closer to Tanni and dropped her voice.

"A ship got through the barrier last week."

Tanni gaped.

"I heard about it this morning," Calandra whispered. "The barrier has been having outages. It was only a small one, a fishing vessel, no women, so they Redeemed the men and put them up for auction down in Haven."

"That's why Adonia announced the blackout on lightstones," said Tanni, realization dawning on her face.

Calandra nodded. Over the last several years, there had been bans on more and more devices that drew power from the Heartstone. The latest measure meant a return to oil lamps for everyone in the trades, except for those who did the bulk of their work at night, like bakers and sweepers. Even people in the palace and other government positions were restricted to the use of a few hours per evening, and then only for official tasks. Some devices, like quartz datastone readers, created their own power. But the lightstones drew from power generated by the Heartstone.

Tanni regarded the subdued fire of the Heartstone.

"Do *you* think you can do it?"

Calandra twisted her braid around her hand, then released it. The void sucked at her insides again, and her throat tightened. She closed her eyes and took a breath, then opened them. "I honestly don't know. Not right now, certainly. But in five years and with the added strength of the consort bond?" She shrugged. "Maybe. I've already done things that even Thea has been surprised at. Like healing the breathing stones."

She'd been particularly proud of that one. It was rare for a stone healer—or any healer—to have much dexterity with air, so over time the stock of masks they used to convey humans long distances underwater had become depleted as the stones had worn out and were unable to retain oxygen. But Calandra had figured out how to heal them when she was only nine. Thea, her mentor and a panacea in her own right, had been stunned. And very proud.

Calandra looked up at the Heartstone. Perhaps the adults were right—perhaps she *could* do what so many before her had failed to do. But why wait until she was eighteen, bonded, and had a crazy-making baby on the way? She'd watched the annual Healing Ceremony that summer, though it had had little effect. Her powers were already stronger than any other living undine's. How much difference could the consort bond make when she already outstripped so many others' powers? And how different could it be from healing the breathing stones or imprinting a datastone?

But if she failed . . .

She shoved aside the darkness that furled at the corners of her mind. Before she could think too hard about what she had decided to do, she stripped off her sarong, tossed it behind her, and dove into the pool below. As she fell, she initiated the transformation to *ichthys* state. By the time she hit the water, her legs had already merged into a blue-green scale-covered tail with a large fin where her feet had been, and her skin was covered in slick, viscous gel. Gills that opened on her neck allowed her to dive deep beneath the surface with no fear of running out of oxygen.

She stilled herself in an upright position several spans below the surface. Closing her eyes, she *pulled* the water toward her. Instead of swimming to the surface, she used the water to raise her up, higher and higher, until she burst into the air on a rising column of liquid. As she passed the antechamber, she saw Tanni and Osaze both standing on the ledge with wide eyes and jaws hanging open. She rose through the vast, luminescent space until she was hovering directly below the glowing orb that housed the Heartstone, then used the water to hold her there.

From this close, the sphere filled her entire field of vision, and probably would have blinded her if it had not been so broken. She laid a hand on the crystal casing and closed her eyes, then gently extended an energy line through the broken Tear pendant, up her arm, through her hand, and into the quartz crystal. Finally, her emotions touched the opaline Heartstone.

In an instant, she was suspended in a warm, dark ocean, but not an empty one. The water was suffused with a red ember glow all around her, but more than that, there was a *presence*. It felt like it was speaking to her, surrounding her spirit with acceptance, and joy, and love. It was the most blissful thing she had ever experienced. She wanted to stay in that place forever. But something wasn't right. She reached toward the pain.

Abruptly, the darkness was obliterated by colour and light and sadness. So much sadness. A confusing cacophony of images filled with humans, undines, and creatures she'd only read about in the stones flooded through her mind in a rushing, senseless torrent that left her weeping in jagged gasps. The tower of water collapsed and she plummeted with it until she was swallowed by the Mother's Pool below. Her mind drifted through consciousness, much as her body did through the water.

In moments, Tanni was beside her, shaking her to her senses and pulling her back toward the surface. Calandra followed her friend's flashing golden-orange tail until they reached the ladder that would let them climb back to the antechamber. They both resumed *podia* state and clambered, dripping, onto the ledge. Conscious of Osaze's wide eyes, they wrapped their sarongs around their naked hips before settling onto the floor.

Calandra felt strangely energized. She could sense every place where her body touched cold marble, the hemp bodice pressing against her ribs, the sharp salt smell in the air. Far off up the tunnel, distant voices seemed amplified in her ears. She could even sense a vibrational hum from the Heartstone itself. She looked around in wonder.

Tanni watched her with a furrowed brow. "What happened?"

Calandra stared at the triquetra on the marble floor, considering. The triquetra symbolized many things to her people. The elements. Healing. Eternity. Atargatis, the First Mother.

"I—I'm not certain. There was too much there. It was like the stone was . . . *alive*."

"Don't stone healers treat every stone as if it were alive?"

"Yes, but this was different. It was *more* alive, like it had its own spirit somehow." She closed her eyes, the memory of how it felt to touch the Heartstone still filling her. "A spirit more powerful than what I can manage. Aunt Adonia's right. I'm not powerful enough yet."

A strange tingle hummed throughout her body, residual power activating every cell. She should have felt defeated at her failure, but instead she felt as though she could do anything. "But I think I might be able to, uh, *help* Osaze."

They turned to Osaze, who sat up straight tat their scrutiny.

"Wait." His nostrils flared and he frowned. "What are you going to do?"

3

BONDED

Osaze looked between them with fear in his eyes, then turned back to Calandra.

"Redeemed. That's what the queen did to me before, right? Is that what you mean by 'help'?" He clutched Calandra's arm. "Please don't do it again, Calandra. I—I think I would rather die than have that happen again."

As soon as Osaze touched her, a wave of desperation and fear crashed through her. She put her hands to her ears as though she could physically block out the sudden onslaught of emotion. *Is it happening already? Is this the Madness?*

When Osaze's hand fell from her arm, the emotions subsided. She slowly lowered her hands, staring at the boy. Those feelings . . . they had all come from *him*? Why had she felt them so strongly? Did it have something to do with the Heartstone?

"It's okay, Osaze. It doesn't hurt, does it?"

He shook his head and buried it in his hands. "That would be better. It's worse than anything you can imagine."

Calandra stared at him, stricken. As a rule, undines treated every living thing with respect. She had always been told that Redemption meant saving the men from themselves, cleansing them of impurities they could not purge on their own. But how could it be right to do something to these men that they hated so much?

Calandra's natural instinct was to reassure Osaze as she would any other frightened creature. Humming a lullaby and projecting calm, she took his hand and looked into his eyes.

This time, she was prepared for the emotions, though it took her a moment to organize and funnel their intensity into her opal Tear pendant.

That wasn't what actually happened, but it was the mind trick she used to reduce the flow so she could remain herself while she touched him. After a few minutes, Osaze's pulse slowed against her thumb and his panic receded.

Tanni shook her head. "I'm still amazed every time I watch you do that."

Calandra smirked at the praise. "You'll get it eventually. It only requires spirit to work."

Tanni snorted. "Maybe. Is that what you meant by 'help'?"

Calandra glanced at her friend, then back at Osaze.

"No. But I've changed my mind about that. I don't think I could Redeem him, even if I could figure out the Song. Not now."

She squeezed his hand, and he gave her a small, grateful smile.

How she'd missed his smile.

Tanni pressed her lips together in disapproval, regarding him with distaste and a trace of fear.

"If you don't, he will be found out. We could be exiled or worse, and he'll only be Redeemed again anyway. Assuming he hasn't done something that would earn him the death sentence by that point."

Osaze frowned at Tanni. "Like what?"

Tanni glared at him. "Like disobeying an order. Or neglecting your duties. Or being aggressive. Or showing any emotion whatsoever. Under Redemption, those would be impossible, so anyone who does them is considered a threat and an aberration. Which is why the best thing would be to Redeem you again, immediately. Anything else would risk your life and our freedom. Besides, men are dangerous." She paused, her expression softening to uncertainty. "Aren't you?"

Osaze frowned. "I don't feel dangerous. I've never wanted to hurt anyone. Why would anyone think I'm dangerous?" His eyes widened. "Did I do something I don't remember?"

Calandra shook her head. "I don't think so. It's the way we've done things since forever. You grew up here, you should remember that. But anyway, we still don't know how. And we're not doing it, so that's that."

Tanni frowned at Calandra, then stared up at the domed ceiling of the antechamber. "There's got to be a solution. There's just got to be. Think, Tanni."

Tanni was talking to herself. She must be distraught.

To be fair, Tanni had gotten them both out of plenty of fixes, but she had rarely gotten them in one. Calandra could understand her friend's panic over her mistake. After all, if anyone found out that it was Tanni who had Released Osaze, her promising career as a siren could be over. Calandra couldn't let that happen.

Frustrated, she studied the floor, staring at the Holy Triquetra set in the tiles.

Dark stone against light. Two different minerals, bonded in unity.

"Wait." She looked up at her companions. "I overheard Thea use a song once that I think might help."

Tanni and Osaze both turned to her in interest. "What does it do?"

"I'm not sure exactly, but I think it might create some kind of bond that compels service without trapping the mind. Sort of like an imitation *sklavia* bond."

Tanni's nose wrinkled. "What use would something like that ever be?"

"I think I heard Thea call it the *pisti* bond?"

"The loyalty bond? Huh. Never heard of it."

"It is what happens naturally between a physic and animals or people they heal. But unlike the healing bond, it will not fade over time."

"Like the consort bond. That never fades either." Tanni frowned. "Why don't you try it on me before you try it on him? The *sklavia* bond wouldn't work on me since I'm a girl, but this one might. And if something goes wrong, it will be much easier to explain that than if something happens to Osaze. You could say you were just practising."

"Are you sure? What if I make a mistake?"

Tanni cocked her head and smiled. "I trust you. And if you can figure out how to do it, you could probably figure out how to undo it." She glanced at Osaze and then at the floor. "Unlike me."

Calandra squeezed Tanni's hand. "Don't be so hard on yourself. It was an accident."

Tanni nodded, but her expression didn't change.

Calandra smiled at her friend, tight-lipped, then turned to the boy. Beads of sweat had pearled on his skin, and she knew it wasn't all because of the heat and humidity in this room.

"If I can make the *pisti* bond work with Tanni, will you let me try it on you? It would mean you would be compelled by loyalty to serve me, which might help us fool others, but you would retain control of your emotions and will in all other areas. It would also mean much more work for you. There would be no room for mistakes, Osaze. And if what we have done is ever discovered, we could be punished severely for it, possibly even executed."

Osaze played with his fingers while he considered, then met Calandra's gaze.

"Calandra, you have always been a friend to me. Even without some strange 'mermaid magic,' as my mother calls it, I would do anything you asked me to. If acting the slave prevents me from becoming one in actuality, I will do as you wish. There will never have been a more perfect liar than me."

Calandra frowned. There were a lot of things to unwrap in Osaze's words, but the gist was that he agreed to her terms. She could think about the rest later.

After she'd come to her senses.

Pushing down her misgivings at what she was about to do, she wrapped her hand around the broken Tear at her neck. Her mother had left it for her when she'd gone Mad and fled Sirenia many years ago. With its unique shielding ability, Calandra thought of it as her talisman—she had yet to find another stone like it. But mostly she wore it to remember her mother by—and to remind herself of the cost of failure. She had powers stronger than any healer since the great Nadia kor'Hera. And if she did not find a way to stop the Madness, she could sink Sirenia, as Nadia had sunk Atlantis before her.

The void of her nightmare curled at the edges of her mind like smoke. If she failed, instead of saving her people, she could condemn them all to oblivion—and the thousands of humans now living on lands to the north, west, and south of their island. But she still wasn't powerful enough.

Which was why she had to learn everything, try *everything*. Including this.

Taking a deep breath, she turned to Tanni. She took both of her friend's hands and looked into her eyes.

"I think it requires that we both give love while the bond is being formed."

At Tanni's solemn nod, Calandra closed her eyes. Acting partially on instinct and partially on the remembered snippet she'd heard, she reached out with spirit and poured all her love for her friend through their physical connection, then sang two wordless lines of music.

The two threads of spirit—hers and the one Tanni had spun—wove together and interconnected, overlaying and melting until they joined into one. Then the unified line returned to both of their bodies, fading but not breaking.

Calandra opened her eyes in wonder. In the corner of her mind, she had a new awareness—emotions that were not hers, though they did seem similar at the moment. "You . . ."

"I can feel you," Tanni whispered, staring at Calandra with round eyes. "I can feel you in my head."

They stared at each other in shock. Slowly, as the realization of what had happened washed over her, Calandra smiled. Where the cold void had whispered only moments ago was now a soft, warm presence, like an echo of how it felt to touch the Heartstone. She was no longer alone.

"I don't think that was what I meant to do. But I'm glad of it." She released her friend's hands and they threw their arms around each other.

"Me, too. Now we will never be apart."

Tanni sat back on her haunches and glanced at Osaze. "But I don't think that will help him. Even though I can sense you in here"—she touched her temple—"I certainly don't feel any extra compulsion to serve you. If you shared that with Osaze, would you be able to help him control his emotions that way? Do you think that would be enough to help him stay safe?"

Calandra frowned uncertainly. "I—I don't know." She looked at Osaze, whose brow was furrowed in worry. "I'm sorry, Osaze. I failed. I created a bond, but not one that would help you play your part." Tears pricked her eyes. "I don't know how to help you."

Osaze took several long deep breaths while he regarded Calandra.

She struggled to maintain control for his sake, but a few tears slid down her cheeks anyway. She could see only one other solution to his dilemma.

"The only other option is to help you escape."

Osaze shook his head. "No."

Calandra and Tanni both blinked at him in surprise.

"No," he repeated. "My mother is here in the palace. She still works as a governess at the Academy, no?"

Tanni nodded confirmation. Urbi had worked in the palace since she had been brought to Sirenia almost thirteen years ago.

Osaze continued. "It is my duty to stay with her. I am her only family. Besides that, where would I go? I have spent my whole life on this island, but I know only those in the palace. My father was lost to me in Africa even before my mother and I were brought here. There is no way to escape the island completely, not for humans like me—and I will not let you risk yourself trying to help me. No. This is the agreement I will make with you, Calandra."

He took her hand in his and placed his other hand on top. His hands were warm and surprisingly dry.

"Take me to someone who will Redeem me again." He took a breath, jaw clenched, then soldiered on. "When you have learned how to do what it was you thought you could do, find me. Free me. Give me the chance to give you my heart without giving up my mind."

Calandra wept freely now. Even Tanni, who rarely displayed such sentiment, wiped at her eyes.

"If you're sure."

Osaze squeezed her hand. "Hey," he said gently, ducking his head to meet her gaze.

She looked at him in confusion. There were tears in the corners of his eyes, but his expression was full of concern. For her.

"It'll be all right," he said. "I trust you. You promise to do this, don't you?"

Calandra blinked in shock. An Unredeemed male was supposed to be angry and violent. But Osaze, rather than fight against a fate he abhorred, comforted her instead.

She pulled her friend to her in a hug. "I promise."

*

CALANDRA tried to send Tanni back to her dormitory so she could face Thea alone, but Tanni refused.

"As soon as Osaze is Redeemed again, he will answer every question they ask. I don't want it to look like I was trying to hide anything and escape the consequences." She glanced around the antechamber. "Nor do I want them to ask too many questions."

She gave Calandra a meaningful stare, and Calandra swallowed.

"Good point."

They found Thea in the Archive, surrounded by drawers and shelves full of datastones of every type of crystal, poring over an unfamiliar script embossed on the surface of a large stone reader on top of a cedar table. The Academy's headmistress flicked her finger across the surface of the hexagonal rock crystal slab and the raised luminescent letters changed to new characters. Her curtain of straight silver hair obscured the back of her green floor-length healer's tunic to her waist. Despite being the oldest person Calandra had ever met, there was still iron and vitality in her tall thin frame.

Calandra and Tanni stood at attention behind her with Osaze between them. Calandra held his hand.

Thea spoke without turning around. "What are you doing out of bed at this hour, cadet?"

She straightened, then turned around and inspected them, her hooded jade-green eyes widening only slightly when she saw three of them standing there. A panacea's fire opal set in the centre of a golden triquetra dangled from a hair chain in the centre of her forehead.

The three teenagers bowed their heads slightly and touched their bunched fingertips to their foreheads in respectful salute. Thea's gaze flicked to Calandra's Tear and her and Osaze's conjoined hands, then over each of them in turn.

"Calandra. Osaze. As well as Cadet kor'Zelia. What is the meaning of this?"

Calandra lifted her chin and looked directly into her mentor's face—much younger-looking than her years—as she explained the night's adventure up to the point of running into Osaze in the Grotto. Thea listened without interruption, occasionally glancing at the nervous Osaze, until Tanni spoke up and claimed responsibility for Releasing him.

Thea's sharp green eyes snapped to Tanni's face, then she stepped toward Osaze, looking the tall teenage boy in the eye. Restrained fear and determination coursed through Calandra from his touch, but Thea would sense it from him without that. The *daskala* nodded.

"How did you Release him, cadet? Please show me."

Tanni's eyes widened. "I—I don't know, *daskala*, and that's the truth. I was trying to copy something I read in one of my mother's stones, a memory-erasing song." She glanced at the floor and twisted her fingers together.

Thea tilted her head. "That is not a song for the inexperienced, either, and should be used with caution."

Tanni nodded, not looking up. "I know. I'm sorry, *daskala*."

Thea placed her finger on Osaze's forehead and sang a short trill of notes. His eyes glazed and the boiling cauldron of emotions he'd been containing went as still as water in a bowl.

"Now, cadet, please try again."

Calandra let go of Osaze's hand and hers felt cold—but not as cold as her heart at his blankness. She blinked back moisture and watched Tanni.

Tanni put her finger on Osaze's forehead and tried several times to do what she'd done in the garden, but nothing happened.

Thea waved dismissively to indicate that Tanni should stop. "Give me your hand, cadet."

Tanni held out her hand

Thea took it, then looked in Tanni's eyes. "Do you remember how you Released young Osaze here, or don't you?"

Tanni bit her lip, then shook her head. "I don't. I swear it. And even if I did, I wouldn't do it again."

Thea kept Tanni's gaze and hand for several more moments. Calandra thought she seemed a touch disappointed, which made no sense.

"You speak truth." Thea dropped Tanni's hand and turned toward her work. "Neither of you are to speak of what happened tonight to *anyone*, ever. You are both to report to Daskala Lida for a strapping immediately. Calandra, you will be on scullery duty for three months. I will be speaking with Queen Adonia in the morning about posting guard outside your door at night to prevent further escapades. Cadet kor'Zelia, Daskala Lida will determine your penance, and tell her I said not to make it too light. And one more thing."

She turned to look at them both. Calandra shifted on her feet, refusing to glance at her friend because she knew she'd have to look past Osaze's stiff profile beside her.

"You two are no longer permitted to spend time together. If I hear or see so much as a whisper about you seeing each other outside of normal duties, Cadet kor'Zelia will be expelled. I'm sure neither of you want that to happen."

Tears pricked Calandra's sinuses. "For how long?"

Thea arched an eyebrow. "For as long as one of you is a student at the Academy. Understood?"

Calandra swallowed and nodded, her own grief matched by the turmoil of Tanni's emotions in her mind. She wanted to yell and scream about the unfairness of it all. The thought of losing access to her closest friend was worse than seeing Osaze Redeemed again. How was she supposed to Release him again on her own? It would be five more years until the bonds were taught to her.

Tanni had matching tears in her eyes. At least they had their secret bond. At least they had that.

As they walked stiffly together toward Daskala Lida's chambers to receive their punishment, Calandra said in a quiet voice, "Perhaps we did the wrong thing, telling her."

Tanni shook her head, gaze downcast. "I think she did us a favour."

Calandra frowned. It was the harshest punishment Thea had ever dealt her. "How can you say that?"

"Can you imagine the punishment Adonia would have doled out if she didn't think Thea had dealt with this infraction severely enough? Unauthorized Release is a capital offence for adults. Sure, I did it by accident and I'm only fourteen. But it could have been so much worse."

Calandra nodded thoughtfully, breathing deeply to keep her emotions in check. Now she understood. If Thea hadn't dealt so harshly with them, Tanni would most likely have been expelled and had to return to Haven.

"I suppose I understand that."

Tanni shook her head again. "I'm not sure you do. One thing I've already learned about the bonds is a *sklavia* bond can only be Released by the one who holds it. As far as I know, what I did tonight shouldn't have even been possible."

Calandra stared at her friend, wide-eyed. "Can you imagine what Adonia would do if she found out?"

Tanni raised her eyebrows. "Why do you think Thea told us not to tell anyone?"

Calandra stared straight ahead. Perhaps Thea had been kind, after all.

*

DASKALA Lida gave them the hiding of their lives, not made lighter by them waking her up to do it, then told Tanni she would mete out the rest of her punishment in the morning. Tanni and Calandra parted ways with Tanni outside the Siren house mother's door, neither of them wanting to test their new restriction and risk making it worse.

As Calandra made her way back to her bedchamber—wincing every time her sarong moved over her tender backside—she passed Osaze being accompanied back to the *tapeinos* cadet quarters by a siren. She tried to meet his eyes, but he ignored her with the unfocused stare of the Redeemed.

She lay in bed for hours, clutching her mother's Tear next to her heart as silent tears slid down her face. Everything that had happened that night had been her fault. She had botched everything, just as she'd always feared she would. This time, Tanni and Osaze had paid the price. What would happen if she couldn't learn to use her powers well enough or went Mad and failed at her ultimate duty—saving the Heartstone, and her people?

She thought of Osaze, his gentleness and earnestness, and the parting image of his unfocused eyes burned into her soul. She mourned the loss of Tanni. Even though her new awareness let her pinpoint Tanni inside the palace from where she lay, she'd never felt more alone. Eventually, she drifted off to sleep and found herself back in the cold abyss under the weight of her unmet duty, with Osaze's name at the top of the list of those she must save.

And then *he* was there—the strange undine man. Smiling at her with his mouth, but not from his golden eyes. Something about him intimidated her, but she refused to let herself be intimidated by any male, especially one in her dreams. She squared her shoulders and frowned at him.

"You are wondering how to gain control of your powers," he said without preamble.

She thought about ignoring him or denying it, but what was the point? This was nothing more than a dream, and the slippery logic of dreams fuzzed her will to keep her more rebellious thoughts to herself.

"You know, I shouldn't even be talking to you. An Unredeemed male. I could get in big trouble."

The corners of his mouth curved under his trim goatee.

"And who will report you?" He indicated the blackness around them. "Certainly not I. I exist only in your mind."

She crossed her arms and cocked her head, studying him.

"Have you ever been Redeemed?"

His expression became stony. "Redemption is for humans."

"Redemption is for men. To make them safe. It just happens that the only men are human."

Thinking of Osaze's dread, she wondered again at the morality of it. Uncrossing her arms, she shifted her gaze from Damon's face to his bronze chest.

"And one of them is my friend."

"All humans should be controlled," he replied nonchalantly, drawing nearer. "They have not the patience nor discipline to control themselves. And *I* am not human, yet I am male."

She looked up at him, eyes narrowed. "I can see that. What are you? I've never seen an undine with golden eyes."

He smiled knowingly. "Not human. But I could be your friend."

That same feeling of security and warmth from their first encounter enveloped her, as though he were projecting it from himself intentionally. She frowned, wanting to accept it and shake off her heavy heart, but not daring to trust him yet.

"What do you want from me?"

"I want to help you."

Damon came near enough to touch her but didn't, pausing before her with his arms to the sides in a placating gesture.

She wrapped her arms around herself and glared into the blackness beyond him. "Yeah, well, you can't. Not unless you can tell me how to control powers that could sink an island and heal the Heartstone without going Mad."

"Little lark," he said, amusement dripping from his voice like honey from a spoon, "that is exactly what I intend to do. You have a difficult road ahead of you. You shouldn't have to do it alone."

Her gaze snapped toward his, and as soon as their eyes met, the light from his golden irises melted something inside her.

"You can help me heal the Heartstone?"

He leaned over her and the water between them warmed.

"If you let me keep visiting you, I'll show you how to do things you never dreamed possible. I swear it." He held up his hand with the palm toward her in an invitation to take it. "Do you agree?"

She stared at him, mesmerized by the swirling golden orbs.

"Who are you?"

"I," he said, "am the one who is going to help you change history."

Without once looking away from his face, she wove her fingers through his and golden sparks flowed between their hands. The abyss melted away and shifted until they were hovering in some underwater ruins, the sense of fear and oppression melting with it. Suddenly his plan, whatever it might be, seemed like an excellent idea.

"When do we begin?"

4

THE WATERBOY

Five Years Later
Somewhere in western England
January 15, 1799

ZALE TEAGUE STARED AT THE people on the other side of the glass, not really seeing them, focusing instead on keeping himself suspended more or less upright so they would have a good view. That's why they were here, after all, to see the Waterboy—the half-man, half-fish merfreak. For a threepence, they could stare at him for a few minutes and talk about him for a lifetime.

Zale might be unusual to them, but after five years of staring through these glass walls, every face looked the same to him—every gaping jaw, every wondering stare, every frightened, delighted scream. Every mother hustling her small child out of the tent while craning her neck to stare at him in horrified fascination.

Through the cold safety provided by the glass, he'd seen it all. And he welcomed it. The repugnance, the obsession, the terror were no more than he deserved—but not because of his hideous deformity. The true abomination within this tank lay inside his soul.

He could call down lightning from the sky. Only a god or a demon could do that—and since his father had ended up dead, and his friend blinded, he knew which side he landed on.

He hadn't intended to do those things. But intended or not, he'd done them, and learned the steep price of giving his emotions free rein. So now he climbed into a tank every afternoon and stayed there, hiding in plain sight, until the watchers cleared out and went home to their beds. Then Zale would join Eric and his family for supper at their *tan*, the Romani name for the low tents they called home.

Eric had been the one who'd found Zale, exhausted and half-dead, on the bank of a stream in Cornwall, miles from the home he'd fled in shame. Eric hadn't blinked at Zale's tail, hadn't even commented when it melted back into the legs of a seemingly ordinary human boy.

Most importantly, Eric had never asked what demons haunted his past. He'd just fed him, clothed him, and offered him shelter with his family if Zale would be willing to earn his keep. And by "earn his keep," Eric had meant "let people stare at him for money."

At the time, Zale had only just realized the connection between his flares of distress and the frightening natural consequences—how the lightning always came when he called it, but not to do his bidding. It did as it wished, like the surf that pounded the cliffs of Penzance near his home.

He'd had no control of it. And his father had died.

Someone tapped at the glass. Zale blinked and focused on the face of a boy, about eleven or twelve, with a thatch of wheat-coloured hair and a slim build. When he realized he'd caught Zale's attention, the boy's face split into a crooked grin.

For a moment, it was like a spectre from his own past had come to torment him—a ghost of the person he'd been *before*. He met the boy's eyes, which were brown to Zale's vibrant green, and glimpsed the curious wonder of a child who has retained his innocence. It was like looking into a mirror through time.

The boy put up his hands, palms out, fingers extended—first both hands, then a single finger, and then he pointed at himself. *Eleven*.

Zale smiled and held up his slightly webbed fingers to indicate his own sixteen years. The boy jumped up and down, a grin splitting his face, then turned to two village women who stood behind him. The ragamuffin child jabbered at one of them excitedly, pointing at the tank.

Unlike Zale's typical audience, the boy seemed to see him as more than a mere curiosity. Zale put his palm flat against the glass in acknowlededgement. The woman, most likely the child's mother, seemed only mildly interested in the boy's chatter. She flicked her gaze at Zale, then crossed her arms and waved a dismissive hand at her son. The boy came back to stand in front of the tank and smiled at Zale, who smiled back. Then the boy drew a rather grotesque image of a merman monster with fangs in the condensation on the glass and proceeded to make faces at Zale.

Zale snapped out of the moment and closed his eyes. As long as he was in this tank, he'd never be more than a freak on display, less than human. And that was fine. It was what he wanted, wasn't it? A chance to do penance for his evil deeds? To obliterate the painful memories beneath the emotional lashings he got day in and day out?

Then why did he never feel cleansed?

When he opened his eyes again, Eric's grown daughter, Josefine, was shooing the two women and the boy out of the tent. Once the canvas flap closed behind them, Josefine turned to face him and made a chopping motion with one hand onto the other palm—the time's-up gesture that signalled the end of the customers for the night—before ducking through the entrance herself.

Zale surfaced, pushing his shoulder-length blond hair out of his eyes. He hauled himself up onto the wooden bench along the top edge of one side of the tank. Within moments, his gills had flattened against his neck, his tail had melted into human legs, and his mucosal layer had reabsorbed into his skin. If someone saw him like this, they would have no clue that he was anything other than human—except for the iridescent green of his eyes, which he had been told shone softly in the dark.

He descended the stairs on the back of the tank and then dried himself with the soft cotton towel that he had left on a small table for that purpose earlier. He grabbed his breeches from the pile of clothes on the table and pulled them on, then became aware of someone's presence in the room. Odd. He hadn't heard anyone enter.

"I'll join you for supper in a few moments, Eric," he said without turning around as he pulled on his stockings.

A woman's voice replied.

"I'm afraid supper will have to wait."

Back erect, Zale swivelled toward the intruder, his shirt bunched over his hands.

The young woman glanced at his bare chest, raising her eyebrows and biting her lip on a smile. She crossed her arms and nodded appreciatively.

"Well, aren't you all grown up now? After five years, I suppose that was to be expected."

Zale gulped and stared. For a brief, breathless moment, he wondered if this was what drowning felt like. Everything about the apparition before him seemed dipped in sunlight. Bronze-tipped halo of dark-brown corkscrew curls pulled back with combs, radiant deep bronze skin, gold braid on her elegant tawny silk pelisse, and eyes that refracted light like melted gold. Her clothing and posture bespoke a lady, but her lack of chaperone and warm brown skin implied something else. A lady's maid on an errand, perhaps? Zale wasn't sure what to think. There was something familiar about her, but he couldn't place it.

Under her frank appraisal, embarrassment that had long since ceased plaguing him when he was in the tank warmed his face. He hurriedly worked his shirt over his head. Then, with a stumbling flourish, he gave the young woman a deep, sloppy bow.

"The show is over for the night, uh, mistress." Best to err on the side of caution. "You'll have to come back tomorrow."

The girl—or was she a woman? It was difficult to tell—pulled herself up and met his gaze.

"I'm not here to see you *perform*, Zale Teague. I need to speak with you. It is a matter of some urgency."

She had his attention now.

"How do you know my name?"

She took a step toward him. "I know a lot of things about you. That your father died in an accident at the Madron tin mine when you were ten. And that you ran away from home when you were eleven. It would seem that since then, you have taken up with the gypsies and have been exposing yourself for money for the pleasure of others." She frowned in disapproval, but then cast a sorrowful glance at the tank. "Has it helped?"

Zale scowled and ignored her question. He snatched his brightly patched waistcoat from the table, continuing to dress with jerky movements.

"Who are you? What do you want from me?"

She took another step toward him and he tensed. She was very near him now. It had been a long time since he'd stood so close to a stranger.

Again, that look of sorrow filled her eyes.

"Oh, Zale. You truly do not know me? You once made me a lavender crown and we pretended that I was the Lady Marian, and you were Robin of Locksley on an adventure to save me. And Robbie was—"

"Little John."

He searched her face in disbelief. He had known only one other person with eyes that colour—but except for those molten irises, this young woman looked nothing like the dark-haired, fair-skinned girl he had grown up with in Madron.

But who else would remember playing Robin Hood with him and Robbie Cox in the fields of Cornwall?

"Talwyn?" he offered, memory flooding him.

He could still picture Talwyn as he'd seen her last, standing on the bank of a stream calling his name, the metallic zing of electricity from the bolt of lightning he'd accidentally called to save her from the now-fleeing bullies still permeating the air. On that fateful day five years ago, life as he'd known it had ended. It was when he'd discovered what kind of monster he really was.

The girl smiled, revealing perfect, white teeth. "You *do* remember."

He gaped. "How can that be? Talwyn was—well, she looked different than you. And she was not a lady."

She waved a dismissive hand. "This face is only flesh. Like you, I am not all that I appear to be. And in this form, you may call me Abela."

Zale shook his head, trying to still his whirling mind. "What do you mean? Who are you really?"

Abela drew an impatient breath. "I don't have time to explain everything right now. Please trust me. I am the same girl you knew growing up in Madron. And I have been looking for you. It's your mother. She has disappeared, and I believe she may be in trouble."

Zale gulped. "My mother?"

A sudden breeze stirred the tent flap and the temperature in the room dropped several degrees.

Abela flicked her eyes toward the movement, then turned a hard stare toward Zale.

"She is like you, Zale. She is an undine—an ancient race of water people created as guardians of the deep. She was supposed to help you learn to control your powers. I can see that she did not. Perhaps you fled before she had the chance."

"An un-what? What are you talking about?"

Abela sighed and crossed her arms.

"Zale, you are unique. And not in the way you think, not a . . . a freak to display. You are *special*. Your parents raised you in Cornwall to protect you. There are people who would kill you if they knew of you. Frankly, I'm surprised you have survived this long, Mr. *Waterboy*." She quirked her lips. "Then again, I suppose it did take me five years to find you, and I knew who I was looking for. Thank Elyon that I found you first."

That last bit didn't seem to require a response, which was good, because Zale felt like a fish that had suddenly been thrown into the desert.

Abela frowned at him. "It would seem that you disappeared before your mother could tell you any of this. But I don't have time to explain everything right now. She needs you. You might be her only hope."

Zale's normally mundane life had been sucked into a whirlpool of chaos.

"I—I don't believe you. Who are you? How do you know of me and my mother? How did you find me?" An alarming thought gripped him, and the face of the brother of the boy he'd blinded glared at him in memory. "Did Gryffyn send you?"

The panic tickling the edges of Zale's mind only made him more afraid. His control was slipping. He had to calm down. He *had* to. He'd spent years disengaging himself from emotions of any kind, and in moments, Abela—Talwyn—whatever-her-name-was—had revived every one, along with the danger they presented.

The dull roar of a rising wind outside echoed the swirling in his gut. He backed away from the strange young woman—could she really only be a year older than him?—and tripped on a stool, catching himself from falling by grabbing the table. Thunder boomed outside, and the water in the tank began to boil. When he pulled his hands from the wood, his blackened fingerprints were seared into it.

Abela rolled her eyes. "Oh, for the love of Elyon. Not again."

From her reticule, she pulled out a thin silver cylinder that appeared to have a glowing red ember on one end of it and touched it to his forehead. Instead of burning him, the fire felt cold.

His thoughts fuzzed and her image began to blur.

Cold rhymes with gold. Like her eyes. Is that a miniature dragon?

Zale's world went black.

5

THE ANGEL

Zale awoke to Abela's beautiful, worried face only inches above his own. She was kneeling beside him, patting his cheek and whispering in restrained urgency. When she saw that his eyes were open, she leaned back on her haunches with a relieved smile.

Zale sat up. "What happened to me?"

His head throbbed. He touched the back of it where a large goose egg had formed.

Abela looked sheepish. "I, uh, used the mindover. I only meant to calm you down. I must have done something wrong, because you passed out."

She noticed him nursing the bump and her hands flew to her mouth.

"Oh, no! I'm sorry. That must have happened when you fell. Here, let me help."

She looked around the room and spotted the washstand and basin near the back of the tent. With surprising grace, she dashed to grab the cloth on the stand, dampened it with the water from the pitcher, then came back and made to put it on the goose egg.

Zale flinched away. "What's a 'mindover'?"

Abela's face scrunched. "Mindover? As in 'mind over matter?'"

He stared at her blankly.

She shook her head. "Never mind. It's something I'm not supposed to talk about. Or show you. Or use. Now may I? That looks rather nasty."

She indicated his head with the cloth.

He gave a slight nod, then bent his neck so she could reach the injury more easily. The pressure was uncomfortable at first, but the cool water did make it feel better. She dabbed at the bump with gentle movements.

He was very aware of the warmth of her hands and the proximity of her body beneath the rustling silk of her long-sleeved pelisse and gown. She smelled like a wild wind whispering through heathered fields of adventures in far-off lands. Despite his travels with the band, he felt like a backward, unkempt country bumpkin.

Voices came from outside the tent as two men passed. ". . . strangest thing I've seen in my life. That wind came from nowhere, and went back there just as suddenly. It didn't seem natural. What do you make of it, Sal?"

"All I know is that my wife's best copper kettle was ruined when it was tossed against a tree, and my supper along with it. The canvas for our *tan* is probably somewhere in Wales. Thankfully, no one was hurt."

"Aye. I hope Eric will know more about it. Or Josefine. She talks to spirits, so maybe she has some answers."

"Perhaps you're right . . ."

The men moved on. Abela dabbed at his head a few more times. He could tell she was looking at his face as much as the bump, though.

"I'm sorry," Abela said at last. She sat, letting her hands drop to her lap. The cloth was now soiled with dirt from his head, but no blood. "This is all my fault."

Zale frowned and gingerly touched the bump. "I'll recover."

"No, not only for that." Abela avoided his gaze, looking like she was trying to gather her thoughts. "That day with Gryffyn and the others, when you saved me—"

Zale looked at her sharply. That had been Talwyn. Could this strange girl be telling the truth? Was she somehow also Talwyn, his childhood friend?

"—I was meant to be watching you. You were my responsibility, but I let myself get detained by that blackguard, Gryffyn Cox. By the time I had dealt with that situation, you were already gone. If only I'd done a proper job, you wouldn't have had to live like this"—she indicated the tank—"and perhaps your mother wouldn't have gone missing either. I'm glad I've finally found you, because now I can try to make it up to you. If you'll let me. Are you able to stand yet?"

Zale shook his head in denial of her story, not as a response to her question—and instantly regretted it. He put his hand to his forehead to stop the world spinning, then squinted at her through the pain.

"Talwyn was only, what, twelve or thirteen at the time? Why would she—you—why would you feel responsible for what happened to me? And how could it be possible that you are Talwyn?"

"We don't have time for this," she muttered with a low, exasperated growl. Abela gave him a sideways look and sighed. "I can see that I will need to make time to convince you if you are to come with me."

She stood, unfolding with the grace of a cat.

"You were on the way home from the market alone. I had gone into the woods near Chyandour Brook ahead of you, intending to check for danger and tell Berian if I found any."

"Reverend Berian, the Methodist minister? How do you know him?"

Abela nodded. "I told you. I'm Talwyn. Or used to be."

Zale set his jaw. She watched him, pacing in the limited space offered by the tent's viewing area.

"Gryffyn, Willie Prouse, Jory, and Robbie surprised me. Robbie didn't really seem to want to be there. He'd always looked up to his brother so much, and I think he'd convinced Gryffyn to let him come that day. You remember, right?"

She glanced at Zale. He said nothing, following her movements through narrowed eyes.

She continued pacing, laying the cloth on the washstand as she passed.

"Gryffyn decided to initiate Robbie into his little gang by trying to get him to take advantage of me. Robbie wouldn't help the boys, but he didn't help me either."

She frowned at the ground.

Zale gritted his teeth. In his mind's eye, he could see Robbie Cox standing near the path, fidgeting irresolutely while Gryffyn and his gang forced kisses on Talwyn. Could it be possible that one of them had spread the story so this stranger would eventually hear of it?

Abela's voice sounded distant as she retold the tale, like she was reliving it in her mind, not the melodramatic tone of someone relaying a piece of gossip.

"Part of my job is to let situations play out so a person's true character may be revealed, so I waited and went along with it. But Robbie never found his courage. Not that day."

She put a hand on Zale's arm and he met her gaze.

"Then you came along and stood up to them for me—just you against four nearly grown boys. By then, the situation had escalated beyond my control. What you did—calling lightning to hit that tree to make the wasps chase off the boys—I knew at that moment why you were the one who had been chosen. But then you disappeared." She frowned. "Did you . . . run away?"

Zale's mind reeled. She had described exactly what had happened.

When he'd tried to save Talwyn from the gang of bullies, he had been overpowered and restrained. Gryffyn had been about to haul Talwyn off, threatening Zale's life if he ever told anyone. At his most desperate to save her, the lightning had come, knocking down a large wasp's nest from a nearby tree. The swarm had driven them all into the water.

It was the first time in his life that Zale had been immersed in water—there'd been no room for a tub in their small hut, and his mother had always warned him not to go swimming, citing a boy of his acquaintance who'd drowned when he was young as the reason. Zale had thrashed about in the brook, fearing the water had sealed his doom. Then his deformity had been revealed for the first time—to him and to everyone else present. The sight of his tail and gills had scared away the boys.

Not Talwyn. She had stared, but she hadn't fled.

Zale did.

As he'd watched the burned and sightless Robbie Cox flailing on the stream bank, the weight of what he'd done fell on him, nearly crushing him. He realized with dawning horror that the lightning that had struck the explosives shed at his father's workplace the previous year hadn't been an act of God, as everyone had murmured with hushed tones and quickly averted eyes whenever he or his mother had approached. It had been his fault. It had to be—it had felt the same.

He wielded terrifying elemental powers that he couldn't control. He was a monster and a freak, and he had done horrible things.

He'd originally meant to return home, but then he realized that he could just as easily kill his mother as he'd killed his father and injured Robbie. And knowing who he was and what he'd done, he couldn't bear to face her, or anyone else who knew him, ever again. So he'd run back to the water to hide. In a way, he hadn't left it since.

It seemed that hiding hadn't been enough. His past had found him anyway.

"Talwyn?" Zale blinked at the girl before him as though seeing her for the first time. "Is it—can it really be you?"

She smiled in relief. "Yes. But my real name is Abela. Now come. We need to go." She extended a hand toward him as if to take his. "Now. Before your keeper comes looking for you."

"My—my *keeper?* What are you talking about?"

The sound of an approaching conversation came from outside.

Abela glanced toward the tent flap, then back at Zale.

"*Please*, Zale. Every moment we waste is another moment your mother is in danger. I'll explain everything later. Right now, we need to go. But you must choose this. I can't make you do it."

Zale shook his head in bewilderment, and—*blasted bump on the noggin*—once again had to steady himself with a hand to his head.

So much was happening so fast. So much he didn't understand.

"I left to keep my mother safe. If I go back, she'll be in danger from me."

Abela's eyebrows rose. "What on earth are you talking about? Zale, if I'm right about what I think happened to your mother, you might be the only one who can save her. With the help of your sister."

"My—my *sister?*"

He'd known his parents had had a daughter before he'd been born, but that they'd lost her. They barely spoke of her to him. How would Abela know about her?

Abela stood in front of him and took his hands, hauling him to his feet. Her fingers were soft and strong at once

"I know it's a lot to take in. But Zale, it's me. I baked you and your mother honeycakes after your father died. At Christmas, our families would share a meal together. You gave me a red ribbon when you were eight. I wore it every day until the Davis's pig ate it."

She started laughing at the memory, a bubbly giggle that was interrupted by a snort—a ridiculous laugh he'd heard a thousand times before.

Zale stared at her in wonder.

"Talwyn?"

Abela nodded, getting her mirth under control.

It had to be her, though he couldn't see how. But if he could change into a water boy, could it be possible that Talwyn could change into Abela?

Now that his mind accepted her story, her urgency passed to him through her fingers.

"What has happened to my mother?"

"I'll explain on the way. We must go immediately. Come." She began tugging him toward the tent flap.

Zale resisted. "Wait. Let me grab my things and say goodbye to Eric and Gio and the rest."

He couldn't leave without telling his Romani family that he was going.

Abela shook her head. "You can't. He won't let you go. He—"

The tent flap opened, and in walked a powerfully built man in a leather waistcoat and breeches. His black hair would have brushed the top of the door had he not ducked to get through it. Eric.

When he saw Zale, Eric's coal-black eyes lit up and his faced cracked in a jovial grin.

"There you are. I was beginning to think the wind had blown you away. Are you coming for supper or not, lad?"

Zale's resolve faltered. He had come to love this man. But his mother still took first priority.

"Sorry, Eric. I was coming to find you. I have received word from . . ."

Zale turned to introduce Abela, only to discover she was no longer there. He glanced around and saw her squatting behind the wooden cart that the water tank sat on. It seemed unusually dark around her, though Zale could still see her easily. She put her finger to her lips to indicate that he shouldn't mention her.

This girl kept getting stranger.

"From whom?" the big man frowned and began to follow Zale's gaze.

Zale stepped toward Eric and clapped him on the shoulder, successfully distracting him.

"From . . . my mother. One of the customers today was an old friend of mine from home, and she . . . brought a letter." Zale silently prayed that Eric wouldn't ask to read it. "Apparently, my mother is ill, and I must go attend her. It seems that it is time for us to part ways at last."

He swallowed the lump that had appeared in his throat.

Eric's black brows drew together. "And you trust this friend? You're sure she's telling the truth?"

Over Eric's shoulder, Zale caught the echo of Eric's question on Abela's shadowed face.

"Yes. I do. If I hurry, I should be able to catch the morning mail coach."

Abela smiled at him warmly. Zale's insides gurgled pleasantly.

"Your mother's ill, is she?"

"So it would seem. The matter appears to be quite dire."

"Interesting. Well, this is unfortunate." Eric rubbed his stubbly chin, then, with a smooth motion, his hand closed on Zale's arm in a vise-like grip. "I don't think so."

Zale looked between the hand on his arm and Eric's face. "What do you mean?"

Eric snapped a thick, hinged bracelet made of a polished green stone with gold end caps onto Zale's wrist. As soon as it touched Zale's skin, the world darkened and got colder. Eric pushed the two sides together and they clicked, locking the bracelet into place.

Zale tugged at his arm, trying to pull it free, but Eric's grip was unbreakable.

"What is this? What are you doing to me?"

"I've been told this bauble will negate any fireworks you might try to pull on me," said Eric. "Unfortunately, you do not yet have my permission to leave."

"Your permission? What are you talking about? Eric? Uncle Eric? Let me go."

Zale pushed against Eric's chest with his free hand.

Eric twisted Zale's arm behind his back, then grabbed his other wrist and pulled both arms behind him, forcing them upward until Zale stopped struggling.

"See, the problem is that most of us think we are masters of our own destinies."

Eric loosened his leather belt with one hand and lashed it around Zale's wrists, then patted him on the shoulder as though it were a job well done.

"It is a clever illusion, no? But it couldn't be further from the truth." He pushed Zale toward the tent flap. "Especially for you. *Son.*"

This betrayal was more than Zale could process. *Has the world gone mad?*

"Where are we going?"

"You've gone and ruined the plan, Zale. If you'd only waited a few more months . . . The Master has plans for you, you know." Eric sighed. "Now that you know the truth, I have to ask him what he wants me to do with you."

He propelled Zale through the door and out into the night.

Zale didn't know what Eric was on about, but he knew he didn't like the sound of it.

"What are you talking about? What master?"

White light flared around them, coming from everywhere at once. Zale cringed at the intense radiance, and Eric used his free hand to shade his eyes.

An enormous tawny lioness bounded out of the brilliance from behind them, two feathered wings folded next to her sides. She batted at Eric with a powerful forepaw, knocking him to the ground. Then she turned eyes the colour of molten gold toward Zale, and, in Abela's voice, said, "Hop on."

Zale glanced at Eric, who was pushing himself unsteadily upright. Without thinking too hard about it, he did as the lioness commanded, clambering up on her shoulders—none-too-gracefully with his hands tied behind him. She loped into the night, darkness gathering around them like a cloud, though that didn't affect her sure footing any. She didn't stop until they were inside an empty barn in a nearby field.

"Get off, please," she said, sounding winded.

Zale was only too happy to oblige. He scrambled off the beast's shoulders, then turned around in time to see her transform into the girl from the tent.

Zale and Abela stared at each other in silence, then Abela sprang into action, loosening the belt from Zale's hands and tossing it aside.

Finally, Zale found his voice.

"Who . . . what are you?"

"I am Abela of Bayithel. I am your Guardian. But we must go quickly, now. Your jailer won't be far behind us."

She withdrew a fine silver chain from around her neck, at the end of which hung an odd silver pendant. It was a series of nested rings, wheels within wheels, all spinning in multiple directions. At its centre was a tiny round gem that radiated a soft red-gold light. She cupped the pendant in one hand and extended the other hand toward Zale.

"Come here, please. This hasn't had much time to charge, but we should be able to jump far enough to get out of immediate danger."

Zale stared at her, trying to piece all the confusing events of the evening together.

"I *did* see a dragon. Kind of. It was you."

Abela's mouth turned up on one side.

"A dragon? That's a new one. I do know a dragon, though not the one you're probably thinking of."

He blinked at her.

"Which one would I be thinking of?"

She gestured impatiently for him to take her extended hand.

"I don't actually bite."

The shouting from the direction of the Romani camp was getting louder. Zale glanced in that direction, pain pinching his heart. Pretty sure he would regret this later, Zale stepped forward and took the proffered hand.

Abela smiled at him and squeezed it. "I'm more like a sphinx. My people are called lumasi. Humans call us cherubim nowadays—though they often get a few things wrong."

He squinted at her. "You're an angel?"

She shrugged. "In a manner of speaking."

"Guardian angel, huh?"

Events from their past and from this night started to click into place in his head. As outrageous as her claims were, his eyes and his heart confirmed their truth. Zale looked at their clasped hands uncertainly.

"You might want to guard yourself. I'm kind of a dangerous guy to have around."

Abela regarded him steadily. "I'm willing to take my chances. Now let's go save your mum, shall we?"

Zale pressed his lips together and nodded. "Where are we going?"

She smiled. "To see an old friend in Bristol."

Abela blew on the pendant in her hand. The wheels began spinning, slowly at first, then faster and faster until they blurred into a single solid shape. The gemstone gave a brilliant flash of golden light.

The barn disappeared.

*

Eric burst into the barn in time to see his quarry wink out of existence. Behind him, his men fanned out into the building to check for people, but Eric knew it was pointless now. He scowled.

Josefine came to stand beside him, slapping the coil of rope in her hand against her long skirts, her dark eyes flashing.

"Where did they go?"

"Blinked. They could be anywhere in England."

He kicked at some straw in frustration. Travel by chariot—the travelling device these creatures used—was untraceable, and limited only by the energy of the device and the skill of the user. With a powerful enough chariot, you could walk across the world in a single step. The lumasi woman couldn't have had a very big one, but it had been big enough.

"The Master's not going to be happy about this," his daughter said with a worried expression.

Josefine was right. Eric considered not mentioning it to his superiors, but discarded the idea immediately. As dangerous as it would be to tell the Master, it would be more dangerous if he discovered it later on his own. The key was to control *how* the Master found out.

Eric spied his discarded belt and picked it up, then tugged both ends with a decisive snap.

"Pack up. We're going to Bristol."

6

THE WAGER

Sireniapolis, Sirenia
May 19, AD 1799/14 Tauros 4155 EK
Panselinos

No one can heal death.

The words of warning kept circling through Calandra's brain as she stared at the earthen pot nestled between her folded legs, the marble rim of the Fountain of Atargatis cold against her thighs through her bleached linen tunic. The terracotta coffin contained the herbaceous corpse of what had once been some kind of fern. To Narcissa and the circle of whispering novices and apprentices who watched, she projected calm confidence. But inside, her gut was clenched to the hardness of stone.

It's only a plant. A dead plant. It can't feel anything anymore.

In the five years that Damon had been training her, she had exceeded her undine instructors' expectations many times—but never Damon's, who only goaded her on to learn more. But lately, she had been getting worse, not better. A month ago, she wouldn't even have balked at the challenge before her. That was before she had tried to heal the rabbit.

She shuddered every time she thought of the gory end to which she had condemned the poor creature, and the scornful words Damon had showered upon her about her lack of control when she'd told him about her failure. Ever since then, her ability to manipulate all the elements had been affected, but none more than spirit. The timing couldn't have been worse—only weeks remained before she came of age, and one month before the Redemption Moon that would provide her a consort and the Summer Solstice when she would, at last, lead the Healing Ceremony in the Mother's Heart.

Heal the Heartstone? Lately, she hadn't even been able to heal leaf blight. But if she couldn't heal a plant, how was she ever going to repair the damage to the ever-fading Heartstone?

What is wrong with me? I've healed plants before. I can practically do it in my sleep.

But not dead ones.

The question is—is this plant truly dead?

Somehow, Narcissa had sensed her weakness and, as usual, pounced. Calandra knew the wager was a trap, a bid for her cousin to negotiate more favour with her mother, the queen. If Calandra failed, Narcissa would say she was too weak to heal the Stone and shouldn't be named Opal Princess, the title of the heir to the throne which Adonia had yet to officially bestow. And if she succeeded, Narcissa would say her power was *too* great, that the risk of her going Mad at any moment wasn't worth any potential benefit gained by having a healer of her power lead the Healing Ceremony—never mind what having a Mad queen might do to Sirenia.

Calandra didn't care one iota about the throne. But she couldn't afford to be out of control when it came to her healing abilities, and she couldn't avoid the niggling thought that she was still not powerful enough to do what must be done. Not with a dead rabbit staring at her every time she closed her eyes—and Osaze's unfocused gaze accusing her every time she saw him in her cousin's wake.

She glanced toward where Osaze stood near the Grotto palace entrance next to her bodyguard, a stout middle-aged Portuguese *tapeinos* guard named Domingo that Adonia had assigned to her. Narcissa had acquired Osaze as her bodyguard over two years ago, as soon as he'd gained his *ichthys* pin. She didn't hold his *sklavia* bond, though. Calandra had long ago found out that his bond would be held by the palace bondmistress, the same as the bonds of all the other unmarried men.

Since the night Calandra had tried to heal the Heartstone, along with her desperate research into how to prevent the Madness, she'd been searching for any hint of knowledge about how to Release a man whose bond she did not hold. She'd found answers to neither, not even when she'd finally been instructed in the use of the bonds a few months ago. As a future physic, she was one of the few women on the island who would be permitted to temporarily Release a man without a permit by having his bondmistress transfer the bond to her first—under certain rare circumstances—but all she'd learned still gave no indication how Tanni had been able to Release Osaze all those years ago. When she'd dared ask

Thea about it again, the *daskala* had simply snapped a cryptic comment about not poking her nose where it was likely to be bitten off and changed the subject.

To make it worse, since she would not be permitted to hold a *sklavia* bond until she was either engaged or had reached the age of majority and permitted to own a bodyguard, she had no way to experiment. She dared not practise on just anyone, because success on a stranger could spell disaster. She trusted Osaze. Mostly. She had no way of knowing that the gentle boy she remembered was not the exception to the rule. And she doubted that Thea would be so gracious for a second infraction, especially when Calandra should know so much better.

Gracious. Huh. Grace *still required a high cost.*

Tanni's emotions swirled in a corner of her mind like kelp in a current, somewhere southeast of the island where she was on patrol with her pod. Over the years, they had developed codes that would allow them brief, clandestine meetings in hidden nooks and crannies—but their time together was never long enough or often enough, and constant fear of discovery tainted each sweet moment with bitterness.

Calandra had asked Tanni a few times if she thought she might be able to figure out what she had done to break Osaze's bond, but Tanni refused to even talk about it. She was still game to help Calandra in most things, but when it came to topics that might get her suspended from the siren corps, she had a firm no-swimming policy.

Calandra studied the potted plant between her bare knees. Blackened fronds rattled faintly in the summer breeze, no hint of viability remaining. A whiff of urea assaulted her nose. What had Narcissa done to this poor thing?

"What are you waiting for, Calandra?" Narcissa goaded, sneering. "I thought you said healing a fern would be easy. How will you ever heal the Heartstone if you are so easily cowed by a mere plant?"

The princess stood above Calandra, her arms folded across her turquoise-blue siren cadet's tunic, her alabaster face distorted by a gloating smile. A red hibiscus in Narcissa's intricately plaited blond hair marked her as the heir presumptive, formal or not.

She could have the title, as far as Calandra was concerned. She only wished her cousin were better suited to rule. But she'd be chained if she'd allow Narcissa to think her weak. Maybe she could use this stupid wager to her advantage.

Calandra glared at Narcissa and adopted a bravado she didn't feel.

"Do you want me to heal this fern or spar words with you, dear cousin?" Narcissa barked a laugh.

"Frankly, I think you too weak and dim-witted for either, though I seem to be the only one who can see it. This is your chance to prove it to the world."

Afternoon light poured through the open windows and glass ceiling, glinting off the water and scattering diamonds onto the faces of the ring of students in dripping swimming outfits that surrounded her. Nervous, excited whispers passed between the girls like the tropical birds that flitted between the fruit trees in the atrium. Hovering behind them, Osaze's mother, Urbi, stood in anxious silence, as transfixed by the confrontation as her charges.

Calandra arched a brow at her cousin. "And if I succeed?"

"I already told you. You can have your pick of my closet. The last time I looked into yours, I was almost embarrassed for you. Not that I fear giving up any of my gowns today."

Calandra shook her head. "No."

"No?"

"You heard me. If I wanted something as frivolous as a tunic, I could have one. Aunt Adonia would see to it. I want something else."

Narcissa frowned. "Really."

Calandra gave a firm nod. It was worth a shot.

"If I win, I want to trade bodyguards with you."

Narcissa's nostrils flared. Her gaze flicked toward the two *tapeinoi* standing at attention at the edge of the courtyard. Calandra knew Narcissa had only wanted Osaze because of Calandra's connection with him. But, try as she might, she had never been able to find a legitimate reason for Narcissa to let him go.

Until now.

A sliver of doubt crept into Narcissa's expression. She dropped her gaze to the plant, seeming to reconsider.

"Come now, Narcissa." Calandra narrowed her eyes. "If I am risking a week of cleaning lavs for you, you must risk more than a pretty gown for me."

Mari, a sixth-year siren cadet and Narcissa's ever-present shadow, shook her head.

"That plant is deader than my great-grandmother," she scoffed. "You'll be off the hook for latrine duty for sure, Narcissa."

Narcissa smiled with renewed confidence and tilted her head at

Calandra.

"You think I don't know about your infatuation with my *doulos*? Fine. I agree to your terms on the condition that when you lose, you never try to take him from me again by any means. But I have little to fear. Osaze will be crossing *deiktes* with me later, not you."

Trust Narcissa to think that sparring with Osaze would make Calandra jealous. While Calandra's ability with *Tropos Hydor Zon*, the Way of Water, was passable, she did not have near the obsession with studying combat that her cousin did. She saved that energy for more scholarly pursuits. But then, if Calandra's skill with the elements were as limited as Narcissa's, she'd probably spend more time in the training ring, too.

Calandra smiled sweetly. "Don't worry, cousin. If you enjoy sparring with him that much, I'll let you borrow him once in a while."

Narcissa narrowed her eyes and said nothing.

Calandra frowned at the pot. This plant was further gone than any she had worked with before. The fern's fronds were nothing more than rattling, skeletal stems with leaves she dared not touch, lest they crumble off.

She glanced up at Osaze, whose unfocused stare condemned her by its very lack of accusation. For five years, she'd been looking for her chance to fulfill her promise to him, but the timing had never seemed right. Not to mention, Narcissa blocked her desires at every opportunity. At last, she could get one step closer.

If only she could do the impossible.

What if Narcissa were right? The stronger Calandra had gotten, the more the abyss pulled at the edges of her mind every time she healed, furling darkness that urged her to release the control she'd struggled so hard to gain. She had been too afraid to tell anyone, even Tanni, in case it were a harbinger of approaching insanity. Tanni still thought she'd made up Damon to get rid of the nightmares in the first place, not that Calandra could blame her. A male undine? Maybe she *was* going Mad.

She shook her head. No. Not yet.

Calandra placed one hand a few inches above the stiffened stems. She dangled the other in the cool water behind her.

Meg, a seventh-year stone healer acolyte who would soon be taking her adept's test along with Calandra, arched her black eyebrow and adjusted her posture in imitation of Daskala Thea. Though her thick straight hair was black instead of silver and she was not as tall, Meg's resemblance to her great-aunt was almost spooky.

"Feel the plant's energy," Meg intoned, her voice throaty and melodious like the headmistress's, her narrow dark green eyes intense. "Find the spark of life that still exists, deep in the roots. Do you *feel* it?"

The girls tittered, covering their mouths as they glanced nervously around to see if any of the *daskalas* had been near enough to overhear. Meg peeked at Urbi shame-facedly, but the Yoruba woman's black eyes never wavered from watching Calandra.

"Spark of life?" Urbi muttered in her native tongue. "Surely no life remains."

Calandra caught Urbi's eye. She had never told the woman about her promise to Osaze, but Urbi had always held a special place in her heart. The feeling seemed to be mutual. At any rate, Urbi would be well aware of the kind of treatment that Narcissa gave her servants.

Calandra nodded toward the tall, somewhat chunky woman and responded in the same language. "If there is, I'll find it. I promise."

Urbi nodded, then wrapped her hand around the strings of red and white beads she wore around her neck, lips moving in silent prayer. Calandra thought she heard Urbi invoke Yemaya, who, as far as she could tell, was the Yoruba name for Atargatis. She sent up a little prayer herself. She could use all the help she could get right now.

Sweat trickled down Calandra's back and soaked through the fabric of her *tsiraki's* tunic into her healer-green acolyte belt. She pressed her lips together and closed her eyes, concentrating on Tanni's emotions. Her friend seemed calm and controlled, exactly how she usually was—an anchor in the storm.

A pale child near the front with two long saffron-coloured braids stood up on her toes.

"You can do it, Calandra."

Calandra smiled at the girl, who looked like she was about seven years old—a second-year novice, at most.

"Thank you, Melany."

Melany gasped, then whirled to the girl next to her.

"Calandra knows my name!" she whispered loud enough to be heard out in the city. The two girls giggled until one of the older acolytes shushed them.

Calandra grinned, then moved her hand closer to the fern, drawing in water from the fountain through the fingers of her other hand. She closed her eyes and inhaled deeply. The clamouring emotions from the girls pounded at her mind—curiosity, nervousness, anger, fear, excitement, victory.

The noisy whispers—both audible and emotional—faded away as she concentrated. She reached for spirit with authority as Damon had so often told her to do, but it eluded her, fading into a sea of molasses-thick darkness.

Blinking away the tears pricking her eyeballs, she tried again, but it slipped through her fingers like an eel. Her heart thumped against her ribs as she fought the urge to release control of her powers, to give in to . . . what? She didn't even know, and it was the not knowing that terrified her.

Gritting her teeth, she reached for spirit once more and this time took hold. It fought her, but she maintained control and the darkness dispelled enough to allow her to focus.

She established a starting point for her empathy in her broken Tear pendant, then extended her awareness from the opal to the fern, creating an invisible energy line only she could sense. She let sensations from the plant pool in her chest and settle in her gut.

She could *feel* the water she channelled soaking into the loamy earth in the pot, diluting and flushing the salts from the uric acid that saturated it. She sensed the swarming microbes in their infinitesimal universe. She followed the paths of the plant's roots, now acid-burned, withered, and as dry as its leaves. She searched for the plant's pain—for where there was pain, there was life—but everything she touched had lost the ability to feel.

Silty water trickled out of the drainage hole and onto the marble between her legs, but she ignored it. Becoming increasingly desperate, she stretched her senses along each channel, looking for something, anything, she could use to—

There.

She stopped, holding her awareness where she had Seen it. At the tip of one branching root grew a tiny new shoot with live cells. They were dehydrated, but maybe, just maybe, it was enough.

She quivered in indecision, fearful of destroying what remained instead of healing it. The memory of being inside the Heartstone flashed through her mind and a sense of peace filled her. She relaxed.

Instinct took over.

Opening her eyes, she placed a finger on the fern's delicate crown, careful not to damage the leaves. Drawing on the water behind her, she pulled the aqueous energy through her trailing fingers into her body and then injected it into the plant, healing and hydrating the damaged live cells first. Seconds later, she began reconstituting the withered roots, using the living cells to reignite the cellular processes.

The outcome was assured now, but she never grew tired of watching it. She peered at the plant, eager for the change she could feel beneath the surface to spread to the skeletal remains above. Each revived cell's energy strengthened and cascaded to its neighbours, the effect multiplying and advancing until—in what seemed like an instantaneous rejuvenation—the fern's dried leaves freshened to a plump, velvety green, springing erect with renewed vigour.

Calandra poured one last pulse of energy into the fern and watched the leaves broaden and increase, new fronds emerging from the crown at an unnatural rate, bushing out the plant until it was more full and lush than seemed possible.

The novices let out a collective gasp and babbled with excitement and admiration. Urbi covered her mouth with her hands, staring at the plant in awe. Meg smiled in unabashed wonder.

Deeply satisfied and completely exhausted, Calandra drew her hand from the pool and cupped the lip of the pot between her palms, tension draining from her shoulders. She closed her eyes and carefully withdrew her awareness along the energy line into the stone, and then retracted it fully into her heart. The emotions of those around her dulled to an incoherent whisper, present but unremarkable, like the sound of the ocean pounding the shore in the distance beyond the iron-latticed windows.

Finally, she blew out a long breath and admired the miracle before her. "I did it."

Narcissa's arrogant smile fell into a disappointed frown—she must have thought victory was certain. She'd probably been dousing that fern with urine for a month to set this up.

Mari looked momentarily impressed. She glanced at Narcissa's face and her shock disappeared, replaced by folded arms and a stern set to her lips like her idol's.

Melany grinned and crossed her arms in mock authority.

"Told you you'd do it."

Calandra met the girl's crinkled emerald eyes, forcing a smile past the lethargy that now plagued her, a common side effect when she healed lately.

"It would appear you were right."

"Do what?" came an imperious voice from behind them.

7

THE HEADMISTRESS

THIS TIME, THE DISTINCTIVE THROATY voice came not from Meg, but the real Thea. The crowd of girls flowed aside to allow the headmistress through, separating like waves before a ship's bow. Her panacea's triquetra swung gently on its hair chain as she walked, the fire opal aflame in the light, her sculpted face framed by the curtain of her long silver hair.

The headmistress scanned the scene with a gaze as unfathomable as a deep-sea lagoon. Her consort and bodyguard, Gerrick, a wiry man whose features appeared somewhat skewed to one side—though he would have been handsome as a younger man, none-the-less—waited at attention behind the girls with Urbi, as was proper.

Thea turned to Calandra, her dark eyebrow arched exactly as Meg had imitated. One of the younger girls stifled a giggle. Thea glanced at her sharply and the child ducked her chin, her face aflame.

The *daskala* then turned her formidable grace toward Calandra.

"What did you do, *tsiraki*?" She somehow commanded an answer by her very posture.

Under her mentor's gaze, Calandra felt a rush of shame that she had used her gift—"a rare and precious thing," as Thea had so often reminded her—for something so frivolous. She drew a deep breath.

"I—I healed this fern, Daskala Thea."

Melany bounced on her toes. "She didn't only heal it. She brought it back to life!"

The other novices gasped. Calandra, who had often felt the receiving end of Thea's authority, knew that Melany's tender age would be the precocious child's saving grace for speaking out of turn.

Thea turned a baleful glare on the girl, and the child's freckles stood out like mud splattered on bleached linen. But the *daskala's* lips softened

53

with the hint of a long-suffering smile.

"No one can heal death, Melany. But if anyone could, I believe our Calandra might be the one to do so." She turned a stern face back toward her prize pupil. "Though if that were true, we have far better uses for her talents."

Calandra met her mentor's gaze, refusing to look away. She hadn't done anything wrong, exactly, but she expected Thea would find some menial task for her to perform as penance for her wastefulness anyway. Narcissa snickered, and Mari echoed with a shaky laugh.

Trembling slightly, Urbi stepped forward and touched her bowed forehead with her bunched fingertips in a respectful salute.

"If you had been here, *daskala*, you would have seen it was a matter of honour for Calandra," she said in Greek. "She had no choice."

"Oh?" Thea's eyebrow arched again as she glanced between Urbi and Calandra. "Please explain."

Urbi squared her shoulders. "Thank you, *daskala*." She glanced at Narcissa, whose eyes were throwing daggers at the human woman. "Princess Narcissa claimed that Calandra should be banned from marrying and bearing children, lest she destroy the Heartstone instead of healing it. Such a thing seems too cruel to wish upon any woman."

A hint of sadness touched her lips.

"And," Melany added, "she called Calandra a harpy who forced her own mother to the Madness."

Thea's eyes snapped toward Narcissa, her face harder than the visage of the statue behind Calandra.

"Is this true, *tsiraki*?"

The word seemed designed to remind Narcissa that here, she was a student like everyone else, not a princess.

Narcissa stiffened, glaring sullenly ahead. "Everyone knows that when a panacea bears a child, she goes Mad."

"Not all of us," Thea reminded her. "I have not, and I have three grown daughters with daughters of their own."

Narcissa's jaw worked. "Fine. *Practically* everyone. If Calandra bonds a consort, she could endanger us all with the very power she gains by it. Perhaps Mother should rethink her strategy to repair the Heartstone, not put so much faith in one person. That's all I meant."

Meg frowned. "Calandra is not the only new talent about to join the ranks of healer adepts."

"No, but she is the only one Mother cares about," Narcissa retorted, then stared fiercely at the orange tree in full bloom beyond the fountain.

Thea frowned. She glanced around at the dozen or so pairs of wide green eyes watching the scene as though noticing them for the first time. The novices' swimming attire was in disarray, their wet hair in tight braids. They had obviously come directly from the water.

"Aren't you novices slated for scrubbing the Pool of Atargatis today? Work duty isn't finished for another hour. Surely your tasks can't all be completed already?"

Thea eyed Meg, who had been supervising the work on the koi-filled pool outside until the disturbance in the Grotto had brought her charges running. Thea's great-niece had the good grace to look abashed.

"Megara kor'Sibylle, please return the children to their chores at once."

Meg cast a regretful glance at Calandra and Narcissa, obviously wanting to see how this played out. But she touched her forehead respectfully and began herding the younger girls down the flagstone path toward the water garden terrace in the outer courtyard, hushing Melany's protests.

Urbi fell into place beside Meg, seeming relieved that Thea had spared her a reprimand. The woman had been a governess at the Royal Academy since before Calandra had been born and was quite familiar with the undines' powers of healing—but even she kept glancing toward the fern and then Calandra as though unnerved by what she had seen. And was that a glimmer of hope in her eyes as she spared a glance for her son?

Once the younger children were out of earshot, Thea turned the considerable weight of her emerald-hard glare on Narcissa.

The acolyte fidgeted uncomfortably. "*Daskala*, I—"

"Silence."

Thea didn't raise her voice, but that one word fell like a whip. Narcissa closed her mouth and clasped her hands behind her, looking as though she were steeling herself for the inevitable tongue-lashing.

Thea glanced between Narcissa, Calandra, and Mari, then held out her hands toward Calandra.

"The fern, if you please, *tsiraki*."

Calandra unfolded herself from the ledge of the fountain and handed the headmistress the pot in one graceful motion. Thea examined it, sniffing and grimacing at the overpowering odour of urine that still remained, then regarded Calandra over the whispering fronds.

"How did you heal this?"

Calandra swallowed. "It wasn't dead. There was a hair shoot on one of the roots. I—"

"You brought that plant back from a hair shoot?" Even Narcissa sounded a little awed by the admission. "See, this is what I mean. Her power is simply too great to risk—"

"Did I not tell you to be quiet, child?" Thea arched her brow at the princess.

Narcissa clamped her mouth shut and fell back into her waiting posture, but her jaw worked and her nostrils flared.

Narcissa's power could fit into a nautilus shell—the only reason Adonia was even considering Calandra for the throne—so it was no wonder the princess had thought the plant was completely dead when she'd brought it to Calandra. In fact, if she weren't the eldest daughter of the queen, she would likely have been schooled in Haven as a weaver or some other trade more suitable to her talents instead of staying in Sireniapolis to train as a siren. It was fortunate that she had even enough ability with Song to achieve any kind of skill in that.

But as the probable future queen, she did not need to be able to stun a whole ship full of men with spirit as a siren or craft Tears as a stone healer. At most, she had only to worry about the one man she would eventually bond as King Consort, which would amplify her powers enough to take care of any other necessity. And she *did* need the combat, navigational, and political training siren warriors received.

Thea nodded, giving the plant an appraising glance before flicking her gaze toward Narcissa.

"Your *highness*"—the word nearly solidified, it was so cold—"perhaps you would consider returning to your duties at the lavs. I would hate to hear that Daskala Lida had extended your assignment there for another two weeks due to . . . *negligence*."

Narcissa's jaw dropped. "Two more weeks? That's ridiculous! I have already been on latrine duty for the past three weeks in a row. Cleaning lavs is for servants and *douloi*! My mother would never—"

"Your mother will abide by your house mother's—and my—decision," interjected Thea with a voice like iron, "and I'm afraid another *three* weeks are certain now. Be thankful I don't intend to tell your mother about your part here today. If the queen knew what you said about your cousin . . ." She let the threat hang in the air.

Narcissa's face went as red as the flower in her hair. Calandra almost felt bad for her. Almost.

The princess looked like she wanted to object again, but instead she dropped her gaze, turned to Thea, and touched her forehead with her bunched fingers.

"*Daskala*, may I be excused to resume my duties?"

Thea's nostrils flared in amusement. "As you wish, *tsiraki*. Do be sure to use the *proper* disposal vessels this time."

She tilted the pot toward the girl to emphasize her point.

Narcissa cast an irate glare at Calandra before twirling on her heel and marching toward the colonnade leading into the palace, her stance as regal as she could make it. When she reached Osaze and Domingo, she paused. Stiff-backed, she nodded curtly at Osaze, said something Calandra couldn't hear, then left. Domingo turned an enquiring gaze toward Calandra and she nodded, then Domingo followed the princess out.

Calandra watched her cousin's retreating back and bit her lip to stifle a smirk. No sense inviting more of Thea's ire than necessary by gloating. She was now one step closer to freeing Osaze. She did not yet hold his Redemption bond, but at least he was now in her charge. She could begin to work out what she must do—and hope the palace Mistress of Bonds wouldn't notice if she successfully Released him. With so many other bonds in the bondmistress's possession, surely she wouldn't?

Thea followed Narcissa's actions without comment, only glancing at Calandra with a curious expression. She turned to Mari next.

"And you, Tsiraki kor'Ana? Why are you here?"

Mari flushed like a cornered eel. "I, uh, I'm—" She closed her mouth, touched her forehead clumsily, then spun and practically fled on Narcissa's heels.

Calandra stood erect and kept her expression neutral, painfully aware that the round of dismissals had not included her. Alone with the headmistress but for Osaze and Gerrick, who waited patiently at the side of the flagstone path until his mistress had need of him, she wondered what her own house mother's justice would be. Since the headmistress and the Healing House's mother were one and the same, she knew she wouldn't have long to wait to find out. She thought it best to jump in before she could be reprimanded.

"*Daskala*, I am sorry. I never should have—"

Thea cut her off with a shake of the head. "I am not angry with you, child."

"You're not?"

"For healing a plant? Whyever would I be angry about that? 'All life is precious,' is it not? And what is a life restored?" Thea prompted, referring to one of the first-year apprentice rote memory lessons.

"'A life restored restores the healer.'"

Calandra had always wondered at that saying. Even now, exhaustion weighed her down like a heavy woollen blanket. All she wanted to do was go back to her room and sleep for the rest of the afternoon. Other than that day when she'd touched the Heartstone and felt so wonderfully alive, she had rarely experienced the energy that others reported after healing.

"Precisely," Thea said, as though the matter were settled. She gave the fern in her hand one last admiring look and then set it down near a brilliant clump of birds-of-paradise beside the walkway. "There is a matter I need to discuss with you."

"Oh?" Calandra wasn't sure if that was good or bad news. It seemed to have little to do with the fern.

The quartz-encased rainbow opal Tear in Thea's silver wristband vibrated, and a thin-sounding voice emanated from it.

"Port Physic Bay to Thea."

Thea pressed her index finger to the stone to unlock the communication channel, then raised the bracelet to her mouth.

"Thea here. Go ahead, Heo."

Calandra frowned. The Harbour Physic sounded rushed. Even stranger, Tanni's emotions through the bond were turbulent and upset, and were now coming from the bay. In the next moment, Calandra knew why.

Heo spoke again. "We've got a situation down here. Patrol pod tried to save a dolphin cow-calf pair. We've got the calf and an injured siren. Come quick. I'm going to need help for this one, and I can't raise Niobe."

Thea's expression looked grim. "I'll be right there."

Calandra gulped. Could Tanni be the injured siren? It was difficult to tell from her friend's emotions whether they were caused by pain or merely worry.

Thea turned to face her student.

"You're coming, too. Time to earn your physic ring."

The world turned to ice. With wooden movements, Calandra followed the older woman out of the garden. Images of the dead rabbit's staring, blank eyes flashed through her mind.

Yes, she had healed a plant.

But she did not feel anywhere near ready to heal a person.

And what if that person were Tanni?

8

THE DOLPHIN

The streets of Sireniapolis were swollen with festival-day traffic—brightly dressed ladies and their families coming or going from paying their respects to the Mother at the Temple of Atargatis in the lower city. Savoury smells and last-minute haggling between household servants and the street merchants vending food for the evening feast filled the air. Children swam in the canal running along the outer edge of the Street of Pearls, the main road that defined each gently curved tier of the city. Beyond the city stretched the Paradise Valley, with its rolling green hills, patchwork fields, and irrigation canals flowing down to the Atlantic Ocean.

Calandra bit back her frustration as she walked next to Thea along the flagstone sidewalks that would take them to the Lower City. She normally loved the opportunity to be out on the streets during Panselinos. Even without the festive atmosphere, the view of the white stone city with its canals and waterfalls and the eroded black rock spires that guarded the valley would be enough to lift her spirits.

But now, as Osaze cleared a path through the bustling crowd for her and Thea, with Gerrick a vigilant escort behind, she resented every obstacle that delayed her from reaching Tanni for even a second. Gerrick's gaze roved about in an unfocused way, his *deiktis* staff doubling as a walking stick.

They hurried the mile down to the bay, taking the more direct route of the bridges and steep flights of stairs between levels rather than travelling by canal boat or rickshaw down the four tiers of the city. Adrenaline had subverted Calandra's fatigue, and a storm thundered in her heart the entire way. Tanni's turbulent emotions, usually something she could notice and keep at a slight distance—like looking at the contents of a clear glass jar on a shelf—were all she could think about.

By the time they reached the brick-paved square that hosted both the Court of the Redeemed and the Physic House, Calandra was convinced that Tanni was on death's door. She feared she would be required to save her friend's life in order to earn her physic ring. But she didn't think she could do it.

If that's what Thea asks of me, I'll . . . I'll . . .

Calandra didn't know what she'd do. If Tanni were injured, she couldn't refuse to heal her. She'd hate herself forever. Her pulse raced, and she prayed fervently for the injured siren to be someone else. Then she punished herself mentally. A failure to heal another woman would not be much better than losing Tanni. But if it were someone else, at least she could step aside and delay her Physic Trial for another time, letting more experienced— and assured—hands do what must be done.

What other time? The Heartstone Healing Ceremony is in a month. You can't afford to be a coward, Calandra kor'Delphine. There's no time.

The security hut in front of the Physic House came into view and the bands of anxiety around Calandra's lungs tightened.

"Are you sure I'm ready for this, Thea?"

Thea kept her urgent pace, but tilted her head at her *tsiraki*. "How many live cells remained in that fern when you began?"

Calandra shrugged. "I don't know. One, maybe as many as five?"

A stunned expression crossed Thea's face. "Five cells . . . ?" She shook her head. "Remarkable."

Calandra put a hand on her mentor's arm.

"A fern is not a rabbit, *daskala*. And a rabbit is not a person. How dare I try to heal anything greater than a scratched finger if my power could do more harm than good?"

Thea turned a level gaze toward her student. "You have healed many rabbits and other animals, too. I have seen you dissolve tumours from chickens, drain abscesses in dogs, clear colic in horses, and even cleanse the sacred fish of parasites. You *know* what you're doing, Calandra. You have a more acute sense of empathy than anyone I've ever known, your mother included. When you choose to use it."

Calandra frowned, but nodded. Thea gave a nod like a judge's gavel and turned to speak to the siren on watch duty. Calandra gazed around to distract herself. Behind them, Osaze and Gerrick stood motionless and emotionless, as was to be expected.

There were only two structures on this street, standing opposite each other across an enormous pounded-dirt square with no adornments or gardens of any kind. The square was practically barren now. Most of the fish vendor stalls near the quay had already closed so the merchants could spend the festival with their families. But next month during the Redemption Moon, when the new crop of men was harvested, this place would be filled with half the city.

On one side, the marble Court of the Redeemed far overshadowed the much plainer Physic House in grandeur. Its frieze depicted scenes that romanticized the Commission of Atargatis to Redeem men. Marble columns of muscular human men held up the roof on either side of the wide steps. In comparison, the simple straight lines, smooth face, understated mouldings, and arched windows of the medical bay built out into the water made it look like a plain, matronly older sister who was too practical and busy to worry about the fripperies of adornment.

Romea, the siren singer on watch duty, waved their group through the door into the stone building. Calandra's throat tightened as the moment of truth approached.

The interior was cool, with high ceilings and walls of pale stone. Afternoon sunlight angled through large copper-latticed windows along the wall and fell in dappled patches on the double row of empty beds, about two dozen in total. A large wooden door in the wall to the right of the entrance hung open, and sounds of splashing came from the water pens in that part of the building. But what drew Calandra was not the sound, but her infallible inner locator—the secret bond she and Tanni shared. She was soon running along the wooden walkway directly to where Tanni swam in a pen with her hands on a dolphin calf, surrounded by bloody water. Another siren whom Calandra didn't know by name was with her, helping her hold the calf still and humming a soothing melody.

"Tanni!"

Tanni twisted to look at her, not breaking contact with the calf. "Heo's tending to Danai. Help me."

A weight lifted from Calandra's heart. Tanni was fine. She ignored the pricking of her conscience that she should not be so relieved by that.

Thea had caught up in time to hear Tanni's explanation. She took in the situation with the calf, who was missing a large piece of her side and was barely conscious, in a single glance.

"Calandra, you help here. I will see what has happened to Danai."

Calandra nodded, not even bothering to strip her tunic as she turned and stepped down the ladder into the pen, disturbing the water as little as possible with her entry before changing to *ichthys* state.

Tanni and the other singer moved aside to allow her access to the dolphin's head. They were doing as they had been trained, keeping the injured calf sedated with Song. The calf's eyes were glazed, but that was probably from lack of blood, not sedation. Calandra cupped her hands on either side of the dolphin's face. As soon as she touched it, the full extent of the damage hit her in a blast that left her feeling nauseous.

Tanni frowned in concern. "What's wrong?"

"She's just . . ." Calandra looked at her friend, the void tickling at her mind even more forcefully than earlier. "I don't know if I can do this, Tanni."

Tanni laid one hand on Calandra's arm.

"Just do your best. We're here to help. Tell us what to do."

Calandra looked at her friend, thinking. Physic healing required earth, water, and air, which she could easily handle, but also spirit, which was the area she struggled with most when healing animals. She'd managed to grasp spirit earlier with the plant, but that healing had required her to use the element very little. This was totally different. What if she couldn't grasp it again? Or couldn't maintain control for the full duration of the task?

Wait. Since sirens only used spirit, perhaps they *could* be of use.

Calandra nodded and turned her attention to the calf.

"You," she said to the other woman. "Support her tail."

The singer did as she was instructed. Calandra indicated that Tanni should come support the calf's head, and then she moved to the side where the injuries were the most serious. She looked at the wound with misgiving.

"Do you know what happened to her?"

While the ways of nature were harsh, undines did not usually interfere when one animal made prey of another. Each species had the right to eat.

"Humans," said the other siren, the disgust in her voice plain. "They didn't even want her. They were after a school of fish, and she and her mother happened to be in the way."

Calandra's gut clenched in rage. She frowned and glanced at Osaze, who had taken up position on the walkway, observing her with the detachment of the drugged. She shook her head, pushing away her fears at what he might do when she eventually Released him. Would he be the same person she remembered? Or would he have become like the men they worked so hard to protect themselves from, the kind that would kill a dolphin and her calf while fishing and would murder you in your sleep if given the chance?

No time for moral questions now. Right now, this baby's life needed saving. And she was the only one here who could do it.

"I need both of you to keep her calm, just as you have been doing."

They nodded, taking up their humming once more.

She closed her eyes and gently placed the tips of her fingers on the healthy skin on either side, as close to the wound as possible without causing further discomfort. Despite the sirens' soothing Song, she was nearly overwhelmed with the dolphin's panic and pain. She wrestled to regain control. A cool hand touched her forearm and the emotional maelstrom subsided. She looked up to see Tanni with one hand on the dolphin's head, the other on Calandra's arm, never stopping the wordless vocalizing that calmed both the animal and herself.

"Be water," Tanni said, then went back to humming.

Calandra gave a brief nod of thanks, then closed her eyes again. This time, she could feel the energy of Tanni's spirit added to her own.

The *Tropos Hydor Zon* explained how water could be likened to the energy used to end a conflict or manipulate the elements. *Water can be guided, but water can also guide. It can fill a vessel, lift a vessel, or crush a vessel. It can rend holes in the earth in sudden violence or move mountains with the patience of ages. Spirit gives life, and water heals it. Be water.*

When Thea or the other *daskalas* explained what this meant, they always talked about flowing with the elements and guiding them to where they needed to be to bring balance. But Damon had taught her that to manipulate the elements, she had to bend them to her will like the ocean controlling a boat in a storm. In his time, he said, back in the days of Atlantis, the healers had merely to think about what they wanted, and they could close even the direst of wounds.

She desperately wanted to command that kind of power. It made sense that techniques that no one had used in millennia were the only thing that would save her people, and she was determined to master them. She held her breath and reached for the elements. Earth, water, air. Now spirit, the key component she would need to See what she was doing.

This time, I'll do it.

But spirit—the most basic element in the Matrix of Creation—would not be grasped. Instead, she once again fought the warm darkness that pulled at her senses, a whispered suggestion to release instead of hold. Was it her mind playing tricks on her? Her heart thumped in fear, and the darkness and exhaustion clouded her mind. Shaking her head, she focused her inner Sight and tried again, adding the strength of Tanni's spirit to the claim. When it still didn't work, she glanced at the other siren, who stopped humming when she saw Calandra's frown.

"Lay your hand on my arm and share spirit with me," Calandra said.

The siren nodded and did as she was asked. Calandra tried again with their triple cord of spirit brought to bear. Punching through the confusing darkness, she grabbed hold of the final element she needed, holding onto it with fierce determination. She stretched her awareness through her mother's broken Tear into the dolphin, which began thrashing and squealing in pain.

"Calandra?" Tanni's eyebrows bunched.

Calandra frowned, concentrating, *willing* the flesh to heal. The calf bucked and heaved, screaming.

"Calandra!"

At Tanni's cry, Calandra pushed herself away and watched helplessly as the two sirens attempted to calm the baby once more.

Thea appeared at her side, treading water with small movements of her greenish-silver tail, her silvery hair floating on the surface like a cloud and obscuring the clinging short grey linen bodice she'd stripped down to. She gave Calandra a troubled look, then swam over to the dolphin. Heo appeared on the calf's other side. At Thea's command, the four women placed their hands on the calf and closed their eyes.

The dolphin relaxed and went silent. The flesh began to regenerate over the exposed ribs, closing the open wound in minutes.

"That's enough for now, Heo," said Thea, pulling away. "We will heal the rest later. She needs to rest and regain some of her strength."

Heo nodded and backed away from the calf, who continued to bob at the surface, eyes drooping closed. Heo asked the two siren women to submit to a cursory examination. They swam toward the walkway and each let Heo place her palm on their forehead for a brief internal diagnostic before climbing up the ladder.

Thea turned her piercing emerald gaze on Calandra.

"What went wrong this time?"

Calandra's tears mixed with the salty water on her already-wet face.

"I almost killed her."

9

THE JOURNEY

Four Months Earlier
Somewhere in Western England
January 1799

ZALE SAT IN THE REAR-FACING seat of the mail coach, trying to make sense of everything Abela had just told him. She sat across from him, staring at the little wheeled device she called a chariot that was suspended by the chain she held in both hands.

Zale still caught his breath at the memory of the single step that had taken them from the barn to the middle of an open field. After an initial jump that had moved them only a day's journey toward their goal, Abela had been unable to make the chariot work again. In between his questions, she kept fiddling with it.

"So, let me get this straight." Zale licked his lips. "You're an angel—"

"Cherub."

"Fine, *cherub*, who has been assigned to me as a guardian since I was born. Reverend Berian was meant to be watching my mother. And your, um, 'father,' Mr. Penrose, who wasn't *really* your father, because your kind aren't born, they're *made*"—he still couldn't wrap his mind around that one—"was supposed to guard my father."

"Doing good so far." She frowned at the chariot and blew gently, but after a few weak spins, the wheels stopped gyrating. She gave a frustrated snort.

"And my mother has been missing since soon after I left, and Berian has no idea where she went."

Zale swallowed a lump in his throat. He'd left to protect his mother, but Abela had said that she'd left to find him and had never come home. He wondered what had been happening to all the money Eric had supposedly been sending home to help support her.

Abela's golden gaze flicked toward him. "That's right."

"And you've been looking for me ever since that day with the wasps."

For the first time, she dropped her gaze, then looked out the carriage window at the passing fields. "Yeah, it sounds like you've got it."

"What I still don't understand is, if you're an angel . . . uh, *cherub*, and you had one of those all along"—he pointed at the chariot—"why did it take you so long to find me? And who is after my mother?"

Abela turned large earnest eyes on him. "Not only your mother. You and your sister, too. And technically, they found you, but they must have thought that keeping you imprisoned would be easier if you didn't know it."

"Right. Eric."

Zale frowned at the green stone bracelet he still wore, a storm brewing in his belly. Abela had offered to figure out a way to take it off, and he had declined. It might represent Eric's betrayal, but it also helped him keep his fearsome powers in check. No answering clouds, wind, or rain arose out of nowhere in response to his inner turmoil. He felt safer with it on.

He picked at the hemp bracelet with the striped brown river stone woven into it on his other wrist. It had been a gift from his mother. If he'd had this green stone bracelet when he'd discovered his abilities, he never would have left home. Maybe his mother would have never gone missing. What else could have been different?

His gut clenched. He stopped fidgeting and stared up at the ceiling.

Abela sighed and slipped the necklace chain over her head, letting the gyroscope drop beneath her clothing.

"How well do you know your Bible?"

Zale blinked at her. "What?"

"Greek mythology?"

Blank stare.

"*Any* mythology?"

Zale shrugged. "My mother taught me some of that stuff when I was a kid, but that was a long time ago. Why is that important?"

Abela frowned. "It's important because in order to answer your question about who is after you, you first have to understand who you are and why you are so special. And to do that, you have to understand the history of the races."

Zale leaned back against the hard bench and made an encompassing gesture.

"We won't reach Bristol until tonight. So I've got nothing but time." He patted his empty pockets and gave a wry smile. "Literally."

Abela giggled at his attempt at a joke and it ended in a small snort.

"Yeah, we'll have to do something about that at some point. After we see Berian so I can replenish my purse."

She had been reticent to hire a seat on the mail coach, since it had used up nearly all of her remaining money, but she had justified it to Zale—and herself, probably—by claiming the urgency and secrecy of their mission. Walking in the open would have taken too much time and been too con-spicuous. The mail coach, though open to other passengers, was the safest, fastest way to travel—and they'd had the good fortune to arrive from their jump only a mile outside of Gloucester, walking into town minutes before the coach came through the night before.

There had been other passengers in the coach for the first part of the night, so he'd had little opportunity to ask questions. At Abela's insistence, he had dozed until the change of the horses, at which point the other passengers had inexplicably decided to exit the coach. No new ones had gotten on, despite there being several waiting at the post. Zale was certain Abela had had something to do with that, though he'd no idea how she'd managed it.

Zale's stomach grumbled. The last thing he'd eaten was a hurried breakfast of cold cuts and stale bread that Josefine had fed him yesterday morning, and it was nearly time for breakfast again.

"Do angels—*cherubim*—do cherubim eat?"

"When we take on flesh, we do. I'm sorry, I didn't have much extra money to buy food, but I did get these." She reached beneath the seat and pulled out a small cloth-covered basket. She opened it and pulled out two soft boules of bread and two wedges of white cheese. She handed a chunk of cheese and some bread to Zale, and he accepted gratefully.

"So," he said around a mouthful of bread, "are you going to fill in the gaps in my sorely lacking education?"

Abela swallowed a mouthful of food and rested the back of the dainty hand holding her cheese on her lap.

"After the universe was organized from chaos, or its basic elements—"

"Wait—when the *universe* was made? We have to go all the way back to Creation, here?"

Abela cleared her throat and smoothed her skirt.

"Yes. We do." She gave him a level stare. "Now, may I continue?"

He raised an eyebrow, then flipped a hand in a resigned gesture that said *by all means.*

She eyed him for another moment, then continued.

"As I was saying, after creating the universe, Elyon—the Almighty—made several races to populate it. First he made seraphs, born of fire. They are the ones that humans typically refer to when they think of angels, by the way. He also made my people, born of light, and yours, the undines, born of water. Lastly, he made humans, born of earth, whom he called the crowning achievement of Creation."

Zale chewed slowly. "Reverend Berian said God formed Adam from the dust and breathed his spirit into him."

Abela's face lit up. "Yes!" She jabbed at the air with her cheese. "Exactly. The breath of Elyon's spirit is in all, giving life and order."

Zale smiled, glad he had paid attention in Sunday school once in a while—in between making faces at the girls and dipping their hair in ink. He cleared his throat. He had been quite the handful.

Abela took a bite of cheese and swallowed.

"Elyon created each race for a specific purpose. Seraphim were to serve as his messengers and warriors and as princes of the dominions. Cherubim were meant to be guardians and protectors of his holy places, specific people, and to be the throne-bearers of Elyon. And undines were to guard and keep the oceans and the passage to the underworld."

"Wait—the underworld? Do you mean hell?"

Abela tilted her head back and forth as she considered his question.

"Well, 'hell,' as you call it, is now *part* of the underworld, but originally, Tartarus was meant only to be the place where chaos—the unordered elements of the universe—had been contained, kind of like an elemental storage room for Elyon to draw from as needed, if you will."

Zale shook his head. He wasn't sure he followed, but didn't know if an explanation would help.

"Go on."

Abela looked at him skeptically, then continued.

"Elyon placed humans, the youngest of the races, over all the creatures of the Earth and placed each of the other races in their service—not to obey humans, but to protect them and help them fulfill their duties in obedience to Elyon. Unfortunately, some of the seraphim didn't understand why they must serve such a naive, ignorant race—one bound to the Earth, no less—when they themselves had abilities and beauty that nearly rivalled that of Elyon himself. There were differing opinions about how to remedy the situation."

Zale frowned. "Oh?"

"Yes. One of them, a seraph known as Kesbeel, the right hand of Elyon, thought that, in order to become worthy of his esteem, humans only needed knowledge. So he sent his accomplice Gadreel to offer it to Eve in the Garden of Eden, humanity's nursery. That was when things went horribly wrong."

Zale frowned, searching his memory. "I thought the serpent's name was Lucifer?"

Abela nodded. "Christians now call him that. But they use the same name for several other seraphim mentioned in their Scriptures. I'd prefer to be specific."

Zale dipped his chin. "Fair enough."

Abela finished off her cheese, then transferred her bread to her dominant hand.

Zale leaned forward, fascinated. While he'd heard Reverend Berian preach the bones of this story from the pulpit, there were certainly some details that had been missing. He wanted to discredit the whole thing as a tall tale—but after what had happened last night, and the fact that this strange story was the first thing he'd ever heard that explained his own existence, he couldn't help but believe it. And if he needed proof, he need look no further than the golden-brown girl with the eyes of a lioness before him. His mouth went dry as the image of the sphinx jumping toward him from brilliant light popped into his mind.

Abela continued. "Humans were not yet mature enough for the knowledge they received. Not only that, the disobedience of the first humans cursed all flesh, making it mortal."

"That hardly seems fair to humans. They were all cursed because of the disobedience of a couple? What about the seraphs . . . seraphim? That race?"

Abela sighed. "Few humans have been able to throw off the mantle passed on by their forebearers. Unfortunately, rebellion against Elyon is rebellion against order, and a spirit in rebellion is tainted by chaos, tugging it closer to the Abyss than to the throne of Elyon. Thus, men were cursed with physical death."

She paused, and her expression became downcast.

"Hundreds of seraphim followed Kesbeel in a rebellion against Elyon and were defeated. They and the impertinent Gadreel were imprisoned in the Abyss, a place at the edge of chaos, to await judgement—though Elyon the Merciful still gives them a chance to repent, even now."

A look of wonder filled her face as she pondered that. She gave her head a shake.

"Despite the potential consequences, later, hundreds more seraphim, led by a seraph named Semyaza, left heaven to give humans more knowledge they were not yet ready to learn, but with intentions even less pure than Kesbeel's had been. They gave only enough knowledge to make humans easy to control, and set themselves up as gods and goddesses, taking the worship of humans—rightfully meant for Elyon—for themselves. They even married humans and had children by them. In the end, they, too, were imprisoned in the Abyss, and the spirits of their children—giants who harassed and hunted humanity nearly to extinction—were bound to the Earth without physical form. You call them demons."

Tears glistened in her eyes.

"Their stories—or stories inspired by them—have survived in the ancient religions of the world. You know them under names like Zeus, Shiva, and Ishtar."

Zale frowned. He'd heard of Zeus. The other two, he wasn't so sure about.

"This is quite the story, but other than my people's origin, I don't understand what any of it has to do with me."

Abela shifted in her seat and looked out the window.

"After the rebellion, Tartarus became the place of confinement, not only of the rebellious human spirits, but also the rebels of the other races. Undines were the keepers of the Abyss, responsible for maintaining the barrier that confined all those awaiting judgement."

She turned to face him.

"Over time, the undines have forgotten their purpose, and the barrier has weakened. There is a human secret society known as the Order of the Ascension of the Grigori that believes the confined spirits should rule humanity, that only the fallen seraphim offer men *true* knowledge and power, which they claim Elyon has tried to conceal."

She shook her head sadly.

"Foolish, blind men."

Zale clutched the last hunk of his bread, his mouth too dry to take another bite. "Why do you say that?"

She looked at Zale.

"The Order has made it their mission to free the spirits who have been confined there. In order to do that—in order to break the chains that bind their chosen masters—they need you and your sister. If they can't get to her, your mother will probably do. In the meantime, your mother is serving as bait."

What she had told him had his mind spinning. He shook his head.

"Why us? If there is a whole race of people like me somewhere"—his heart leaped at the thought—"then what makes my family so special?"

"Because," Abela said, "in order to free the Grigori, the Order needs to destroy the barrier, which requires both a powerful male and powerful female undine. You and your sister are the most powerful of either that have been born in three millennia. And, in your case . . ."

Abela fidgeted with the sleeve of her pelisse and looked out the window into the darkness.

Every nerve in Zale's body tightened to the point of snapping.

"What?"

"In your case, you're the *only* one to have been born in that time."

Zale felt as though he had just learned to breathe and had simultaneously forgotten how.

"What do you mean?"

She touched his knee as though trying to soften a blow.

"Zale, you are the only male undine in existence."

Zale stared at her. *I'm the only one?*

The carriage slowed to a stop, and a couple of bangs on the door indicated they'd reached their destination.

Abela's face tightened—most people would probably not have noticed, but Zale, who had made a career out of studying people's expressions, certainly did.

"What's the matter?" he asked.

She started. "Pardon? Nothing. C'mon." She opened the carriage door and pointed for him to precede her. "Let's go find Berian."

10

TOOLS OF THE TRADE

Bristol

ZALE SAT IN THE BACK pew of the small but airy church, its cream-coloured walls making the room seem more spacious than it was. Abela stood near the front of the room beneath a high raised pulpit, speaking with the imposing Reverend Berian. While Zale waited for her signal to come forward, as he'd been instructed, he took in the building's clean lines, the smooth columns that supported the roof, and the elegant dark wooden benches that furnished the hall. An enormous octagonal window in the ceiling illuminated the space with soft daylight from the late afternoon sun.

Abela's and Berian's voices rose and fell several times but were mostly restrained to urgent whispers. Zale couldn't make out much. At one point, Abela handed Berian her chariot—she had said she'd intended to ask Berian to look at it and figure out why it wasn't working. Berian didn't seem to want to give it back, and Abela looked less than impressed.

Then Abela said something that caused Berian's attention to snap in Zale's direction. Zale shifted uncomfortably and fidgeted with the stone bracelet. How could he have never noticed that, under Berian's thick, heavy eyelids, the minister's eyes also glowed that molten gold colour? With his black suit stretched over his ample middle, the reverend looked like a round, black raven. Or a bulldog who had gotten into the coal scuttle.

Berian turned his attention back to Abela, whose arms were crossed.

"Wait here," Berian commanded in a carrying voice. He fixed another baleful stare on Zale, then turned and marched out a side door, tucking the chariot pendant into his breast pocket.

The moment he left, Abela whirled and hustled toward Zale.

"Let's go."

"What?"

Zale stood, but not quickly enough for Abela. She grabbed his elbow and began pushing him out the door.

"We can't be here when he gets back. Let's *go*."

When they reached the cobbled pavement outside, Abela broke into a trot. Far from the awkward gait of most ladies in a gown and heels, she somehow retained her cat-like grace. Zale jogged to catch up, following her through a maze of streets and alleys until she reached a street near the River Avon. She stopped, and he leaned against a stone wall, breathing hard.

"What was all that about?" he said between gasps.

She shook her head, her hands braced on her knees. "Let's just say Berian isn't going to be as much help as I'd hoped."

Zale frowned. "Why not? Did he say? And does he know where my mother is?"

"It's personal. Not exactly. And maybe," she said, ticking off her responses on her fingers as she gave them. "As I feared, the Order discovered your mother's location and they were already closing in by the time you . . . disappeared. Berian helped her escape and remained behind to throw them off her scent—and to keep an eye out for you. She took passage on a ship to Barbados, and he was to follow and meet her there. He suspects she probably intended to return home, perhaps to recruit help in finding you. However, he hasn't heard from her in over three years. He has gone to Barbados and several other islands in the West Indies, but has found nothing."

"So why hasn't Berian gone to . . . wherever my people live?"

Abela shook her head. "It's not that simple. While the undine realm can access both the spiritual and material planes, creatures from outside it cannot enter without a special key, which Berian does not have. But you do."

Zale blinked. "I do?"

"Of course."

Abela pointed at the small, plain-looking brown stone bead woven into the hemp bracelet on his arm. The bracelet had been made for him by his mother and had worn remarkably well over time. It was a little snug, but he never took it off—just as she'd warned him not to. He looked at the flat, oval-shaped bead in wonder. Stripes of dark brown wavered across the cream-coloured surface. It looked like a stone you would find in any stream or river, completely unremarkable. Its only value to him had been in the giver.

"This?"

He held up his wrist to show her.

Abela nodded. "One of your mother's powers is creating special patterns in stone. She has keyed that to allow you to cross the barrier into the realm of your people. That means—"

"—we can look for her there." Zale grinned, his heart pumping with a rush of energy. "Do you know where it is?"

"Approximately." Abela looked hesitant. "There's another problem, though."

"What?"

"Berian wouldn't give me any money. We're broke, we have no chariot, and Sirenia is on the other side of the Atlantic Ocean."

"Sirenia? Huh." Zale rolled the word around on his tongue, trying it out. "Sirenia. I like it."

A cracking sound caught his attention, and he turned to see some children sitting on a stoop, crushing walnuts into a bowl, then making fun of the way the wrinkled meat looked before they ate it.

Standing abruptly, Zale grinned at his guardian.

"As for the trip across the Atlantic, leave that to me."

*

ZALE spent the rest of the afternoon playing a shell game on various street corners of Bristol, entertaining gullible citizens out of their farthings and pennies. He hired a street urchin named John as a shill, and the lad threw himself into the role like he was born for it. The coins the boy earned didn't hurt any either.

Abela refused to participate.

After watching several rounds of wagers, she pulled Zale aside as he settled on another potential location.

"You have to stop. You are swindling these people, Zale. That is like stealing and lying at the same time. There is no way I can be a part of that. And I don't want you to do it either. We must find another way."

"What other way?"

He held out his hands wide, inviting alternative suggestions, the three undamaged walnut shell halves he'd collected from the children in one open palm, and a small round pebble he'd found in the other.

"Trust me. This works. And I never take much. What little my clients lose, they can afford to. And it is not much payment to ask for the service I provide."

Abela rolled her eyes, her arms crossed. "What service? Thievery? Most people are quite willing to pass on that."

Zale drew himself up.

"I am *not* a thief. Though I do know a fair bit about pickpocketing."

Abela gave him an incredulous look. "You do hear yourself, right?"

Zale smiled cheekily and shrugged.

"I didn't say I would do it, only that I know how. The service I provide is entertainment. I bring some cheer to my customers' otherwise-dull lives. It's like when people used to pay to stare at me, except this way is more fun. For me." He cocked his head in thought. "And probably for them."

Abela snorted. "'Customers.' Huh." She picked up one of the shells and examined it, frowning. "How did you learn to do this, anyway?"

Zale brushed the dust off of a piece of wood covering a water barrel on the sidewalk.

"A few years ago, one of the walls of my tank cracked. It was three months before they were able to find a way to repair it. I spent that time under the tutelage of Eric's nephew, Gio. He taught me everything I know." He fidgeted with the shells. "Literally. These are my only useful skills. It's tough to learn much while you're floating in a tank for the better part of every day."

He glanced away, wondering what Gio was doing now. The boy had been his closest friend. Had he been in on the hoax, too?

Sitting down on a wooden crate, he arranged the three shells on the water barrel lid like a chorus line of small turtles ready for a show, and grinned up at her, tamping down the shame and sorrow the conversation had produced. Abela had powers and fancy gadgets, but what good were they now? And how dare she look down on the one way he had to earn some honest money without revealing their secret?

"So, are you going to help, or not?"

Abela turned away, her expression cloudy. "I can't."

"Can you at least stand over there and attract potential customers, then?" He pointed a short distance away.

"And how am I supposed to do that?"

"Oh, just stand there and watch. Trust me, if I don't draw a crowd, you certainly will."

Abela looked dismayed. "What do you mean by that? I chose this appearance so I would be inconspicuous."

Zale raised an eyebrow. "A beautiful African woman dressed in silk in Bristol, one of England's prime slaving ports? Very inconspicuous."

Abela's lips clamped shut. Her face first went very pale, and then flushed a deep rosy brown. The space around her dimmed.

"And what," she said, in a voice as thin and cold as winter sunlight, "is that supposed to mean?"

Zale rubbed the back of his neck and avoided her gaze.

"It means that you're, erm, very pretty." He eyed her outfit. "And your dress confuses people."

Her blush deepened. She glared at him, then huffed and walked off in a different direction than he'd pointed. However, when she turned around at approximately the distance he'd requested, Zale rubbed his chin on his shoulder to hide a smile. With her folded arms, set jaw, and fierce glare, she looked like an angry tigress—but she was doing as he'd asked.

Zale turned to the young boy who had paused to inspect the walnut shells in curiosity. "Would you like to see how it works, lad?"

John nodded eagerly, the brim of his cap bobbing like a duckling.

"Yessir. Please, sir."

Good lad.

With the ease of a skill he'd never stopped practising—the game had been a good way to pass the time on the road or with his mates in the morning—Zale's hands began their choreographed dance with the shells and the pebble—*where could it possibly be?*—while he entertained the gathering crowd with witty patter. He always let his mark think they had a chance to win, first by letting John win something, and then losing a low wager with his target to convince them to wager a higher value coin, which he would then win. After a couple of rounds of that, it was time to find a new location, with new customers.

Abela continued glaring at him, and he didn't try to stop her. Glaring at him was less likely to get them arrested than glaring down the curious, and often rude, glances and whispers of the middle-to-upper-class citizens who soon joined her—leaving a safe distance, of course, in case her race might be catching.

Zale caught her gaze, her eyes glimmering with moisture. He paused his spiel, wishing his prediction hadn't been correct. She whirled and walked away down the street.

He pressed his lips together, then went back to the game.

11

THE TEMPLE

CALANDRA FLOATED IN THE CLEAR water of the temple pool in *podia* state with her eyes closed, legs crossed in front of her. She held her breath until red spots appeared behind her eyelids and her body's natural reflex took over. As her legs fused into her *ichthys* tail and her gills opened to relieve her burning lungs, she opened her eyes and sat on the bottom of the marble pool, her fin undulating in the gentle movement of the water. Through the twisting cloud of blond hair around her and the rippling surface of the pool, she could see the white marble statue of Atargatis in *podia* state stretching to the temple's vaulted ceiling, lit by the torches that rimmed the open-air chamber.

Tanni settled onto the floor of the pool in front of her, a question in her shining dark green eyes, her *ichthys* skin glimmering in the torchlight. She still wore her siren's tunic and hemp diving belt, the quartz-encased fire opal Tear laced onto the left shoulder glowing slightly in the evening gloom. She signed and mouthed, *Ready to go?*

Calandra looked around. By this point in the evening, the pool was nearly empty of worshippers. Most would have gone home to begin the Panselinos feast. Thea had given the Mother only the most perfunctory of respects before beginning the trek up the mountainside with Gerrick. She'd given Tanni a look, then deliberately turned away as though to say she hadn't seen a thing, throwing a warning over her shoulder for Calandra not to stay too long or she would miss the feast. Calandra sent a grateful thought after her foster mother, but she could read between the lines—*Adonia will be displeased if you're late.*

Tanni had stayed behind with her, but had respected Calandra's need for privacy, choosing a spot on the opposite side of the idol to do her duty. Calandra performed her libations and dip in the pool in relative privacy, begging for the goddess's forgiveness for her failure and offering promises to do better.

Now, feeling no less responsible, she knew she could wait no longer to return home. What had she been waiting for? *Him*, she admitted to herself. She'd wanted to tell Damon what had happened, have him exonerate her somehow. If she'd recreated the sensations of the void, maybe he'd come to save her from it as he had so long ago.

Foolish. He'd never appeared to her while she was awake. Only a chained fool believes she is being trained by the ghost of a long-dead prince that only visits her in her dreams, and then believes he would be lenient on her failure.

The fear and frustration of the sick bay pen filled her, and she was once again choking on bile as the dolphin thrashed at her inadequacy. She had been doing it exactly the way Damon had said, or so she'd thought. When she'd told him what had happened with the rabbit, he had frowned and told her she must have gotten it wrong, then scolded her with icy silence. Her stomach twisted at the memory, and even more so because she had felt shamed by a man. Yet today she'd nearly done the same thing. What was she doing wrong?

From the bottom of the temple pool, she gave Tanni a signal and flippered toward the surface a dozen or so feet above, pushing through the fatigue that had been plaguing her all day. Tanni followed suit. They dried off in silence in the torchlight by the edge of the pool, using the provided linen towels. *Douloi* in white robes came and collected the soiled linens and brought Calandra her clothes, bowing deeply and backing away before turning.

As Calandra pulled her tunic over her head, she could feel Tanni's gaze on her, studying her. She ignored her friend's unspoken question.

"Ready?" Calandra asked brusquely as she fastened her belt. She glanced toward the pillars of the entrance, knowing Osaze stood waiting beyond. "Osaze needs to eat."

Unless they were given permission to voice personal needs, a *doulos* would starve or run themselves to death in service to their mistress. In all the confusion of the afternoon, Calandra had not had time to go through her standard permission contract with Osaze. And he had certainly never been allowed to say anything out of turn while in Narcissa's service.

Tanni's brow furrowed. "So you don't want to talk about it at all?"

"About what?" Calandra feigned ignorance, blinking at her friend as though nothing were wrong.

Tanni folded her arms.

"Of all the people in the world, you know I'm the one person you can't fool, Calandra kor'Delphine. Something happened in that pen today, and it was different than other times I have seen you heal. I don't know what it was, but I think you do. And I want to know if that's why it didn't work."

Calandra whirled on her friend.

"I'm not strong enough. That's why it didn't work. I tried to control the elements, but I couldn't. Is that what you want to hear?"

Tanni recoiled. "Control? Since when do you approach healing by trying to *control* anything? How is that 'being water?' Water guides and is guided, remember?"

"Guide, control, what's the difference? The point is that I failed. I couldn't do either one. If it weren't for Thea stepping in, I would probably have killed that calf, and all your efforts to save her would have been for nothing."

Calandra strode to the outer patio of the temple ziggurat and indicated that Osaze should follow her. He stepped into place behind her, as was proper. The staircase torches had already been lit to prevent missteps among the late worshippers and their human *douloi*.

Tanni caught up to her in a few strides, and they began descending the steep stairs side-by-side.

"There's a big difference between the two with spirit. I'm not a healer, but I'm sure that the elements react differently based on—"

"You're right. You're not a healer. So stop telling me how to do it."

Calandra wouldn't have needed their bond to feel her friend's spike of hurt. Tanni only closed her mouth and looked straight ahead as they jogged down the west side of the temple structure. They passed some ascending white-robed *douloi* carrying amphoras of water to replenish the pool after the day's festivities.

When they reached the bottom, the temple market stalls were boarded up or closed, their purveyors gone home to spend Panselinos with their families. The silvery disc of the full moon was peeking above the black boulders on the east side of the bay. Calandra took in the flickering lights of the homes between them and the twater and let the moonlight soak into her skin. She sighed and turned to her friend.

"Look, I'm sorry. I . . . I shouldn't have snapped at you. It's been a long day, and I know it has been for you, too. I've had far too many reminders that this"—she indicated the rising moon—"is the last *panselinos* before Adonia will have me try to heal the Heartstone, and that

I am still woefully inadequate to do so."

Tanni cocked her head. "You won Narcissa's wager. Osaze is finally free of her. I thought you'd be happier about that."

Calandra nodded. "I am. But that raises more problems, doesn't it? How do I get his *sklavia* bond transferred to me so I can Release him? And how do I know that if I Release Osaze now, he'll still be . . . you know . . . like he used to be? I've learned a lot since I was thirteen, Tanni. The reasons we've been given about why men must be Redeemed—they're not wrong. Look at the dolphin. No Redeemed man would ever be so callous or inhumane."

Tanni frowned. "True. Unless their mistress ordered them to be so. I've learned much, too. And I have often wondered if robbing someone of the capability to possess evil intent is truly more merciful than simply punishing someone who acts with evil intent, as we do for women when the need arises. When we Redeem a ship of slaves to the Mother, how can we say we are truly freeing them?"

"This from you, whose mother was killed by humans? Things *have* changed."

She raised a hand to hail a rickshaw that sat parked on the street corner near the canal.

Tanni shrugged uncomfortably, her eyes even darker green than usual.

"I'm not saying I want to be bosom friends with a freeman. I'm merely saying that, well, sometimes I see more similarities than differences between us and them."

Calandra glanced over her shoulder at Osaze, then leaned closer to her friend as the rickshaw pulled up to the curb.

"Does that mean you'll help me figure out how to free Osaze?"

Tanni hesitated, lamplight reflecting off her black braided hair and singer's medallion.

"Look, I've told you that I don't know what I did, and I wasn't lying."

Calandra raised a placating hand. "I know. But could you at least give me a hint? Give me the stone you got the idea from. Give me something to work with. Between that and what we now know about the bonds, I'm sure I could do it with a little time."

The rickshaw pulled up to them, pulled by two strapping *douloi* in the half-robes of civil servants.

Calandra climbed in and looked at her friend, who stood waiting on the sidewalk. "Aren't you coming?"

"Not in this one." Tanni shifted her feet. "You haven't officially earned your healer's rings yet, Calandra. Thea may have given us grace tonight, but I don't want to risk it further."

Calandra nodded. "I understand." She studied her friend. "Look, I've never been this close before. I'm not asking you to do anything to compromise your position, Tanni. I would never do that. But I have to keep my vow. It's been too long. Besides, if I fail to heal the Heartstone next month, I may no longer be in a position to help him. Who knows what will happen to him then?"

Tanni hesitated, then nodded. "Okay. I'll have it delivered to you."

Calandra smiled and reached out for Tanni's hand.

"Thank you."

Tanni took it and squeezed it. "I miss you."

"And I you. But I'll soon earn my rings, and then we will no longer be bound by the mistakes of our past."

Tanni glanced at Osaze. "Won't we, though?"

Before Calandra could respond, Tanni strode off toward the rickshaw stand.

Calandra swallowed, then told Osaze that he should take the seat beside her. After he climbed in, she leaned forward and gave instructions to take them to the palace. At that moment, the sky opened in a torrential warm monsoon rain.

Calandra studied her one-time friend's muscular leg next to hers, then glanced at the backs of the two *douloi* pulling the cart. Water made miniature rivers down the valleys on their skin, yet they ran as though it were a pleasant winter evening.

Tanni's words reminded her of one of the last things Osaze had said to her with his own will: *Let me give you my heart without giving up my mind.* She shivered at the implications—Osaze had cared for her. She had always been told that men could not truly love. Yet she had been sure he had loved her a great deal, just as she had cared for him. Would he still feel the same way about her if she Released him and he found it had taken her five years to fulfill her promise?

Cautiously, she opened her heart to See what she could sense from him. She had never done this with a Redeemed man before and didn't know what to expect. On the surface, there was only a vague sense of duty and obligation, like someone pressing through a grey fog.

Without warning, his gaze snapped toward her.

"Do you need something, m'lady?" he asked in a voice as smooth as buttered coffee and as flat as her diving knife.

The uncharacteristically focused expression in his black eyes startled her. Had he felt what she was doing?

"N—no, thank you, Osaze."

He touched bunched fingers to his forehead in salute, then faced forward to his duty.

She sat back in her seat and watched the festival lights flicker on Osaze's close-cropped hair. When he'd spoken to her, it was almost as though she could feel the old Osaze, but she knew that had to be an illusion, a product of her own wishful thinking. She thought about diving further beneath the surface of his mind to find out, but decided against it.

There were some questions to which she wasn't sure she wanted to know the answers.

12

THE TEAR

CALANDRA SAT AT THE HEAD table in the Great Hall, took another sip of wine, and watched a group of plant healers do a water dance in the centre of vaulted room. The dancers tumbled and gyrated between streams of water they pulled and manipulated from bowls on the floor.

Everyone at the feast appeared to be having a good time except her. Her aunt's tinkling laughter carried over the crowd. Across the banquet hall, Adonia gossiped with two ladies of the court, a goblet in one hand and an ostrich-plume fan in the other, her auburn hair aflame in the lamplight. Adonia's current favourite *doulos* stood behind her and made sure she never ran out of wine. Cain, that was his name. Maybe. It was difficult to keep up with Adonia's flings. Ever since the queen's consort had passed away several years ago, it seemed she had taken a different man to her chambers every week. Most of them looked not much older than her daughters.

Calandra dismissed such unkind thoughts. Losing a consort was difficult. Many women took comfort where they could. Calandra doubted that Adonia would rush into bonding another, if indeed she ever did. She already had two daughters and a niece and probably felt the throne was secure. Her only real pressing concern was the faltering barrier.

Calandra had been sensing an increasing desperation behind her aunt's not-so-subtle promptings of late. It was a pressure that Calandra felt nearly as strongly. She had heard enough of the kind of havoc humans could wreak upon their own kind on the islands to their west. She had no desire to see what they would do if the peaceful undine race were exposed to their view.

A teenage *doulos* stepped up beside her with an amphora of wine, but she waved him off.

Hebe, Narcissa's younger sister and the princess who most strongly

83

resembled their mother, followed his retreat with her eyes, smoothing her red hair. She leaned toward Calandra.

"You should ask Mother if you could bond *him*. I bet he'd make pretty daughters."

Hebe's friend Alexandra, the daughter of one of the ladies with which Adonia was holding court, tittered from her other side. "I bet he'd make anything look prettier. Like my couch."

The girls broke into a chorus of raucous giggling.

Calandra rolled her eyes and gave the girls an indulgent smile. "Do you two ever think of anything besides boys?"

Hebe nodded. "Sure, lots of things. Jewellery, gowns, parties. Anything fun."

"Boys are the *most* fun, though," interjected Alexandra, and Hebe nodded agreement.

Calandra frowned, wondering how the girls could see ogling the pliant males that served them as entertaining. Perhaps because their mothers still kept them so closely chaperoned. Normally, Calandra enjoyed Hebe's bubbly, silly conversation, but her heart wasn't in it tonight. She glanced back at Thomas, the night shift bodyguard she had sent for when they had arrived back at the palace. Osaze had looked ready to sleep on his feet, so she had dismissed him to his quarters for the night. Her own exhaustion was creeping up on her. She stood and excused herself from the girls' conversation and retreated through the doorway near the head of the vast semicircular room, Thomas falling into place behind her.

She'd only taken a few paces down the hallway that was the quickest route to her chambers when she reached the door that led to the Heartstone Observation Chamber. She paused. She used to spend hours in this chamber, poring over old datastones she had found in the Archive and contemplating the puzzle of how to both complete her destiny and simultaneously prevent insanity. But she had not set foot in the room for many months, shame at her recent failures keeping her away. And, she had to admit to herself, she no longer felt the comfort of its presence that she used to. Instead, as time had gone on, her soul had been consumed by shame and guilt every time she saw it, much as she had been by the sight of Osaze and the reminder of her unfulfilled promise to him.

She hesitated outside the door of the chamber. The pulsing heart of the stone tugged at her soul, and a whisper of the warmth that had once enveloped her at its core called to her.

"Stay out here," she told Thomas. "I'll only be a few minutes."

He nodded and took up position by the door. She lifted the brass latch and slipped into the room.

"I wondered if I might see you here," Thea said.

Calandra jumped, startled. Her eyes quickly adjusted to the dim light, and she spied Thea and Gerrick sitting at the oblong walnut wood conference table. It looked like she had interrupted a conversation, or . . . Calandra blushed. Consorts weren't usually much for conversation.

"Am I interrupting something? I only wanted to . . . to see it."

Calandra took a hesitant step toward the floor-to-ceiling curved window that ran the length of one wall of the room. Beyond it, moonlight scattered from the tiled walls of the Mother's Heart and filled the interior of the Observation Chamber with a soft glow. She couldn't see the Heartstone from this distance, as it was above her line of sight, but she could tell from the level of light alone that it had dimmed even since she had seen it last.

Thea stood. "No, it's fine. I'm glad you're here, actually. I have something for you."

Calandra turned from the window in surprise to face her mentor.

"You do?"

Thea came and stood beside her, reached into her pocket, and pulled out a small silver ring with a green jade teardrop cabochon-cut stone set into it.

Calandra gaped. "My plant healer's ring? But . . . I haven't taken the trial."

Thea smiled. "Narcissa's test with the fern was much more severe than any I could have devised for you. Here."

She proffered the ring in her fingers.

Calandra extended her right hand, and Thea slipped it onto her middle finger. It fit perfectly.

Thea raised her voice to be heard behind her, but didn't turn.

"Gerrick, come here," she said in her consort's native Gaelic.

After forty-five years on Sirenia, Gerrick could manage a fluent but heavily accented Greek, but he and Thea often spoke Gerrick's native tongue, or sometimes even English, when alone with family.

Gerrick moved around into their line of sight and bowed slightly.

"Yes, mistress?"

"I require a specific memory stone from our chambers. The green jasper Tear I keep on the third shelf tagged 'student records.' Please fetch it immediately, husband."

Thea was the only person Calandra had ever heard refer to her consort as "husband," at least in her presence. It held a much different connotation than the more usual "*doulos*"—warmer, more personal. She'd asked Thea about it once, in private.

"He shares my bed," her foster mother had responded archly. "He deserves a different title than a bondsman fit only to muck stables and bear heavy burdens."

Sensing the matter was closed, Calandra had never brought it up again. She chalked it up to one of Thea's idiosyncrasies. It would make no difference to a consort one way or another what his mistress called him—any difference in nuance in the address would be for Thea alone.

Gerrick bowed again.

"Yes, m'lady." He spun on his heel and hurried out of the room.

Calandra pulled her hand toward her and examined the stone in the dim light.

"You are not pleased?" Thea's voice was gentle.

"I am, *daskala*. Thank you. It's just . . . this feels like a turning, like something has changed. Perhaps it is because I am one step closer to my destiny. And my doom."

"You are so certain of your own doom?"

"Aren't you? In all my research, I have found only three panaceas who have succeeded in not going Mad, and you are one of them. Three in three thousand years. Today, Narcissa threw that old saying at me, the one that says 'a healer who gains a suckling loses her sense.' Yet you have three grown daughters and seem in complete possession of your wits. And I am no closer to solving my problem than when I began."

Calandra clenched her fists.

"Only two weeks until my birthday, a month until the summer Redemption Moon, and a few days more until the summer solstice. Adonia has already told me that I'll be leading the circle at this year's Healing Ceremony. She'll probably choose a consort from the Redemption harvest and have me bonded the very next day so I'll be ready."

She stepped toward the window and the slightly pulsing red light of the Heartstone opal came into view. She gasped. It appeared to have very little life left.

"Not that I can blame her. If that is the only way to heal this, then I will do what must be done. Even if it means an early retirement to the Abyss, as Narcissa claims she foresees for me."

Thea shook her head. "Narcissa—and that old nursemaid's proverb—are wrong, you know. It is not child-bearing that brings the Madness."

Calandra's heart skipped a beat and she whirled to face the older healer.

"You know what causes the Madness?"

Thea touched a wilting water lily in the bowl of flowers on the table, and it surged back to full freshness.

"Not precisely. But I know what does *not* cause it. And I have my suspicions regarding what does."

Calandra tried to control her excitement. "Is that how you have managed to avoid it? And why have you never mentioned it before?"

Thea turned toward her, her eyes shuttered in caution.

"As I said, I only have suspicions, some of which I have worked out over the years since your mother left. I never told you because I was not—still am not—certain. And, if what I suspect bears even a grain of truth, the consequences to Sirenia could be catastrophic."

"Worse than a Mad panacea?"

Thea frowned.

Calandra leaned toward her mentor.

"Narcissa was right about one thing, *daskala*. If the Madness does take me, I could endanger everyone who lives on the island." She lowered her voice. "I confess I agree with Narcissa about me bonding a consort. I know I need as much power as possible if I am to succeed in healing the Heartstone, but what if, instead, I destroy it and everyone I hold dear?"

She thought of the exhaustion that pulled at her every time she healed, or attempted to heal, a living entity—a symptom she had reported to no one for fear it might be one of the first signs of her fall from grace.

"My studies made it clear that the more powerful the healer, the more quickly she declined. What if, with my strength, I lose my mind so quickly that we have no warning, and with no one strong enough to stop me? What gain could possibly be worth that?"

She thought of the other benefits a consort offered and dismissed them. What good were companionship, service, and children if one were not in control of one's mind? She shuddered at the thought. She could think of no worse fate than that. But what if she bonded no one and failed to restore the Stone? From the looks of it, it wouldn't last another year until next summer's solstice. Did she dare risk failure now for fear of a Madness that may not even come?

Thea put a hand on Calandra's knee.

"Your mother did not destroy anyone."

"No, she didn't. She just left."

Calandra couldn't keep the bitterness from her voice. Even if Delphine were Mad, what mother abandons her child?

Thea frowned and hesitated.

"Calandra, there is something I need to tell you."

Something about Thea's tone made Calandra's heart pick up speed. "What is it?"

Thea indicated the chairs. "Perhaps you had better sit down."

Swallowing hard, Calandra obediently took a seat next to the table. Thea turned the chair beside it to face her, then sat. Light from the window beside them lit half of Thea's face in sharp relief against the shadow it cast on the other.

Her mentor looked as if she were searching for the right words.

"I have reason to believe that your mother may not have been Mad when she left."

Calandra stared. *Could it be true?*

"Didn't my aunt declare her Madness for public record?" She had looked it up to be sure.

Thea nodded. "Oh, yes. Delphine hadn't been gone a day before Adonia had updated the stones. There is something else. I cannot be certain, but I think it may be possible that your mother was pregnant."

Calandra's eyes widened. "So . . . so I could have a sister?"

She contemplated the implications. Not only had she lost the support of her mother, but she could also have a younger sister out in the world somewhere. Assuming her mother hadn't gone Mad and killed them all.

"Or a brother."

Calandra's mouth fell open.

"A . . . a brother? Why would you possibly guess that?"

Thea smoothed her robe. "As I said, I cannot be certain. And I ask that you keep these conjectures between the two of us. But if Delphine were pregnant with a boy, she may have fled to protect him. As a panacea, she would be able to tell."

"So you're saying my mother hid a pregnancy and abandoned me to have her baby somewhere else? Why? She would have been safer here, and so would her baby, boy or girl. What kind of person does that?"

Calandra blinked furiously to hold back the tears that threatened. All this time, she had thought her mother had been going insane and had left to prevent the fate she herself feared unleashing. But if Delphine hadn't been losing her mind—

Thea's voice was quiet, sad. "The kind of person who loves her children very much."

Calandra shook her head. "That doesn't make sense at all."

She studied the bowl of lilies, not needing to look at Thea to feel her pity and compassion.

Gerrick entered the room and closed the door, then came toward them and bowed, offering Thea a linen-wrapped Tear.

"I have the stone, m'lady."

Thea smiled and accepted the package, then pulled a dark green jasper teardrop from the cloth wrapping. "Thank you, husband."

Gerrick bowed again, his face as placid as ever, and resumed his waiting position a short distance away.

Calandra startled. Her emotional shield had weakened in her distress, allowing the emotions of her companions to intrude on her senses. She felt something from Gerrick she had never known in any consort before—pleasure and affection, even *ownership*, toward his mistress. She stared at him. His expression had never changed, never once revealed what she thought she'd sensed. He noticed her looking and the warmth was immediately squelched, replaced once again by blankness, but tainted with something else out of place—fear.

Thea noticed Calandra's expression and hesitated, glancing between her and Gerrick. "I understand your confusion, child. I have something for you that I hope will help."

Calandra glanced at the jasper Tear in confusion. "The memory stone?"

Thea laughed, but it seemed strained. "No, that is so I may record the passing of your first and second Healer's Trials."

Calandra frowned. "I don't understand. My second one?"

Thea pulled a hexagonal tablet of transparent rock crystal from her tunic pocket and cradled it in her palm. She laid the memory stone inside a shallow depression in the bottom corner, pressed her thumb against the green jasper, and Sang a short trill. The crystal clouded slightly and its surface wriggled to life, stretching outward to form raised, glowing characters that displayed the information she had requested. She raised the tablet slightly toward her mouth and spoke to it.

"Calandra kor'Delphine has passed her plant healer's trial on the *panselinos* of Iyar in the year 4155 EK, known as May the nineteenth of AD 1799 by the Gregorian calendar. So it is written."

As she spoke, letters bulged from the stone's surface, and with the final command, flattened slightly to indicate that the recording was complete. She sang a different triplet of notes and the stone tablet flattened and became transparent again.

Calandra bit her lip.

"I . . . I don't . . . Thank you, Daskala. But that was only my first ring. And I certainly didn't earn my physic ring today. Did I miss something?"

Thea gave a thin smile. "Yes. The reason I came to find you this afternoon was not to break up a silly wager. And it will also complete the stone healer's trial nicely."

Thea reached into the pocket of her overtunic and withdrew something in her fist. She extended her hand and opened her fingers to reveal a shimmering green shard of opal that seemed to have all the colours of the Atlantic Ocean flashing in its depths.

"I've been carrying this around all day."

Calandra gasped and her hand flew to the broken pendant at her neck.

"My mother's Tear. You have the other piece." It was part exclamation, part question.

"Go on. Take it." Thea smiled.

Calandra hesitantly took it from Thea's palm, treasuring its weight in her own.

"How did you . . . ? Did you have it all this time?"

"Yes. Your mother gave it to me before she left. She said that it was to be yours when you were ready to gain the rings. Even at such a young age, your potential was clear. She knew you would become a panacea like her. Gerrick, please help her."

Gerrick stepped around behind Calandra, and she lifted her braid so he could reach the clasp of her necklace, which he quickly released. When he placed the pendant and chain in her waiting palm, his hand brushed hers, and a jolt of emotion shot through Calandra like a lightning bolt. Calandra's eyes widened and she froze. He gulped, stepped back, and quickly regained his placid control—but Calandra had already Seen it.

Gerrick was emotional—very emotional. He was nearly full to bursting with pride and affection for . . . for *her*. Never, in all the years she had known Gerrick, had she felt true warmth from him, which was only to be expected. Like all other Redeemed men, he was obedient and submissive to a fault, as was befitting the consort of Sirenia's First Healer, archon of the Royal Council, and the Headmistress of the Royal Academy. In fact, he was the most well-trained consort Calandra knew.

Why was she suddenly sensing emotions from him? Had he somehow broken his *sklavia* bond? Was that even possible? And if so, wouldn't Thea know about it?

Another thought occurred to her. Perhaps Thea did know. After all, if Calandra was correct, how could Thea not? Calandra's chest tightened with both alarm and excitement. Could it be that Thea had already done what Calandra hoped to do with Osaze? Calandra dared not say anything until she knew for certain. If she were wrong, the consequences could be dire.

She took a breath and turned a blank face to Thea. The *daskala* was not as empathic as Calandra, and much better disciplined at using her mental shield. Calandra hoped Thea had not even noticed her brief moment of alarm, or the low-lying distress she buried now beneath the wonder of holding both pieces of her mother's Tear in her hands.

Thea's eyes glittered and she pulled a stone healer's ring from her pocket, holding it in readiness, the blue opal teardrop in the setting gleaming with promise.

"Well, what are you waiting for? Heal it."

Thea sounded as eager to see the stone restored to wholeness as Calandra felt. Or perhaps Thea's emotions were mixing with her own in her heart.

Calandra moved to join the pieces, but Thea leaned forward and laid a warning hand on Calandra's arm.

"You should wait until you are in private before you read it. I suspect your mother left a message on there that you may not wish others to hear."

Calandra nodded, eyes and heart full, her exhaustion falling away from her like a dropped cloak. She held the two pieces together and they snapped into place. There was not even a chip missing—evidence of a deliberate separation by a skilled stone healer. She reached for earth to heal it, grateful that stone healing, at least, was something she could still easily do. She did what she always did when working with stone—envisioned how she'd felt when her mind had touched the Heartstone. From the sphere on the other side of the glass wall, she thought she sensed an answering flicker of warmth and smiled.

Closing her eyes, she reached out from her heart's energy centre toward the stone shards to begin the process of repairing what was broken, reconnecting links in the water-saturated silica structure.

Delphine had been thinking of her before she had fled. Perhaps her mother *had* left for a good reason. Perhaps this Tear held the answer for which Calandra had been searching all these years.

Perhaps, just perhaps, she was not fated for insanity after all.

13

THE MESSAGE

CALANDRA PRACTICALLY RACED TO HER room, restraining herself to a fast walking pace for Thomas's sake only. Once they reached her chamber, she left him posted at the door, closed it, and dove for the quartz reader she kept on her nightstand.

Biting her lip in nervous anticipation, she placed the Tear on the reader, put her index finger on it, and sang the password she had set as she'd healed it. The crystal's transparent surface darkened and danced to life in a bas-relief of a woman's face—her mother, Delphine kor'Helena. When Calandra was young, she used to stand in the Hall of Ancestors and stare at the painting of her mother—the only representation of Delphine that Adonia had allowed to remain on display—trying desperately to find some answers in the image's flat green eyes. As soon as her mother began speaking in the recording—when she heard her own mother's voice for the first time in her memory—tears tracked down Calandra's face. She wished the readers would display colour, but even a ghost-like representation of her mother was better than none at all.

"Calandra, if you are seeing this before my return, it means that my plan has failed. I am sure you have many questions, but the first thing I want to say is this—I love you. I always have and always will. Everything I have done has been to help you and our people."

Calandra drew in a breath. Plan? What could she mean?

"Many years ago, I began searching for answers to the problems that plague our people—why can we not produce boys? Why do our most empathic healers go Mad? Why is the Heartstone failing, despite our best efforts to repair it? I found an ancient datastone in the heart of Atlantis that I believe revealed the answer. For safekeeping, I have left it in its original location, which is much more secure than anywhere else I could devise."

The screen changed to show a map of the ruined Atlantis. Calandra recognized the building marked with a blinking arrow from old datastone records she'd read. It was the Archive, a library large enough to have had its own building on the Old Island. Her mother was right about security—technically, her people were not forbidden from entering the waters of Atlantis, but few ever did. Grief and superstition had colluded into rumours of it being haunted, even among her erudite kind—but then, even the most intelligent could be swayed by plausible-sounding fears, and the humans among them introduced many. In reality, the only creatures haunting the ancient stones were sharks and other wildlife—no small threat, to be sure, but completely material. Calandra had long ago learned how to deflect any would-be animal marauders' dim interest in her with the persuasion of Song and a well-aimed stream of water.

Delphine's face came back onto the screen.

"In order to prove my theory, I must leave. If I am right, what I have discovered could change everything. But no one will believe me unless I prove it. Not even Adonia."

Her mother's effigy looked and sounded sad.

"If I have not returned, that does not necessarily mean I was wrong. Something may have happened to me. Find the stone. See for yourself. The truth has been hidden in darkness for far too long, and we must bring it into the light."

Her visage got larger, as though she were leaning toward the recorder.

"I believe in you, Calandra. If I have failed, it is up to you to show our people the truth. Men are not our enemies, nor our servants. They were meant to be our partners. Find the stone, look *beneath* the surface. It holds the answers I dare not leave here. Goodbye, my daughter. I love you."

Her face moved off the screen sideways, as though she had stepped away from the data recorder's field of vision.

Calandra's stomach churned and her breath came in gasps. What her mother was saying about men was complete and utter heresy—yet they were the same questions Calandra had been asking for the last five years, since that day when Osaze had given himself up. Delphine said she thought she'd found the answers, but then she'd disappeared and never returned.

Perhaps her mother *had* gone Mad, as she'd been told. But if she had actually become an apostate, maybe that's why Adonia was so quick to claim she had gone insane. Calandra clenched her teeth. She wasn't sure which would be worse—knowing her mother was crazy, or knowing that she'd left in full possession of her wits but had been exiled as a heretic.

And *then* gone insane.

Yep. That would be worse.

A man with a strong jaw and appealing features came into view. Calandra had no idea who it was, though he did look vaguely familiar. He began speaking in Cornish. Calandra hadn't realized she'd heard the language before, but she both recognized it instantly and understood it perfectly, so she'd had to have heard it at least once in her life.

"Cali . . . um, Calandra, it's um, me. Your dad. Kenver." He looked off-camera, his visage in profile on the stone. "Are you sure this strange contraption will work? Nothing seems to be happening."

Delphine's voice sounded indistinctly. Kenver nodded and turned back to face the recorder.

Calandra almost turned it off. There was something . . . *wrong* about the man who spoke. Something in his voice, his manner, the way he seemed so uncertain. But . . . he was her *father*? She stared at the stone, entranced.

Kenver cleared his throat. "Cali, my pearl, you are the most beautiful child I have ever seen. I can hardly bear to leave you behind, but your mother has convinced me that it is necessary."

He needed convincing? The implication that Kenver's mind had been free and that he did not necessarily defer to her mother made her mouth go dry.

Kenver continued. "Your mother tells me we are to have a son." He smiled proudly.

Calandra frowned.

"I hope, before too long, we will return with your baby brother, and we will be a family again. He will be the proof of what your mother has discovered. But if you see this first, I pray you know that I wanted to be a father to you. A real father."

She paused the message. *A real father?* What did he mean? Undines barely even used the word *father*, as the men that sired them had very little to do with raising them. Thea had been like a mother to her, and she supposed that that made Gerrick her foster father. But he had never once spoken to her as Kenver did in the message.

Kenver's face—her *father's* face—looked unbearably sad. That was an emotion she had seen on only one other man—Osaze, when he was still a boy, before he'd been Redeemed. It was when he had realized that after he was Redeemed to the Mother, he would no longer get to live with his own mother.

"Don't worry, you won't miss her," Daskala Lida had told him with a pat on his head.

Her words had brought no comfort, and Osaze had been less than his usual cheerful self for days, often appearing with red, puffy eyes.

It was the same genuine sorrow she saw on Kenver's face now.

My father's face.

She touched the reader, tracing the temporary frieze of her father's features in wonder.

Osaze had cared for her. Kenver had sorrowed to leave her behind, just as her mother had. As freemen, they had felt the same emotions that women would. She could no longer believe that all men were defined by their warlike tendencies. Couldn't they, like women, feel love, compassion, and hope? Had what she'd been taught been wrong? And what did her mother conceiving a boy—which Thea had surmised and her father had confirmed—have to do with any of this? On the other hand, how many men were like Damon—cold, distant, with a hint of violence in everything they said or did? Damon may not be human, but that didn't make him safe.

She twirled the two new rings on her middle finger, the blue opal teardrop of the stone healer ring nestled next to the green jade that represented plant healing. She knew now why she had procrastinated so long on fulfilling her promise to Osaze. Fear.

Oh, sure, she had excuses, but she knew that if she'd been determined, she could have found a way around them before now. But as time had gone on, she had been afraid that when she Released him, he would be different than the boy she had known—that he would fulfill all the worst things she had been told about untamed human men, and she would no longer be able to see him as the affable, affectionate boy she had grown up with. The longer she had waited, the more she grew afraid that he would also hate her for dragging her feet—or her fins, as the case may be. Her heart beat faster as she thought about it.

Her gaze lingered on her father's face, then she pressed her index finger to the memory stone and sang a trill to blank the screen.

Osaze may very well resent her for waiting so long. If so, it was no more than she deserved. But if her mother had been willing to risk so much to discover the truth, surely Calandra could also face the dangers of keeping her word. Osaze was her friend, and she had made him a promise. She intended to keep it at last using the fastest method possible. First thing in the morning, she would go find the palace bondmistress and convince her to give Calandra his bond, then Release him.

For now, she needed sleep.

The exhaustion hit her hard. She laid the reader and Tear on her nightstand, stripped off her gown, and threw it on the floor, too tired to even get up and hang it in the wardrobe. She lay down on her bed, her thoughts still swirling madly.

She had begun to wonder if sleep would even find her tonight when she drifted into unconsciousness.

*

Narcissa stood as still as a statue in Calandra's wardrobe, her legs cramping from staying in one position for so long. For once, she was appreciative of her snobby cousin's pedestrian tastes. She'd had plenty of room to hide amongst the handful of garments—a few apprentice tunics, a couple of festival and court gowns, and some swimming clothes—that were all her cousin kept in here. She'd come close to panic several times since Calandra had entered the room, but luck had favoured her and she had remained undiscovered.

Not only that, she was certain Calandra had brought her the very thing she was looking for—leverage to use against her, and possibly an escape from the onerous latrine duty. She hadn't heard everything in the Tear's message, but she'd heard enough to know that Calandra wouldn't want her to have it. Narcissa certainly hadn't found anything else in the sparse furnishings in her cousin's room to help her cause.

Calandra was notorious for her insomnia, and despite the wine she'd drunk, it still seemed to take an extraordinary amount of time before her breathing became even. Narcissa waited for what felt like an eternity—but was probably only about fifteen minutes—after she thought Calandra had fallen asleep, then slipped out of the wardrobe, using all her stealth to prevent the door from clicking as she closed it behind her. With painstaking slowness, she crept over to the nightstand, picked up the necklace, and moved toward the door.

Calandra stirred and muttered something that sounded like "mother" and "message." Narcissa froze with her back to the brass-worked door, holding her breath as Calandra settled into a new position. When her cousin's breathing had evened out once again, Narcissa opened the folding chamber door, stepped backward through it—

And bumped into the solid wall of a man's back. She whirled.

Startled, the *taps* turned around, eyes narrowed, hand on his sword hilt. When he saw Narcissa, his brow furrowed in confusion.

"Your highness?"

Narcissa willed her heart to stop racing as she closed the door. She put on her haughtiest air, hoping the several glasses of wine she'd seen Calandra imbibe at the feast worked in her favour.

"Clumsy oaf. Watch where you're going!"

The man gave a perfect, deep bow and salute.

"Yes, your highness. My humblest apologies."

Narcissa inspected him as though he were a revolting specimen of sea cucumber, then whirled and stomped down the hall to her room.

Quietly, though. If she woke Calandra, her ruse would be for naught.

Her guard stepped aside to admit her without comment. The loathsome Domingo had been relieved of duty at midnight, with orders to present himself to Lida, head of the Siren House and the palace piper in charge of work detail, in the morning for a new assignment. Narcissa would be chained if she'd take any castoff of Calandra's.

Calandra should be getting my castoffs, not the other way around.

"I'm the heir-apparent and the daughter of the queen," she muttered. "Who is she? The daughter of a crazy person"—she clutched the Tear in her hand—"and a traitor, that's who."

If Narcissa wanted Osaze, she deserved to have him, and that was that. Calandra had no right to say otherwise.

When she tried to read the message on her own reader, she was foiled by the password. What had Calandra sung? After several attempts, she got it right. As she watched the heretical message, a delicious feeling of delight came over her. This was exactly the kind of leverage she needed, and then some. This wouldn't merely knock Calandra down off her pedestal of perfection and let Narcissa get Osaze back—it would probably get her cousin jailed, thereby removing the threat of her powers—and her claim on the throne—entirely.

"We'll see what the *daskala*'s pet does about this, won't we?"

Narcissa marched out of her room with renewed purpose. The guard fell automatically into place behind her.

Her mother needed to see this.

FOUND AND LOST

Damon was brooding tonight.

Calandra found him in the ruined building she had come to think of as his house, though she was fairly certain that it was actually some kind of archive, with its broken columns around a wide courtyard of crumbling paving stones and its tumbled shelves of datastones. His muscular bronze back was toward her and his hair floated around him in a dark cloud. He seemed to be contemplating a wall mural. Tropical fish in a rainbow of bright colours swam among the columns and sea plants undulated from cracks in the floor.

It had taken Calandra a while to figure out where this place was. One day in her history lesson, the image that Daskala Persephone displayed on the large obsidian wall reader felt familiar, like she had been there before. In the image, the buildings were above the surface and filled with people on foot wearing stately shawls and tunics.

The city was Atlantis. And it was the same place she and Damon inhabited together in her dreams. Only now, it lay at the bottom of the ocean somewhere to Sirenia's northeast, its majestic architecture crumbling into ancient history.

When he sensed Calandra, he turned away from the painting of Atargatis and her consort, Hadad, bestowing blessings of food and wealth on the undines. The trench between his brows flattened slightly. He smiled, but it didn't reach his golden eyes.

"Calandra, my lark, you have come at last. What kept you?"

As always when she was with him, she felt a strange yearning to be nearer to him. She swam a few feet closer, then stopped. Even in her dream state, her attraction to him seemed dangerous and unnatural. Men were to be commanded, not sought after.

"The Panselinos festival, *daskalos*."

He smiled. "Yes, of course. How could I forget that the hour of your triumph draws so near? One more month until you will heal your Heartstone. Come, sing me a song to celebrate."

As though of its own accord, her mouth opened and she sang him a song of love and loss. It was sad, and by the end, she was weeping.

She had never heard the song before, but that was always the case when she sang for Damon. It was like he gave her the song he wanted her to sing, and she was merely a conduit for it. It didn't have to make sense. This place had its own rules, like the fact that she could sing underwater at all, or could feel tears running down her cheeks. This was a dream. Merely a dream.

Damon swam toward her and brushed the tears away with the back of his hand. The heat from his body warmed the space around them. Calandra's stomach clenched.

"Why are you so sad tonight, my little lark?"

Sad? Was she sad? Oh, yes. She had been sad. She remembered now.

"I have failed again, *daskalos*. I tried to heal a dolphin calf, but . . . the elements escaped me. I nearly killed her."

Damon's lips curled up in a dangerous smile. He cupped her chin in his hand and tilted it up to meet his golden eyes.

"With so little time left until your great service to the goddess"—the smile twisted into a mocking sneer—"you can't afford to fail. You are of two minds, struggling between a spirit of weakness and a spirit of strength. You must be stronger than that which weakens you."

Calandra's face burned and she dropped her gaze. How did he know? She had told no one, not even Tanni, that every time she healed, she fought the impulse to surrender her power completely, to release control instead of take it. She feared what might happen if she ever succumbed to those whisperings of madness, the tug of the void at her soul. But each time, it was more of a battle—and as he spoke, she knew it was that battle that had cost the rabbit's life, and nearly cost the dolphin's.

Calandra hung her head. "I—I know. I'm sorry. I will do better."

He scowled. "See that you do. Your people's fate depends on it."

Shame choked her. He ran his hand down her arm to her hand, then noticed the rings and lifted it for a better view.

"These are new."

Calandra dared a smile as she remembered.

"Yes. I defeated Narcissa in a wager about a dead fern. And I healed my mother's Tear."

She gasped as she remembered the Tear.

"My mother! She wasn't Mad. She left me a message."

He raised an eyebrow and his golden-eyed gaze roved over her face.

"Is that so? Please, do tell."

"She, um, said she thought she knew what caused the Madness. And why we can't have boys." It was difficult to grasp the memories, like pulling fish from a barrel of oil. "She thought she was pregnant with a boy. She left a stone for me here, in Atlantis, to tell me more."

She looked around at the toppled shelves in wonder. All this time, she could have been right beside a message meant for her and wouldn't have known it. *Couldn't* have known it—the only substantial thing in this hall of shadows was Damon himself. If she tried to touch anything else, her hand would go right through, as though her surroundings were made of water.

Damon's eyes widened slightly.

"A boy child in Nadia's lineage." He rubbed his chin. "Very interesting." He tucked a strand of blond hair behind her ear. "And he would be your brother. I wonder if he has received an equal share of power?"

That idea had not occurred to Calandra. Besides Damon, the only men in her experience were human, and while a human male could be capable of great acts of physical strength, she had never seen one display any ability to manipulate the elements.

"Undine men have powers? But of course they would. You do."

She held her breath, hoping he would finally confirm or deny whether or not he were, in fact, an undine.

Damon smiled in knowing amusement and said nothing. He still held her hand, rubbing her fingers between his own, a not-unpleasant sensation.

"I sometimes forget how young you are and how little you know. When I reigned, humans would pray to me for calm seas and for favourable winds, even for rains in season. And they were right to do so, as I could grant it if I wished. When it came to fire and air, there was very little I could not do. If I wanted something, I could have it. No one could stand in my way."

He closed his eyes, as though basking in the memory.

"How I miss those days."

Calandra had so many questions for Damon, like how long ago he had reigned, and how the humans had even known of him, for it sounded like he meant humanity in general, not only the ones that had been brought inside the barrier. He had often expressed his ideas that humanity as a race needed to be ruled, that without guidance, they were listless, savage, and lost. That they craved something to worship, and the undines should be using that to their advantage. But whenever she began to ask anything of Damon's past, he chided her for impertinence and changed the subject. She decided to risk a question, anyway.

"How did you become . . . like this? And how is it that you and I can speak?"

She expected him to frown and snap at her, as he usually did. But instead, he regarded her thoughtfully.

"I once loved an undine woman. She was a great deal like you—bold, beautiful, and extremely powerful. I . . . made a mistake. She punished me for it by confining me to the Abyss."

He was a prisoner? That was news.

"But should you not be dead by now?"

He smiled patiently. "The flesh I wore has died, yes. But my true form is spirit and cannot die. Sadly, though, I am tied to this wretched ruin. She weakened the chains that keep me captive when she collapsed the island on my prison, but she did not break them, more's the pity. I had merely wanted to rule with her, together. She could not see the vision I held."

Calandra gaped as she put pieces together.

"You . . . you were Nadia's consort? You're *Alessandro?*"

Damon nodded.

"That was my name then. To you, I am Damon. As to how it is that we are here, together, I have had much time to ponder that. I believe it is because you are so powerful, just as she was, and because you are her descendant. Your spirit has found mine because we belong together. You call me to your dreams, and I come."

He cupped her cheek.

"It is sometimes disconcerting how much you are like her. Perhaps this is my chance to make right what I did wrong all those years ago."

She called to him? She had always thought he had drawn her into his presence. Undeniably, they had a connection that defied explanation.

Hesitating, she laid a hand on his chest and shivered at the solid warmth.

"What did you do that was so terrible?"

He grasped her arms and drew her toward his mesmerizing eyes. Dark hair and blond floated in symphony in the water around them.

"Nothing deserving of the fate I received." He sighed. "It doesn't matter anymore. What matters is that I get a chance to be better, with you. If we were together, there is nothing we could not do. It's what you want, isn't it? To be with me?"

Calandra nodded a head that felt too heavy.

"If you were my consort, I'm certain I would have enough strength to heal the Heartstone."

He smiled widely. "And so much more. But your Heartstone is a start."

"But how can we do that? Adonia intends to bond me to a consort after the next Redemption Moon so I will be prepared for the Healing Ceremony. And you are, well, you're a . . ."

"Prisoner?"

"I was going to say *spirit*, but both are an issue."

Was it even possible to bond a spirit? Then again, a spirit had been training her in her dreams for the last five years. Who could say what was or was not possible?

"You must come to Atlantis." He clasped his hands behind his back. "I believe that if you came to me, we could be joined and I could be freed."

Calandra swallowed. Even in the thick heaviness of her dream thoughts, something about this terrified her. Maybe because she could never sense what lay behind that beautiful face, and it left her feeling adrift. On the other hand, she already had one reason to go to Atlantis. If freeing Damon and bonding him as consort were what was necessary to heal the Heartstone, wouldn't whatever price she must pay be worth it?

"Why don't we try it now?" She lifted a trembling palm toward his forehead.

He caught her wrist and pulled it away, his face darkening like a thundercloud, then returning to its normal brooding expression so quickly she doubted what she had seen.

"You are not really here, my dear. This place exists only in the dreams we both share. I do not even know if this is a true representation of the city as it is now. You *must* come to me."

Calandra's insides shrank. Her mother had left a message for her in Atlantis, but as much as she wanted to find it, the thought of encountering Damon in the flesh—if he had flesh—left her ice-cold, at the same time as it set her body on fire.

She hesitated. "How do I know that what you are telling me is true? Are you saying Nadia went Mad from a broken heart?"

If Thea were correct and Nadia hadn't gone Mad from bearing her several daughters, was it possible that the Madness was caused by matters of the heart?

Another thought occurred to her—if Damon were Alessandro, did that make him her ancestor, too?

Damon took both her hands and squeezed.

"I do not know why she went Mad, and that is the truth. But I would have done anything to prevent it, if I had been free to do so. Just as I would do anything to make you happy, my lark."

He lowered his head and kissed her. Calandra didn't know what he was doing at first. She'd heard of kissing but had never seen anyone do it. It was an act that happened solely in private, when an undine took her pleasure with a man—or a woman, as sometimes happened.

She could see why. Her insides had become molten and flowed in directions she didn't understand. She did not want the kiss to end. But eventually, it did, leaving her gasping and breathless—and feeling strangely dirty, like his kiss had left a residue on her soul.

He smiled at her.

"Let that be proof of my intentions. Once you free me, you will finally know how a woman is meant to be loved by a man. I cannot wait to show you."

She stared at him, struggling between bliss and disgust. Ancestor or no, Damon was still her best hope at gaining the power she needed to fulfill her mission. Then she looked into his golden eyes and forgot why she was resisting in the first place, the lethargy returning.

"Okay. I will come to you. Perhaps, after we heal the Heartstone, we can find my family."

She could hope.

He was fading from view, as were the broken columns and walls of the building. "And be together forever."

"Forever," she said mechanically, her hands grasping nothing.

Soon, she drifted through the waves of the sea of dreams.

*

CALANDRA was awoken by steady pounding on her chamber door and muffled voices outside.

She dragged herself out of the depths of sleep and cracked her eyelids open. Light harpooned her vision. She winced and blinked, then grabbed last night's crumpled gown from the floor and wriggled into it, letting it hang on her without belting it. Then she opened the door.

Tanni stood on the other side trying to stare down Osaze, who returned her glare with a look of placid obstinance.

"She is not to be disturbed," he insisted, his voice calm but determined.

Tanni looked annoyed.

"Did you not hear me? Queen *Adonia* sent me. The queen's orders supersede Calandra's, I don't care who you are."

Calandra cleared her throat. "And what does Aunt Adonia want?"

Tanni started and turned toward Calandra but looked no less irritated. If anything, her frown deepened as she planted her fists on her hips.

"What did you do this time?"

Calandra shook her head, trying to focus. Why was everything so bright? "What do you mean?"

"Adonia sent for us both to meet her in the Observation Chamber. You were supposed to be there fifteen minutes ago, but apparently, Osaze refused to let the messenger disturb you."

Osaze spoke as though by rote. "My mistress is never to be disturbed in the morning for anyone less than a *daskala*. A thousand apologies, mistress."

He touched his forehead and bowed to Calandra with proper obeisance, but the mechanical tone of his voice made the penitent gesture somewhat ludicrous.

Calandra cast a bleary glance at the man. She really needed to review his permissions.

"It's okay, Osaze. Tanni always has permission to see me. And in the future, please notify me if a messenger arrives."

Osaze bowed and saluted, then resumed his waiting posture.

The world came into clearer focus as the events of yesterday popped into her head. Dismay overcame her as she remembered she had planned to find the palace bondmistress and Release Osaze first thing this morning, which would require at least some time to allow him to come out of it and then talk through what they were going to do next. She glanced at Tanni's expectant face and sighed. Apparently, that would have to wait.

She gestured to the room. "Would you like to come in while I dress, Singer kor'Zelia?"

Tanni looked up and down the hallway, then stepped into the room and closed the door behind her.

Calandra stripped the gown from her body and threw it into the soiled linens basket for the palace servants to collect.

"Any idea what Aunt Adonia wants?" she said over her shoulder. She found a clean apprentice's tunic which she belted on, and then began working on her hair.

"No, but she didn't look happy. What happened last night after I left the feast?"

"Nothing. I left soon after you did. I have no idea what's going on."

Calandra remembered Thea's parting gift with a rush of adrenaline.

"Wait! Something did happen, but not something bad. I can still hardly believe it myself. Thea gave me my plant healer's and stone healer's rings."

She offered her hand to Tanni to inspect them.

"She also had the other piece of my mother's Tear, and I healed it."

Calandra reached for her throat to show Tanni her pendant and grasped nothing.

"Oh, yeah, I left it on my night—"

Her gaze flew to her side table, but all it contained was the rock crystal reader. She frowned.

"Where did it go?"

She ran to the bed and looked all around the furniture, even checking under the mattress and ripping the linens off the bed. Tanni watched her in bewilderment.

"Calandra, what in the name of the Mother . . . ?"

"My Tear! It was right here last night, but now it's gone. I *know* I left it here. It was the last thing I did before I fell asleep."

Her brain scrambled as she tried to think of what might have happened to it. Had someone sneaked in and stolen it? How could they, with Thomas and Osaze on duty? But Osaze would have only arrived within the last hour, and Thomas would be in his quarters sleeping by now. She didn't have time to send for him to find out about possible intruders—it would have to wait until she'd found out what Adonia wanted.

She froze. If that stone fell into the wrong hands . . .

Tanni looked concerned, but tapped her leg with her hand, tension flowing through the bond. "I'm sure it will turn up, but we're keeping the queen waiting. We can look for it later."

"You don't understand." Calandra stood on shaky knees. "That stone had a message from my mother. And what she said?"

She looked her friend full in the face.

"It could change Sirenia forever."

15

THE LESSON

Calandra filled Tanni in on her mother's message on the way to the Observation Chamber. She kept her voice low enough that Osaze, who followed behind them, wouldn't be able to hear.

When Calandra finished, Tanni let out a shaky breath.

"Oh," was all she said.

Calandra knew the message's implications would not be lost on her friend.

"Wait—you have a brother?" Tanni said a little too loudly. She looked as incredulous as Calandra had felt at first.

"Shh. Maybe. Assuming he's still alive out there."

They fell silent as a group of acolytes passed them in the hallway on the way to their morning lessons.

When the students were out of earshot, Calandra continued in a whisper. "Since my mother hasn't returned, I can only assume that something must have happened to her. I need to find out what, and where my brother is—if he's even alive. And hope he knows the secret of his own existence."

Tanni frowned.

"How are you going to do all that, with the Redemption Moon, your impending bonding, the Heartstone, and"—she flicked her thumb at Osaze, shielded from his vision by her body—"to deal with? It's not like Adonia is likely to let you go chasing off after the sister she declared a madwoman."

Calandra reached for her pendant and then remembered that it was missing. Her fist closed on empty air, and she clenched it hard.

"I don't know," she said through gritted teeth. "But I'm going to have to figure something out. Once the Heartstone has been repaired, perhaps I can take a voyage. My brother might be alive but have no way to find

106

us, so I need to find him. I also need to find the answers my mother was searching for. Right now, the only lead I have for both is the datastone that my mother mentioned."

"The one in Atlantis?"

Calandra nodded, avoiding her friend's gaze.

Tanni grabbed Calandra's arm, pulling her to a stop.

"You're going after it, aren't you?"

Tanni already looked resigned to the answer she knew was coming, but Calandra answered anyway.

"Yes."

Tanni threw her hands up in the air and spun toward the windows lining the corridor. She put her hands on her hips, sighed, and turned back to face her friend.

"So when are we going?"

Calandra grinned in thanks, ignoring the worm of guilt eating at her gut for not mentioning Damon.

"I'm working on a plan. But we'll have to discuss it later, okay?"

Tanni rolled her eyes in mock exasperation, but she chuckled. "You and your plans."

Calandra laid her hand on the handle of the Observation Chamber. Tanni didn't need to know that her plan involved a certain dream spirit whose intentions she questioned more every time they met. She suddenly remembered last night's kiss. She blushed and put her other hand to her mouth, then covered her momentary discomposure by flashing a cheeky smile at Tanni.

"We'd be nothing without you."

Tanni laughed, then quickly composed herself in preparation for facing the queen. Calandra pushed the door open and they stepped into the chamber.

They froze in their tracks, Calandra's danger sense on high alert. Entering the room was like swimming into a cave full of jellyfish. Only she wasn't sure where the stinging tendrils were pointed.

Queen Adonia stood at the floor-to-ceiling curved glass wall with her back toward them, her arms folded across her petite frame, staring up into the vast chamber beyond. Her simple white morning tunic and the thick red hair flowing loosely down her back marked her hurried and early rising after the late night of revelry.

Narcissa stood with clenched hands on the other side of her mother and Thea stood near the table, her relaxed posture hiding the unease that

Calandra could sense in her. Gerrick, Cain, and two *taps* guards stood near the back wall of the room, all with the unfocused stare of the Redeemed. Brilliant sunlight refracting from the rock crystal tiles in the Mother's Heart chamber bathed the entire scene in soft white light through the filter provided by the glass.

When Calandra and Tanni entered, Adonia turned, dismissing their salutes with an imperious wave of her hand.

"Come. Join me."

Calandra indicated that Osaze should stand with the other men at the back, and then she stood between the queen and Tanni, who had adopted a soldier's stance of ready ease.

She had seen the Heartstone only last night, but in the blinding light of day, the blackened surface of the sphere was even more alarming and ugly. She stiffened and forced herself to stare at the dark shadow above their heads.

Beside her, Tanni drew in a soft gasp.

Adonia considered the stone with an air of cold consideration.

"We are running out of time." She turned to face her niece directly. "Which is why it is time for you to stop delaying the inevitable. We need you to embrace your destiny, Calandra. Our greatest stone healers and panaceas have exhausted themselves with trying to repair the Heartstone. You can see how successful they've been."

Adonia indicated the orb with a casual gesture and strolled toward the table.

Calandra pondered her aunt's words. "It is only one month until the next Redemption Moon and my bonding. What can I do in the meantime?" She tried not to think about what being bonded to a stranger might be like. It was not her place to decide who her partner would be. She didn't have that luxury. Adonia would choose, just as she had directed every step Calandra had ever made. And Calandra would fulfill her duty. A memory flashed through her head from her dream. Had she promised Damon he could be her consort last night? She flushed, but the thought faded as quickly as it had come.

Adonia pierced her with eyes as sharp as a jade spear.

"You can stop letting fear hold you back and earn your physic ring, for one. Your power has been growing, but still, you let doubt prevent you from completing the triquetra."

Calandra glanced at Thea, whose golden triquetra set with a panacea's fire opal dangled from a hair chain in the centre of her forehead, as always.

"Yes," said Adonia, following her gaze, "Thea told me you earned both your green jade and blue opal rings yesterday, but failed to earn the red jasper and thus the panacea's triquetra. She seems to think you have the skill but lack only the confidence. Do you want to know what I think?"

Calandra's gut clenched, but she dipped her chin respectfully. "Please, your majesty."

Adonia smiled, but it was not a pleasant one. "I think you've been lacking the proper motivation."

Calandra hadn't the slightest idea what her aunt could be getting at.

"You." Adonia beckoned Osaze with a jerk of her hand, and he came to stand before them. Adonia pointed at the chair. "Sit down, *doulos.*"

Osaze sat, staring straight ahead. Adonia instructed him to hand her his sword, remove his gauntlet, and put his arm on the table.

Narcissa stepped forward. "Mother, what are you going to do? I thought this was about the—"

"*I* am going to do nothing." Adonia turned her piercing gaze on her daughter, then extended the sword hilt toward her. "*You* are going to chop off this man's hand."

Tanni drew in a sharp breath, and Calandra felt as though her heart had stopped.

Thea stood very still. "Adonia, what—"

The queen held up an imperious hand of warning, and Thea fell silent.

Narcissa, who had gone very pale, shook her head and ignored the proffered weapon. "You can't be serious. Why would you ask me to do such a thing?"

"Because, dear daughter, you want to be queen someday. And queens must sometimes make difficult, and even ugly, choices for the good of their people."

She raised her other hand and let a dark green opal Tear pendant drop to the end of its chain.

"And because you, and every woman in this room, has either seen the message this contains, or, I presume, knows of it."

She cast a pointed look at Tanni, who flattened her lips and nodded.

"And I need to know who among you believes this blasphemy, and who remains loyal to me, to our people, and to Atargatis."

Calandra stared at the swinging pendant, unable to speak.

My mother's Tear! How did she . . .?

She glanced at Narcissa, and the guilty look she got in return confirmed her suspicions. Her cousin looked like she would do almost anything to undo what she had done if it would remove her from her predicament.

"My arm tires, Narcissa. Come. Prove your loyalty."

Adonia had always had the air of one who expected instantaneous obedience, which was understandable. But Calandra could not remember her ever making so nonsensical of a demand before.

"Your majesty, please," Calandra began, and faltered when Adonia's attention snapped toward her.

Calandra took a deep breath, trying to project calm, but her stomach churned like the whirlpool of Charybdis. She'd have to rely on other methods.

"You don't need to do this. This has nothing to do with Osaze, or Tanni, or anyone else in this room. The message was for me. Let me suffer the consequences, not him or"—she flicked her gaze at her cousin, frowning—"anyone else."

Adonia's gaze grew even sharper.

"Oh, these consequences *are* yours, my dear. But you are not the only one here who must learn a lesson." She turned back to her daughter. "If you refuse to learn yours, I shall have to think of something more severe."

Narcissa eyed her mother, then took the sword as though it were an electric eel that might shock her. Osaze still sat on the chair, his arm extended, seemingly oblivious to what was going on around him. Narcissa turned to face him, planted her feet, and adjusted her shaking grip. Her pale, clammy face held an expression of horrified determination.

"Adonia, I must object," said Thea.

The monarch turned to glare at her.

"Have you forgotten to whom you speak, Councillor? You will address me properly."

Thea's eyes widened at the rebuke. She had known Adonia since the queen had been in the nursery, and when in an informal setting, they often addressed each other by their given names.

"Fine, then, *your majesty*, this seems nothing but cruel. If this man is to be mistreated, there needs to be a good reason for it. I should not need to remind you that *douloi* have rights."

Adonia seemed to grow somehow, as though she simply took up more space in the room. She glared at each of them in turn, ending with Thea. Though the queen was a full head shorter than the healer, she seemed to look her straight in the eye.

"You dare to demand a reason of me? Does that mean you are partial to my sister's lies?" She thrust the jewel into Thea's face. "Do you believe that men should not be our servants, but our *partners*?" She spat the word as though it were venom. "As though they were capable of reason and rational thought, let alone love? Look at your consort, Thea."

She pointed at Gerrick, who stood there with a blank, stoic expression. Thea hesitated, then glanced at him.

"Would you trust decisions of council or even your own household to such a creature?"

Thea reddened slightly, closed her eyes and took a breath, then opened them and met Adonia's gaze.

"My loyalty has ever been, and will always be, to the preservation and safety of our people. As to Delphine's message, I have nothing to say. It would bear further study to determine the truth or falsehood of it."

"No! We need no further study." Adonia turned to Calandra. "We *need* a panacea skilled enough to guide and power the healing of the Heart-stone. And we need a future queen"—her gaze bore into Narcissa's—"who leads with decisive action, not deceit and petty trickery."

Narcissa flushed and took a step backward as though struck.

Without warning, Adonia grabbed the sword from Narcissa's trembling hands with both of her own, whirled while raising it above her head, and chopped off Osaze's hand in one lightning-fast motion. Tanni maintained her at-ease posture, but her face lost its rosy undertone and her jaw tightened. Narcissa's hands flew to cover her mouth, but she dropped them to her sides and began swallowing convulsively.

Osaze didn't flinch, merely let out a small grunt. Thea leaped forward to attend to him and Adonia extended the sword toward her heart. Thea froze.

"Back off, healer," Adonia said. "You are not to touch him. If he is to be healed, it will be by Calandra."

Calandra watched Osaze's lifeblood pulse out onto the table and run onto his leg, then drip onto the floor. She couldn't make herself move.

16

THE PHYSIC

ADONIA TURNED HER FACE TOWARD Calandra, the sword she still pointed at Thea keeping the healer from interfering.

"You care for this man, don't you? I remember how you used to play as children. If you don't heal him, he'll die. Are you going to let him die, Calandra?"

Calandra took a halting step forward, dumbly picking up the severed appendage. It felt strange, like it should be alive, but was now only a mockery of a living thing. She squatted in front of Osaze, took his arm, and held the two pieces of his flesh together. But her heart was racing so fast that she couldn't feel the energy she needed to heal him. Not even the treacherous swirling darkness touched her.

"I need my Tear," she said. "I can't do this without it."

"Really?" Adonia mocked. "A man's life is on the line, and you will fail again because of a silly stone?"

"It is how I focus my energy."

Adonia's jade eyes glinted. "Perhaps this will help you focus."

She put her finger on Osaze's forehead and sang a short sequence of notes. Osaze's eyes grew bright and he began screaming. He grabbed his bloodied limb in his other hand, staring dumbly at the place where his hand should have been, a wordless cry of torment tearing from his lips.

Adonia had Released him.

Osaze swallowed his scream and began panting. Calandra squatted in front of him, her thoughts slow and sluggish. *I need to focus. Keep it together, Calandra.* Images of the rabbit and the screaming baby dolphin filled her mind.

Osaze's gaze fell on her, then the severed hand she held, and his face contorted in pain and confusion. His good hand shot out and closed around her throat. Through gritted teeth, he choked out, "Make . . . it stop. Put it . . . back."

Tanni, Thea, and Gerrick leapt forward to restrain him. Narcissa stood motionless, eyes bulging like a blowfish.

"What have you done?" Thea shouted at Adonia as she and the others tried to pry him off her.

Lights were dancing in Calandra's vision when they finally ripped Osaze's hand away from her throat. She gulped air like a fish on land—being breathless was not a thing she had ever truly experienced before. While Tanni and the other human guard held Osaze's arms, her attacker shouted curses at her, Adonia, and everyone in the room.

Adonia's face remained impassive. "You see, this is what we are freeing them from with the bond. Calandra, Redeem him. Save him from his pain and anger. Surely you can do that much?"

Calandra rubbed her throat, the muscles already cramping. She stared at the man whose night-black eyes glared at her with the berserk intensity of a shark who smells blood in the water. She had never Redeemed a man before, though she knew how, in theory. She hummed to try her voice box, put her forefinger on his forehead, then sang the line of music the way she had learned it.

Immediately, Osaze's eyes lost focus and his taut muscles relaxed. She felt the pull of his spirit toward hers, but not the gentle bond of sharing she had with Tanni. This was more akin to holding something of him in her hands, like a tether.

Once he stopped resisting, the others stepped away from him.

Adonia nodded approval.

"Very good. Now heal him."

Osaze's flailing had caused him to lose blood even faster, and his complexion turned ashy.

Calandra put her blood-splattered hand on his arm again. This time, she could *feel* him. She held the severed hand in place, closed her eyes, and took a breath.

Something was missing.

Calandra looked up. "I need water."

Tanni snatched up the wide, shallow glass bowl of lilies from the centre of the conference table and hurriedly scooped out the flowers, then brought the bowl to her.

"Where?"

"Put my foot into it."

Tanni pulled off Calandra's sandal and gently lifted her foot, then placed it into the bowl on the floor. Her heel rested on the edge.

She closed her eyes and began to extend the energy line from her heart into Osaze's wrist. Not wanting to take chances, she called the elements to her as she usually did, preparing to battle for control. But there was something different this time. No tendrils of warm darkness furled at the corners of her mind. The elements, even spirit, snapped to do her bidding, as though they were eager—or afraid. Calandra blinked. What was different?

But although the elements were firmly within her grasp, she could barely sense the pieces inside Osaze that she needed to mend. She could feel the parts of Osaze's arm that were shrivelling and the hand flesh dying from lack of nourishment, but as far as Seeing the places she must heal, it was like looking through a gauze veil.

Frustrated, she glanced at Osaze. His head lolled slightly and his eyes glazed.

"Stay with me, Osaze," she said, releasing his arm to give him a light slap on the cheek. His eyes focused on her, and she stared into them, trying to give him her strength.

I'm sorry, Osaze. I'm sorry you had to go through this because of my failures. I'm sorry I had to Redeem you again. I'll fix this. I'll fix it all.

The image of him when he'd been Released—eyes manic with pain and blood lust—flashed into her mind and she nearly lost the connection. She grabbed hold of it with her mind and that's when she felt the *pull*, that familiar tug to surrender control. But she couldn't fail again. Not this time. Not when he was beginning to wobble in his seat from the blood loss. He was like a helpless bird with a broken wing. And she knew how to heal a broken wing. She *would* heal it.

She drew in the water's energy and extended her awareness into Osaze's flesh. This time, she *ordered* the elements to do her will.

To her surprise, they obeyed with a speed that nearly overwhelmed her. She barely had time to direct the sudden influx of energy to where she needed it most.

After a momentary struggle, she gained the upper hand. Breathing deeply, she poured energy into the wound, beginning the labourious process of reconnecting bones, blood vessels, and other tissues. Occasionally, Osaze let out a low moan or a grunt, but other than that, gave no indication he was in any discomfort at all.

Time stood still around her. Thea and Tanni had been speaking gentle encouragement, but their words slowed and stopped. She could no longer hear Narcissa's panicked breathing, or the occasional clink of the guards' armour. There was only her and Osaze, her spirit mingling with his flesh as she drove the elements like a pack of wild creatures, forcing them to knit the tissue together.

At last, she released the elements and pulled the last vestiges of her energy line back into her heart, then closed it off.

She opened her eyes. "It is finished."

The world abruptly resumed motion in supersaturated colour and sound. Though she had just woken up, Calandra was completely exhausted. She felt like she could go back to bed for the rest of the day. At the same time, the same hyperawareness that had buoyed her after she'd tried to heal the Heartstone flooded through her. She did not even need to look around to sense the relieved sighs from Tanni and Narcissa, the tension draining from Thea, and Adonia's nod of victory and approval. But there was something different about the feeling, too, something harsher. Beyond the glass, the Heartstone pulsed sadness.

"I knew you could do it, Cali," said the queen, once again the doting aunt. "But you'll understand that I can't let you have your mother's Tear again until it has been blanked."

Calandra felt strangely detached, but some part of her balked at the queen's statement.

"Please, Aunt Adonia," she said evenly, meeting her aunt's gaze with a level stare. "Let me keep it. It is the only recording of her I have."

Adonia tsked at her. "Now, now, why would you want to keep the ramblings of a madwoman? I think not. And you can forget about any thought of finding the datastone she mentioned."

She drew a chain from her neck and let it hang from her hand. A blue aquamarine Tear dangled from the glinting silver.

"I had it blanked years ago. She always did think she was cleverer than me."

Blood whooshed through Calandra's ears like ocean waves. Could that be the stone? She had no way to know. The stone readers did not show colour, so she would have to find the place her mother had shown her in the message to know for certain. But Adonia obviously didn't want the contents of that stone found, so it seemed likely that she was telling the truth.

As the queen replaced both chains around her neck and lifted her hair out of them, Calandra's heart fell. She felt outmanoeuvred and without options. Her only hope for finding her family was on those two stones.

Thea stepped forward.

"Your majesty, perhaps I could blank the stone for you? I could blank only the parts of the message that are inappropriate. Delphine was the girl's mother, after all."

Adonia gave the healer a searching stare, then nodded and handed her the green opal Tear.

"Very well. But splice carefully."

Thea pressed her lips together, cupped the stone in her hands, and closed her eyes.

While she worked, Adonia watched not the healer, but the healer's consort, with a musing expression. Gerrick continued his attentive, waiting posture, staring straight ahead. Sweat beaded on his forehead. Once again, Calandra sensed an unexpected spike of fear from the man.

When Thea opened her eyes, Adonia extended a hand for the Tear.

"Let me see."

She pulled a handheld reader from a shelf on the back wall and placed the Tear on it, then scanned through what remained of the contents. When she finished, she nodded and met the healer's gaze.

"You did well, Thea. Very well. You surprise me."

She set the reader back on the shelf and handed Calandra the Tear, who clasped the stone to her heart.

Thea raised a questioning brow. "Why does my loyal and precise service surprise you after so many years, your majesty?"

"Because I just realized something I should have seen years ago."

Adonia closed the distance between herself and Gerrick with a single step, unsheathed her belt knife and raised her hand to strike in one fluid motion.

Gerrick flinched.

As soon as he did, all the colour drained from his face. A wave of fear and dread rolled from both him and Thea.

Adonia dropped her hand and turned toward Thea with a grim expression.

"How long has Gerrick been Unredeemed?"

Thea looked toward her husband, her expression betraying none of the fear she radiated.

"Unredeemed? What are you talking about?"

After so many years of restraint, his alarm was apparent only by the dilating of the eyes, the quickening of his breath, and—

"See?" Adonia crowed, crossing her arms. "His hands shake like palm leaves in a trade wind. Guards!"

"No!" Thea pleaded, her composure gone. She stepped toward Adonia. "Don't hurt him. Please!"

"My dear councillor," Adonia said, giving Thea the same unpleasant smile she had bestowed upon Calandra earlier. "The guards are not for him. They are for you."

With that, she turned to Gerrick, placed her forefinger on his forehead, and sang the Redemption Song.

Gerrick's face went slack and his posture relaxed. Thea's eyes welled with tears, but she stood tall and offered no resistance as the *taps* guards put green feldspar handcuffs on her.

"He has served with me for forty-five years." Thea's voice quivered slightly. "What harm do you think he might do now, when we are both old and frail?"

Adonia snorted. "Old? Yes. Frail? Don't mock me. And it is *your* seditious actions that concern me most."

She flicked her wrist, and the guards led her away.

Calandra stared after Thea in shock, unwilling to believe what had just happened.

Adonia turned and inspected her niece.

"I can see that you were unaware of Thea's deception. And what do you think of your mother's foolish ideas?"

Calandra shook her head. *Forty-five years? Gerrick had been Unredeemed their whole marriage?*

"I—I don't know, Aunt Adonia. How can we be sure she is wrong if we don't at least try to find out what she knew?"

Adonia glared at Calandra from only a slight advantage in height, but she may as well have been on a ladder. Abruptly, her expression softened.

"She already told me, back when she first found this blasted stone. I'll tell you what I told her—if you continue down this road, you will cause our civilization to collapse as surely as Nadia sank Atlantis. Delphine didn't listen to me, and we lost many sirens putting down the rebellion that ensued. Including Singer kor'Zelia's mother." She glanced at Tanni, then back to Calandra. "When your mother saw what she had done, she fled like the coward she is."

Calandra felt like she had been punched in the gut. Tanni's emotions through the bond were not much different. No one had ever told them what had started the rebellion that had killed Tanni's mother. The history stones always glossed over that little detail—which was probably how Adonia wanted it. Now that she knew, Calandra almost wished it had remained a secret.

No, it was better to know. Even if the truth hurt.

Adonia placed a hand on Calandra's shoulder.

"You don't want to have that kind of blood on your conscience, do you, my dear?"

"Of—of course not, your majesty."

Adonia pressed her lips together.

"I thought not. Your mother's radical ideas have already caused enough trouble on Sirenia. I don't intend to allow another rebellion to take hold." She took both of Calandra's hands and stared earnestly into her eyes. "You need to decide whom you will believe, Calandra—the madwoman who abandoned you as an infant, or the aunt who raised you as her own. Whose side are you on?"

Calandra swallowed, trying to work some moisture into her mouth. How could she possibly respond to that question?

Suddenly, she felt the weight of the task that she had been given as though it had been laid upon her for the first time. At that moment, she would have given up every ounce of her power if it meant she did not have to make decisions about who was right and who was wrong, or have the fate of a single person laid at her feet. The truth was, no matter whom she chose to believe, the lives of everyone on Sirenia were already on her shoulders. And saving them was the task she had been groomed for her whole life, whether by her aunt or, apparently, her mother. But how could she know who was right?

In the end, what did it matter? Adonia was the queen, and the ultimate responsibility for what happened to Sirenia was hers. Calandra was her subject, a tool to be used, not someone required to make life-or-death decisions for the good of their nation.

She ignored the quiet hesitation at that reasoning. Being absolved of responsibility felt too good.

"I have no intention of instigating a rebellion, your majesty. I remain loyal to you, and will continue to obey you with every ounce of my heart. I am yours to command."

Adonia smiled. "Excellent. Today you have proven your loyalty, Calandra, as well as earned the last ring you needed to become a panacea."

Adonia jerked her head, and Cain stepped forward and handed Calandra a red jasper physic ring. Numbly, she took it and slipped it onto her middle finger with the others.

"Now," Adonia continued, "all that remains is for you to be bonded and you will be able to repair the Heartstone. I have decided that we will not wait to see what the Redemption Moon supplies." She indicated Osaze, who still sat in the middle of a drying pool of his own blood.

"I have chosen this *doulos* as your consort. The bonding will happen the morning of the Summer Solstice while the nation is in the city for the festival, to be followed by the Heartstone Healing Ceremony. Until then, you will train him in service, as he has only ever been trained in guard duties."

Like most undines, Calandra could understand any language she'd ever heard, but Adonia's words washed over her like waves on the sand, changing everything while appearing to change nothing.

Narcissa, who had been watching the entire scene in silence, spoke up in a shaky voice. "Mother, I thought you promised the *tapeinos* to me."

Adonia regarded her daughter with a placid stare. "You think I do not see why you are interested in him? Foolish girl. First, you must learn to use the power you already have wisely before you will be ready to strengthen it with the help of another. Pettiness is no way to lead. Now be gone, daughter. I am sure you have latrines to clean."

Narcissa's face darkened in shame and rage. She cast a look that could flay skin at Calandra, then gave her mother a salute, spun on her heel, and left the room.

Adonia turned back to Calandra.

"Well?" the queen demanded. "What do you say? Are you not happy to bond a consort as desirable as this?"

"Thank you, your majesty," Calandra murmured, managing a clumsy salute.

Adonia smiled. "You're welcome. Come, Cain," she said to her pet. "Gerrick, report to your quarters and await further instructions."

She waited for Gerrick to salute, bow, and leave. Casting a final triumphant smile at Calandra, she swept out of the room in a swish of linen, Cain following in her wake.

Tanni and Calandra blinked at her retreating back, then turned to the blank-faced Osaze. She now held his Redemption bond, what she'd hoped for for so long. But instead of setting him free to choose his own path, she was now destined to marry him.

"Mazel tov," Tanni said as they stared at Calandra's consort-elect.

Calandra couldn't think of a thing to say.

17

THE GYPSY

Four months earlier
January 1799
Bristol

ROBERT COX TUGGED HIS TOP hat lower over his eyes and adjusted the collar of his black woollen great coat to stand up around his neck against the chilly breeze that blew down Broad Street. He kept his gaze straight ahead of him as he trailed behind his brother and sister-in-law. Each time Amelia pointed out some object she wished to stop and admire in a shop window, the corners of Gryffyn's handsome mouth tightened in impatience.

Near the street corner ahead of them, a small crowd gathered around a young gypsy lad playing a street game.

"Look, Gryffyn." Amelia tugged on her husband's arm with a pink-gloved hand. Dark ringlets framed her round, china-doll face inside a matching pink silk bonnet poking out from the hood of her green wool cloak. "Let's have a bit of fun. Come, place a wager."

Gryffyn frowned and surveyed the scene, his strong jaw working, then put on a charming, indulgent smile. "Your parents are expecting us at five o'clock sharp for tea, and your mother takes a very narrow view of tardiness."

"Oh, pshaw." Her face pinched in disdain. "Mama can wait a few minutes longer. Early or late, she would not be happy, either way."

Gryffyn harrumphed. "That's the truth. All right, my dear. We shall at least watch."

Amelia smiled in unaffected delight and led the way to the front of the crowd of onlookers.

Robert moved to follow and stepped aside to allow a distraught-looking, finely dressed African woman passage into the street. Her eyes were downcast, and he got the uncanny feeling she was attempting to escape notice, just as he was, with as little success. He glanced around to see if she were in any danger. Seeing no pursuers or molesters, he glanced at her retreating form. She looked back over her shoulder and their eyes met—just for a moment—and then she continued on her way.

Robert started. Her eyes had been a luminous amber colour, the same as Talwyn's had been. He stared after her, but her head of dark, springy curls soon disappeared into the milling crowd filling the market street. He gave his head a shake and turned around, working his way toward his brother's black top hat, which was easily visible at the front of the crowd.

She's gone, Rob. After all these years, why won't you admit she's dead? You let her die.

He and his flayed conscience wedged in uncomfortably beside his older brother, unsurprised that he had not been consulted on the matter of stopping.

Despite the fact that he and Gryffyn were ostensibly business partners—the sign above their office door did read *Cox Bros Shipping* after all—Gryffyn seldom consulted him about anything. Robert was surprised that he even pretended to listen to his wife. Then he reminded himself that he should never underestimate his brother's desire to ingratiate himself with the powers that be—in this case, Amelia's father, the not-so-silent partner and primary underwriter of their shipping company. While she may have thought she married for affection, Robert knew that to Gryffyn, it had been more of a business contract than an affair of the heart. Gryffyn wanted the financial security she brought to the table, and Mayor Albright had wanted the prestige of having his daughter marry into old money, even if their father's lands and title had passed to their older brother, James.

Not for the first time, Robert thought how she had deserved so much better than his brother. Just because Gryffyn was the middle son of a lord did not make him a gentleman—though he knew how to put up a good pretence when he desired. Enough of a pretence that Amelia seemed as yet unaware of the type of man to whom she was bound. If only Robert had been of age when the transaction occurred, perhaps he could have saved her some of the future inevitable heartache for which he was sure she was destined. Though he had his own dark secrets, he was certain he would have been a more suitable partner to Amelia than his arrogant bully of a brother.

Robert's intentions were completely altruistic, of course. It had nothing to do with her rose-petal lips or big, dark eyes or the maddening scent of lilies that followed her like a cloud.

No. After what he'd allowed Gryffyn to do to Talwyn, the dark-haired girl he hadn't stepped up to defend all those years ago and who had disappeared that same night, he had vowed never to stand by and let another be hurt again when it was within his power to do something about it, and that included what his brother might inflict.

In this case, despite his best efforts, Robert had been unable to stop it. However, since they had been married six months ago, Gryffyn had behaved with almost admirable civility toward his wife. From what he'd told Robert, he'd even given up philandering in the gentleman's club. Mostly.

Frowning, Robert followed Amelia's gaze to the gypsy lad. The young man's engaging smile, confident manner, and rich voice elevated his patter from a game into an adventure, like he was letting the spectators in on a secret. A young boy in a brimmed cap stood before the barrel, concentrating on the shells with rapt attention.

"Watch the pebble, lad. Is it 'ere?" The young man lifted a shell to reveal a blank board where the pebble had been only moments ago. "No, if you thought 'twas there, you'd be wrong."

The street urchin's mouth hung open in astonishment.

The gypsy brandished the pebble between his thumb and forefinger. "Here it is."

The boy gasped. Amelia gave a delighted laugh and covered her mouth with her hands.

The gypsy kept eye contact with the boy.

"Now watch closely, lad, for the next time, you shall have to tell *me* where it is."

He made a production out of putting the pebble under the left shell and rearranged the order of the shells several more times, moving them forward and back, then lining them up in a row in the centre of the makeshift table. Robert kept his eye on the shell he thought contained the pebble.

"Well?" The blond gypsy indicated the shells with a flourish. "Where is it?"

The boy pointed directly at the shell hiding the pebble. The gypsy lad looked disappointed as he lifted the shell to reveal the prize and handed a small silver coin to the urchin.

"You 'ave a good eye, young man. Care to try yer luck again?"

The boy looked at his coin, considering it, then shook his head.

"That doesn't look so hard," Robert heard himself say. "I'll play."

"Of course, sir. The wager is a . . ." The gypsy lad looked up at Robert's face and trailed off. ". . . a thre'pence."

At the sight of the lad's face, Robert froze. He was used to people reacting to him that way. After catching a glimpse of the scars that puckered the flesh on the right side of his face—the scars that constantly reminded Robert of the cost of doing nothing, and the chance he'd been given to make up for his mistake—the next thing they usually did was look away, which was how he preferred it. But the gypsy lad did not.

The gypsy and Robert stared at each other, Robert rendered speechless by brilliant green eyes exactly like those of the boy that he would never forget. Could it be? Robert studied the young man, comparing him to the memory of his childhood playmate. But no—this lad's nose was crooked, his eyes too close together, and his ears stuck out and looked all lopsided. And he was decidedly chubby. Other than his colouring and approximate age, he looked nothing like Zale Teague.

Robert shook his head to clear it. *First Talwyn, now Zale? You've been seeing their ghosts for so long, you're beginning to see them in every face.*

"Well, lad?" Robert cocked his head and scowled. "Did you get enough of an eyeful yet? Are you ready to play?"

"Aye, sir."

The lad's thick Welsh accent was further confirmation that Robert's mind had been playing tricks on him—Zale had grown up in Cornwall, just as he had, and had spoken with the local rural dialect of the common folk.

Amelia turned her pretty eyes toward Robert with a teasing smile.

"Are you certain you can keep your eye on the ball, Mr. Cox?"

Robert frowned. "My eyesight is just fine, Mrs. Cox. Thank you for your concern."

Amelia bit her lip and exchanged an amused glance with her husband. "Confident enough to make it a shilling?"

Gryffyn frowned. "My dear, 'tis bad enough to risk even a thre'pence on this scoundrel. Besides, this vagrant boy probably has no shilling."

The lad's jaw tightened, and he fidgeted with a rich-looking green-and-gold bracelet he wore, frowning at the water barrel he was using as a table.

"Sorry, sir, I 'ave only a—"

He opened his palm and stopped. A well-worn shilling lay on his hand. He stared at the coin.

The boy closed his jaw, wrapped his hand around the coin, and squinted up at Robert. "Aye, but I don't think I'm willing ta risk it with someone as keen as yerself. You'd win, for certain, and I'd 'ave no supper. Care to try yer luck for sixpence, instead?"

"Did you steal that shilling, boy?" Gryffyn interjected, pulling out his pocket-watch and inspecting its unique stone face.

Robert cast a long-suffering look at his brother.

The lad gave Gryffyn an iron-eyed stare and pocketed the coin, then turned back to Robert.

"What say you, sir?"

Gryffyn guffawed, tucking his watch back into his waistcoat pocket.

"Come, Robert. Leave off this nonsense and let us go. Mrs. Cox's mother is expecting her for tea in one minute, and the business I have with my father-in-law cannot wait."

Amelia pouted prettily at her husband. "Oh, but I was so looking forward to seeing your brother's keen-sighted prowess, Mr. Cox. He has told me such tales of the things he's seen. Or *almost* seen." She turned to Robert, her dark eyes wide and innocent. "Such fantastical things. Surely, if he can discern the supernatural, he can win a mere street wager."

Robert schooled his face into a neutral expression. "I am sure I do not know to what you are referring."

"Oh, come now, Mr. Cox." Amelia indicated his face. "You know, the demon who gave you those scars."

Robert's face grew hot, and he mentally cursed the fair, freckled complexion that gave away every tremble of emotion he experienced.

After what had happened in the woods all those years ago, Gryffyn had bullied the boys into telling a concocted story of a freak lightning blast interrupting an innocent walk through the trees as the cause of Robert's injuries. Robert had once made the mistake, in a somewhat tender moment between himself and Amelia—before she'd become his sister-in-law—of telling her the truth behind his scars. He'd told her of Talwyn, and Zale, and the lightning and the wasps. He'd told her what Willie and Jory had said about a demon appearing in the water.

Before he had finished and could tell her what he feared had become of Talwyn and Zale at the hands of Gryffyn and his friends—for the demon could only be another ridiculous tale they had made up to absolve themselves of responsibility, or so he hoped—she had laughed him into mortified silence. Then she had gone straight to Gryffyn with it, who had convinced her that Robert had lost not only his looks that day, but his mind as well. In fact, Gryffyn insisted on the lie with such earnestness that sometimes Robert wondered if Gryffyn had begun to believe it himself. He certainly did not seem half so tormented by that night in the woods as Robert was.

Not that he'd expect that of Gryffyn, no matter what he might have done to Robert's friends.

Friends. He mocked himself. *Does a friend do nothing while his friends are attacked? Does a friend go along with a lie to protect those who have hurt them?*

He scowled at his sister-in-law, whose delight at his discomfiture was plain.

"I assure you, dear sister, that my eyesight is excellent and my mind intact, no matter what my brother has told you. Fine, to please you, I will play. But only if the boy puts up his shilling."

The lad considered it, then gave Robert a crooked smile.

"Aye, sir, I can't turn down the game." He turned his charm toward Amelia. "And I'd 'ate to disappoint such a lovely young miss as yourself."

"'Tis *Mistress*, lad, and don't you forget it."

The boy feigned shock. "And all the unluckier gentlemen in Bristol are the worse off to be deprived of your fair comp'ny, I'm sure, madam."

She preened at his flattery.

Gryffyn shifted his weight impatiently. "Hurry up, then. Let's get this over with."

Robert pressed his lips together at Gryffyn's rudeness, then turned and presented his own shilling to the gypsy lad, folded it into his palm, and crossed his arms. He nodded his head to begin.

Beside Robert, Gryffyn stood in stiff displeasure, and Amelia folded her hands in front of her in tense anticipation. Out of the corner of his eye, he spotted the beautiful African woman standing at the edge of the crowd, concentrating on the gypsy lad. He barely had time to wonder at her interest when the young man began the game.

Robert concentrated on the lad's movements, watching as he pushed shells forward, pulled them back, and lifted them up, giving a continual pattering narrative to accompany his motions. When the lad stopped and lifted his hands, Robert pointed at the shell containing the pebble.

"That one."

He grabbed the shell and turned it over to find barren table underneath.

Amelia bit her bottom lip, not quite hiding a smile.

Gryffyn pressed his lips together, casting a look of scorn at Robert, and held his arm out toward his wife.

"Come, Robert. Let us waste no more time on this tomfoolery."

Amelia placed her hand in the crook of Gryffyn's elbow, gave Robert an amused glance, and let her husband lead her away.

Robert turned back toward the lad and handed him his coin, who looked genuinely surprised as he accepted it.

"I'm sorry, sir, better luck next time. Care t'wager again?"

"There will be no more wagering today," came a deep voice from behind Robert.

He whirled to find a rotund man in a black cleric's suit standing behind him. It took a few moments to recognize the jowly face.

"Reverend Berian?" Robert bowed. "What are you doing in Bristol?"

A flurry of movement behind him drew him back around in time to see the gypsy lad and the African woman running into the entrance of an alley down the street. Before they disappeared into it, the blond lad glanced at Robert one last time, but he looked different. Gone were the crooked ears and the pudgy cheeks. In their place were strong features that bore an uncanny resemblance to one of the ghosts that haunted him.

"Zale!"

Robert ran toward the alley, but by the time he reached its mouth, it was already empty.

"'Tis no use, sir," said Berian from beside him, patting his breast pocket. "They've stolen back their chariot." He put his hand in his trousers pocket and his eyebrows drew together in a bushy grey line. "And mine, so it would seem."

Robert started and turned, amazed at the old gentleman's speed.

"How did you—?"

He shook his head. That didn't matter. What mattered was whether or not his mind was playing tricks on him. Was Gryffyn right? Was he truly going mad at last?

"Tell me, and this may sound strange, but did that boy resemble—" He swallowed. "Did he look like Zale Teague to you? The boy who disappeared near Chyandour Brook five years ago?"

Berian laid a hand on his arm, his face grave. "Aye. It was him. And I believe he may need your help."

Robert's mouth went as dry as chalk. He stared at the minister, completely dumbfounded.

"That . . . that *was* Zale? He isn't dead?"

Berian shook his head. "No, he is not. And you must help me keep him that way."

Robert turned back to stare at the empty alley.

He had never been so happy to see a ghost in his life.

18

THE REVEREND

ROBERT SET DOWN HIS CUP of tea in the saucer on his desk and stared at the golden-eyed cleric across from him. He'd arranged to have Reverend Berian meet him at his office after his social obligation at the Albrights had been fulfilled. He'd passed a rather dreadful hour at his brother's in-laws' house, but several cups of tea and Mrs. Albright's raspberry scones had calmed his nerves somewhat.

Zale Teague was alive, and according to Mr. Berian, in need of his help. Before he'd even heard Berian's request, he knew what his answer would be. Of all of the charitable deeds he'd gone out of his way to do over the years, this was the one that would be required of him above all—he owed Zale too much to refuse.

But now that they were crammed into the gloomy closet that passed as his office and he'd heard Mr. Berian out, Robert sat in stupefied denial. He searched the minister's expression for some hint of amusement and found none.

He did not want to accuse a reverend of dipping into the communion wine, but the things Berian had said in the last ten minutes were so far-fetched that Robert was having a difficult time believing them, like a country woman's admonishing fairy tale come to life. He thought longingly of the brandy in his cupboard, but pushed the thought aside. This story was hard enough to accept with his mind clear.

"You are quite serious? All this time, Zale has been alive, but has been travelling with a band of gypsies? And not only travelling with them, but their captive?"

Reverend Berian nodded. "So it would seem. I had almost lost hope of finding him again, but today, he arrived as an answer to prayer."

"Indeed."

Robert folded his hands in front of him and contemplated the meaning of the reverend's words. Since Zale lived, that meant Robert's fears about the crimes his brother may have committed, or what he himself had allowed through inaction and silence, had been groundless. *No, not groundless. How did Zale come to be imprisoned by gypsies? And why would a gypsy band imprison him, anyway?*

The air in his dark wood-panelled office seemed thick and close.

"And Talwyn Penrose? Do you know if she also lives, perhaps with these same gypsies?"

Berian cocked his head and stared at Robert as though the reverend could see straight into his tortured soul.

"I'm sorry, Robbie—er, Mr. Cox. Miss Penrose is gone, though you could say that her spirit remains with us." His voice grew gentle. "However, I want you to know that her fate had nothing to do with you. Her destiny was of her own choosing."

Robert clenched his fingers against the backs of his hands, staring out the window at the overcast, darkening sky above the river.

Talwyn is dead.

No matter what the reverend said, Robert could never fully absolve himself of responsibility for her fate. If only he'd done something . . .

"And you believe Zale is still in some kind of danger?"

Berian shifted in his leather-padded wooden chair. Robert would have expected the chair to complain under the weight of a man of his stature, but it made barely a sound.

"Yes. He escaped his captors, but the men who kept him will not let him go so easily. They will arrive soon, if they have not already. We must leave immediately."

"'We?' As in, you and I? Where on earth do you intend for us to go?"

"No, no." Berian waved his hand. "Mr. Teague and I."

Robert released his hands and picked up his teacup, regarding the impatient-looking cleric over the china rim before taking a sip.

"Forgive me, Reverend, but Zale and his companion did not seem eager to speak with you earlier. Are you certain that Zale trusts you?"

Robert had never had reason to distrust Berian when he was a child, but that had been before his eyes had been opened to see how evil could hide in the most innocent of guises, and demons could live even in country brooks. Gryffyn had never liked the reverend, but that no longer counted for much in Robert's books. If anything, it was a mark in the reverend's favour. His father had tolerated him as a man of the cloth, but Robert had no distinct memories of personal interactions with the man, good or bad.

However, Berian could just as easily be trying to get to Zale for his own ends. For that matter, perhaps it had been Reverend Berian that had caused the beautiful African woman's distress, for it was when Berian had appeared that she and Zale had fled. Robert had no idea why Zale was so valuable to the gypsies, and maybe to Berian, but he didn't want to be the one to cause the lad further grief. Robert pondered the implications and wondered whether he would have the nerve to confront even a cleric in the name of righteousness, should it become necessary.

Berian fidgeted with his teacup.

"Ah. His companion. Yes. I believe that Zale's mistrust originates with her. A simple misunderstanding. However, I will soon resolve the situation, and then I shall need passage for the both of us to Barbados. You have a ship leaving for that destination in the morning, I believe?"

Robert jerked his head up. "How did you know that?"

"I have made it my business to be constantly prepared for this very moment for several years."

"And why is that, pray tell? Of what interest is the lad to you?"

Berian smiled. "It is not so much the boy, but his mother, who interests me. You are probably aware that Delphine Teague has also been missing for several years?"

"Indeed." Robert nodded. It had been one more addition to the self-flagellating litany that he recited before bed every night.

Involuntarily, Robert touched the ridges of scarred flesh along his right temple and cheek. As hideous as he knew his face to be, were it not for Delphine, his disfigurement would have been much worse. While he had been writhing in the madness of pain, she had come to the manor and offered her healing services. To this day, he had no idea what was in the poultices and salves she had used, but when she had finished, not only had most of the burns on his face healed, but he could see. The local doctor had called it miraculous, and Robert knew that it was—a miracle that had come through the hands of the woman whose son he'd failed to save. He would be forever in her debt for what she had done.

"Is this an affair of the heart, Reverend?"

Berian gave a small smile. "You may think of it that way, if you wish. At any rate, I believe that Mrs. Teague can be tracked down from the vicinity of Barbados with her son's help. Now that he has been found, I want to waste no time in beginning."

"Ah." Robert picked up a quill from his desk and fidgeted with the sharpened tip, frowning. "And you are hoping to gain passage on my company's ship, I take it?"

Berian smiled with full, pink lips, his hooded eyes squinting to slits through which gleamed a bare glimmer of gold. The smile transfused his rather unattractive features with warmth.

"I am more than happy to pay for our way. But I knew you would understand. A man who has been given a second chance can't help but extend grace toward others. Wouldn't you agree?"

Robert steepled his fingers and replied only with a small tilt of his head. There was something about Berian's brusque, assuming manner that rubbed Robert the wrong way. He couldn't identify exactly what troubled him, only that he knew Berian was not telling the whole truth. And he had learned the hard way that he should always listen to his gut.

A sharp rapping at the door yanked the attention of both men toward it. The shadows on the other side of the frosted panes of glass revealed the silhouettes of a tall, husky man and a petite woman in the hallway beyond.

Robert frowned and stood.

"What the devil? It's after eight in the evening."

Berian also stood. "Don't answer it. I have an ill feeling about those two."

Robert scowled at him. "Watch yourself, sir. Man of the cloth you might be, but you have no right to tell me how to conduct my business."

"Suit yourself." Berian picked up his bowler hat and tucked it under his arm. "I will wait in the next room until you have sent them on their way."

Robert, having reached the door, watched Berian enter Gryffyn's office, wondering why the man didn't wait where he was. With a quick shake of his head, he opened the door.

"Good evening, sir," said the hulking, dark-haired man on the other side. He didn't even blink at Robert's scarred face. "I am looking for Mr. Cox."

Robert took in the man's worn blue velveteen jacket and dark features, and the woman's bangles, bohemian clothing, flashing black eyes, and long dark curly hair tied with a red scarf. Gypsies. He swallowed.

"I am he."

"Ah," said the man. "Mr. Gryffyn Cox?"

"He is my brother, and he is not here. May I pass on a message to him?"

"Ah, no, no." The man stepped back and rubbed his neck.

The woman looked . . . relieved?

The big man tucked his hand into the front of his brown waistcoat.

"Only tell him that Eric stopped by, and I will come to see him again in the morning."

"May I tell him what this is regarding? If you wish to ship something, I can see to it."

Eric looked thoughtful. "Tell him the package I had has gone missing, but a search is underway. I will speak with your brother about it in person tomorrow. Perhaps by then, all will be in order. Good evening, sir."

He touched his bare forehead with a little salute and a sloppy bow, the woman gave the briefest of flippant curtsies, and they walked away down the hall.

Robert closed the door, shaken. What was the likelihood that a pair of gypsies should show up on his doorstep on the very night Zale Teague had appeared on the streets of Bristol and wish to discuss a missing package with only his brother? In light of what Reverend Berian had revealed, Eric's visit and message implied two things.

One, that Berian had been right about Zale escaping from gypsies— for what other *package* might Eric have been referring to?

And two, that his brother had known about Zale's whereabouts all along, and had possibly even been responsible for them, for why else would the report be going to him? And if that were true, what nefarious scheme was Gryffyn involved in? Whatever it was, Robert would not be responsible for letting Zale suffer at his brother's hands any longer. But neither would he unwittingly put him into unknown danger in Berian's either.

Robert strode to the door of Gryffyn's office and wrenched it open.

"All right, sir," he said to the surprised man on the other side. "You may take passage on the *Atlanta*, on one condition."

"And what is that?" Berian said, frowning.

"Before you embark, I want a chance to speak to Zale. Privately. I will be waiting for you at the ship come dawn. If he wishes not to go, or not to go with you, then I will ensure that his wishes are met."

Berian's brow furrowed, but he nodded and fidgeted with his hat.

"Thank you, lad. I knew you were the one to ask."

"Don't thank me, sir. I suspect you may regret my generosity 'ere you reach Barbados."

Berian cocked his head. "Why is that?"

Robert cocked a brow. "Because, by my brother's direction, the *Atlanta's* first stop is Africa. Thereafter, her cargo will be slaves."

19

THE ATLANTA

"WHY DO WE NEED TO find a ship again?"

Zale squinted over the pile of nets at the large boat next to the pier. In the grey predawn light, he could make out *Atlanta* on her bow. Her masthead was a depiction of the Greek goddess for which she was named. Men bustled up and down the gangplank bearing bundles of supplies for making way.

"Can't we use one of those chariot thingies and—poof!—be there?"

He grinned as he thought of Abela's face when young John had given them the pendants he'd lifted from the reverend when the man hadn't been looking. She hadn't known whether to be grateful or to scold the child for pickpocketing. In the end, she had simply paid him a shilling for each and sent him on his way, the lad more than satisfied with the trade. Now they had not only Abela's chariot, but a spare. If only Abela could get them to work.

Crouched beside him on the pier, Abela growled with a resonance that surprised him.

"I told you. Barbados is too far away for chariots of this size. They will only take you short distances, and there is too much ocean between here and there to make it feasible."

"That's not a problem for me," he whispered with a grin.

She rolled her eyes. "Bully for you, Waterboy. But would you really want to try to keep me afloat if something went wrong and we were stranded in the middle of the Atlantic?"

Zale sobered. "No. But couldn't you at least zap us onto that ship? Why do we have to sneak on?"

"We're not going to sneak on. We'll be there for months, and the last thing we want is to be caught as stowaways. No, we'll pay for passage using the money you won last night."

Her mouth twisted in distaste, but she said nothing further about the means to their desired end. Over the course of the evening, Zale had won them a tidy sum from sailors and gentlemen in their cups, using the shell game and, at the pub later, his skill at cards—a game for which he'd always had an uncanny knack. Abela had been less than thrilled at the methods, but she couldn't argue with the results.

"We simply want to make sure no one sees us embark."

"Like Berian?"

"Especially Berian."

"And why is that, exactly?"

Abela ignored his question, glancing up and down the street. The only other people were the sailors and dockers loading the ship from a wagon on the quay.

"Okay . . . now!"

At her command, they straightened and walked hurriedly to the dock, approaching a man with a corked barrel over his shoulder.

"Excuse me." Abela waited regally as the man stopped and turned to face her. "Where may I find the captain?"

He scanned her from head to toe, and his face twisted into a sneer. "What's it to you, girl?"

Abela's nostrils flared. "No business of yours, sir."

He studied her for a moment, then scowled and jerked his head up to the quarterdeck. After casting a surly glance at Zale, he stomped up the gangplank without another word.

On the deck above them, a barrel-shaped salt of a man with greying red hair caught into a queue by a black ribbon stood overseeing preparations. The worn but well-cut blue coat he wore, brimmed black cap, and air of authority all indicated that he was the one they were searching for.

Abela smoothed her skirt. Zale wished he'd been able to find a nicer waistcoat for himself than this patched, worn thing, but there was nothing for it. Abela's fine clothes made her stick out like a nun in a brothel, and his ragged ones made him look like a fool in a mummer's play.

With as much dignity as any lady, Abela walked up the gangplank. Zale followed her as she wove between men hauling bags, barrels, and wooden crates of food, water, and trade goods. Some of them leered, some of them ignored her, and a few cast curious glances at them both. They did make a bit of an odd pair.

When they approached the quarterdeck, the captain took notice of them.

"You, there! What are you doing here?" the captain called down to them, pointing and looking at Zale.

Zale looked uncertainly between the captain and Abela.

Abela took a step forward and cleared her throat. "My friend and I would like to book passage to Barbados. May we come up to discuss it, sir?"

The captain looked askance at both of them, then nodded assent.

When they stood before him, he looked them up and down. "Can you pay?"

"Yes, sir," Abela said. "We have a guinea each for our passage."

The captain looked amused. "A whole guinea? And how do you plan to cover the rest?"

A tall man resembling an upside-down mop, with stringy greying black hair in a thin queue, an awkward gait, and a cruel set to his lips, walked by and leered at Abela.

"Oi can think of a way."

"Mr. Crow!"

The man turned to face the captain with a sloppy stance of attention. "Aye, cap'n?"

"Is that any way to address a lady?"

Mr. Crow snorted. "A lady? 'Ow can she poss'bly—"

The captain leaned into the taller man's face. "I may not have gotten to choose my first mate, but that does not make you any less subordinate to me. And I *will* have proper manners on my ship, especially from the officers. Is that understood?"

Mr. Crow regarded the captain with hard eyes, shifting a toothpick from one side of his arrogant grin to the other. "Aye, Cap'n Meredith, *sir*."

Captain Meredith glared at Mr. Crow, then gave him a dismissive nod. Crow cast an angry glare at Abela before shoving his hands in his pockets and walking away, whistling as though nothing untoward had even happened.

Captain Meredith turned his attention back to his guests.

"This ship has limited berths, and frankly, is no place for a lady such as yourself. The lad, I might be able to put to work, but you, Miss . . ."

"Bethel," Abela said with a slight curtsy. "Miss Abela Bethel."

The captain nodded. "Well, Miss Bethel, I'm afraid this voyage would not be suitable for you at all."

"And why is that, sir?"

"Because . . ." He took off his hat and repositioned it. "This is a slave ship."

He looked away, avoiding her gaze.

Abela stiffened and frowned. "And you think that would not suit me because . . . ?"

"Well, er, the smell. It is something like you've never known. Most men can barely handle it. And then there's your, well, your complexion, miss."

The outspoken Crow walked by again on the way to the officer's quarters, a crate of rum bottles in his arms.

"We can't be 'avin' any misguided notions of do-goodin' and incitin' a slave rebellion at sea, mind."

Captain Meredith cast a scowl at his first mate's retreating back, but said nothing.

Zale caught sight of a tall man with skin as dark as pitch on the lower deck peeling potatoes. While the man worked diligently at his task, he seemed to be paying close attention to the proceedings on the quarterdeck. Zale wondered what his status amongst the crew might be.

Abela noticed the man, too, regarding him with a steady gaze before turning her attention to the captain and giving him a warm smile.

"I assure you, Captain Meredith, it would be counterproductive to my purpose to incite a rebellion at sea. It is of the greatest urgency that Mr. Teague and I reach Barbados. And I'm not even certain why Mr. Crow would think I could possibly be a threat."

She took a step closer to the captain and looked up into his blue eyes. "Do you see me as a threat, sir?"

Captain Meredith cleared his throat. "No. No, I suppose not."

Zale stifled a smile. If only he knew to whom he spoke.

The captain continued thoughtfully. "You might even have a calming effect on the slaves, you might. 'Tis my first slaving voyage, but I've heard that they get some mighty strange ideas in their heads about the ways of the white men. That alone might be enough to justify the cost of your passage."

Abela nodded gravely. "I will do what I can, sir."

He nodded as though that settled it.

"And I am happy to work for my fare," Zale interjected. He had perked up the moment the captain had suggested it. The chance to gain some useful skills seemed like a godsend.

Captain Meredith raised an eyebrow. "And what use could you be, lad?"

Zale considered. Playing shells and cards didn't seem particularly worth mentioning, but he supposed he wasn't completely without mentionable qualities. "I'm quite agile. And I see exceptionally well in the dark. Also, I'm used to not sleeping much at night. I'd make an excellent night lookout."

"Aye, and you're lithe and light enough, too," said the captain, considering.

Mr. Crow came back from the cabin with empty arms and stood beside the captain.

"And wha' of that fancy bauble of yours, eh? Why not pay with tha' and be done with it?"

Zale covered the green stone bracelet self-consciously, his gut clenching. The very fact that his anxiety sparked no answering weather phenomenon confirmed how necessary it was.

"No, sir. This bracelet has more value to me than mere money. It . . ."

He glanced sideways at Abela. She would not like the tale he was about to spin, but he recognized the greedy look in Crow's eyes. He needed to put him off the track. Perhaps he could tell only a partial lie.

"It was a gift from my mother, and I will need it to find her once we reach our destination. It is not for sale." It was true of one of his bracelets, anyway.

Abela's eyes narrowed, but she said nothing.

"Mr. Teague," came a pleasant male voice from behind Zale.

Zale started and whirled to find Robbie Cox standing behind him. The young gentleman was still dressed in a finely cut greatcoat, his top hat tamped onto his burnt copper hair, just as he had appeared yesterday afternoon. The scars obscuring the freckles that should have covered his entire face were drawn tight with exhaustion.

Captain Meredith stood a little straighter and bowed. "Mr. Cox. I did not expect to see you before we embarked. To what do we owe the pleasure?"

Robbie bowed his shoulders toward the captain.

"Captain Meredith, the pleasure is mine. Rest assured, I have not come to check up on you. I know our property is in very capable hands."

Captain Meredith relaxed slightly. "Thank you, sir."

Robbie turned to Zale. "I have been searching everywhere for you. Who would have imagined I would find you on my own ship? You've lost your Welsh accent, I see. And your Cornish one. No more funny ears either. You're quite the chameleon, aren't you?"

Zale swallowed, staring at the face that had haunted his nightmares for five years, seeing double with the image of a blistered, blinded boy standing on the edge of a stream. Robbie really could see, couldn't he?

Despite what had happened yesterday afternoon, Zale still almost didn't dare believe it possible.

"What's a chameleon?" he asked stupidly.

Robbie—probably Robert now—smiled, and it made the skin beside his right eye pucker. Still, it was a kind smile, holding no threats.

"A chameleon is a lizard that can take on the colours of its environment at will. I saw one that had been brought back from Madagascar. I don't know how you did it, but you had me quite fooled yesterday. How does one appear fat one moment and fit the next?" He glanced at Abela and flushed, lifting his hat briefly as he bowed. "Good day, Miss . . ."

"Bethel," she replied with a perfunctory curtsy.

Robert nodded and turned back toward Zale.

Zale had no idea what Robert was talking about. Until now, he'd assumed that Robert and Gryffyn hadn't recognized him because he must have changed such a great deal in five years, and had been thanking God—*Elyon*, as Abela called him—ever since. If he'd been able to disguise himself, he would have, but there had been no time. The last people he'd expected to appear on the streets of Bristol had been the Cox brothers.

Over Robert's shoulder, he noticed Abela biting her lip and understood. *Born of light.* She'd created a burst of light when she'd saved him from Eric, and a pocket of darkness while hiding from him. She must have some kind of light-bending abilities—which she had conveniently neglected to mention. That's probably where the mysterious shilling had come from, too—it had been only a sixpence when he'd pulled it from his pocket.

Why, the hypocritical minx! Berating me for lying, and then this . . .

To Robert, he said, "A trick of the light, I'm sure." He put on the Welsh lilt again. "Though I freely admet ta speaking 'owever pleases."

Robert's eyes widened, then he laughed. "Very good, old man." He clapped Zale on the shoulder. "Brilliant."

Zale, unsure of what to make of Robert's behaviour, laughed uneasily. "Why were you searching for me?" *Not for revenge, I hope.*

Robert glanced at Captain Meredith, Mr. Crow, and Abela, then wiggled his fingers to draw Zale aside. They walked together to the other side of the deck. Abela frowned, but waited where she was.

Once they had achieved privacy, Robert leaned against the rail.

"It is good to see you after all these years. You have no idea what gruesome fates I had concocted for you in my imagination."

Zale's throat closed. "I—I suppose I would have deserved them. Is that why you are here now?"

Robert looked confused.

"Deserved them? What on earth do you mean? You have no idea how overjoyed I was to find that you were alive!"

Zale blinked, trying to make the world make sense. "You mean, you thought I was dead?"

"Of course. Everyone did, though no one knew what had happened to you. I blamed myself. And still do, for Talwyn."

His voice sounded haunted, and he gazed over the grey waters of the sea. Somewhere beyond the overcast sky, the sun was rising.

At once, Zale understood. Robert hadn't blamed him for the blindness. He hadn't seen him transform into a mer-freak in that stream. He didn't even know what had caused the lightning. While Zale had been torment-ing himself over the fates to which he'd condemned his father and Robbie, Robert had been tormenting himself in much the same way. He glanced at Abela. There was no sense in trying to explain Talwyn to Robert right now. Or any of it. And, as relieved as he was to find that his own guilt had been lightened somewhat, Robert was right—he *had* been to blame for what had happened to Zale and, by extension, Talwyn.

He narrowed his eyes at the young gentleman.

"Why are you here? To keep me from taking passage on your ship?"

Robert's gaze snapped back to the present. He blinked in surprise.

"Not at all, though that does answer the question of whether or not you want to go. I came to warn you that Reverend Berian paid me a visit last night, as did two gypsies. Everyone seems quite interested in finding you. Berian booked passage for you and himself to go to Barbados on this very ship."

Zale blinked. "He did? Why would he want to do that?"

A mellifluous baritone behind them replied, "To find your mother."

Robert stiffened, then stepped aside, turning to face the speaker.

Reverend Berian gave them a tight-lipped smile, a black valise clutched in one hand. An alarmed-looking Abela stood beside him.

"Hello, Mr. Cox." He bowed and lifted his hat to Robert, then turned his golden-eyed gaze on Zale. "Hello, Zale. We have a great deal to discuss."

20

UNREDEEMED

Calandra kept herself together until she was safely back in her quarters. After what had just happened, it seemed wrong to leave Osaze standing guard outside the door as though everything were perfectly normal. She brought him into her room and gestured for him to sit on the room's only chair, which sat at the desk she used for her stoneworking projects. He sat stiffly in front of the desk supporting an orderly arrangement of tools and geodes. She lowered herself onto the edge of the disordered bed.

Only then did she let herself cry.

Tanni had offered to come with her—with her last healer's ring, the sanction on their time together had officially been lifted—but a messenger had arrived and summoned the singer to a meeting with Despoina Cleo, Adonia's Mistress of Sirens. Calandra was mildly relieved. After finding out that her mother was basically responsible for Tanni being an orphan, Calandra didn't know if she could face her friend. Tanni had looked shaken, too. Maybe they both needed a little time alone to process.

Not that she believed Delphine had instigated the rebellion on purpose. However, it would seem her ideas had done so somehow. But then, how would Calandra know? Delphine kor'Helena might be her mother, but Calandra didn't know the woman at all.

Calandra rubbed the Tear in her hand with her thumb, taking comfort from the smooth, glossy surface. She should try to be thankful that Adonia had left her any bit of her parents at all.

Wait. Would she have deemed her father's image *appropriate*? Or had he been erased when Thea blanked the stone?

Swiping at her wet cheeks and sniffling, Calandra picked up the reader on her nightstand and placed the Tear into it. She unlocked it and her mother's face bubbled into view.

140

Calandra froze the message and stared at her mother.

"Who are you, really? And how am I going to find you now?"

Her vision blurred with more tears. She blinked them back, then let the message play.

Her heart broke as she watched the sparse remaining fragments of her mother's message.

"Calandra . . . I love you. I always have, and always will. . . . I believe in you. . . . Goodbye."

All that remained of her father was a frozen relief of his face wracked in sorrow. Much like Calandra felt now. Sorrowful and violated at having so much taken from her by force. She didn't blame Thea for the loss— without her mentor's intervention, Calandra would have nothing left of her mother and father at all.

Osaze shifted position, and Calandra looked up. He had been so still, she'd nearly forgotten he was there. The image of his face as it had appeared only an hour ago flashed through her mind—a Released man in extreme pain, manic but inhabited—and compared it to the placid, bovine-like expression on his face now. She thought of Gerrick, his eyes glazing as the light of intelligence was snuffed from them by Adonia. She understood at last how he had been different, and why she had always been drawn to him despite his maleness. He had been a very good impostor, but somewhere deep in her empathic soul, she had recognized his differentness and loved it, loved him, even as she refused to acknowledge it. And now she had lost him, too.

Her mother's message had been gutted of substance, leaving only fragments of the heart, but Redemption stole both heart and substance from men.

Abhorrence flooded through her. For the first time in her life, she couldn't stand the pliant obedience she knew Osaze would offer her if she told him to do anything at all. She wanted to smack that dull expression off his face and have him respond as she knew Damon would—with justified anger and the intention to defend himself. But she could feel that thin tether in her mind, like a thread tied a little too tightly around her finger. She knew that any part of him that might respond that way was held securely in the grip of the *sklavia* bond.

A bond she finally held.

Jumping up, she crossed the floor in three strides, put her finger on his forehead, and Released him. Then—her still-tender throat reminding her that this could go poorly—she stepped back a few paces and watched him.

He blinked slowly and looked around, as though the world were coming into focus for the first time that day. After several seconds, his gaze settled on her. He stared at her and said nothing.

Calandra grew uncomfortable.

"Osaze? Can you hear me?"

"You healed my hand." He held up the arm, still bare of a gauntlet, which Calandra had forgotten about and left in the Observation Chamber. "But the queen cut it off. Not you."

Calandra's heartbeat quickened. "Yes, that's right. What else do you remember?"

"I—" He pointed at her neck. "I hurt you. I'm sorry."

Calandra gasped. He was sorry? If the first emotion he felt was regret, perhaps this could work.

Osaze abruptly stood and started pacing, rubbing his face and his head and muttering to himself. Calandra overheard snippets of muttered words and occasionally names. She shifted her feet, anxiety tightening her chest. Had the events of the morning been too much? Should she have waited until some time had passed, so . . .

So *what* could happen? Under the *sklavia* bond, Osaze did not have the luxury of processing traumatic events. Or any events. And who knows what he had experienced in the six years since his Redemption?

"Osaze?" Calandra's voice trembled slightly.

What would she do if he began yelling or ran away from her? If Adonia discovered what she had done, all hope of ever finding her mother, father, or brother would be truly lost, along with her freedom.

"Osaze, please sit." She put a hand on his arm, projecting calm through her touch as much as she was able to in her tense condition.

Osaze whirled to face her, intensity defining the lines of his face.

"Calandra. I—I remember. I *remember*." He gripped her arms above the elbows and stared into her eyes, emotions waging war in his expression and through his touch. "I remember *everything*."

Gone was the veil that had dimmed her ability to See him earlier. Calandra didn't turn off the onslaught of anger, pain, embarrassment, shame, and more that flowed through his hands into her mind, but she did gather them up into a ball and hold them slightly removed from her heart so she did not get swept away by them.

He deserved to feel these things. And she felt it was a penance of sorts for her to feel them, too. In a way, it was a heady, intoxicating revelation— Osaze could *feel*, just like he used to do. It was as though she was seeing him for the first time. Though if she were wrong—if he turned out to be as dangerous as she'd always been told men were . . . she would do what must be done and Redeem him again.

For now, she let him keep his hands on her arms, staring up at him as he floundered in the waves of his awakening. It occurred to her that she might be his only anchor in this storm he was experiencing. She pushed aside her own distress and gathered calm to herself, breathing deeply and humming a Song designed to soothe.

After several minutes, his breathing slowed and his hands relaxed their iron grip. Osaze was tall, and Calandra's neck had begun to ache from the strain of maintaining eye contact. But she waited until he released his grip and stepped back before she stopped singing and lowered her head. She examined her arms and rubbed them where he'd been holding her—the red skin was already darkening into bruises in places. How was she going to explain those?

"I have hurt you again."

Surprised, Calandra glanced at Osaze. He indicated her arms with his chin.

"It is of no consequence." Calandra moved to her wardrobe and opened it to retrieve a long-sleeved tunic. If only physics could heal themselves. "And no more than I deserved."

"Why would you say such a thing?"

Calandra turned to face him and was struck silent by the image. She really *looked* at him for the first time in a long while—the sleeveless linen tunic of his *tapeinos* uniform giving sharp relief to the dark oiled leather of his baldric across his muscular chest, the silver single *ichthys* pin on his shoulder which denoted his rank as a human guard, his one remaining bronze gauntlet wrapped around muscular ebony arms, and his face . . . his face, twisted in concern and confusion, but not the confusion of the Redeemed. His face was *alive*. She had never seen a sight so wondrous.

In that moment, she knew why her mother and Thea had left their consorts Unredeemed. She had only held the will of another for less than an hour, but it had chafed at her mind every second. How had her people ever come to believe that fracturing a man's mind was the right thing to do? Had the evil of men been so potent as to justify the cost?

"I—I can't get over you like this, Osaze. You are . . ." She stepped toward him and touched his arm to confirm that she was awake. "You are a miracle. I should have found a way to Release you long ago."

Her eyes moistened, and she blinked.

He reached up and wiped away the tear, then smiled. That smile was like the sun rising over the ocean. She'd forgotten how much she loved it.

"You kept your promise, Cali," he said. "I knew you would. You did the best you could."

"Did I, though?" Calandra wrapped her arms around herself. "I wonder."

Osaze sucked in his lip, then released it. "One thing I have always known about you, Calandra, is that you fulfill your duty. I remember . . . I remember—"

He squeezed his eyes shut and pressed his palms into them as though in pain.

Calandra reached for his temples in concern, ready to alleviate what she could. He shook his head and she dropped her hands.

After a moment, he took a breath and his face relaxed.

"I remember too much, and not enough. But I do know this. We cannot live in the time that has gone before. All we have is this moment. And in this moment, you, Calandra of the undines, have kept your vow. I am forever grateful."

Calandra nodded and turned back to her wardrobe, pondering what he'd said. The only long-sleeved tunic she had was an apprentice tunic. She sighed as she took it off its hanger. Now that she was an adept, she would need to get a new wardrobe. She made a face. She detested fussing with clothes.

"We are going to have to figure out what to do now."

She hung the fresh tunic on a hook on the wardrobe door.

"I mean, do you still want me to use the *pisti* bond to help you? Turns out, I got it right after all, just not what it was supposed to do."

She stripped off the tunic she wore and threw it in the soiled clothes basket, then wriggled into the white tunic.

"Or should I help you escape at last? I believe I could find a way to do that now."

Buckling on a girdle—at least she had an embossed green leather one instead of the healer-green apprentice hemp—she turned to face Osaze. His cheeks were darker than usual, and he was smiling again, shyly.

"What?" Calandra stared at him staring at her.

"There are some things about you that have changed since the last time I could speak to you this way. But you are still very beautiful."

An unfamiliar rush of heat crept up Calandra's neck. While undines usually went about clothed, they had no taboos against nudity, especially among intimates. Clothes were usually more practical or decorative than for modesty's sake, and many of their fashions left little to the imagination, anyway.

It wasn't the nudity that embarrassed her. It was having a man appreciate her body in that way that was new. Despite the discomfort, she decided she liked the feeling. It gave her the same tingling in her belly she had felt when Damon had kissed her.

Damon! What would he say about her betrothal and everything else that had happened today?

She wondered if she could find a way not to tell him. She often struggled with remembering the details of her encounters with the water spirit when she awoke, but she was always disquieted by dreams of him. She used to think it was because he was an Unredeemed male. Now, grinning up at Osaze like silly Hebe and Alexandra ogling a boy, her pulse racing in her ears, she knew it couldn't be that.

A gentle tapping at the door startled Calandra out of her foolish trance.

"M'lady?" came a girl's voice.

Calandra's heart started doing laps inside her rib cage.

"Uh, just a minute!"

She waved and mouthed at Osaze, whose eyes had widened in alarm, to indicate he should go sit in the chair again. He planted himself there and took on the unfocused gaze of the Redeemed just as Calandra reached the door. Satisfied he was ready, she opened it.

A palace serving girl—a short undine of medium-brown complexion with a long black braid, dark-green eyes, and a simple, indigo linen robe— stood on the other side with a tray of food. She gave Calandra the small, saluteless bow that was permitted when someone's hands were full.

"Excuse my interruption, m'lady, but Queen Adonia has appointed me as your lady's maid. She said I was to start by bringing you and your man breakfast. My name is Judith. May I come in?"

Calandra managed a strained smile that she hoped covered her panic. She also hoped this girl had no ability of any kind with spirit, or the pretence would be for nothing.

"Thank you for the breakfast, but I have no need of a lady's maid. Let me take that from you and you may resume your previous duties." She reached out to take the tray.

Judith's eyes widened, and she refused to relinquish her burden.

"Her majesty, the queen, gave me the instructions herself. I dare not disobey her."

Calandra sighed. Arguing with the girl would not solve the problem. She would have to speak to Adonia if she wanted the situation changed. The last thing she needed right now was another set of eyes upon her and Osaze—especially someone with unproven loyalties. But what could she do?

Over her shoulder, she threw Osaze a wide-eyed, intense look she hoped communicated both her feeling of helplessness and the warning to be careful, then stepped away from the door to let Judith enter.

The girl—who was probably in her early twenties, in actuality, but her face, voice, and petite stature made her seem younger—gave another bow, then took the tray and set it on the desk beside Osaze. While Judith had him in her field of view, he kept his expression blank, but as soon as her back was turned, he cast a frantic look toward Calandra.

Judith turned from the desk and, free of her burden, gave a proper bow and salute.

"Do you need anything else, m'lady? Perhaps I could help you with your hair? I'm quite good at hair."

Calandra smiled politely. "I'm sure you are, and perhaps I will have you help me later before dinner."

Judith looked pleased. "Thank you, m'lady."

Calandra cast about for a reason to send her away, even for a few moments. She spotted the basket containing her discarded gown and tunic.

"There is something you can do. Please take my soiled linens to the laundry. I will likely be gone when you come back, but you may put my bed back in order." The linens were still in disarray from her wild hunt for her Tear that morning.

"Yes, m'lady."

Judith bowed respectfully again, then quickly gathered the linens and left with barely a whisper of her bare feet on the marble floor.

Calandra let out a breath she hadn't realized she'd been holding, then turned to Osaze.

"Judith is going to make it very difficult for us. I will see if I can get Adonia to change her mind about my 'need' for her, but she has been so cagey lately that it may not work. After what happened with Thea this morning"—she felt a twinge as she thought of her foster parents, but pushed it aside—"she'll probably be even worse. She might even have sent Judith to spy on me."

Osaze stood and took her hand. It felt different than when Damon did it. It was more reassuring and natural somehow.

"It's okay, Calandra. I know this will not be easy. But what I must do now will still be better by far than walking around like a machine, a prisoner in my own mind."

"A—a prisoner? Is that how it felt? Like you were trapped?"

His face contorted and he looked away. "I don't want to talk about how it felt."

Calandra squeezed his hand. "I wouldn't want to do it again either. It was so . . . wrong."

Without warning, the door burst open and Tanni rushed into the room. Calandra and Osaze dropped their hands as though burned and each assumed a posture that would be expected of a Redeemed attendant and his mistress, but it was too late.

Tanni stood there, glancing between them.

"I see," she said. "Well, you two are going to have to be a lot more careful than that. Especially now. Adonia has started testing the *sklavia* bonds of all the men in the palace." She gave Calandra a warning look. "And she wants you to help her."

Calandra looked at Osaze, whose grim expression matched the apprehension in her heart.

What were they going to do now?

21

THE ROUNDUP

When Calandra and Osaze arrived in the Observation Chamber, Adonia was sitting at the table, wrapping up a meeting with the Royal Physic, a middle-aged woman named Evadne. Adonia looked up at Calandra and beckoned her to join them. Osaze took up position at the back wall next to Cain and Evadne's consort, a man with the warm brown skin and high cheekbones of the lands to their west. He looked not so different from Evadne herself, who must have had male ancestors native to the Western Lands, as so many on Sirenia did. Calandra noted with surprise that Gerrick also stood in the row of attendants.

Calandra stopped just short of where the queen and physic sat. She saluted, but remained standing. Adonia did not invite her to sit.

"Calandra," Adonia said, "you should know I have appointed Evadne as acting Headmistress of the Royal Academy. She is unfamiliar with Thea's record keeping system, so Gerrick will be assisting her. However, if she has need of you, you will also do as she requires, as long as it doesn't interfere with the task I am about to give you."

Calandra nodded. "Yes, your majesty." To Evadne, she said, "It will be a pleasure to help you, healer."

She bowed and saluted to hide any emotion her face might betray at the lie. She had nothing against Evadne, but she couldn't bear the thought of Thea's imprisonment, nor the cause—especially as she was now intentionally guilty of the same crime and was questioning its legal validity.

The queen continued. "That brings us to our next task. Calandra—"

The door opened and Narcissa entered, glancing at Osaze along the back wall and giving Calandra the evil eye before saluting her mother respectfully. A *taps* Calandra didn't recognize followed the princess in and took his place with the other men.

"Ah, Narcissa, you are just in time," said the queen, noting the new bodyguard without comment.

"What is this about, Mother?" asked Narcissa.

"I was about to explain our new security protocol. In light of this morning's events, we will be testing the Redemption bonds of every man in the palace today. I have already had Despoina Cleo give the order to begin gathering them into the Great Hall. We must be sure there are no other traitors in our midst. Calandra, you will be the one testing the bond."

Calandra nodded, her mouth dry.

"Yes, your majesty. Though I have a hard time believing that even those few who know the Song of Release would risk it. Surely Thea was an exception to the rule."

Adonia cocked her head. "I dearly hope you are right, niece. But it is best not to take chances."

Calandra drew a deep breath to calm the turmoil in her belly. Without turning, she could sense Osaze's spike of fear. She would have to give him some tools to control that. A physic like Evadne would be able to sense emotions, though Calandra hoped the physic's powers were nowhere as sensitive as her own.

However, any suspicion Evadne may have had was disregarded when Adonia ordered her consort to be the first to be tested. Evadne looked affronted by the implications against her loyalty, but simply nodded at Calandra and stepped back. Her heart racing, Calandra placed her finger on the forehead of Evadne's consort and performed the Redemption rite while Adonia looked on from her chair at the head of the table. Nothing happened.

Calandra let her arm drop. "He was already bonded, your majesty."

She stepped back, not daring to glance at Osaze, who stood beside the man she'd just tested.

What if Adonia suspected she had Released Osaze and took it upon herself to test his bond? The *sklavia* bond would only be created if a man were Unredeemed, and she would know from the moment she created it that Calandra had Released him.

Oh, how she wished she could talk to Thea! She desperately needed her foster mother's advice. How was it that Gerrick had been able to hide his status for so long? And would Thea make the same choice again if she knew she would be found out in the end?

Calandra wondered what Adonia planned to do with Thea now, but dared not bring it up. The penalty for Thea's crime was death. Calandra's chest tightened. She felt as though she had lost her mother and father, the only ones she knew and loved. If Adonia intended to punish Thea to the full extent of the law, Calandra didn't know what she would do.

Evadne glanced toward the queen, and Adonia dipped her chin.

"Thank you, healer. Your prompt obedience is noted, and appreciated. You may go."

Evadne saluted and murmured her thanks, then moved to leave.

"And Evadne?" Adonia added.

The healer paused expectantly. Adonia bestowed her with a gracious smile.

"This is meant to be a day of rest, so do not burden yourself overmuch with your tasks today. They will wait until the morrow."

Evadne smiled. "Thank you, your majesty."

She gave a departing bow before retreating, her consort and Gerrick both trailing after her out the door.

A siren singer knocked and entered, then bowed and pressed her bunched fingers to her forehead in a crisp salute.

"Your majesty, Despoina Cleo is here to report."

Adonia stood and smiled. "Excellent. Send her in."

Adonia's Mistress of Sirens entered the room with the controlled confidence of an orca matriarch. Her royal blue knee-length dress tunic girded with an ornamental wide tooled-leather sword belt and greaves only enhanced her natural air of authority. The *despoina's* close-cropped silver hair framed a high-boned dark face hardened by both weather and experience. She was fiercely, magnificently beautiful.

Cleo presented Adonia with a precise, crisp salute. "We are ready to begin, your majesty."

"Thank you, *despoina*." Adonia turned to the remaining women. "One more thing."

She nodded toward a servant standing at the back wall, and the girl stepped forward and offered Calandra a small abalone box. Calandra glanced up at the queen, who nodded.

Calandra swallowed, trying to work moisture into her mouth. Taking the box, she worked the lid off.

Inside, strung on a fine short chain, was a gold triquetra pendant set with a fire opal in the centre—the panacea's emblem.

"Thank you, your majesty," Calandra said, her voice cracking.

It made her think of Thea, and her heart pinched. She betrayed nothing of her pain, though, giving her aunt the appropriate bow and salute. The girl took the necklace and helped Calandra put it on. It hung well above her mother's Tear on her décolletage.

Adonia smiled warmly. "You're welcome, child. It suits you."

Then her smile became laden with longsuffering for the task that lay ahead, and she turned to include the others.

"Let us begin, shall we?"

She led the group into the Great Hall, which was already crowded with queues of women and men criss-crossing the vaulted triangular auditorium-like room. They entered near the narrow head of the space. Adonia led the way up the steps of a raised stone platform, which held three intricately carved seats. Hebe sat in one of them, playing with her braids while she waited.

"Mother, what's going on?" Hebe asked as soon as Adonia drew near.

The queen gave her younger daughter a tight-lipped, indulgent smile as she sat down beside her.

"You'll see."

"Cissa?" Hebe asked, leaning forward to look at her sister.

"Wait and see, Mother said," Narcissa snapped, taking the other chair.

Hebe made a face at her sister and leaned back in her chair, continuing to fidget with her braids. Calandra stood beside the queen's chair. Osaze and the other men lined up behind them.

The room echoed with the undulating murmurs of a crowd of people. Calandra surveyed the activity. Palace staff and *douloi* mingled with ladies of the court and their consorts in serpentine queues, snaking around the carved marble pillars that lined the walls. Sirens posted near the entrance to the pillar-defined vestibule along the curved back wall directed incoming traffic toward the appropriate line. Through the north-facing floor-to-ceiling windows at the back of the room was a magnificent view of the city and lush, green valley. The marble walls of the courtyard gleamed white in the morning sunlight.

Calandra spied Tanni across the room among the sirens, trying to bring some order to the chaos, and gave her a nod. Tanni returned it without even pausing in the instruction she was giving to some unattended men—stable workers, by their clothing—filing into the room to line up next to a pillar.

Near the bottom of the steps that led to the platform, a small table had been set up. A stone healer scribe sat at the ready with a rock quartz data recorder fitted with a pink quartz Tear. An assistant waited beside her, looking around the room in annoyance. She'd probably had far different plans for her first of *panselinos*—as had everyone else in attendance, Calandra would wager.

Despoina Cleo stood on the top step of the stage in front of them to calm the room. Calandra stared past the silvered head of the Mistress of Arms at the masses of people. While many of the men were escorted, there were a significant number of men without female chaperones. She didn't see the palace bondmistress anywhere, and wondered what would happen if she did successfully create a *sklavia* bond today. Would she be required to keep it? She squirmed at the thought.

"I still don't understand why I need to be here," muttered Narcissa, slouching in her seat.

Adonia gave her daughter a stony stare. She seemed about to chastise Narcissa, then pressed her lips together.

"I suppose you don't. Run along. Go do whatever it is you have to do that is more important than the security of the nation you intend to rule. Calandra certainly doesn't need your supervision."

Narcissa's nostrils flared. She glared at her mother, then sat erect and faced forward, hands clenching the arms of the chair, making no move to leave.

Adonia looked away, a small, triumphant smile on her lips.

"May I go, Mother?" Hebe asked sweetly.

Adonia cocked her head at her. "Of course you may, my heart. There is nothing for you to do here, anyway."

Hebe grinned, and Narcissa stared at her with narrowed eyes. As Hebe passed behind their mother's chair, she stuck out her tongue at her sister, then hurried out the door toward her quarters while Narcissa scowled.

Cleo didn't whistle or yell, simply stood at the front of the stage and surveyed the room until all the murmuring voices fell silent in expectation. If her powerful presence weren't enough to command attention on its own, the gold triquetra set with four pearls that denoted her rank, attached under the siren's Tear laced onto the left shoulder, alerted everyone to who she was.

Once all eyes were on the stage, Adonia stood. Cleo stepped to the side to not obstruct anyone's view of the queen.

"Welcome, my people." Adonia moved forward to stand at the top of the steps. "Thank you for attending me on such short notice, especially on the first of *panselinos*." She smiled.

A few ladies of the court snorted somewhat resentfully. They looked much less bleary than Calandra was sure they felt, though she didn't bother to check with her empathy. Their servants and *douloi* must have been busy this morning to pull that off.

Adonia's voice, projected with a siren's skill, echoed around the vast room.

"It has come to my attention this morning that we have allowed ourselves to become careless in protecting our ways and have thus left ourselves open to danger from within. This screening is the first of what will become a regular security ritual here in the city. Do not fear."

She looked around at the crowd, where several women with anxious expressions had begun whispering.

"I have no concerns over your loyalty to me or to our people. But since prevention is better than a cure, we will be doing this testing on a regular and random basis from now on. Thank you for your cooperation."

She sat, and a wave of murmured responses rose in the air, quickly dissolving into cacophony as Despoina Cleo gave instructions on how to proceed—couples first, then the labourers and other *douloi*. When Cleo turned and saw Calandra still standing beside the queen, she gestured her forward impatiently.

Calandra took up position beside Cleo as the first couple stepped forward and the scribe recorded their names. Then they moved forward a few steps to stand before Cleo and Calandra, who placed her forefinger on the man's head and completed the Redemption ritual. Cleo nodded and they departed, only to be replaced by another woman and her consort.

Calandra shifted her feet and stared across the heads of the hundred or so people filling the room. The back door of the vestibule opened to permit entry to a new group. Through the windows, she could see even more people crowding onto the portico and into the courtyard beyond. She recognized several ladies of the upper-class families who lived on Sireniapolis's highest tier near the palace, each of them demanding an explanation from the poor singers assigned to cover the door. Calandra couldn't hear what was being said, but their body language spoke volumes.

Calandra's heart fell. Adonia wasn't only screening the palace inhabitants. She had called all the members of the city to come for testing.

It was going to be a long day.

22

THE COUNCIL MEETING

By the end of the day, the faces of the men and women who had presented themselves before Calandra blended into a featureless blur. Adonia allowed her short breaks for meals, and once gave her a half-hour break so the royal tailor could measure her. When the grandmotherly woman, whose name was Dorothea, noticed the bruises on Calandra's throat and upper arms, her eyes widened in concern.

"Sparring practise," Calandra offered as an explanation.

Dorothea clucked and muttered, but otherwise said nothing and went back to her measurements.

They found another freeman that afternoon, an old man who worked in the palace kitchens. Upon investigation, Despoina Cleo discovered that his bondmistress had died several years ago, but no one had realized it as she did not live in the palace—she was simply the dealer who had sold him to the palace kitchens in the first place and had neglected to transfer his *sklavia* bond to the royal Mistress of Bonds. Adonia looked thoroughly annoyed by that, but did not send for the bondmistress to reprimand her, which was odd. As Calandra thought about it, she realized she hadn't seen Mistress Margaret for quite some time.

It was late in the evening by the time the head cook, who was human, was presented to the queen and *despoina* for her statement. The cook said she had noticed very little change in his performance around the time of the woman's death, only a short period of confusion before he resumed his duties. If anything, it had been nice to see a sense of humour appear—something she found not at all odd, but rather encouraging.

"'Twas a nice change, it was. The men here are always so serious. It was nice to have a man who could see the bright side, for once."

Adonia met the cook's earnest assessment with stony silence, then

154

admonished her not to speak of this to anyone and dismissed her to her duties. She then gave a strict order of silence on the matter to her advisers. Soon after, she dismissed her retinue, including Calandra, and retired for the night. Calandra gratefully did the same, trying to ignore the prickling irritation at the back of her mind that represented the man's bond. At the moment, she could do nothing about it. Perhaps tomorrow, she could find Mistress Margaret and transfer the bond to her.

By the time Calandra returned to her room, the torches had been lit in the halls, but her room was bathed only in moonlight. A woven hemp cot had been placed against the far wall. Judith, barely awake, sat in the chair, which she had moved near the window in order to use the light of the moon to see the needlework she held. She jumped to her feet the moment Calandra entered, laying her work on the chair.

"It is so late, m'lady. I wondered if you would ever return this evening."

She busied herself with loosening Calandra's hair and combing it out. She had a slight Turkish accent, and Calandra wondered where she had acquired it.

"I thought you said you wanted help to dress for dinner."

Calandra sighed, a profound heaviness burdening every motion. She had dismissed Osaze after the brief evening repast she had taken with her aunt and cousin earlier. He'd been replaced once again by Thomas, who now stood outside the door. Her consort-elect had kept his expression as neutral as the Redeemed should throughout the long day, but she had been grateful on his behalf that he would soon get to rest. Still, Calandra hadn't been able to help but feel a pinch of jealousy that his task for the day was done, while she'd had several more hours of work to look forward to.

"I didn't really have dinner."

"Well, you're right beat, aren't you? Here, let me take your tunic. There is a nightdress laid out on the bed for you. What would you like me to do with your apprentice tunics? Shall I donate them to another student?"

"If you do that, I shall have nothing to wear until my new clothes arrive."

Judith's eyes widened. "But they already have, m'lady."

She opened the wardrobe and stepped back as though revealing a treasure.

In the silvery light of the moon, Calandra could make out three elegant new tunics hanging there—a floor-length gown and two more practical knee-length ones—along with two new beautifully embroidered linen girdles and a large, brilliant green shawl embroidered with purple shells, fish, and tridents and embellished with pearls along the edge.

"Tailor Dorothea brought these herself, said they should fit right proper, and she would bring the other clothes when they were ready."

Calandra, too exhausted to even comment, merely nodded, wriggled into the nightdress, and fell onto her bed. By the time Judith had closed the wardrobe, crawled into her pallet, and whispered, "Goodnight, m'lady," Calandra was already slipping into a deep, dreamless sleep.

*

THE screening began again early the next morning.

Calandra had already eaten and been at work in the Great Hall for at least an hour when Adonia appeared, full of energy and renewed purpose.

"I've called an emergency meeting of the Council for later this afternoon," she said. "Hopefully, the out-of-town archons who came to the city for Panselinos will be able to attend. You and Narcissa will be there, too."

"Yes, your majesty," Calandra said, then turned to the weaver's assistant who was next in line, placed her finger on his forehead, and sang the required notes.

Late afternoon became early evening, but Adonia delayed the meeting to ensure Calandra could complete her task. Her voice box raw and her feet aflame, Calandra gratefully sank into her designated chair in the Observation Chamber and accepted a cup of hibiscus tea from a serving girl. She thought of poor Osaze, who had been standing for as long as she had, and wished she could offer him a seat. Instead, she asked the girl to offer him a cup of tea, also. She hoped he liked hibiscus tea, because he would be expected to drink it once it was offered.

It struck her how odd it was to be considering the personal tastes of her bodyguard—she'd never in her life had to do that before. But rather than being burdensome, she found it rather exciting. She didn't know what kind of tea Osaze liked. What else about him did she not know?

Calandra sat next to the empty seat that Adonia would take if she ever sat down. Narcissa sat on the other side of it, avoiding her cousin's gaze. Despite Adonia's protestations yesterday, she had excused herself to perform other duties only an hour into the screening, and hadn't stayed past her initial announcement this morning, letting Cleo supervise proceedings. Once Narcissa's mother had left, within minutes, the princess had done the same. Calandra wondered what her cousin had been up to in the meantime. Probably sparring with Mari—both in and out of the water, judging from her wet hair. Narcissa had made no secret of her desire to be selected to lead a pod for next month's Redemption Moon harvest. Despoina Cleo had yet to announce who would be permitted to go, but the event was traditionally the graduation ceremony of a siren cadet. For a cadet to lead a pod was another matter entirely, and Calandra thought her cousin had a better chance of being accepted into the Weavers' House than that.

Six of the remaining chairs in the Observation Chamber were filled with six of the island's twelve councillors, primarily those that lived right in Sireniapolis and were therefore near enough to attend on such short notice—with the exceptions of Hypatia, the grey-clad councillor from Trinity, and Iris, archon of Fire Lake. Thea's empty seat matched the hole in Calandra's heart. The councillors' *douloi* and consorts lined the back wall, their discretion guaranteed. Other attendants, if they had any, waited in the hallway outside.

Adonia went through some preliminary greetings and a recap of the weekend's events, then presented her plan. She paced up and down in front of the glass wall of the Observation Chamber as she spoke.

"Given what has happened in the last two days, I intend to check the bond of every man on the island."

Calandra didn't need to look around to notice the surprise and even irritation among the councillors. So much had happened in the last several days, her reserves were depleted to the point that her shielding had suffered. She felt constantly under attack from the emotions of those who surrounded her. She closed her eyes and rubbed her temples. What she wouldn't give for the chance to go for a swim in the bay. It had been far too long.

Hypatia, a willowy woman wearing a finely cut simple grey robe, her black hair in a plain, unadorned bun at the back of her head, stood and addressed the queen. Her hooded eyes were shuttered in caution.

"How do you see us going about this task, your majesty? Our resources in Trinity are already stretched too thin, what with the extra boundary patrols our sirens must take on these days. How are we to manage what will surely be a public melee such as this?"

Adonia, her own hair caught up in a lavish arrangement of curls and pearl-encrusted metal bands, dressed in a fine turquoise-blue silk tunic gown belted with a linked silver girdle—in other words, looking every inch the queen she was—raised an eyebrow at the archon of the small fishing community.

"Never fear, Councillor kor'Fotini. If my sirens can manage the task of bringing in all of Sireniapolis in only two days, I am sure we can make do in your village. However, I will bring a pod of sirens to assist the effort."

Narcissa blinked in surprise. "Mother, there are thousands of men on this island. A trip like this would take weeks! What about the upcoming Redemption Moon and Summer Solstice?"

Adonia put on a long-suffering smile.

"Preparations for the festival will remain in the capable hands of the steward, cook, and Mistress of Festivities. My time will be far better spent connecting with my people and presenting them with the Saviour of the Heartstone and her consort-elect."

Narcissa's expression darkened. "So Calandra is to go, too."

Calandra sat erect, dread blooming in her stomach like creeping red algae. She did not like the sound of this.

Hypatia, who was still standing, frowned.

"With all due respect, your majesty, your daughter is right. This is much too large a task for a single person, or even the two of you, to carry out. Perhaps you could appoint extra bondmistresses to travel the island to complete the task for you."

Adonia shook her head.

"If recent events have taught me anything, it is that the only way to be certain of something is to do it myself. Thea's error represents not merely treason, but a very dangerous idea, an idea that could upset the very fabric of our society. Can you imagine what would happen if others took it into their heads that men need not be tamed by the *sklavia* bond? Violence, crime, and all the things that pervade the human world, but which are so rare here, would escalate. It could be another Fire Lake."

Calandra glanced around at the troubled expressions on the councillor's faces. Fire Lake, the artisan community and mining town on the caldera lake of the same name in the island's centre, had also been the staging point for the rebellion that had taken place when Calandra was a baby. *The one that is my mother's fault.* She swallowed the lump of emotion that tried to choke her.

An older woman in an eggplant-coloured gown—the archon of the town in question—stood and gave a small cough.

"No one wants that, your majesty. But would it not alert the population that there is something greater afoot if you were to go around performing this task yourself? Imagination could create causes and incite ideas far more dangerous than the truth, and in my village, the imagination can run very long. We must always be wary of producing any excuse which could be used against us by the—"

"I have everything well in hand, Councillor Iris." Adonia's lips pressed together and she scowled at the woman, who looked chastened. Adonia's expression softened. "However, I will be sure to consult with you later about any extra measures you would suggest."

Iris nodded and sat, looking less than satisfied.

Calandra frowned. There was more going on between them than had been said. And what was it that Adonia had prevented Iris from saying?

Adonia continued, speaking to the room.

"This will be an official state visit. Every person on Sirenia will be required to come pay their respects to the queen, princess, and the newly betrothed panacea and saviour of our people. And every *doulos* who is not bonded as a consort will have his bond transferred to my niece."

Soft gasps circled the room. Calandra's mouth had never been so dry.

Narcissa straightened and frowned. "So I am also to go? Would it not be far better for me to remain here and train to take the consort ship? And why should Calandra take so many bonds?"

Adonia stopped her pacing, leaned on the back of her chair, and pinned her daughter with her eyes.

"Narcissa, it is, unfortunately, no secret that you have little power with Song. While the *sklavia* bond does not strengthen an undine's powers like the consort bond, it does provide a certain amount of, shall we say, *enhancement*, as Calandra discovered yesterday. And even you have enough power to implement it."

Narcissa lifted her chin. "But the effect of the *sklavia* bond is minimal, isn't it? I thought for most women, they don't notice any difference at all."

Adonia arched a brow in acknowledgement. "For most women, that is true. But Calandra is not most women."

Calandra blinked. Is that what had happened? Is that why she had finally been able to use the elements with such authority and speed to heal Osaze's hand?

Narcissa's eyes widened and she stared at Calandra, but didn't have a chance to speak again before Adonia continued.

"In fact, I had originally considered giving one out of three of the bonds to you, as a means of strengthening your power. With enough of them, even you should notice the effects. But, unfortunately, before you are given power, you must prove you deserve it. And you have proven repeatedly that you do not. Not yet." The ice in her voice softened slightly. "So I am giving you another chance. Please don't make me regret it."

Narcissa's jaw tightened, and Calandra sensed anger and shame emanating from her cousin in waves. She almost felt sorry for Narcissa. The burden that Adonia had lain on her shoulders was as heavy as the one she had given Calandra, only in a different way. For the first time, she had a twinge of true empathy for her waspish cousin.

Adonia turned to her niece.

"You, Calandra, need to heal the Heartstone. I intend to give you every advantage in completing that task, which is why the bonds will be transferred to you. After you have succeeded, we will disperse the bonds among the regional bondmistresses once again, perhaps in combination with a celebratory tour."

Hypatia nodded thoughtfully. "I believe that could work, your majesty, but it will still be a bureaucratic nightmare. Not every unmarried man's *sklavia* bond is held by each community's Mistress of Bonds. How will you transfer the bonds of those whose bondmistresses you cannot find?"

Adonia shrugged. "I suppose they will remain as they are. If they cannot be Redeemed, that means they are secure and their current mistress lives."

She resumed her pacing.

"The benefit of each individual transfer is small, and I suspect that the number of men whose mistresses cannot be found will be, also. But I believe I will take your suggestion about an added bondmistress at each village. The purpose will not be to take the bonds, which is Calandra's duty, but to randomly test them after we leave, as we will continue to do here in the city. While I don't want to transfer the *sklavia* bonds of the consorts of loyal citizens, if any woman is likely to be tempted to Release a man, it is one who fancies herself in love with him, after all."

Adonia glanced at her niece, and Calandra's heart stuttered.

Hypatia hesitated, and Iris broke in.

"We have been told for eighteen years that Calandra kor'Delphine already has enough potential to heal the Heartstone. Once she is bonded, won't the *syzagos* bond offer her sufficient increase of power for what she may still lack?"

Adonia's glacial green glare landed on the councillor, and Iris paled.

"You forget, councillor, that my sister"—Adonia's expression tightened slightly—"was nearly as powerful as my niece and yet failed in her duty."

Calandra wondered if that were true. Everyone knew that any undine chosen to participate in the Healing Ceremony must be bonded to a consort. But if her mother had let her father's mind remain Unredeemed, would she have also neglected to bond him as a *syzagos*?

Iris was not to be deterred. She cleared her throat.

"But why must we go through this labour-intensive exercise for so little potential gain?"

"Have you forgotten that our best efforts for three millennia have done little more than slow the damage to the Heartstone?"

She eyed the women in the room, who shifted uncomfortably.

"I thought not. Not only that, but as you can plainly see, it seems unlikely that the Stone will last even one more year. If it is not restored on the upcoming solstice, we will have much bigger problems on our hands than ensuring the security of the bonds." She paused, gazing through the glass at the decaying Heartstone. "Every potential advantage I can offer to Calandra will be given to her."

The archon nodded and folded her hands in front of her, flicking a cursory glance at Calandra, who met her gaze, undaunted.

Adonia continued in a quiet voice like iron.

"Besides, if someone I trusted as implicitly as Thea kor'Aglaia could commit treason right here in the palace, we must be certain that no one else has gotten it into their heads to do the same. We have also recently discovered that men can become free for other much more innocent reasons, such as carelessness. In these dangerous times, with the barrier weakening, we must be extra vigilant to protect ourselves. There is no use in putting so much effort into maintaining our borders if we expose ourselves in our own homes."

The other councillors nodded. Iris said nothing, her expression thoughtful. Calandra wondered if the Fire Lake councillor were worried that the investigation would stir up old resentments in her community—but if the resentments still existed, that was all the more justification for Adonia's concerns.

"As you say," said Hypatia. "Protecting our people and healing the Heartstone are of utmost priority, and this plan increases the chances that Calandra will succeed. 'A well-tied hook catches more than a torn net,' so we say in Trinity. I will give you every assistance, your majesty, and look forward to having you visit our humble community."

Each councillor present put forth similar sentiments. Calandra kept her face placid as Adonia nodded and murmured thanks.

Narcissa, for some inexplicable reason, looked almost excited. She was probably just happy to get out of latrine duty.

But Calandra had little thought to spare for her cousin—not when she would soon have not a single thread spun of nettles in her mind, but a whole bundle of them. On the other hand, if those nettles would truly help her accomplish her task, as Adonia had said, she could find little reason to object. A little discomfort was a small price to pay for fulfilling her duty. Besides, Atlantis was northeast of the island by several hours. Perhaps she would be able to find a legitimate reason to visit there while they were on their tour and check to see if Adonia had been telling the truth about the aquamarine, or perhaps find other helpful knowledge in the ruins.

Damon's face appeared in her mind in a cloud of swirling dark hair, and she cleared her throat in discomfort.

She looked up. Adonia stood watching her.

"Is there a problem, Calandra?"

Calandra shook her head. "No, no problem. When do we leave, your majesty?"

Adonia arched her brow with a thin smile. "Tomorrow."

*

CALANDRA lingered in the Observation Chamber, pretending to ponder the Heartstone, as her aunt, the councillors, and their escorts filed out of the room for dinner. She hoped to get a few minutes to speak with Osaze alone. Narcissa also held back until the only four people in the room were the two cousins and their *taps*.

Abruptly, Narcissa rose and came to stand in front of Calandra, intercepting her view. Calandra met Narcissa's narrowed eyes.

"I see what you're up to," Narcissa said.

Calandra kept her eyes on Narcissa, but was suddenly very aware of Osaze at the back of the room behind her. Had Narcissa discovered what she'd done?

"What do you mean?"

"At every opportunity, you rob me of what is rightfully mine. Well, consider this fair warning. You have messed with the wrong princess. And I *will* take it back."

Calandra relaxed slightly. Narcissa didn't know.

She put her hands on her hips.

"Is this about Osaze? It was your own ego that lost him. If you could for one minute put your duty before your personal desires, perhaps Aunt Adonia would start trusting you with the power you crave." She leaned toward her cousin. "That's the problem with power, Narcissa. Those who want it are usually the last ones who should have it."

Narcissa's eyes widened, reminding Calandra once again of a blowfish.

"Are you trying to pretend you don't want power? Ha! I see through your masquerade, Calandra. You love being the centre of attention and getting anything you want and having everyone on this island fawn over you and hand you power on a silver platter. You might have Mother fooled, but you don't fool me."

Calandra sighed, weariness dragging at her.

"You're wrong. You don't know anything about what it's like to be me. I grew up wishing I had been born a stoneworker's daughter, and the only stones I need heal would be to craft beautiful objects for people to enjoy. But that is not my course. And sitting in the cesspool of your own misery should not be yours. You could do great things, Narcissa, if you would stop looking only at yourself."

Narcissa drew herself up, her face reddening. She bent down into Calandra's face.

"I don't care how much power you get," Narcissa spat. "You could absorb the power of the sun, and it wouldn't make a difference. Healing the Heartstone will not make you the heir. You will *not* take my throne, Calandra kor'*crazy*. I know what you're up to, and I'm watching you."

With that, she stomped out of the room, her guard following obediently behind.

"She thinks I'm out to steal her throne?" She shook her head. "That's the last thing I want—though the thought of *her* occupying it does terrify me." Calandra turned to face Osaze, who looked slightly shaken. "Sometimes I wonder what star was out of alignment the day she was born. And she calls my mother crazy."

Osaze came and sat in the chair beside her, looking grateful to be off his feet.

"Either way, that is one more set of eyes turned in our direction. I must confess, Cali, this is much more difficult than I thought it would be." His shoulders slumped. "I don't know if I can live like this. It has not yet been two days, and I feel on the edge of discovery at every moment. I got lost on the way to my quarters last night. I had to pretend to be on an errand for you until I found them. And I discovered that my bunkmate is a terrible conversationalist."

He gave a wry smile at his attempt at humour and Calandra chuckled, but the joke felt hollow.

She took his hand to comfort him, and the full scope of his exhaustion and distress washed over her like a breaking wave, and then receded as she strengthened her shield. She wished she could offer him some hope that things would change, that it wouldn't always be like this, but she really couldn't see a way to make that be true.

Then a thought occurred to her. Perhaps she *could* offer him some hope, or at least some relief. It was risky, but it might be worth it. She smiled.

He glanced at her and raised an eyebrow. "What are you thinking about, Calandra?"

She patted his clasped hand with her free one.

"A really stupid idea. You're going to love it."

23

THE CRYSTAL CAVE

CALANDRA TOOK OSAZE BACK TO her room, sent Judith out to bring a tray of food for their dinner, then quickly changed into a short swimming skirt and bodice. She eyed Osaze critically. *Douloi* never went swimming, so he didn't have any special clothes. He would probably have to go naked.

"Do you know how to swim?"

He blinked at her.

"What? Swim? Why would I?"

She shook her head. "Some of the humans do. I can manage it with legs instead of an *ichthys* fin for simple things, like floating and treading water, but I've seen some women who are quite strong swimmers, though they must stay near the surface to breathe. I thought perhaps you had learned as a child."

She checked the blade of her diving knife, then tucked it securely into her belt.

"No, I didn't." He looked very nervous. "What is this stupid idea of yours?"

"Just wait. You'll see. Do you like hibiscus tea, by the way?"

He gave his head a shake. "What? It's okay, I suppose. I don't know. Why?"

"Well, what kind of tea *do* you like?"

He shrugged in frustration. "How would I even know, Calandra? I don't remember the last time I had tea before today. Why are you asking that?"

She paused and frowned, biting the inside of her lip.

"I realized today that I don't know much about you anymore. And I want to. Is it okay for me to ask questions like that?"

She suddenly felt shy.

165

He gave a small frown. "I suppose so." He flopped on the bed, propping his body up with his arms. "Honestly, I don't know much about me anymore either. So when I figure out the tea thing, you'll be the first to know."

That dampened Calandra's exuberance somewhat. How sobering, to not even know what kind of tea you like. It was one thing for Calandra to be asking Osaze about himself, but for him to not even know the answers?

Her heart fell like a lead weight as she realized how very much was taken from the men on their island. But what could she do about it? She couldn't overturn her entire culture. It seemed her mother had tried, and all that had happened was that people had died.

Suddenly, her original idea—to use a breathing mask to take Osaze for a swim in the bay—seemed ludicrous. How could a swim make you forget your problems when you didn't even know if you liked to be in the water?

Her recent words to Narcissa lodged in her mind. In whose best interest was it to keep Osaze here, trapped in this life? His, or hers?

She reached a decision.

"I've got a better idea. Come with me."

He heaved himself off the bed. "Where are we going?"

Calandra strode out the door without replying. He sighed and fell into place behind her.

She led him to the tunnels and hallways that descended into the bowels of the mountain below the palace. When they reached the fork that led to the dungeons, she paused and gazed yearningly down the stairwell, long enough to sense Thea's steady presence and a bored siren on duty. She *would* go talk to Thea, but not right now. She turned the other way down a hall and continued down another set of stairs.

They hadn't seen anyone else for at least two levels when they passed the last landing that was lit by torches. Calandra could easily see by the light filtering down the staircases, but Osaze had to keep his hands on the walls and slow his pace to prevent stumbles.

"Calandra, where in the names of all the gods are you taking me?"

Calandra threw a curious glance over her shoulder. Which gods did Osaze worship? The same ones as his mother, probably.

"You'll see. We're almost there."

At the bottom of the ninth flight of stairs, they entered a narrow, dark hallway that descended with a gentle slope. The sides were smooth but the floor had elegant embossed scrolls for traction. Condensation beaded on the walls and the air smelled old and musty. This level had probably been hewn by master stoneworkers and stone healers millennia ago, but

Calandra was sure no one had used it for hundreds, perhaps thousands of years. She had discovered it in the night-time wanderings that she often used to fill the many hours when she wasn't sleeping, and she and Tanni had sometimes used it for secret meetings after their forced separation.

The only light came from one tiny lightstone on the stair landing, which released a dim blue glow. Calandra struggled to see in the gloom. She knew that to Osaze, it would be as black as night.

"Put your hand on my shoulder. I will guide you."

He did as he was told. Through the physical contact, she could tell that he was less than happy about this trek into darkness, but she also sensed his trust in her. It made her both pleased and sad as she grieved the sacrifice she would make by doing what was best for him.

They reached a wooden door with a rusted iron padlock. The dim light outlined a defunct, blackened quartz print reader beside the door, which is how it had been when Calandra had first discovered this place. She supposed that at some point in the far distant past, the reader had malfunctioned. The padlock had probably been meant to be a temporary measure of security, but for some reason, the reader had never been repaired. Probably because no one except her and Tanni had used this room in her lifetime.

Calandra wrapped her hand around the lock and within seconds had nudged the tumblers so that it fell open. The door resisted her push to open it into the room beyond, and she heard the welcome sound of stone scraping on stone. The chunk of rock she had snugged up against the door the last time she left was still there, which meant her hiding place remained secure.

The space beyond the door was darker than night, even to Calandra, but as soon as they stepped over the threshold, gentle blue-white light flooded a crystal-encrusted cavern, emanating from the large pool of water only a dozen feet or so beyond the door. The quartz reader had malfunctioned, but the motion sensors still worked.

Behind her, Osaze stopped. She turned and saw him looking around in wonder.

The room had been a natural cave that Sirenia's ancient engineers had pressed into use as a boat shed. The walls and vaulted ceiling still bore their original shapes, and enormous purple amethysts on a bed of white feldspar quartz grew in hexagonal clusters from nearly every surface. She had only ever taken a few of them for herself, not wanting to raise suspicions as to the source. She preferred to enjoy them here in their natural environment, anyway. Since so many of them remained, she imagined that the cavern's original users may have felt the same way.

Along the edges of the pool under the surface, automatic lightstones had been installed. Since no one knew of them, they had not been disconnected when Adonia had put the blackout into effect years ago. Light refracted through the deep green pool and glimmered off the crystals lining the walls and ceiling in a spectacular, spellbinding display.

In the centre of the pool, raised out of the water by hand-turned lifts, were two small bronze-sided submersibles. Calandra had never used one, fearing the consequences if she were discovered, but she had often sat in them and tried to decipher what all the different controls did. She had gone through a period of pestering some of the siren cadets about it on the odd occasion after she had been allowed to look inside a siren submersible, but had backed off when they grew suspicious, turning instead to dry texts in the Archive and using them to familiarize herself with the vehicles and try to tune them up a little. She hoped she'd understood what she learned well enough to operate one now. As gifted as she was at healing, mechanics were not her strong suit.

"What is this place?" Osaze asked, awe filling his voice as he stepped slowly into the room. He looked like he was trying to see everything at once.

"I believe that it was once where the palace vehicles were stored, but no one has used it for as long as I've known about it."

She laid the open padlock on the floor in the hallway outside and closed the door.

"It is so beautiful," he murmured.

Calandra let Osaze continue his open-mouthed exploration of the room while she covered their tracks. She squatted and laid her hand on the door near the bottom. Closing her eyes, she concentrated until she could See the lock. Channelling both air and earth, she gently pulled on the iron with her mind until it bumped against the outside of the door, then dragged her hand—and the lock with it, as though by a magnetic field—up the door until it reached the latch.

Now for the tricky part. After a moment of concentration, she manoeuvred the lock until it was in position, then pulled it down. The latch rattled as the hook fell into its eye loop.

Panting, she paused, pulling her hand away from the door. This kind of stone work took an immense amount of concentration, since it was all done by feel, but it was necessary. She didn't want anyone to be able to piece together what she had done. When she'd caught her breath, she replaced her hand on the door. Within seconds, the lock swung around and clicked closed. She moved her marker stone—a chunk of lava rock the size of a melon—in front of the door once more, then turned to find Osaze watching her.

"What are you planning, Calandra? You must tell me."

"I realized something tonight, Osaze. It doesn't matter that I have Released you. It doesn't matter if I find out all there is to know about you. You are still a slave."

Slave. *Doulos*. When had enslaving someone come to equate freeing them?

"If I keep you here, you would be trapped in a life not your own, forced to behave as others expect, continually in fear of being re-Redeemed, and without autonomy to find out what you could have done differently. You would be like Gerrick, living a lie for your whole life. You know, I don't know what kind of tea Gerrick likes either? And he's the man I've probably been closest to. What does that say about me?"

"That may be true, but—"

"I could hide you in the country—my family owns some farmland in the mountains, though I've only been there once. You would have more freedom, but you would still not be free. You would constantly risk discovery by the staff. No, the only place you can truly be free to live your life is among your own kind. So that is where we are going. I am going to help you escape, *truly* escape."

Her throat closed on the last. Even though she had not really had access to her friend Osaze for years until yesterday, she had always known where he was. And despite their limited interactions since she had Released him, she had begun to think that her duty to marry might not be so bad if it were to a man with whom she could enjoy spending time. She would miss him, she knew she would. But this was what was best for him, and she had a duty to more than only herself. She had promised him she would help him, and this was the best help she could think of.

Osaze, who had drawn nearer to her with every word she'd said, now stood breathtakingly close. She could smell the harsh soap they gave the *taps* to use mixed with man sweat and leather oil over the salt in the air.

"Are you finished?" he said.

Not trusting her voice, Calandra nodded.

"I must ask you, Calandra, do you intend to give me a choice in this? Or do you still see me as your *doulos*?"

Calandra blinked in surprise. "Haven't you heard anything I've said? This is all about your choices. I want to give you the choice to be your own person and control your own destiny. Which you will never be able to do while on Sirenia."

"Hmm. Can't I?"

He turned abruptly and took a few steps to stand at the edge of the pool, crossing his arms and studying the raised submersibles.

"Do you want me to go?"

No. Never. "It doesn't matter what I want. Helping you leave is the right thing to do."

He turned to face her. "If what I want matters, why doesn't what you want matter?"

"Because . . ." Calandra struggled to find a reason. "Because I am bound by duty, which matters more than what I want."

"Indeed. Always, so it would seem."

He took several steps toward her until he was once again standing within arm's reach, but this time, something about the way he was looking at her made her insides liquefy. How was it that men could do that?

"Has it occurred to you, Calandra kor'Delphine, that I may also be bound by ties no one could force upon me?"

His voice was soft, gentle. She had never heard a man speak like that, not even Damon, and it made some part of her yearn for this moment to stretch. But she had no idea what he meant.

"What sorts of ties?"

24

THE DOULOS

Osaze's up-slanting black eyes studied hers like he was searching for an answer to a question Calandra hadn't heard. He abruptly glanced away. Maybe he hadn't found it. Or had, but hadn't liked what he'd seen.

"What would happen to you if I left?" he asked. "Surely Adonia would know you had something to do with it."

Calandra shrugged. "I'm not sure, but I'm certain she won't harm me. Not until I heal the Heartstone, anyway. That might give me enough time to set plans in place to escape, too."

She had never considered what her life might be like after she completed the duty she had been raised for. She was not even sure Adonia had, even if she did name Calandra the Opal Princess—Adonia was young, and the need for an heir was remote. However, once Calandra's crime was discovered, the chances of her surviving her aunt would also be remote.

But now, Calandra had a new mission from her mother. If she could escape Adonia's justice long enough to complete it, her life's purpose would be fulfilled and she could return to face her sentence. If Adonia didn't condemn her for treason, perhaps she could move to that country estate. The thought of life on a farm sounded pretty good right about now. There was even a great source of marble in the nearby quarry for her stoneworking hobby.

Osaze squinted at the submersibles. "Don't you need a . . . a *consort* to do that, to heal the Heartstone?" The word sounded bitter. "Isn't that why you need me?"

"Adonia will find me another consort."

Calandra studied his back with regret. She would marry whomever Adonia chose for her, short-lived though the union may be. But no one else would be Osaze.

"Of course she will," he muttered.

She remembered the words he'd once said to her about giving her his heart, and how convinced she'd been that he had cared for her. He couldn't possibly wish to stay here for her though, could he? They had been friends, certainly, but his freedom surely outweighed their friendship.

After several more moments, he turned to face her.

"My mother. I want to see her. Would that be possible?"

So that's what he'd meant by ties. Of course.

Calandra pondered his request. "Of course you may see her, but . . ." She frowned. "She can't know you are Unredeemed, Osaze. It would endanger her as well as us."

He looked disappointed, but nodded.

"Do you only want to see her before you go? Or will you choose to stay for her?"

He met her eyes. "I choose to stay. I know the cost. But I, too, am bound by duty. My place is here."

He looked like he wanted to say more, but he didn't.

Calandra nodded. "Okay. Well, if that's the case, then I need to teach you how to protect yourself. You're not an undine, but I have a few mental tricks I think even humans can use to make sure other healers can't sense your emotions."

"Okay."

Calandra went through the process of how to draw calm to himself and then project it, and had him practise. After a half-hour of that, he seemed to be grasping it somewhat. She had to work a little harder to sense what he was feeling.

"I think you're getting it," she said, smiling.

He smiled in response to her praise, but she could see how tired he was. Her own fatigue pulled at her like a warm, heavy blanket.

"I think that's enough for one night. You will have plenty of chances to practise while we are on the road for the next few weeks."

"Right you are. I suppose we should go get some rest."

"Right you are," she said, imitating his deep, velvety baritone as best as she was able.

He laughed, and her heart melted. It was like seeing a glimpse of the old Osaze again.

She hesitated. "There is one more defence we could use."

"What's that?" he asked, still smiling.

"Remember the bond that I created with Tanni all those years ago?

The one I made by accident?"

He nodded, uncertainty filling his face. "The . . . *pisti* bond. You said you got it wrong, that it didn't compel loyalty."

"I thought I had. But when I finally learned of the bonds, I discovered that the bond I created is not taught. The loyalty bond I was trying to create is what is used for consorts, the *syzagos* bond. It gives the undine access to the additional power available from the consort's spirit, while simultaneously creating a deep bond of loyalty toward the undine mistress on behalf of the consort. That is why Adonia chose you for me. She equates physical strength to strength of spirit. And in the past, it was found that undines who shared an existing emotional bond with their consort had their powers amplified even more."

Calandra thought about the different types of bonds, and wondered if that had always been the way undines were married, even before they had lost the ability to produce their own males. Would not a male undine want his powers amplified as well? Perhaps a bonding between two undines allowed power to flow in both directions? Since human men didn't have powers, they would receive no benefit.

Not to mention that every other man on the island was Redeemed, with no will of their own.

"Do you share an emotional bond with me, then?" he asked lightly.

"Of course I do." She frowned. "What a ridiculous question. I have recently discovered I have a brother, though I have never met him. As a child, though, you were like a brother to me, or what I imagine having one would be like."

He had that look of disappointment again. She couldn't figure him out, which was rare. She could read his emotions—though not as easily as before, and mentally applauded him for working on his shield—but she did not understand their origin.

"At any rate," she continued, "what I created with Tanni, the *pisti* bond, does something else. It's like the bond of friendship, but much more intimate. I can feel her and she can feel me at all times. I always feel exactly where she is. She's that way."

She pointed backward over her shoulder along the mental compass needle toward her friend to prove her point.

Osaze smiled.

"Our emotions can affect each other, too, like we can help each other calm down or bring each other up, even if we're not together. We can also share anxiety, but there is a way to protect yourself from that, too. It might be helpful for you and I to—"

She stumbled over the words, suddenly realizing that what she was about to ask might be taken as an invasion of privacy. Certainly, if anyone other than Tanni had asked to share this kind of bond with her, she would have been extremely uncomfortable.

"To share a friendship bond?" he finished for her.

She nodded and started playing with her braid, feeling very vulnerable.

He gave her an amused smile.

"Do we not already share a friendship bond?"

"Of course we do, but . . . I only thought that . . . this is a little different because . . . oh, forget I said anything."

He put his hand in front of her lips. "After all that work you did trying to get me to hide my emotions, now you want direct access?"

"I'm the most powerful empath on Sirenia." She shrugged weakly. "I'd probably feel them anyway as long as you were within shouting distance of—" She broke off when she saw the twinkle in his eyes and sensed the amusement rolling off of him. "Wait, are you teasing me?"

He chuckled.

"You *are*, aren't you? Why, Osaze, you little . . . giant . . . wonderful devil, you."

She laughed, and so did he, a deep belly laugh she'd never heard before. He'd been only a boy the last time she'd heard him laugh like that.

"I missed you. So much."

His smile turned soft. "I missed being with you like this."

The way he looked at her made her stomach start doing that thing again.

He took her hand.

"I remember that you and Tanni held hands, like this."

He took her other one and intertwined his fingers with hers.

"Tell me, what else do we need to do to create this bond?"

She swallowed, mesmerized by his black eyes.

"You . . . you need to project spirit into me, which you can't do. And love. Maybe this won't work. I forgot about the use of an element."

"Isn't love felt by the spirit? Won't it be enough to project that, the way you taught me to project calm?"

"Maybe. It's worth a try."

Her stomach did a dance in her abdomen. She'd thought her reactions to Damon had been because of some kind of magical influence he held. Now she wondered if all males of any race had those powers.

Osaze hesitated. "If I change my mind later, can you unmake it?"

Calandra studied the crystals on the far wall, thinking.

"I believe so. I've never tried before, but I believe I can figure out how to reverse it." She met his gaze. "And if you ever change your mind about . . . about staying, the offer I made today will still stand. I will help you leave."

"I won't change my mind about that."

Calandra's heart gave a little flutter. She pushed it aside. His choice had nothing to do with her. Duty and friendship. That's what they shared. Was it not wondrous enough that a man could fulfill that?

"Let's try it. Do you think you can? Perhaps think of your mother, or something or someone else you care about."

"I will see what I can do," he said gravely.

"Okay." She gathered spirit energy into her chest in readiness, preparing a line of empathy. "Close your eyes."

He obeyed, and she followed suit.

"Begin."

Through their hands, she felt his trepidation and uncertainty fade, melting beneath the outpouring of love that pulsed through him. She didn't know what he was thinking of, but she was nearly overwhelmed by it. He was not manipulating spirit, but she could sense his spirit inside the emotions and thought that this would work.

She extended her own line of spirit to touch his and concentrated on her feelings for Osaze while she Sang the notes. The boy who brought her a different red thing each year on her birthday because he knew it was her favourite colour, or who juggled stale rolls to entertain the kitchen staff. The boy with the easy smile and buoyant spirit who always knew how to make her laugh. The man with the belly laugh who chose to stay, who *chose* to risk his freedom because—

Chains of Prometheus! Osaze *loved* her!

Her eyes snapped open. She studied his face. His eyes remained closed and a small smile curled his lips. As their spirits mingled, she knew the truth—he wasn't *finding* those feelings and projecting them toward her. That was how he truly felt about her.

She was not sure which wonder was greater—that he loved her, or that she loved him back.

She finished singing the rite in awe. The combined thread of their spirits retracted into each of them and faded, but didn't break, leaving behind an awareness of the other. He opened his eyes and stared at her, both of them stupefied by the truth they could now sense within the other's heart.

As though it were the natural consummation of their new communion, their mouths met in a simultaneous response. This time, Calandra knew what to expect, or thought she did. But as her blood surged through her veins and every cell tingled with electricity, she thought she might finally know what it was like to wield fire.

Several minutes later, when they came up for air, she realized she'd had no idea what a kiss could be like.

Nor, apparently, love.

They stared at each other, holding hands, and then Calandra giggled.

"Do you remember that time when you were helping Cook Marta make biscuits for the siren cadets, and you accidentally used salt instead of sugar?"

"And then Tanni told me that if I ever did that again, she would melt me with her mind." He laughed his deep belly laugh. "I remember. Do you remember that time we visited the source of the Light Canal and Narcissa dared you to jump from that cliff into the pool in *podia* state? I couldn't believe you did it, but you screwed up your face, jumped off that rock, and made the biggest splash I had ever seen."

"It was like I forgot everything I learned about diving." She shook her head at herself. "I had a red backside for weeks. Good thing I never agreed that I'd stay in *podia* when I got down there." She giggled. "Do you remember that time I taught you to swim?"

His brow furrowed in confusion. "You never taught me to swi—"

The final word was cut off as she pushed him into the pool. She dove in after him and brought him to the surface, her arms hooked beneath his from behind.

"Just relax. I've got you."

He stopped flailing and spit water out of his mouth. She helped him hook one hand on the edge of the pool, then swam to his other side and showed him how to move his hand and legs—she changed her tail back to legs for a few minutes to demonstrate—to create upward resistance to the pull of gravity. After a minute, he released the rock ledge and managed to keep his head mostly above water.

"You learn fast."

He grinned. "It has always been in my best interest to do so."

"Well, then, we might have a hope of pulling this off."

He smiled, his gaze wandering over her face and neck and down into the water where the lights lit her twitching tail and swimming outfit.

"I have rarely seen you like this, all . . . fishy."

Calandra swallowed, self-conscious. She brushed the leathery gills on her neck, then held out her hand and examined her glimmering skin.

"Is it too strange?"

"Only strangely beautiful."

He bent his head to kiss her again, but lost concentration on what he was doing and bobbed beneath the surface. He resurfaced amidst a flurry of splashes, flails, and laughter. She put a steadying hand under his arm until he regained control.

"Let's save combining two things at once for the next lesson, okay?" she teased.

He grinned. "Okay. So what else can you teach me?"

She laughed. "All right, you need to learn how to float, which takes much less energy. Lie back, like this . . ."

*

IT was nearly third watch by the time Judith heard Calandra creep into the room and collapse into bed. The healer smelled of saltwater and wet hemp. Judith sat up groggily from her cot as though she had just been awoken.

"Can I help you, m'lady? It's late enough the owls have gone back to bed, I'm certain."

"No, no," Calandra mumbled. "Go back to sleep, Judith. Goodnight."

"Goodnight."

Judith lay down and made a pretence of falling back to sleep, struggling not to drift off in actuality while she waited to be certain that Calandra was no longer conscious. Then she pulled out the communication stone which she kept under her pillow at night, hummed quietly to open it, and whispered her report into it. It would be encrypted and transmitted automatically and waiting for her superior to review in the morning.

Gratefully, she allowed herself to fall asleep at last.

25

AT SEA

Four months earlier
January 1799
Atlantic Ocean

Within the first day at sea, Zale came to miss the peace and quiet of his tank.

He thought he had known what it was like to be crammed into a small space with far too many people while living with the Roma. Apparently, he'd had no idea. He'd also never been actively trying to avoid any of them for any significant length of time.

After an initial hurried private conference between Abela and Berian—which had involved a great deal of urgent whispering and frustrated arm-waving—all three of them had taken passage on the *Atlanta*. Zale had agreed to work as crew to cover what they could not pay for—namely, Abela's place. However, Robert said he wouldn't hear of it and gave them all complimentary passage.

"Erm, not to appear ungrateful, sir," Zale said, "but could I work on the crew anyway?"

Both Robert and the captain raised askance eyebrows.

"What on earth for?" Robert asked.

"I want to learn to sail."

Robert and the captain exchanged glances.

"I'll leave it up to you, good sir." Robert tamped his top hat onto his head. "I must away to other duties so you can weigh anchor."

"Aye, sir," the captain said through his bushy moustache. He gave Zale an appraising look. "All righty, lad, I'm always happy to have another pair of willing hands."

He'd been put to work right away, cleaning everything from pots to cannons. He was tempted to complain that his duties had nothing to do with sailing, but he was too grateful for the excuse they gave him to avoid his travelling companions.

It soon became obvious that whatever initial truce Berian and Abela had reached was both tenuous and temporary. Every interaction they had seemed marked by tense words followed by uncomfortable silence. Zale couldn't have cared less, if only they hadn't put him squarely in the middle of their squabble, whatever it was.

On his second afternoon on the *Atlanta*, Reverend Berian approached Zale and asked him about the green bracelet.

Zale curled his hand around it protectively. "It's something Eric, um, gave me."

Berian gave him a shrewd look. "'Gave,' is it? Huh. Well, lad, if you ever want to have a hope of saving your mother, you're going to have to take that off and start to get right comfortable with the gifts God has given you. Might as well start now. May I?"

He extended a hand expectantly, and Zale pulled his arm toward himself.

"There are far too many souls on this ship to risk. Wouldn't you agree, sir?"

Berian frowned and opened his mouth to speak.

"Quite," interjected Abela, coming up behind the reverend and putting her hand on Zale's arm. "Come along, Zale. I need you for something."

When they reached the opposite side of the deck, Zale glanced down at Abela.

"What do you need?"

Abela smiled.

"Nothing. I like getting the old codger's goat. He shouldn't be pressuring you to do something you don't want to do—it's not our way. However, since we're going to be stuck on this ship together for the next several months, I could take this time to fill in the gaps in your education. There's a lot you don't know, and someone should really teach you. Might as well be me. What do you think?"

"Will you tell me how spirit beings can 'take on flesh,' as you call it?"

"No."

"Or about your interesting magical devices?"

"No."

She looked exasperated. Glancing around to make sure no one was close enough to overhear, she leaned toward him and lowered her voice.

"I meant about *you*. And the undines."

"Do you know why I'm the only male undine alive?"

Abela pressed her lips together. "Yes, but I'm not going to tell you that."

Zale looked at her, mouth agape.

"So by 'educate,' do you mean that you'll basically torment me with all the things you know and I don't? That sounds like a barrel of fun. I mean, you're a bloody ang—"

She put her hand in front of his mouth and he cut off.

"Language," she admonished, looking around, as though it were the curse word that had caused her alarm.

"Sorry," he muttered. "And I think I'll pass."

"You—you can't *pass*! This is important, Zale. The fate of your mother rests on you knowing these things. The fate of your people!"

Zale stared at her in horror. That was way more than he had signed up for. He still wondered how he was going to do anything to help his mother, and now his entire *race* needed saving? He didn't even know if his mother would *want* to see him again after he'd run off without a word, but he owed it to her to help her. What did he owe the rest of his kind? Nothing. That's what.

"You were saying about pressure?" he said in disgust.

Abela's eyes widened in comprehension. She put her hands up as though to ward off the consequences.

"I'm sorry, Zale. That was too much, I know it was too much. I never should have—"

Fortunately, Crow barked an order at him, and Zale happily sought out the cook to obey it.

He spent the next hour peeling potatoes for supper alongside the thin black man he'd noticed the day before. The man sat on a stool peeling potatoes with a wooden-handled knife while smoking a cigarette. When Zale sat on an overturned bucket beside him and asked his name, the man looked surprised, then respectfully introduced himself as Smith. Zale, grateful to have a regular person to talk to who wouldn't hound him about his powers or his obligations—who didn't even know of them, which was refreshing on its own—was soon chatting with him like they were old friends.

Smith wasn't the man's real name, of course. He was a slave, he said, originally from the Gold Coast. Smith relayed how, before he'd embarked on his own first voyage across the Atlantic, a sweaty little man with a cross around his neck had thrown some drops of water on his head and said many words he hadn't understood at the time, but that thereafter he'd been known as Ebenezer Smith.

"Just Smit'," he said, white teeth flashing from a deep ebony face.

A breeze from the English Channel blew Zale's loose hair into his face, and Smith offered Zale a length of cotton string from his pocket. Zale took it with thanks and tied his hair back into a queue, then picked up his knife to continue peeling.

"Smith?" He cocked an eyebrow. "What's your real name?"

Smith shook his head, chuckling. "It not matter. You not be able to pronounce it."

Zale smiled. "Try me. I've always had a knack for languages."

Smith took a drag from his cigarette and regarded Zale.

"Very well, *obroni. Me din de Kofi.*"

It was the first time Zale had heard an African language spoken, and he needed more words than that to begin to pick it up.

"That doesn't seem so hard, *Kofi,*" he said, copying the man's inflection perfectly, swallowing the *k* and making the *o* long.

Smith's grin widened in surprise. "Ah! Very good. Most white man, dey say 'coffee'. It is not de same.'"

"And why were you called Kofi?" Zale threw his potato in the bucket of water with the other peeled ones, then grabbed another from the pile at his feet. "Tell me in your language."

Kofi watched him through slitted eyelids. "Why," he said in his own tongue, "because I was born on a Friday, of course."

Zale smiled, deciding to risk a few words. "Well, Kofi the Friday-born, *me din de* Zale Teague."

He was rewarded by his new friend's eyebrows climbing nearly into his hairline. Kofi offered him a drag of his cigarette, and Zale politely turned him down.

"'Tis your pleasure, and none of mine. But I thank you for your generosity."

Kofi chuckled again. "I like you, *obroni.* But ye best call me Smit' most o' de time. De master wouldn't take kindly to it if he heard me called by anyt'ing else."

Zale nodded. "And who's your master?"

"Ah, dat depend." He waved his finger at Zale as though he knew a secret. "A Bristolian man named Donovan own me, but he rent me out, see, as de cook's helper an' a translator. It not so bad, but de cap'n an' Mr. Crow, dey wouldn't like it no more dan Donovan for us to be talkin' Twi."

Crow walked by and yelled at the two of them to get back to work, they weren't paid to laze around yammering like penny dockers all day. Kofi flicked his cigarette over the rail into the water and leaned toward Zale, who had already confided that he was only working for a passage to Barbados.

"Pay? Dat's a laugh, eh?"

Zale chuckled and bent his head to his task. They worked in silence until the potatoes were all skinny-dipping in the bucket of water, then Zale stood and stretched. Kofi did the same.

"May I ask you a favour, 'Smith'?"

"Yessir, what can I do for you?"

"When it's only you and me, may we speak Twi?"

Kofi laughed out loud. "You want to learn my language, *obroni*?"

Zale felt suddenly self-conscious and shifted his feet.

"If it's all right with you."

"Oh-ho, *and* you ask my permission?"

Kofi spied Crow returning with a mean look in his eyes.

"As you wish, Zaleteague," he said in Twi. "You are the strangest white man I ever met."

The following weeks and months were an endless cycle of being ordered around by Mr. Crow, being pursued by Abela to learn his people's history, and being hounded by Reverend Berian to take off the bracelet and explore his abilities. One day, he got so angry at Abela for nagging him that he yelled at her and she declared she would never speak to him about it again, if that's the way he was going to be.

The few moments he could spend with Kofi in a day were a welcome reprieve from the expectations everyone else seemed to have of him. He learned of Kofi's wife and son, whom the man hoped to see again one day. He also learned that Kofi had been enslaved on the merest of infractions by a man who wanted to take Kofi's beautiful wife for his own.

"Every place I go, I look for her. That man did not love her. He already has many wives. Maybe he will grow tired of her, I think, and I may see her again. At the same time, I am terrified of seeing her on a ship like this."

Zale nodded, wishing there were something he could say that would help and knowing that those words did not exist.

Zale was soon fluent in Twi and several other African languages. Every time Zale would master a new language—within days, usually—Kofi would shake his head in wonder.

"Surely, this is a gift of the gods," Kofi said in Yoruba.

Zale blushed and went back to his work. He did not know what else to say. But if it were a gift, then Zale was thankful for one gift that would help, not harm, others. And for one friend who made no demands of him.

*

REVEREND Berian remained a mystery to Zale. Perhaps he was uncomfortable with Zale's knowledge of his true identity. Or perhaps he was simply uncomfortable in his human form. At any rate, he struck Zale as someone who would prefer to watch from afar, and every interaction was something he forced himself to make.

Yet he forced himself on a regular basis, at least where Zale was concerned.

Zale had managed to convince the captain to let him take night watch in the crow's nest, which meant he was either asleep or too far away for Abela or Berian to pester for most of the day. Mr. Berian took to waiting for him to appear above deck from his morning's sleep, especially as they got farther south and into warmer climes.

"Mr. Teague," he would say, tipping his hat at Zale.

"Mr. Berian," Zale would return, then he'd shimmy off in another direction to find work to occupy him—and to keep him from having to speak with the reverend further.

Abela would watch without comment. Zale wasn't sure if she were hiding a smile or a frown.

One afternoon, after about a month at sea, Zale was swabbing the deck under Crow's orders when Berian approached.

"Mr. Teague," the minister said, tipping his black hat as usual, as though he had casually come across Zale on his rounds of the deck and not aimed specifically for where Zale had been mopping. "Fine afternoon, wouldn't you agree?"

Zale nodded warily. "Aye, sir. 'Tis."

"I was wondering if we might have a private conference." He pointed to an empty portion of rail, away from prying ears. "I have something of import to discuss."

Zale fought to keep his expression neutral, though he wanted to narrow his eyes and refuse. While the reverend had done nothing in particular to offend him, he didn't like the man, and he thought that Berian's full, pink lips made him look like a fish. Or rather, with those hooded eyes, some kind of lizard.

"Aye, if you think it necessary. I best finish this chore, and then I will meet you there."

Berian nodded and made his way up to the quarterdeck to wait.

When Zale arrived, the reverend was staring intently at an open gold pocket watch. On Zale's soft footfall, he snapped it closed and dropped it into his pocket—but not before Zale had seen that the face of the watch was unlike any watch he had ever known. There were no hands or points to mark the hour. In fact, other than the case, there was nothing watch-like about it. The face had been some kind of multi-coloured stone, red on the outside and with an elliptical band of black down the middle. Gold and green lines radiated from the centre outward. It looked like a strange eye.

Zale pointed at the watch chain. "What is that?"

Berian frowned.

"My business, and none of yours. Now, lad, thank you for coming. I was hoping to discuss plans for what we shall do once we arrive in Barbados. Please show me your bracelet."

Zale pulled the arm with the green bracelet in toward his chest.

"This bracelet again? Do you never think of anything else? I do not want to remove it, sir. I am not a safe person without it."

Berian shook his head impatiently. "Not that one, lad. The other one. The one from your mother."

"Oh." Zale glanced down at the brown stone in the hemp bracelet. "I'll not remove that either."

"Foolish boy. I don't want you to remove it. Just let me see it."

Zale scowled at the reverend's chastisement, then shrugged and held out his wrist.

Berian put on the glasses that hung from a chain around his neck, perching them on the end of his nose, and tilted his head back to inspect the bracelet through them. He held Zale's arm and angled it back and forth as he perused the stone, touching it and even bending down and licking it.

Zale yanked his arm away. "What is the meaning of this, sir?"

Berian took off his glasses and regarded Zale with a steady golden gaze.

"I was trying to determine the exact coordinates where your mother might be located. Imprinted stones often hold a resonance with the healer who made them. However, I can detect nothing. Either Delphine is well hidden, or she is dead."

He looked out to sea, then gave his head a shake.

"Ridiculous of me to be upset by that. She is one of the few who would ascend. I have been in this form too long, and it is affecting my judgement."

Zale studied the man. Did Berian have feelings for his mother? He shuddered internally.

"Wait. I thought you knew where my mother is? That she is on Sirenia?"

Berian shook his head.

"That is only where I hope she is. We won't know until we get there. Nor will we know what else we might find. Which is why I must urge you once again, lad—take off that shackle and learn to use your abilities. Stop running from who you are and embrace who you were meant to be."

Zale shook his head vehemently. Josefine had once told him something nearly identical while trying to convince him to get into that tank. She'd said she'd done it to help him, but it turned out she had been tricking him all along. He was done with letting others tell him who he was supposed to be.

"If who I'm meant to be destroys all those I love, then I'd rather not. And Abela said you were not supposed to pressure me to do something I don't wish to do."

Berian growled, and it resonated low in his chest like thunder.

"That air-headed cub."

He glanced around for Abela, but she had gone below decks.

"'Tis not pressure I'm giving, it is assistance." He placed both his hands on the rail and turned his gaze back to Zale. "I have found that sometimes, a strong wind can nudge a human in a direction that leads him aright, when a warm breeze only lolls him into complacency."

"Aye, that might be true. But I'm not human, now am I?"

And with that, Zale walked away, leaving the reverend scowling after him.

26

THE SICKNESS

ZALE HAD FINISHED A SUPPER of salt crackers and dried cod, helped Kofi clean up the dishes and put them away in the galley on the lower deck, and was about to ascend to the weather deck so he could climb the ropes to his nightly perch in the crow's nest when he noticed that his friend looked a little piqued.

"Are you all right, *m'adamfo*?" He put a hand on Kofi's shoulder and a muffled sensation of distress travelled up his arm.

"Yes, yes, *obroni*. I be fine. But I t'ink I turn in early tonight. See you in de mo'nin'."

Zale watched Kofi make his way to his hammock with a scowl. The man kept putting his hand on the cannons and other fixed objects as he passed to steady himself. A sense of foreboding settled on Zale's shoulders, and didn't leave as he swung himself up through the rigging.

The next morning, Kofi and two of the other sailors had fallen ill.

Zale visited Kofi in his hammock, which swung near the bow of the lower deck. His friend looked like he was in extreme pain, holding his stomach and sweating profusely. A metal pail of putrefying vomit sat below the hammock, and Zale covered his nose with his kerchief, fighting stomach spasms.

"Not so fine, friend," he said, shifting his feet.

The ship's surgeon, Mr. Wesley, arrived and began various assessments, laying his hand on Kofi's forehead, pinching the skin on his arm, and lifting his eyelids to look inside by the light of a candle. When he'd finished, he patted Kofi's arm.

"Get some rest, Mr. Smith. I'll speak to the captain about sending extra water for you today. You'll soon be right as pig's feet. In the meantime, I'll send Mr. Cogger to help move you down to the sick bay."

Wesley left to tend his next patient, and Kofi chose that moment to heave over the side of his hammock into the pail. Zale cringed.

It was a relief when Crow stomped toward him from the wardroom in the stern and spotted Zale standing there.

"Teague! Ye don't need to watch that Negro flay the fox all mornin'. Git your arse to the galley to 'elp Cook."

"But I'm on my way to bed," he objected. "I've been up all night!"

"Then I guess ye'll be up a little longer, won't ye?"

Zale glanced at his friend one last time, who seemed oblivious to his presence, then hurried aft to the galley.

When breakfast had been served and Zale was released by the cook— "Yer barely standin', y'are!" he said—Zale stumbled back over to Kofi's hammock to check on his friend before heading to his own. Kofi had not yet been moved to the sick bay, and Abela was there, ringing out a cold cloth to lay on his head. He looked worse.

Zale bent near her ear and whispered to her. "Can't you do more than dab his forehead? You're an angel, for crying out loud."

Abela looked weary, and worried, as she shook her head.

"My powers in the flesh are limited. Besides, healing is an undine talent, not a cherub's. I'm doing what I can to help, but it isn't much."

"Undines are healers?" Zale swallowed.

Abela met his gaze. "Yes. And your mother is one of the most powerful to ever live. You'd know that, if you ever let me tell you about your people." Her eyes widened. "Sorry. I forgot. Forget I said anything about that."

She bit her lip and turned back to her patient.

Zale's gut clenched. His mother had certainly had an uncanny knack for healing, but he'd never known there had been anything supernatural behind it. He had only ever seen the destructive side of his abilities. Could it be possible that Berian was right—his powers were not a curse, but a gift? Even so, he had no idea how to heal anyone. The only powers he had ever used had left people hurt or dead.

Kofi retched, and Abela lifted the bucket to put under his face while Zale stood there helplessly. It had been emptied and rinsed since his previous visit, probably by Abela. Zale felt completely useless.

When Kofi had finished, Zale held out his hand.

"Let me take that. I can't do anything else."

Abela cocked her head and held out the bucket. "You're so certain?"

Her words lingered in his mind as he went above deck and tossed the contents of the bucket over the rail, rinsed it with seawater, and returned it to its place, then went to lay down for a few restless hours of sleep. Her words reproved him as he watched Abela, Berian, Mr. Wesley, and several of the other sailors tend to his sick comrades for the next several days. They excoriated him as he peeled potatoes—alone—and served in Kofi's place. They castigated him when he overheard the report that one of the other sick crew members had died.

Finally, he could stand it no more. He marched up to Berian one evening as the reverend stood alone on the poop deck reading his Bible.

Zale thrust out the wrist with the green bracelet.

"Take it off. Tell me how to help Kofi."

Berian looked up, surprised. "It may not be so simple."

"I don't care. I want to learn. I can't let him die."

Berian nodded. "As you wish. But understand, I am not an undine. My powers are different than yours. While I understand your abilities in theory, you will have to be the one to learn how to use them—and it may not be possible to learn quickly enough to help your friend."

Zale gritted his teeth, arm still extended. "Take it off."

Still, Berian hesitated. "Before I do that, you need to calm down. Your concern for your friend is commendable, but the part of your powers you fear is related to your fear and anger. If you would gain mastery over your powers, you must master yourself."

Zale stared at the reverend, moisture gathering in his eyes.

"Take. It. Off."

Berian regarded him steadily.

"Elyon, have mercy," he murmured.

Berian withdrew a small metal rod from his pocket, like the one Zale had seen Abela use when they'd met. He cupped his hands around the bracelet, holding Zale's arm close to his own body to shield what he did from other eyes.

Light glowed from within the minister's hands, though Zale felt no heat. With a click, the bracelet released, the halves swinging open. At once, the world brightened and details came into sharper focus. It even smelled better.

Berian pulled the bracelet from Zale's wrist and closed it, then held it out to him.

"It will not lock until it encircles a wrist. Keep this, in case of emergency."

Zale gave a sharp nod, took the bracelet, and tucked it into his shirt pocket.

"Now, how do I heal Kofi?"

Berian sighed.

"Your mother worked for years to learn the things she knew. It is not something you can simply learn in an instant, and we have no healer to teach you. One thing she mentioned as important is a strong sense of empathy. Since you appear to have that for your friend, you might have a hope. Let's go try it, shall we?"

Without waiting for a response, Berian headed for the ladder. Zale clenched his jaw and followed the cherub below decks.

*

WHEN they reached the rear of the orlop deck where Mr. Wesley had his sick bay, Zale hung back, overwhelmed by the stench of sickness and death. Kofi lay unmoving on a narrow rigid hammock bed, his face grey. Abela was several feet away, tending to another crew member who had fallen ill. Berian stood beside Kofi and took his hand, touching the sick man's forehead in a surprisingly gentle fashion.

Kofi stirred and moaned, calling out a woman's name.

"Ssh, hush, now," said Berian. "You will be at peace soon."

After Kofi had settled, Berian released his hand and came to stand by Zale.

"He is not long for this plane. The veil thins and his spirit becomes restless. If you want to keep him here, you must act now."

Zale stared at his friend stupidly. Kofi looked almost a corpse already. He shivered and his heart raced. The temperature in the hold, already cooler than the upper decks, began to fall.

"What do I do?"

Berian gripped Zale's upper arm. "Look at me, lad."

Zale did as he was told.

Berian fixed Zale with a firm gaze.

"First, hear this. Death is not a thing to be feared. It is not the end. And if you fail now, your friend's destiny does not fall on your shoulders, but his own."

Zale shook his head. "What do I *do*?"

Berian scowled and pressed his lips together, then gave a resigned sigh.

"An undine can manipulate the five elements this plane is created from—earth, air, fire, water, and spirit. Delphine told me that using them was like guiding a horse—easy and pleasant if you and the horse are in harmony, but difficult and unpredictable if you try to control the horse by force or fear. That is why empathy is so important—the elements will not respond if you do not approach them with respect. And if you fear them, they will master you."

Zale nodded. He had often ridden horses while with the Roma, and knew exactly what Berian meant. And his powers had certainly mastered him, many times. Each time, he had been reacting in fear and anger.

He glanced at his friend in the bed and his gut clenched. A wind caught the sails and the floor pitched. Everyone on deck stumbled several steps. Kofi's hammock swayed and he groaned. Zale had to calm down. For Kofi.

He took a deep breath, listening to his heartbeat slow, as he had done for so many years inside that tank. The floor returned to its normal gentle rocking. He looked at Berian, who gave him an encouraging nod.

Abela had come to stand beside Berian. The reverend raised his brows questioningly at her and indicated the other sailor with a slight jerk of his chin.

Abela gave a small shake of the head. "He's gone." She turned to watch Zale with a tight expression. "Zale, what are you—?"

Berian held up a hand and she fell silent.

Zale stepped up to the hammock. Kofi's eyes were open, but glazed and staring. Only the slight swelling of his bare chest and the silent movement of his cracked lips indicated that he was still alive.

Zale put a hand on his friend's chest and jerked it away as though it were on fire. He stared at his palm, but it looked normal. Had he imagined the searing heat that had overwhelmed him the moment he had touched Kofi?

"Zaleteague?" Kofi's eyes focused on him. He continued in Twi. "You know the wife and son I told you about? Their names are Yawa and Malike. If you ever find them, tell them I thought of them to the last. Tell them that I will see them when they come home to rest."

Zale's throat tightened. "You will see them yourself, Kofi. I won't let you die today."

Kofi's face spasmed in pain, and he drew his legs up and clutched his midsection. A moment later, he relaxed slightly.

"We see about dat, *obroni*."

Taking a breath to prepare himself, Zale placed his hand on Kofi's chest again. It was slick with sweat. Again, he felt the searing heat, but he didn't pull his hand away. He closed his eyes and concentrated on the sensations that came through their physical connection.

Heartbeat, fast and hard.

Blood pulsing through veins.

Fire. Fire everywhere. Fire that burns from the inside out.

Fire. That was the element Zale had always used before. The lightning bolts that had set off the explosives at the mine and hit the tree with the wasps had come because he'd called them. Because he'd called fire. He could feel the water in his friend's body a little, but it was the fire that was burning the life out of him. Could Zale draw the fire out instead?

But there was something more. Something that didn't belong in Kofi, that had attacked his friend until he was so weak he could barely move. Infinite swarms of small somethings coursing through his body. The fire was trying to destroy the somethings . . . but it was failing.

Zale swallowed. "I—I can feel something inside him. The sickness. I can feel it."

"Good, Zale," said Berian behind him.

"Can you remove it?" Abela's voice was barely more than a whisper.

"I don't know. I'll try."

The fire was trying to destroy it, but the sickness was destroying Kofi. His friend's face had relaxed, and his eyes were shut.

"Stay with me, friend," Zale said in Twi.

Kofi murmured something unintelligible.

Zale put his other hand on Kofi's shoulder, closed his eyes, and concentrated on the sickness. It appeared as dark flecks in a river of red flame in his mind. He moved through that river of fire—*became* the fire—and, every time he found a speck, he grabbed it and incinerated it between his hands.

Kofi began to convulse. Zale glanced at him, but didn't break contact.

Abela rushed up to the hammock and put a hand on Kofi's head. "He's burning up. Zale, maybe you should stop."

"No," said Berian. "He is succeeding. I can feel Kofi's frequency changing. Can you not feel it, Miss Bethel?"

She looked uncertainly at Berian, then at Kofi. Zale wondered what Berian meant, but after Abela had taken a few breaths, she nodded and stepped back.

"You're right. It's working. Zale, it's working. You must finish it."

Zale turned his attention back to his friend, who was shaking and bucking.

"Not today, Kofi."

He closed his eyes and continued his task. There were not many black flecks left. When they had all been incinerated, he floated in the river of fire. The fire that was still killing his friend. He shrank his awareness back into himself, and along with it, he pulled the heat from Kofi's body through his hands.

He opened his eyes to a world gone red. He barely saw Kofi blink with bright eyes and sit up, or heard Abela gasp. His mind was consumed with fire, and it needed to be released. Red blood pulsed through his ears, and red flames danced before his eyes. A storm brewed in his belly. Stumbling, he staggered toward the ladder and out of the hold, intent on dousing the fire that consumed him.

Bursting onto the main deck, he found sailors running around in terror. Black clouds swirled above them, with lightning flashing so often that it was brighter than the sunny afternoon they had obscured. Zale ran to the rail and was about to dive over the side when a hand on his arm stopped him.

"No," said Abela. "We'll never be able to explain how we got you back."

He stared at her, dimly registering her meaning. Panting, he stared toward the horizon where the black sky and frothing sea collided. The fire refused to be held back any longer. Holding up his hands, palms forward, he pushed the fire as far away from him as possible.

The energy left his body in a rush. He could feel, rather than see, it erupt into the clouds above. The lightning bolt that followed connected the heavens and the sea in blinding brilliance and left every person on deck covering their eyes and ears from the booming explosion. Some of the sailors screamed, and some fell onto their knees and began praying for mercy. All was in chaos. Even Abela cringed away from the repercussions.

Not Zale.

He stared at the place in the sea—at least a half-mile or more away—where he had told the lightning to go. And it had obeyed him.

He had controlled the lightning. For the first time since the day his powers had manifested, Zale did not fear the person inside his skin.

Turning, he caught Berian staring at him with an expression of approval, and something else.

A quality he could only describe as smug cunning.

Why would Berian have an expression like that?

27

MOONLIGHTING

THE *ATLANTA* CONTINUED ON ITS course toward Whydah, one of the busiest ports in the Bight of Benin, with a thriving multi-national slave trade that went back centuries, despite the danger presented by the Bight itself. Kofi said there was some kind of malaise common to the area that caused many deaths, especially among Europeans.

"Beware, beware, de Bight of Benin, few come out, doh many go in," he said in a sing-song voice, then gave a shrug as though to say *I didn't make it up.* "But we not need to worry, now we have a guardian angel here. Right, *obofo?*"

Kofi laughed and chucked his friend on the shoulder, and Zale laughed, too, then grabbed another potato from the pile.

Since Kofi's illness, there had been less of a shadow in the man's smile. He claimed he had died and that Zale had brought him back to life. He'd also switched from calling Zale *obroni*—white man—to *obofo*, meaning angel.

Zale denied his friend's claim.

"It wasn't me, *m'adamfo*. I prayed and I tended you, but you somehow healed on your own."

Kofi grinned and touched the side of his nose. "Yes, of course. Whatever you say, *obofo*. But I tell you dat I saw a light, and a spirit of light who look jis' like you, and he tell me dat it is not yet my time. And when I come back and open my eyes, what do I see but you, looking like de devil is inside you, and de devils inside me are gone. Say what you want. And I will t'ink what I want."

Zale chuckled.

"I guess I can't do anything about that."

"No, you cannot. My body may be owned by anudder, but my mind is my own." Kofi grinned and went back to peeling onions.

It seemed strange to see his friend without a cigarette hanging from his lips, but since his near-death experience, Kofi said he had given them up.

"They make me sick now," he had explained to Zale. "I t'ink dey's telling me somet'ing."

Crow walked by where they were working and scowled. Kofi glanced up at him warily, but did not look away. The first mate had been less than happy that Kofi had been the only ill crew member to survive the flux, and blamed the slave for being cursed with good fortune. Captain Meredith only seemed glad to have not lost all three able-bodied crewmen, and had complimented Kofi on his fine constitution.

"T'ank you, sir," Kofi had said politely. He waited for the captain to return to other duties and then ducked his head to hide his grin of pleasure. He felt in his empty pocket for a cigarette, then dropped his hand with a sheepish grin at Zale. "De mind is willing, but de flesh has bad habits. Is dat no how it goes in de Bible, Zaleteague?"

Zale shrugged. "Ask Reverend Berian. He knows that book much better than I do."

Zale's relationship with both Abela and Berian had altered, too. Berian watched him as closely as he had before, but with a subtle hint of respect in his eyes—and always with that bit of calculation, like Zale were a horse at the races, and Berian was deciding what the odds on him might be. Or perhaps like a minister trying to figure out how to use a natural disaster to fill his church pews.

He would still greet Zale and tip his hat when he was making his rounds of the deck, but he no longer tried to find subtle ways to get him alone, and Zale no longer tried to avoid him.

On occasion, Berian would ask, "Have you tried using your powers lately?"

Zale hadn't. There were few opportunities to do so on this ship, with people around every corner. He was only thankful that his powers hadn't tried using him either. He kept the green bracelet in his pocket at all times, just in case.

"You know," Berian said casually, staring off to sea as though they were discussing the weather, "you might think about bringing us a favourable wind from time to time, if it pleases you. Shortening this journey would let us find your mother all the sooner."

Zale swallowed. That didn't seem too hard.

"I'll see what I can do."

It was harder than he'd thought. Over the next week, he experimented with wind patterns, causing a squall one night that left them all rattled and drenched to the skin, nearly sending several crew members overboard.

"A little more care, please, Mr. Teague," chided Berian as though he were telling Zale to watch where he stepped, lest he stumble.

Zale said nothing, though he would have loved to retort that the whole thing had been Berian's idea in the first place and wasn't he glad he had asked?

He waited several nights before trying again, and that time succeeded in causing a cyclone. He managed to disperse it only moments before it reached their ship, converting the few sailors awake on deck into devout Christians.

Berian only chuckled. The effect of a smile on the man's face was transformative. "I was wrong, lad. Keep it up. We'll make an evangelist out of you, yet."

He walked away and Zale rolled his eyes at the man's black-clad back. But now that he had begun, he couldn't leave the challenge alone. Heeding the reverend's warning, he eased back into his experiments with mixing air and heat, finally settling on a technique that did not require too much of his concentration and seemed unlikely to overturn them.

Weather patterns were not easy things to change, he discovered—at least, not in gentle ways. Chaos was easy enough. The morning the sails billowed full toward the south and sailors scampered over the deck like monkeys to adjust the rigging and take advantage of it, Berian glanced at Zale and gave an approving nod.

For some reason, that pleased Zale, which then irritated him.

Since he'd released the lightning, he would sometimes catch Abela glancing at him sideways. As soon as she noticed him watching, she'd glance away.

She continued to honour her promise not to nag him about his education. Despite the tantalizing clues she'd dropped about his people, he hadn't gone and asked either.

He knew it was mere stubbornness now, but there were already enough things in his life out of his control. He was still trying to get used to the idea that he was some kind of half-breed water spirit, let alone be overloaded with a history he hadn't known existed only a few months ago. Rather than face the accusing, anxious look in her eyes, he'd taken to avoiding her whenever possible.

One day, while he and Kofi were mending rope on the main deck, and Abela sat reading in a chair near the rail of the foredeck, Kofi caught him staring.

"What is it about Miss Bethel?" Kofi asked in Twi.

Zale shook his head in confusion, returning his attention to his work. "What about her?"

"She is very beautiful. And she likes you, I think."

Zale looked over at Abela in curiosity. She glanced up, saw him looking, and gave a small scowl, then went back to her book. Thinking of how he had evaded her yet again this morning, he shook his head.

"Only as a friend. Or maybe an annoying little brother."

Kofi smiled knowingly. "If you say so, *obofo*."

*

THEY'D been at sea for nearly three months, and the coast of Africa had been visible in the distance somewhere on their port side for some time, when Abela appeared in the crow's nest beside him in the dark. He was sitting and looking over the side of the tub at the ocean swells when she blinked into existence, crouched on the other side of the mast with her chariot in her hand. At his startled cry, she put a finger to her lips and pointed through the floor of the landing to remind him of the sailors sleeping on deck in the open air below.

"You got it to work," he whispered, indicating the gyroscope.

She nodded and slipped it over her head, letting it fall beneath the neckline of her cream-coloured muslin dress.

"Berian finally gave in and showed me what I'd been doing wrong. Apparently, these things need to be rekeyed to the body that is using them in order to unlock it. I forgot to do that and it timed out. Resetting it for this form was a bit of a process, but I've got it working now."

She glanced away, and Zale thought she looked embarrassed.

"You know, I understand a lot of languages, but I only understand about half of what you just said. Timed out? Rekeyed? You've never once used a key with it."

Abela gave a dismissive shake of her head, smoothing her dress.

"It's just, I haven't used one of these very often, and didn't do it before I left home, since it was a bit of a—" She broke off, her gaze snapping to his guiltily. "Never mind."

Zale thought about pursuing that with another question, but her closed expression made him think better of it. They sat and stared out to sea. Zale fidgeted with his hemp bracelet, wondering if she expected him to say something about the lessons. Well, she'd pay the ferryman before he would admit that she had been right about him needing them.

He pondered that thought. His mother had told him that the ferryman in that phrase carried the souls of the dead to the underworld. He wondered how that fit into Abela's version of the world. And then he realized that, since she was an immortal spirit, she would never need to pay any ferryman to take her anywhere, and punched himself in the leg for his idiocy.

"I've been told we'll arrive at Whydah any day now," she said, staring out at the waves.

"Not soon enough for me," he muttered. "I'm hoping to get some time on land while the captain is negotiating along the coast."

Abela nodded. "I could use another dress. Keeping this one laundered while on a ship full of men has been an adventure."

"Don't you have a magic trick for that?"

"Even what you see as 'magic' must follow laws, Zale. And some laws are physical ones, such as washing and drying clothes. There isn't a way to shorten that unless you can blow really hard."

"Blow really hard?"

He chuckled at her joke, and she smiled back. They fell into a companionable silence.

The sails still blew full with a following wind, and they were making good time—but the journey felt interminably long to Zale. Once they arrived at Whydah, he'd been told to expect the negotiations along the African coast to take several weeks to several months, and then they would finally embark on the long Middle Passage across the Atlantic. Sure, it had been crossed in weeks by some—but years by others.

At the same time that he awaited arriving in Barbados with impatience, he was also terrified, for the stop that would follow was a home he didn't know, populated by a people he was unfamiliar with that were supposedly just like him.

A thought occurred to him.

"Abela," he began.

She looked at him, her eyes refracting the silver moonlight with a warm, golden cast. She was truly the most beautiful girl he had ever seen.

"Yes?"

"If my mother is on Sirenia, why would she be in danger? Isn't that her home?"

Abela tugged on one of her curls. "She fled from there because powerful people in her country did not like the things she had discovered. It is possible that, if she went home, her reception may have been less welcoming than one would hope."

"*If* she went home? Where else might she be?"

Abela looked at him with a level gaze. "If the Order has her, then she could feasibly be anywhere. Even another plane of existence."

Zale absorbed this new information, his gut clenching.

"Wait. I thought you knew what had happened to her. Can't you and Berian just blink into whatever . . . *plane* you're from and find this stuff out so we know exactly where we are supposed to go?"

"You think it's that easy? Physical forms are not meant for our plane, which means if we go back, we'd have to give them up. Taking on flesh isn't something you can simply *do* in a blink, especially forms expected to last as long as mine and Berian's. It is not our natural state, so maintaining them takes a tremendous amount of energy, as well as a special heart which we integrate with. But creating them takes even more, so it is better to stay in the one you have. The longer you are in it, the easier it is to maintain. Besides, only Elyon is all-knowing, and he doesn't always reveal information when we wish he would, even to us."

"If it's difficult to change, then why did you change from being Talwyn to this?" He gave a vague, encompassing sweep of the hand to indicate her current form.

"Because . . ." She looked like she was searching for an answer. "Because I had to go home and report when you disappeared and I couldn't find you. When I left home to come back here, I couldn't find the heart for that form again."

"Can't you at least communicate with your superiors? Don't they help you in any way? And that still doesn't explain why you don't know where my mother is."

Abela sighed. "Zale, there's something I need to tell you."

Zale's pulse quickened. That didn't sound good. "What?"

Abela smoothed her dress, looking reluctant.

"When you and your mother disappeared, my captain reassigned me. He said if he couldn't trust me with guardian duty, then I needed to spend some time doing other things to refocus my priorities. He had me building spheres." She wrinkled her nose. "I'm terrible at building things."

"Building spheres? What does that even mean?"

"I was making chambers out of—" She stopped and frowned at Zale. "On second thought, never mind. It's one of those things that would take too much work to explain, and I probably shouldn't tell you anyway."

Zale rolled his eyes. "Fine. So how did you get this job back?"

Abela fidgeted with her gown and adjusted her position against the side of the barrel. "I, um, I didn't."

"I don't understand."

"I was going crazy on that construction crew, and I was worried about you. Eric must have had some way of blocking you from our finders, something from the Order, because whenever I checked in with my old guardian crew about you, they always told me they were still looking into it. Years went by. 'Still looking into it' was all they would ever say."

She cleared her throat.

He almost felt guilty for the distress he'd caused her, but how could he have known? And his guilty conscience was quick to remind him that he'd abandoned his own mother, so a childhood friend would hardly have persuaded him to stay. *I was protecting Mother. I would have done the same for Talwyn.* Nevertheless, he still felt annoyed at himself.

Abela continued. "I decided to take matters into my own hands and started going over the data myself. It's difficult to explain how the information is relayed, but what I found was that, every time our finders looked for you, they found nothing. In fact, the *nothing* they found was too perfect—there was a pattern of emptiness that criss-crossed England. And that's when I suspected I'd found you, or maybe Delphine."

"You didn't know which of us you would find?"

She shook her head. "Not for certain. But once I arrived in Gloucestershire and started asking around, I heard about the Waterboy, and then I knew."

Zale sucked on his cheek, thinking. "Does Berian know? About you, I mean."

Abela's face clouded. "Yes. That's why he took my chariot back in Bristol and didn't want me to come. He wanted to send me home."

Zale frowned. "And why didn't you go? You found me. You knew I was safe and Berian was here to help. You didn't have to stay, did you?"

"Yes. I did." Her face held firm resolve. "You see, coming here in the flesh without being authorized, especially after the mistakes I've made—that's a big deal. If I don't prove what I'm capable of while I'm here, this will be my last chance to be a guardian, ever. That's all eternity, Zale. Lumasi are immortal. For my kind, I'm quite young, and I don't relish the thought of spending the rest of my very long life in construction or caretaking or even surveillance or something like that. And after what I've done, I'll be lucky if Gabriel is even that kind."

Zale choked. "Gabriel? As in, the archangel?"

She nodded, somewhat amused.

"The very same, though his real title is a 'Seraph of the Presence.' He is also the one who decides what duties a cherub fulfills." She paused, taking a deep breath. "I've always wanted to be a guardian. Always. But if I mess this up, I'll never get to do it again."

Her eyes glimmered with actual tears, and for a moment, he could see Talwyn in her again. He wanted to reach up and brush them away, but didn't dare. Instead, he laid a comforting hand on her arm.

She was right—she had made a lot of mistakes. But so had he. He could hardly hold hers against her.

"Don't worry, Abela. I'll help you. We'll look out for each other, yes?"

She nodded with a tight smile. "As you say."

"So. Apparently, there are some things you think I should know?"

She blinked. "What?"

"About the undines." He waved a hand at the empty ocean. "I've got a lot of long nights here, and I noticed you don't sleep much."

Catching his gist, she grinned. "It's about time."

She adjusted her position and smoothed her skirts once more, then looked at him with an eager twinkle in her eye.

"Now, have you heard the story of Sybil and Eadwynn and the building of Atlantis?"

He shook his head and held up a finger. "Before you tell me, is there any chance you could blink me out to sea for a swim once in a while?" He gazed longingly at the waves. "All this water, and I can't get anywhere near it without revealing my secret."

She grinned. "I'm sure something could be arranged."

He smiled, too. "Plummy. You were saying?"

Abela's face lit up. She began telling him of a time when humans had actively hunted the undines, and the undine king and queen to whom Elyon had granted a haven of protected island nations that would be hidden from humankind. After that story was finished, she began another, regaling him with tale after tale for the rest of the night.

Watching her, her face alight with her tale, her melodic voice unfolding the story like a song, he was certain he would have thought she was an angel, no matter how they met.

*

ROBERT stood at the rail of the *Prudence*, watching a pod of dolphins frolic in the moonlit ocean. Captain Dubrule joined him on the quarterdeck, clasping his hands as he gazed seaward.

"Fine evenin', sir," the old salt said, chewing absently on a straw.

Robert turned and asked the question that was never far from his thoughts, but which he tried to ask only once a week or less.

"How much longer until we reach Whydah, Captain?"

The captain squinted, and sighed, and rubbed a hand over his beard. "Weel, if this favourin' wind keeps up, I'd say another, oh, three weeks?"

Robert nodded and returned to watching the dolphins.

Three weeks until he had a hope of catching the *Atlanta*.

Three weeks until he could warn Zale Teague of the danger he was in.

He only hoped he wasn't too late.

28

THE CLIMB

June 3, AD 1799/29 Tauros 4155 EK
Sirenia

Calandra stared out the carriage window at the pines, giant ferns, and stately cedars that lined the road, running her fingers along the lines of the panacea's triquetra she now wore as a bracelet on her left wrist. On occasion, a break in the canopy would reveal the mountain falling away toward Fire Canyon with the sapphire thread of the Fire River glimmering below.

In the last two weeks, they had visited the entire western side of the island, travelling along the rocky coast and visiting communities there until they reached Trinity, the small mining and fishing town represented by Councillor Hypatia. The archon had been true to her word, and their time in the idyllic place had been so well organized and streamlined that Calandra had felt as though they were leaving nearly as soon as they had arrived. Beneath broad smiles and heaps of flower-garland necklaces, it was almost like the local people had been urging the royal party on their way. But why would that be?

Judith, sitting next to her on the seat, leaned forward and peered upward out the window for the umpteenth time.

"We're almost there, m'lady." She pointed in the direction she'd been looking. "Fire Lake is at the top of that rise there, see?"

Calandra looked up the road ahead where her maid had pointed. Ever since the road from Trinity had joined the main road up to Fire Lake, Judith had been on the edge of her seat. Fire Lake was her home, she said, and she hoped m'lady would permit leave for her to visit her mother and sisters while they were here. Calandra had acquiesced gladly.

She hadn't been able to convince Adonia that the lady's maid was unnecessary before they left Sireniapolis, so she had been forced to have Judith with her nearly every waking moment.

Osaze, who was with her even more, was doing well with maintaining his pretence of vapidity, but she could feel through the bond how the strain wore on him. She did her best to find a few minutes for them to be alone somewhere every day or two, and sometimes all Osaze did during that time was sit quietly and stare at some soothing scenery. Other times, though . . . Calandra smiled at the memory of secret kisses and whispered promises.

He sat within arm's reach of her now, staring blankly through her from his seat facing her. She longed to reach out and grab his hand, but didn't dare. Instead, she contented herself with daydreams of their last stolen moments and sneaked sidelong glances at his handsome features. On one surreptitious peek, she caught him returning her look—and though his face remained placid, his emotions through the bond were anything but. She glanced away, her cheeks getting hot.

Judith turned from her anxious appraisal out the window and noticed Calandra's face.

"It is a cool evening, is it not? It is making you right rosy. Would you like your cloak, m'lady? I believe we are about to leave the carriages and continue on foot."

"Yes, thank you."

Calandra chided herself for her carelessness. Osaze wasn't the only one who could be the cause of their discovery.

Judith checked out the window again.

"For certain, we'll be stopping soon, and then I shall fetch it from your trunk. I'm looking forward to a swim in the lake myself."

Judith had been correct about their location. Within minutes, the line of carriages reached a wide gravelled lot in the road that had been built on a stone outcrop of the mountain. Tucked into the trees was a small lodging place for grooms and coachman and a stable yard for travellers' horses and carriages, owned by the company that ran the coaches—a vital service for the few who needed transport from the coast to the top of the mountain regularly, but not often enough to justify owning their own transportation or fit enough to walk it themselves. The company's owner had offered her services to the queen and her party for free, of course.

The plateau was only about one hundred feet in elevation from the peak of the island's highest mountain, where they would find the town of

Fire Lake, the artisan and mining community built on the caldera of the same name. Despite the fiery moniker that named the town, lake, and river that flowed northeast from it all the way to Haven, Mt. Melissa had not been active since before the Atargasians had fled the Mediterranean and settled here in ancient times. The elevation made the climate more bearable than the coast in the summer, and the hot spring-fed lake held great appeal in the winter, which made the town a year-round holiday destination for Sirenia's wealthy.

The main road went no higher than this, continuing on around the mountain and following a ridge on the south side until it descended into the Paradise Valley and, eventually, Sireniapolis on the southern coast. Somewhere on that side of the mountain was the small plot that belonged to Calandra, at least in title. It had been managed by a steward for generations.

A singer came to the window to inform them that this was as high as the carriages could go. She wore a green woollen cloak over a moulded leather cuirass and shoulder plates, and a wide leather girdle and sword belt, all buckled over a green tunic. Calandra was surprised the singer was so heavily armoured, but perhaps it was partially to help with the chill in the air. When inland, the sirens often dressed quite differently than when on coast patrol.

Osaze helped Calandra and Judith down from the carriage, his hand lingering on Calandra's for a flicker longer than necessary. She smiled.

Judith hurried to the back of the carriage to fetch Calandra's cloak.

"You there!" she called to two *douloi* standing near the road waiting to assist the arriving party. At her page, the two men came and unloaded the luggage from the rack. She knelt by Calandra's portmanteau and opened it.

The groom—a short stout human woman in shades of brown cloth who seemed more comfortable with animals than people—hopped down from her seat and led the horses to the small stable built on the inside edge of the broad landing. The horses and carriages would be boarded here for the three days that the party expected to remain in Fire Lake, then would carry the party back down the mountain toward Haven for the final leg of their journey. From there, they would sail home along the eastern coast, stopping in at the several remaining communities to complete their island tour.

The sun had already dipped behind the mountain ridge to the southwest and the temperature had begun to drop. Judith had insisted that once the sun went down on the mountain, it would be as chilly as a winter's night on the coast. Calandra had packed the new woollen cloak Dorothea had had delivered before they left, just in case, but as they'd climbed through the hot, muggy air of the valley, she had begun to think her maid had exaggerated. Now, as she allowed Judith to drop the peacock-blue garment over her shoulders and then fasten the gold clasp, she was grateful she had listened.

"Thank you, Judith," she said as the maid finished with smoothing the wrinkles from the fabric.

Judith beamed. "'Tis my pleasure, m'lady."

She wrapped a beige knit shawl around her own shoulders and slung her travel satchel crosswise over her body.

The two porters hoisted the portmanteau of Calandra's belongings from the back of the carriage. Osaze put on his short cloak and carried his small haversack.

Calandra carried only a small purse, the majority of her belongings being in her luggage. Adonia had insisted she bring sufficient clothes to not need to repeat any outfits in a single location, thus the reason for the large trunk. She sighed. She'd much prefer to get by on what she could hold in a satchel of her own.

Not that Adonia would have let her carry her own satchel either.

They joined the group gathering at the meeting place near the foot of the path that would take them up the remaining distance to the town. Besides the royal party and their *douloi* and servants and the remaining bondmistresses and their consorts, there was a pod of sirens in inland green. Some of the sirens had also brought companions, including men and even a few female servants of either race, but most of the dozen soldiers were alone, their belongings in small packs on their backs. The men of their group carried some of the luggage, but most of it was hefted by burly porters provided by the coaching company. The group was assured that whatever did not come on this ascent would be waiting in their rooms within an hour.

Calandra had been surprised to see Mistress Margaret, the long-time Mistress of Bonds for the Opal Palace, among their party when they'd left home. On the boat on the first day of their journey, Calandra had asked the bondmistress if it would not interfere with her duties at the palace to be away for so long. Margaret had harrumphed and said, "What duties? I haven't held a bond there for years."

"What? Why?"

Margaret had stared over the rail, her expression dark.

"Only the Mother knows. Adonia seems determined to put all royal bondmistresses out of a job, not only me. Moving us out to the villages, and still not giving us any bonds. It's—"

She had stopped and blinked at Calandra as though she'd just realized to whom she was speaking, then excused herself and walked quickly away.

Margaret stood in the group of remaining bondmistresses near the way station, her personal *doulos* standing beside her bearing two large canvas-wrapped bundles. She was to remain in Fire Lake. Calandra tried to catch the woman's eye, but Margaret never looked her way. She'd been avoiding Calandra since that conversation on the boat, which only made Calandra puzzle more at what the woman had told her. Adonia was having the bonds of the village bondmistresses transferred to Calandra, at least temporarily. But who had taken over Margaret's duties at the palace?

Calandra caught Narcissa looking at her from across the group. Rather, the princess was looking at Osaze.

Calandra's throat tightened. It seemed unlikely that Narcissa could do anything to make good on her threat of getting Osaze back at this point, but there was something about the coldly calculating way she often stared at him that made Calandra nervous.

Narcissa met Calandra's gaze, her expression becoming baleful, and then pointedly turned away. Her friend Mari followed the princess's lead, as per usual, not even returning Calandra's polite smile and wave.

How Narcissa had convinced Adonia to let her bring Mari as her companion, Calandra didn't know. Perhaps Adonia hoped having a friend there would motivate her daughter to behave more selflessly. Or perhaps she hoped that having an amenable companion would keep Narcissa's temper in check, ameliorating the fraying nerves and tempers brought on by weeks of strenuous travel. Adonia had brought one of her own friends, after all, a noblewoman named Tasia.

Tanni, unfortunately, had been required to stay behind. Calandra had hoped Tanni might have been selected to be in their accompanying siren pod, but after skillfully taking charge of the pod after Rhapsodist Danai had been knocked unconscious in the situation with the dolphin, she had been promoted to rhapsodist herself. She'd also been designated to assist in leading the pods that would be bringing in the ships for the Redemption Moon, and had had to stay in the city to prepare.

Even though Calandra missed Tanni terribly, she couldn't have been more proud. She could sense her friend somewhere far to the south. Tanni's emotions were like a comforting, steady flame in the corner of Calandra's mind.

She pressed her lips together. She had Osaze here and, despite the inconvenience Judith's presence caused, Calandra had come to enjoy the young woman's cheerful chatter and sunny disposition. If the lady's maid were Adonia's snitch, at least she was a likable one. Calandra was far from alone.

Despoina Cleo whistled to silence the group's murmuring conversation, then introduced their guide and gave instructions to stay together with their own travelling companions. She told them that the walk should take about an hour, and reminded her sirens to remain on high alert the entire time they remained in the area.

Calandra frowned. The remaining climb was the same rise as the Opal Palace above the plain of the Paradise Valley, but without the benefit of paved streets, stairs, or the locked canal, the travel time was triple what she would have expected.

And why was the *despoina* emphasizing alertness in this particular community? Did it have something to do with that long-ago rebellion? Surely not.

Calandra sighed. It was Néa Selini, the new moon, which normally would be a rest day, but not this month.

By now, she knew the drill—there would be a welcoming feast tonight that would go until the wee hours. After catching a few hours of sleep, she would be expected to begin receiving people for their screening first thing in the morning. The local Mistress of Bonds would be on hand, either gladly or begrudgingly transferring the bonds of the men linked to her as each man appeared, the timing of which would depend on the *douloi's* shifts at the mine.

By the end of the day, the prickly bundle of threads in Calandra's mind would be thicker, and she would be ready to collapse with exhaustion. Depending on the size of the town, she may need to do it all again the next day. She couldn't remember the last time she had been this tired.

Judith chattered excitedly about the attractions of Fire Lake, pointing out favourite spots or describing local dishes as she climbed, all the while assuring Calandra she would love it. When the exertion stole the maid's breath at last, Calandra sighed in relief. She enjoyed the girl, yes, but the constant barrage could become too much at times.

They reached a particularly steep portion of the trail, and Calandra instructed Judith to go ahead of her. As the maid passed, she slipped on a root and slid a few inches.

"Careful," Calandra said.

She offered the girl a steadying hand, which Judith accepted with a grateful smile. Hitching her tunic a little higher, she continued on ahead, at Calandra's insistence.

As she passed, Calandra noticed a curious-looking tattoo on the girl's inner ankle—so small that it would look almost like a birthmark to the casual observer who noticed it under her skirt. But Calandra had been only a couple of feet away, and she was not a casual observer.

The tattoo was a small quaternaria—a four-pointed cross made of four conjoined *ichthys* fish with a circle binding the curved shapes together.

The only other place Calandra had ever seen one was on Adonia's tiara—the shape represented the monarch, though Calandra did not know why. Why a quaternaria, and not the Holy Triquetra that was so sacred to their people? She had always supposed it was an allusion to the four directions—the queen was responsible for the whole island, after all. But that did nothing to explain why her lady's maid had one tattooed onto her ankle. Had Adonia taken to marking her spies now? It seemed unlikely, especially with a symbol reserved for herself.

The path widened, and Calandra stepped up beside her maid.

"Judith, what is the meaning behind your tattoo?"

Judith started and flushed, looking like she'd been caught doing something wrong.

"'Tis only a compass, m'lady. It is a meaningful shape in Fire Lake, since we are at the centre of the island. It reminds us to look ever outward to our responsibilities."

She glanced away, paying close attention to the path.

Calandra frowned. There was something Judith wasn't telling her, but Calandra left it alone. Perhaps it was Adonia's doing, after all. Or perhaps the shape had another meaning to Judith, as well, but it was too personal to share.

Everyone was entitled to their secrets.

29

THE CRIMINAL

THE NEXT AFTERNOON, CALANDRA STOOD in the town hall, an open-air peripteral marble building much like the Court of the Redeemed in Sireniapolis. The columns and frieze were covered in exquisitely worked details of vines, and the ceiling had been painted in historical tableaux. She stood at the front of the room on a raised platform, staring over a sea of heads and entertaining herself by trying to guess their owners' occupations. Farmers, miners, potters, sculptors, wealthy holidayers. The list went on.

Beyond the colonnade, the town of Fire Lake sprawled in whitewashed elegance, punctuated by the green fronds of palm trees and climbing bougainvillea vines. Behind her lay a well-appointed garden and, beyond that, a stunning view of the lake.

She stifled a yawn as yet another man in the long line before her presented himself to first the scribe, then to her, and she performed the transfer ritual with the local Mistress of Bonds, Lefkia. It was similar to the Redemption rite, only Calandra placed a finger on both the man's and Lefkia's foreheads, then sang the notes. The bond transferred to her without the man ever knowing that a spirit transaction had occurred.

Margaret sat behind her next to Despoina Cleo, watching. In alignment with Adonia's new security measures, she would be remaining behind in the community as a secondary bondmistress.

They had not found a single Unredeemed man in any community they had visited so far, which didn't surprise Calandra. In small towns and villages, it was much less likely that someone would slip through the cracks if their mistress died. The Mistress of Bonds in each town would know every *doulos* within her borders, even the consorts, and would check in on them regularly.

Sunlight poured over Calandra, and the rising heat of the summer afternoon made sweat trickle down her back—though it was still more pleasant than Sireniapolis would be on the first of the month of Didymoi.

She could feel Osaze behind her through the bond. He seemed more alert and better rested than she, though she had no idea how. On the way back to their assigned villa after last night's feast, he had snatched her hand and pulled her off the path to a hidden clearing near the lake. Since it was new moon, the only reflection in the still waters had been a billion stars. The clear night made the brilliant smear of the Milky Way look like a pathway to heaven from the lake below to the sky above them.

They sat and held hands and talked for nearly an hour, dreaming together of a place at the other end of the starry path where Osaze did not have to hide in plain sight, like the human couples Osaze's mother had told him about. Calandra tried to imagine a place where men and women both worked together for common goals, instead of one imposing her will on the other "for his own good."

"What if such a place exists? Or could exist?" Calandra craned her neck at the stars as though they held the answer.

Osaze shook his head. "What do you mean? We cannot leave this place. I know you better than that. You would not abandon your duty."

"No, you're right. Especially now, after having met nearly half of the people who live on this island. How could I abandon them when they look at me with so much hope?"

She swallowed. Some of the women she'd met had had expressions of skepticism, and she could hardly blame them. She was young and small, and why should they believe that she would be the Saviour of the Heartstone?

But for those who believed, for those who had lost daughters patrolling the border and bringing in stray ships that had made it through, they looked at her with a combination of awe and worship. It made her uncomfortable and a little afraid. What if she let them down?

She shook her head.

"What I mean is, what if it were possible to live a life like human couples do, right here on Sirenia? Do you think it would ever be possible to make the whole island see what I have seen, and what my mother and Thea saw? How long would it take to change a mindset that has persisted for three millennia? And how could I make Adonia understand it?"

She glanced at Osaze to measure his response. He was grinning at her and shaking his head.

"What? Why are you doing that?" she asked.

"It is only you. You have been raised to become the Saviour of the Heartstone, and you have never shirked from your duty, which I love. But I love that you want to change your entire nation's thinking even more."

He put his other hand over their clasped ones, and his voice grew husky.

"I will forever thank whichever gods present themselves for having Adonia choose me as your consort, Calandra. I cannot think of any man luckier than I."

"Truly? Not even all the men that get to live their lives as agents of their own will? Perhaps even choose their own . . . 'wives,' was it?"

Osaze's expression grew serious.

"I am not sure any man truly gets to do only what he wishes. And if so, I do not want to meet him. He would be a terrifying person, indeed."

Calandra laughed.

"You are a mystery to me, my betrothed." She lifted their tangled hands and kissed the back of his. "But I am delighted to have the opportunity to try to understand you. I suspect it is a gift that will take a long time to unwrap."

He smiled and kissed her, making her heart race in the most delightful way. When he broke off, he tucked a stray lock of hair behind her ear.

"Let us add 'kissing Calandra by a lake' to the list of things I like, shall we?"

"Done."

They kissed again, discovering new things to like until they got too cold to sit on the wet sand any longer and too tired to ignore their beds, and retired for the night.

Despoina Cleo brought her back to the present with a nudge.

"Calandra, why are you grinning like a porpoise? Stay on task, please."

Calandra nodded, chastened, and went on to Redeem the next man in line, who stood before her without a hint of impatience. As was to be expected.

Cleo arched an eyebrow at her, but said nothing further.

A disturbance near the courtyard steps drew her attention.

Two sirens escorted a well-built blond man shackled hand and foot into the room, urging him along with the ends of their *deiktes* staves. He offered no resistance and walked before them with his head held high. The shouting was coming from the middle-aged woman being restrained by two other singers that followed behind him.

"Please, I beg you, it is a mistake! He is as gentle as a kitten—he wouldn't hurt a soul. Please, you have to understand, he is all I have. He's my only child. Please!"

The pleading continued as the man—a young man in his early twenties, Calandra guessed—was brought to stand before her and the *despoina*. Calandra stared at the man, fascinated.

He was Unredeemed, that much was obvious. His bright-eyed gaze darted around the room as he shuffled forward, taking in all the information he could. That wasn't what grabbed her attention, though. From the moment she'd seen him, she could feel it—there was something wrong with him physically.

As she stepped forward to meet the man, the room and all the emotions that filled it fell away—Osaze's curiosity, Adonia's alarm and . . . *ew* . . . lust, the rasping of knives being drawn, Tasia's tittering, Narcissa's and Mari's fascination. He watched her, his face guarded. She reached up and covered his ears, and he didn't pull away.

As soon as she touched him, she found the problem. She closed her eyes, took a deep breath . . .

And he was healed.

She dropped her hands and stepped back, life flowing through her veins. Sensation crashed in on her like a breaking wave, but the only sound in the room was the man's shrieking mother.

"—is she doing?"

"Silence, woman!"

Adonia stood beside Calandra, authority radiating from her like a furnace. Golden trinkets and bands glinting from the arrangement of her red hair made her look like some kind of fire goddess.

The human woman blinked and paused for breath.

Calandra laid a hand on the woman's shoulder, buoyed by a strange sense of serenity and bliss.

"It's all right. He was missing a bone in both of his ears. He has been deaf from birth, I assume?"

The woman nodded, her mouth falling open. "But . . . how did you know?"

Calandra smiled. "Because I healed him."

The woman gazed up at her son, eyes wide. He stared at her in equal wonder.

"M—Matthew?" She struggled to reach him, but the singers still held her arms fast. "Can you hear me?"

He nodded vigorously. Swallowing, he gave his voice a try.

"Mmmuhnderr?"

It sounded strange, but even still, both he and the woman began weeping joyful tears, broad smiles on their faces.

Adonia frowned. "Very touching. Well done, Calandra. He will make a much better *doulos* now that he can hear. What is your name, woman?"

The woman looked at the queen, though she kept sneaking glances at her son.

"Elizabeth, your majesty."

Adonia pursed her lips. "And you know, Elizabeth, that it is a capital offence in this nation to allow a male to remain Unredeemed past his twelfth year?"

Water sprang to Elizabeth's wide eyes. "He couldn't hear, so I thought it would be fine. He is a gentle soul and no threat to anyone. I mean, he couldn't hear the mermaid song anyway, and he is my son, he would never hurt me. I live alone, and I would have had to buy another man to replace him, so—"

"Enough!" Adonia closed her eyes and rubbed her temples. "Lefkia, what is the meaning of this?"

Fire Lake's Mistress of Bonds stepped forward, her face pale. "I have never seen this man before in my life, your majesty. Elizabeth comes to market every week, but I had no idea she had a son."

The siren on Matthew's left spoke up.

"We found him concealed in the woods near the trail on the far side of the lake, your majesty."

Elizabeth smiled. "Yes, yes. He was waiting, as he is supposed to. If he never came near anyone, he could never break the laws, see? He's a good boy, and wouldn't hurt anyone."

"So you keep insisting," said Adonia. "But the law is the law and it exists for a reason. Our ancestors paid a dear price before they established it, and Atargatis herself blessed it. No one, and especially not a human, gets to break it without consequences. I wonder if he would be so gentle if he thought you were in danger?"

She touched the woman's arm, and Elizabeth started gasping for air. Calandra watched, frozen and helpless, as Adonia used spirit and—was her aunt using *air?*—to choke the woman before their eyes.

Elizabeth's legs sagged. The sirens released her and she collapsed to the floor, clawing at her mouth and throat—but there was nothing to pull away. Elizabeth grabbed Adonia's ankle, but lacked the strength to do more.

Calandra's throat went dry. She stepped toward her aunt, mind scrabbling to find a way to stop what was happening. Despoina Cleo arrested her movement with a warning hand on Calandra's chest, then glared a silent rebuke.

"Your majesty?" Calandra called out.

Adonia ignored her. Cleo glared and shook her head.

Matthew watched, his eyes frantic. "Nar!" he screamed.

He lunged forward and put his chained hands on his mother's shoulders, trying to see what choked her. Then he grabbed Adonia's hand from Elizabeth's shoulder and squeezed. The queen cried out and raised her other hand to strike him.

Wordless sirensong filled the air. Matthew dropped Adonia's hand. His eyes lost focus and an expression of wonder covered his face. One of his siren guards continued singing as she pointed her sword at him, keeping him stunned until the other had grabbed his hand and twisted his arm up behind his back, holding it there in such a way that he would have a difficult time resisting.

Elizabeth knelt on the floor, sucking air into her lungs in ragged breaths.

"He was . . . only . . . defending me."

Adonia shook out her hand, then nursed it next to her chest with the other. She turned a baleful glare on her niece.

"Calandra, Redeem him."

"No—" squeaked his mother and tried to stand, but the sirens pushed down on her shoulders and kept her there. She looked at Calandra with desperate eyes. "Please, m'lady. Please, you must listen. You don't need to do this."

Calandra stared at the man and her sense of calm rippled. He was a man who had obviously been born on Sirenia but had remained free his entire life. And Adonia wanted her to Redeem him. But he wasn't merely a face without a name, one more consciousness to tether to her mind as part of her duty.

Matthew. His name was Matthew.

It was the first time she'd been asked to make someone into a *doulos* who had never experienced it. She thought of how Osaze described it, like feeling trapped. Matthew stared back at her without blinking, his wits lulled into complacency by Song.

Adonia frowned at Calandra. "Well, what are you waiting for?"

Calandra turned to the singing siren. "Restrain him, but please stop singing."

The siren blinked in surprise, and looked to Adonia for confirmation.

Adonia pursed her lips. "What do you intend, Calandra?"

"I only want to let his mother say goodbye," she said over her shoulder to her aunt.

Narcissa, who had been standing back and watching the whole proceeding with her arms across her chest, snorted.

"Since when do criminals have rights? She deserves no such consideration. He has already been free for far too long. Get it over with. Every moment he is free is one more chance he has to—"

"Narcissa! That is enough."

Narcissa scowled at her mother, her face aflame, and closed her mouth.

Adonia nodded to the sirens nearest him. They raised their staves to his chest level once again, and then the singer with the sword fell silent.

Matthew blinked as the stupor faded away, then he focused on Calandra.

Calandra met his gaze. He had eyes the colour of the sky on a winter's day.

"Matthew bet'Elizabeth, I am Calandra kor'Delphine. I must Redeem you now. It is my duty. But I wanted to give you a chance to say goodbye to your mother. Do you understand?"

"No . . ." came a weak, sobbing cry from the woman.

Matthew nodded gravely. He turned to his mother, moisture at the corners of his eyes.

"Goood-my, muhnder."

He used hand signs as he spoke, ones Calandra had never seen before.

Elizabeth lifted an impotent hand toward him, weeping. "My son . . ."

He turned back to Calandra, his eyes filled with resolution. But his knees shook.

Calandra drew a breath and closed her eyes to hold back her own surge of emotion. This seemed so wrong and unnecessary. But she had sworn to obey Adonia and fulfill her duty, and that meant she must do this.

Before she lost her resolve, and before any more time could pass to torment the young man, she opened her eyes and touched his forehead. The rite was over in moments.

Elizabeth surged from the floor and her guards dragged her back.

"Calandra kor'Delphine! How could you do this to me? You must know about the curse, the Madness. Your mother knew. Delphine *knew*. You must not—"

The woman's eyes bulged and her mouth gaped in a silent scream.

Her back arched as though she had been stabbed from behind. Calandra watched in horror as Elizabeth fell onto her face, dead, but with no sign of a weapon anywhere.

Adonia stood with her empty hand extended toward the body as though she had released a projectile, but nothing had left it. And Calandra understood.

Adonia had killed the woman. Calandra didn't know how. All that mattered was the result—Adonia had snuffed the life out of Elizabeth from the inside, without even touching her.

Calandra stared at the corpse, her whole body tense. Her throat tightened like she was being choked again. She'd had no idea that her aunt was so powerful. She wasn't even sure she herself would be able to wield the elements upon someone without touching them. And Adonia had killed Elizabeth with no warning or thought. For the first time in her life, Calandra began to fear what her aunt was capable of.

The courtyard was as silent as a tomb.

Adonia dropped her hand and looked around at the dozens of eyes staring at her. She drew herself up.

"The woman's sentence was death. It has been carried out. Despoina, have her body properly disposed of. And Lefkia?"

The bondmistress stepped forward, visibly shaken. "Yes, your majesty?"

Adonia smiled at Matthew, looking him over. "This one will be coming with me." She turned back to her chair and sat.

Narcissa stepped toward her mother and saluted.

"May I have him, Mother? As a *doulos*? Or"—she drew a breath—"as a consort?"

Adonia flicked her gaze up at her daughter, then returned to watching the sirens drag Elizabeth's body out of the room and escort Matthew away.

"I shall consider it."

Calandra dared one very quick glance at Osaze, who was having a difficult time maintaining his emotional shield. He met her eyes, then schooled his expression into blankness. Calandra tried projecting calm toward him, then abandoned it and worked on subduing her own churning emotions so at least he wasn't being upset by her, also.

She knew what he was thinking, because she was thinking it, too—one slip and that could be the two of them.

She packaged the thread that was Matthew's tether together with the bundle in her mind, putting a mental marker on it so she knew she could find it again if she needed. It was the only way she knew to honour the effort his mother had made on his behalf and the courage he had displayed in the face of his unwarranted doom.

What had happened to Matthew and his mother was wrong. Calandra knew it was wrong, but she didn't know what to do about it. Her aunt was queen, and Calandra was bound to serve her. Adonia had been doing some strange things lately—but each of them could be justified within the bounds of the law or her duty to her people. Calandra didn't like it, but it was not her place to rule the nation. Nor did she want it to be. So what right did she have to question Adonia's methods?

As she resumed checking and transferring bonds from Lefkia, a thought that had been dancing around her brain landed squarely in the middle of it.

Elizabeth had known her mother.

And she had known what caused the Madness. How, Calandra did not know. Perhaps Delphine had shared it with her? And now Elizabeth was dead.

Calandra cast a glance at her aunt, the hairs on the back of her neck standing up. She was fairly certain it had not been Elizabeth's crime that had gotten her killed. It had been her knowledge. Who else in Fire Lake had her mother shared her ideas with? Who else might know what Elizabeth knew?

Calandra looked around at the dozens of people still in the room— women with their consorts or *douloi.* Their hearts and faces revealed confusion, concern, boredom, anxiety, and a host of other emotions about what had transpired and the task that remained incomplete.

But only one person in the room was angry. She stood leaning against a pillar at the back, arms crossed over her indigo-blue servant's tunic, glaring at Calandra.

Judith.

When she saw Calandra's intense stare meeting her own, she turned and fled the hall.

30

LAKE OF FIRE

THE LAST MAN IN THE hall walked stiffly out the door, still grimy from his day at the mines.

Calandra watched him go, the thread that was his tether now anchored in her mind, wishing she could slump onto the marble right where she stood. Her feet ached, her shoulders ached, and her heart ached. She hadn't been able to get the image of Elizabeth's corpse out of her mind all day, or Matthew's blank expression while his mother died before his eyes.

Despoina Cleo dismissed the sirens who had been watching the entrances for the evening, then nodded at Calandra and excused herself. Once she'd gone, Calandra and Osaze were alone in the room, the remaining members of the royal entourage having dissipated to various pursuits after the excitement that afternoon. The aroma of cooking food wafted through the courtyard above the sweet smell of summer flowers, and her stomach growled.

Calandra turned to motion Osaze toward their villa to rest and freshen up for a few minutes before the evening meal and paused with her arm in the air.

Adonia stepped onto the flagstones toward her with Cain and a tall, husky siren singer at her heels. The queen was already dressed for dinner in a floor-length tunic of emerald green silk, accented with a bejewelled girdle and golden hair bands. As she had done in the other communities they had visited, Adonia had spent the morning supervising the Redemption rites, but after the discovery of Matthew, had gone to a meeting with the local council to discuss official matters—and, in this case, probably to call them to task for the breach of security in their domain.

Calandra hadn't expected to see her aunt again until dinner. She glanced at Osaze, whose back was to the queen, and flicked her eyes away before she could be accused of staring. His face relaxed, and he looked as though he were about to speak.

Calandra bowed and saluted the woman approaching his shoulder. "Your majesty."

Osaze stiffened to his normal posture.

Adonia smiled graciously. "Calandra, I need to speak with you for a few minutes. May I accompany you to your villa?"

Calandra blinked, unsure of what to make of her aunt's offer. She sensed no danger or slyness from Adonia, however.

"Of course, your majesty."

The sun had set and Atargatis's star, Venus, hung over the western horizon, eclipsing whatever tiny fragment of moon might otherwise be visible tonight. Fire Lake was living up to its moniker, reflecting a brilliant sunset of reds and oranges that made it appear as though the caldera were filled with lava. Steam rising from the warm water added to the effect.

Calandra fell into place beside the queen as they exited the courtyard for the gravelled lakeside pathway that led to the guest villas. At Adonia's gesture, the singer walked on ahead—near enough to be of use should danger present itself, but far enough to not overhear their conversation.

Osaze and Cain walked a couple of paces behind the two women. Calandra was pleased to note that Osaze's emotional shield was getting better—she could sense his exhaustion and anxiety through their bond, but she doubted anyone else would be empathic enough to sense anything out of the ordinary. Still, she longed to be alone with him in private so they could discuss the day's momentous events.

What a strange thought. She only ever used to feel that way for Tanni, and now she couldn't wait to have a conversation with a man. *With my consort-elect.*

A warm glow eased some of the tension between her shoulders and she looked away to hide her expression from Adonia. Thank goodness her Tear's special properties would shield her emotions. *I really need to get better at this.* She regretted that she hadn't yet figured out its secret so she could make one for Osaze.

The pathway soon took them past the market streets toward the beach, running between the tree-lined lake and some gated whitewashed-brick villas. The villas were owned by a noblewoman in Haven who normally let them out to those on holiday, but the houses were always made available for the royal family when they had need. Adonia's villa was very near the entrance of the path, the next housed about half the siren pod, Calandra and Narcissa and their respective parties shared the next, and the remaining sirens shared a fourth. Each villa was surrounded by an extensive lot filled with lovely trees and gardens, with a pathway leading directly to the lake. As they passed the door to Adonia's residence, it closed behind Cleo, who was staying with the queen.

Adonia strolled with her hands behind her back.

"I want to congratulate you. You did something quite remarkable today."

Calandra cocked her head. "What are you referring to?"

"You healed that man instantly. You did not pause to think about it, you did not need water, and I would wager you did not use that stone around your neck as a crutch. Am I right?"

Calandra covered her Tear with her hand. Her aunt was right—that *had* been rather remarkable. In addition to her aunt's observations, she realized for the first time that she had not had to struggle for control either. The whole thing had happened naturally, almost without thinking of it, and instead of the usual exhaustion that followed, she had felt energized. How had she accomplished it? Had that prickly bundle of tethers in her mind enhanced her powers so much?

"Yes, you are," Calandra said. "I didn't use it at all. As soon as that young man came into the room, I knew what I had to do, and then I simply did it."

"I do not think I have ever seen another healer do what you did today. Well done."

The realization of what she had accomplished was quickly replaced by the memory of what had come after, and the wonder faded. She studied the ground ahead of her.

"Thank you, your majesty."

"Please, we are alone. You need not stand on formality now."

Calandra nodded. "Yes, Aunt Adonia."

Alone? She knew Adonia would not count their two male companions as an audience, as she herself had not for most of her life. Still, she had the odd experience of feeling offended on their behalf.

"Tomorrow is your birthday," said Adonia. "Eighteen. Quite the milestone."

Calandra blinked. With everything else that had been happening, her birthday had completely slipped her mind.

"Yes, Aunt Adonia."

"You have been working very hard for the last several weeks, for which

I am grateful. Your dedication to this initiative has not gone unnoticed. Nor will it go unrewarded."

"Thank you, Aunt Adonia." Where was her aunt going with this?

Splashes and laughter from the lake caught their attention. Several teenage undines frolicked in the fading light, the molten surface of the lake disturbed by their antics. There were few school-aged undine children in the town. Most of them had classes in Sireniapolis or Haven nearly year-round. These girls were likely apprentices to local artisans in some craft or trade guild.

Their group had reached Calandra's villa. Adonia took the path down to the water and paused on the edge of the lake near the hidden sandy clearing in which Calandra and Osaze had whiled away some time the previous night. Their entourage all stopped to wait at an appropriate distance near the trees. Adonia watched the girls for a few seconds, then turned back to her niece.

"This afternoon, I arranged with the local civil archon and Councillor Iris for a feast on the morrow to celebrate your birthday. They were only too happy to put their community's resources at our disposal."

She gave a sardonic smirk that implied otherwise.

Calandra swallowed. The last thing she wanted to do right now was attend another feast.

Adonia raised an eyebrow. "Does that not please you?"

"Yes, of course, your majesty. Thank you. You do me a great honour."

Adonia pressed her lips together and studied Calandra.

"I have known you your whole life, Calandra. I know when you are lying. I also know you have never enjoyed large feasts and festivals, and you have had to endure an exceptional number while we have been travelling. Am I right to surmise that you would prefer to avoid another one in honour of your coming-of-age? You may speak freely with me."

Calandra nodded hesitantly. It had been some time since she had seen this side of Adonia—considerate and selfless.

"I—you are right. I would prefer that we not tax this community with the burden of celebrating my birthday, especially only two days after their hearty welcome to our family. Perhaps we can save any obligatory honours until my bonding ceremony in two weeks?"

Adonia raised an eyebrow with an amused smirk.

"Of course, my child. We will remain here for the extra day, regardless—to enjoy the local amenities, not to work. Even were it not your birthday, you have earned a day of rest. I am sure we will all enjoy the break. If we did not have such a pressing schedule, I would gladly allow you one more."

"Thank you."

"Perhaps we will also combine the birthday and bonding ceremonies with the announcement of my heir."

Calandra nodded slowly. "I'm not sure Narcissa will be thrilled about sharing her event with mine, but—"

"No, not for Narcissa. For you."

Calandra's heart skittered against her ribs.

"What—what are you saying?"

Adonia waved Cain forward and, for the first time, Calandra noticed he had been hiding a brilliant red hibiscus flower in his hands. The queen took it from him and tucked it behind Calandra's ear.

"I have had to face the disturbing truth that my own daughter is not fit to rule. She is too petty and small-minded. You, on the other hand, have only ever done your duty, no matter what has been demanded of you. Each day, I have watched your skills and confidence grow. Calandra, I have decided to name you as the Opal Princess, Heir to the Throne of Sirenia."

Calandra stood frozen, unsure of what to say or think. Opal Princess? She didn't want the throne. But how could she refuse? It was not her decision

"Th—thank you, your majest . . . Aunt Adoni—"

Blood swooshed inside Calandra's ears and a blinding stab of pain bloomed between her temples. She grunted and bent double, pressing her fingers to her head. Osaze stepped toward her, but she waved him off.

"Calandra. What is the matter?"

Adonia pressed her hand to Calandra's forehead. Adonia was no healer, but she did have great power with spirit. She growled.

"I can sense nothing besides your distress." She raised her voice and called the siren. "Singer kor'Dione, go fetch the local physic. She is likely at supper already."

"Yes, your majesty." The sound of the singer's running footsteps faded as she hurried to obey.

As suddenly as it had come, the pain receded. Calandra drew in a breath and straightened, her eyes closed.

"I—I think I'm fine now."

She opened her eyes to Adonia's concerned frown. Osaze's worry was like a storm cloud at the edge of her awareness, but he stayed at attention where he should be. She cast a quick glance in his direction, hoping to assure him that she truly did feel recovered, if a bit out of sorts.

"Sit down, Calandra." Adonia urged obedience with a hand on Calandra's shoulder. "Wait for Healer Doris. She will check you over."

Calandra frowned at the sand. It looked wet and cold. She sighed and did as she was told, and then completed a brief inner self-diagnostic—healers could monitor their own systems, though they could not heal them.

"There's nothing wrong with me. I don't know what happened. I had a sudden headache, and then it was gone. May I go into the house now?"

Adonia's frown deepened. "Osaze, help your mistress to stand."

Calandra growled and held up a warning hand toward him. Why was everyone treating her like a child? *First Adonia gives me the throne, and then treats me like an invalid.*

"I can stand on my own just fine, thank you."

Osaze stopped where he stood, his face neutral, but uncertainty shimmered through the bond.

She was about to push herself up from the sand—*just as cold and wet as I expected. It's probably ruined this tunic*—when sadness fell like a heavy, physical weight on her shoulders, keeping her planted, as though it were a parting gift from the pain. The bundle of fibres in her brain burned, and she pushed awareness of them aside in irritation. She had the irrational urge to lash out at something, but what?

Without warning, she began to weep. Aghast, she ducked her head, sniffled, and wiped away overflowing tears, hoping her aunt didn't notice.

Of course, Adonia noticed.

"What in the name of the Mother, Calandra? Pull yourself together."

"I'm tr—trying. I'm s—sorry."

Adonia cleared her throat, and then a linen kerchief appeared in Calandra's line of sight, dangling from her aunt's fingers.

"There, there," came Adonia's stiff comfort, along with a pat on her shoulder.

Calandra took the cloth and dabbed at her face. She would have laughed at her aunt's awkward attempt at softness if Adonia hadn't been queen, and if she had felt at all like laughing. *What is wrong with me?*

Her face dry, she took a deep, cleansing breath in through her nose. She tucked the kerchief into her girdle, knowing her aunt wouldn't want it back until it had been laundered. The weight she had experienced only moments before was gone as though it had never existed.

"I'm feeling much better now. Thank you."

She stood up. Adonia looked like she would object, then backed away a step and said nothing, her brow still furrowed.

"You're not worried about Narcissa's reaction to you being named as the Opal Princess, are you?"

Calandra shook her head. "Of course not. I know she won't like it, but the decision isn't hers, or mine. It's yours, and she will abide by it, just as I will."

Adonia nodded, satisfied. Then her eyes narrowed.

"Is this because of that crazy woman with the deaf son?"

"What?" Calandra blinked, warm darkness tickling her mind. "No. No, I don't think so. Maybe. I don't know."

Adonia crossed her arms and regarded Calandra for a long moment.

"She committed a serious crime, Calandra. She got what she deserved."

Calandra's gaze flicked to Osaze, who stood beyond Adonia a short distance, then back to her aunt.

"And Thea? She is guilty of the same crime, is she not? Will you also execute her in such an undignified fashion?"

Calandra wondered again at how her aunt had even accomplished such a thing. The control it would have required . . .

"Thea has long been a friend to me, and has given faithful service to the crown in every area but this. Unfortunately, the law is clear, Calandra. Exceptions cannot be made, even for those we care about." A stricken expression crossed her face, then was gone.

"Thea will receive an execution befitting both her station and the depth of her betrayal. After she has assisted you in healing the Heartstone."

Calandra's throat tightened again, and she swallowed the lump that had formed. "And what does that mean?"

"Beheading."

Any hint of softness or warmth had disappeared from Adonia's face. She was once again the queen, cold and merciless and bound by her duty.

"Perhaps I spoke too quickly about naming you heir. When you are queen, you need to be able to make these decisions. Can you?"

A growing sense of desperation clawed at Calandra's insides. She knew it might be foolish to continue this conversation, but she didn't know when she'd have another chance. She couldn't let Thea be executed without even trying to help her.

She worked to keep her voice calm. "Aunt Adonia, Gerrick has never posed a threat of any kind. Before Thea's, um, 'crime' was discovered, Gerrick was a better-trained *doulos* than any other man I have known. I have been around him my whole life, and he never behaved as we have been told freemen would behave. Why can't you—?"

Adonia cut her off with an imperious hand.

"Be careful what you say next, niece. Your loyalty has not been in question, but it could become so."

Calandra frowned and closed her mouth, her gut hard.

Adonia's posture relaxed. "Look, Calandra. It is natural to become attached to the men we bond. You think I do not understand? I do. I mourned deeply when I lost Frederik."

A haunted look flashed through her eyes. A lightning bolt of heart-wrenching grief crackled into Calandra before it was cut off as quickly as it had come.

The queen drew in a breath.

"But let me warn you not to make the mistake that Thea and this Elizabeth have. I can see how fond you have already become of your consort-elect—"

"What do you mean? I—"

Adonia smiled and held up a finger to silence her. "It is obvious, child. Do not worry. I expected as much. And it is to your benefit. Affection strengthens the consort bond and will enhance your powers even more. Just be careful to use the proper measures to avoid conceiving too early."

Calandra's face grew hot at her aunt's implications. "I haven't taken—"

"And be careful," Adonia continued, ignoring Calandra's discomfort, "that affection does not lead you to the erroneous belief that these creatures"—Adonia took in Cain and Osaze with a gesture—"can be elevated above the baseness of their natures. They may be able to pretend docility for a time. But so will an orca when in captivity." She paced to stand before the men and peer at their blank faces. "That does not mean their aggressive, unstable nature has been changed."

The queen stood directly in front of Osaze, studying him. Osaze kept his face blank. Through the bond, Calandra felt a bubble of rage and fear. The longer Adonia stared at him, the tighter Calandra's chest became. She had to distract her aunt's attention somehow.

"But Gerrick never—"

"Enough!" Adonia whirled and pinned her niece with her icy green eyes. "We will discuss this no further. Thea played with fire, and fortunately, the only one getting burned from her actions is her. It could have been so much worse. But if I show mercy to her, what would prevent every other woman on this island who might have a misguided notion of her consort's ability to be tamed from following suit?"

Calandra met her aunt's gaze, not blinking, not glancing at Osaze, concentrating on projecting calm. She pushed her fear and grief—for Gerrick, for Thea, for Elizabeth and Matthew—down into her belly and relaxed her jaw.

"But aren't men intelligent beings with wills and emotions like our own? What right do we have to take their choice from them? How can you know how they would behave if their wills were restored to them?"

Adonia snatched the chain around her neck and pulled the blue aquamarine Tear pendant out of her gown, the one she'd said she'd found in Atlantis.

"You want to know how I know? This. This is how I know!" She shook it at Calandra. "Before I had this blanked, I watched it. The horrors that were visited upon us in the past, the destruction, even the sinking of Atlantis, can ultimately be laid at the feet of men. I will *not* allow something like that to happen again."

Calandra's heart skipped. Had Damon been to blame for the Sinking after all? After five years, she still knew so little about him.

Adonia leaned toward her niece.

"You are walking a very dangerous line, child. You stand in almost the very spot where Delphine asked me these same questions. Because she wouldn't listen, dozens of good women died. And if I ever discover that you have betrayed me, betrayed our people, in the way your mother did or that Thea has . . . after so much evidence to forewarn you and the trust I have placed in you, you will not get something so civil as a beheading."

Adonia's green eyes gleamed red, reflecting the last, fiery shots of dusk. The effect was unsettling.

Calandra nodded and set her jaw, refusing to wilt under her aunt's glare.

The sound of footsteps crunched up the gravel path. Healer Doris had arrived.

Adonia stood back and watched with her arms crossed as Calandra submitted to Doris's examination, answering the physic's questions mechanically. Doris was at as much of a loss to explain the episode as Calandra, and resorted to suggesting some time to rest.

"Yes, yes," Adonia said. "She may have the next day to do as she wishes, and I will alert her maid to keep an extra close watch on her in case of further incidents."

The sound of the women's voices faded as Calandra stared at the glassy surface of the starlit lake, now silent and empty of swimmers. She stared at the sinking point of light that was Venus, praying for answers.

As soon as Calandra healed the Heartstone, Thea was to be beheaded.

She couldn't bear the thought of losing the only mother she had ever known. But she was the Saviour of the Heartstone. She *had* to heal it. She was the last hope of an entire nation. And now she was to be its queen.

She had to be strong. Thea wouldn't want Calandra to shirk her duty for her own crime, regardless of the consequences.

Yes. She had to be strong.

Only, Calandra didn't want to be strong right now. She wrapped her arms around herself, longing to dive into the lake and forget about all of it, simply swim away and hide.

She could heal a man in the blink of an eye. She held the *pisti* bond of the two people she loved most in the world in her mind, plus the wiry bundle of threads that represented a thousand other wills. She was the most powerful healer in three thousand years. She would soon be named the Opal Princess.

But despite all that, Thea was going to die.

At that moment, Calandra wanted nothing more than to collapse into Osaze's arms and weep. He stood only two paces away, but under the watchful eyes of their witnesses, he may as well have been on the other side of an ocean.

What was she thinking? Had her affection for Osaze made her weak? She didn't need his strength, not when she was stronger than him by far already. Frowning, Calandra bundled her churning emotions into a ball and mentally held them at arm's length, then tossed them into the lake. Self-pity was not a luxury she could afford.

She watched the imaginary spot where her ball had landed, picturing bubbles floating to the surface and popping.

Doris's voice intruded on her thoughts. "Calandra, are you listening? You must come into the house and rest."

Calandra turned and regarded the wizened healer. "Yes, of course. Coming."

Another voice telling her what to do. Another person to obey.

What was the point of power if all it did was keep you prisoner?

31

TEAR OF HOPE

CALANDRA ROLLED OVER FOR THE hundredth time. After the light supper Judith had served in uncharacteristic silence, she had gone to bed, on Doris's instructions.

She hadn't slept more than three winks since.

Frustrated, she sat upright. The evening star had long since set, but by the starlight still coming in through the window, she could make out Judith's form on the room's other bed. Osaze slept on a cot under the window near the door—she couldn't see him, but she had been counting his rhythmic breaths for hours, regretting that they'd had no private time before bed. Somewhere in Sireniapolis, Tanni also slept, her glass jar of emotions mellow and creamy.

Calandra grabbed the tunic she'd worn yesterday from where it lay on a chair beside the bed, slipped into it, and picked up the leather girdle, being careful not to let the buckle clink. She caught sight of the hibiscus on the floor. It had been on top of the pile and must have fallen as she picked up her clothes. It looked like a limp red stain, reminding her of the added responsibility that now fell on her shoulders.

She shook her head and stealthily padded to the door on bare feet. These doors swung instead of folded, but the well-oiled hinges let her escape to the landing with hardly a sound. The door to Narcissa's room was open and she paused, listening and probing to see if its occupants were awake. The hazy condition of their emotions and their steady breathing told Calandra that both Mari and Narcissa slept.

She crept down the stairs toward the door. Something moved in the common area, and she froze.

It was a man's form, sleeping on a pallet near the door—Matthew. Adonia must have granted Narcissa's request, at least in part.

Calandra stared at him sadly, wondering if she'd truly done him a favour by restoring his hearing. After waiting long enough for several gentle snores to escape and probing his emotions to check that his slumber remained undisturbed, she slipped out the door and down the stone steps.

The rough gravel hurt her feet, but she didn't care. She had meant to go for a walk, but as soon as the starlit lake came into view, she knew what she really wanted was a swim. Running down the path with sure-footed grace, she soon reached the lakeside and flung her girdle and tunic onto the sand. All she wore now was the Tear, resting against her goosebumped flesh. Ever since the night that Narcissa had stolen it, she never took it off, even to swim. She undid the clasp and refastened it further up the chain so it couldn't come off over her head in the water. Then, with a running dive, she let the water take her.

After transforming, she took a moment to enjoy being enveloped by the primal warmth, then began to swim. At first, she aimed in a wide lap, several hundred spans from the shore. Fire Lake held no threats, and it was deep enough that she did not have to worry about weeds or sand bars once she was beyond the beach area. She swam purposefully below the surface, her sensitive vision picking up nothing but murky green water fading off into blackness.

Eventually, her pent-up energy spent, she curved back toward the town. Predawn light had released a chorus of birdsong. She rose to the surface to enjoy it, floating on her back, propelling herself with the occasional lazy flip of her tail.

Today is my birthday.

For some reason, that made her think of Delphine and Kenver. She wrapped her hand around her Tear, then released it. If only her mother had included more information in her message. Now, Calandra's only lead in the trail to find her family was gone, erased by a woman who seemed bent on obscuring the truth. Her only hope was that she could get to Atlantis and find something else to guide her in the abandoned datastones she saw in her dreams.

What was Adonia so determined to hide, anyway? If the erased contents of that blue stone had been so dangerous, why had they existed in the first place? And if they were truly a cautionary tale, wouldn't they do more good as public knowledge? Was Adonia even telling the truth about what she'd seen?

Delphine had known.

Calandra couldn't shake the feeling that Elizabeth had known.

Who else might know? Surely, her mother hadn't kept information this important to herself.

Calandra reached the village shrine of Atargatis, which had been erected on a stone pier protruding into the water near the head of the Fire River flowing from the lake. Here at the source, the river was a mere stream. The marble portico housed a statue of the goddess in *ichthys* state on a clamshell with her arms extended over the water, much like the one in the Opal Palace. It depicted her holding a fish and a sheaf of wheat in one hand to represent fertility and blessing, and the sceptre of justice in the other, a dove resting on her shoulder. On her forehead, a sculpted Venus Rose was set in the centre of a triquetra hair chain pendant. Next to her lay the effigy of her infant son, Ichthys, cradled in the clamshell with his tail curling over the side.

Trinity's shrine had included both Ichthys and Hadad, Atargatis's consort, the only place besides the crumbling murals of Atlantis that Calandra had seen in her dreams and a few ancient history stones where Calandra had seen the two males represented. She supposed that since the town of Trinity had been named for the three deities, it made sense the community would worship all three. She couldn't fathom what the significance of Ichthys to the people of Fire Lake might be, though.

Calandra stared up at the idol, then dove beneath the surface and swam toward the floor of the lake within the area designated for shrine worshippers, which was marked by floating copper buoys. The priestesses kept this area neat and groomed, and it was very easy to find an appropriately beautiful stone to present to the goddess in offering and supplication. She chose a piece of polished pink quartz the size of a chicken's egg, a perfect hexahedron with points at each end. If it hadn't been a sacred stone, something like this would have been in a gemhound's personal collection.

Surfacing, she changed states and clambered up the lakeside steps of the shrine, a chill morning breeze pebbling her naked flesh, her loose hair clinging to her body in wet ropes. She knelt at the feet of the larger-than-life idol. Touching the crystal to her forehead in salute, she kissed it, then held it next to her heart as she whispered her devotions and prayers.

"Blessed are you, Ishtar of the morning, for you alone bring victory. Blessed are you, Inanna of the evening, for you alone bring love. Blessed are you, Atargatis, Lady of the Sea and Queen of Heaven, for you rule all the world in beauty, wisdom, and truth."

After saying the proscribed greetings to the goddess, she placed the stone in one of the shallow stone basins at the foot of the statue, took one of the supplied brass cups and scooped up some lake water, and then poured it over the stone while she prayed. She pondered her requests for a moment, then continued, murmuring the words in a singsong rhythm that was half singing, half speaking.

For the most part, her prayers were as they always were—requests for strength to do her duty and compassion for those she served, all the more so after Adonia's news—but lately, there had been specific names added to her list of requests.

Thea. Gerrick. Her brother, mother, and father. Osaze. And now Matthew. She prayed a blessing on Elizabeth's soul as she crossed the watery barrier between this world and the next.

Calandra opened her eyes and studied the crystal in its bed of water. Not for the first time, she wondered if the goddess even heard her prayers. What good could an entity carved in stone or far away in the night sky do to help her with her problems? Face burning, she squelched such blasphemous thoughts.

Dawn broke and morning sunlight refracted through the pink stone in blinding glints. Calandra admired the clarity of the crystal and the pleasing geometrical shape.

That was what she loved about stones—they made sense. They followed patterns, layer upon layer of information written in the very chemistry. The pattern formed the stone and the stone could then be utilized for both beauty and function by healers like herself. Each type of stone had unique properties that could be used in special ways like data storage, energy generation, or long-distance communication. Some stones could even be used to hide messages and—

Calandra gasped and sat upright. Of course! Why hadn't she thought of that before?

Opals didn't have the same rigid structure as quartz. They were made from water-saturated silica, and their brilliant play of colour was a visible representation of the somewhat-chaotic layers that made up their form. Layers in which hidden messages could easily be encoded by those who knew what they were doing. It was why opals were a favourite personal datastone.

Opals like the dark green Tear Calandra wore around her neck.

Trying to maintain decorum for the sake of reverence, she fumbled with the clasp of her necklace, thankful she was the only worshipper here. Once she'd released the chain, she cupped the Tear between her hands and closed her eyes, penetrating the structure of the stone with her mind.

She had been right. Beneath the surface message—the information that would be easily accessible by a quartz reader—was an encrypted treasure trove of data.

She opened her eyes and glanced around. The eastern sky behind the town glowed a cheery yellowish pink, but other than the birds and the fish disturbing the surface of the lake as they harvested insects, she was alone. The shrine *douloi* had not even arrived yet.

She picked up the sacred quartz crystal, and, to be extra cautious, held it close to her body to conceal what she was doing. Normally, hexahedrons like this were planed in cross sections and processed to create quartz readers, but a stone healer could use one in its raw state in a pinch. She pressed the Tear against the side of the reader and used her power to funnel the hidden information from the opaline matrix into the crystal.

The six sides of the stone boiled to life in a strange dance of faces, letters, and images with snippets of weak sound. She saw her mother's face and Kenver's, but also other faces she didn't recognize.

". . . might cause the Madness . . ." came Delphine's voice. Her face faded and reappeared. ". . . test this idea . . . the only way . . . heal the Heartstone . . . impossible without . . . organized a resistance . . . seek them out."

Calandra frowned, frustrated at the tantalizing tidbits of information that promised answers without giving any. She didn't understand what she was seeing—it was too chaotic and disorganized when viewed this way. But it was enough to confirm that the Tear's true potential remained untapped—and that her mother hadn't left the data only on the single stone Adonia had discovered.

Breathing fast, Calandra tried to reattach the necklace around her neck, fumbling with the clasp. After botching several attempts in her excitement, she succeeded. She yearned to swim straight back to her villa to fetch her quartz reader, but she couldn't dishonour the goddess by neglecting to finish the religious ritual.

Thanking the Mother more fervently than she had in years, she picked up the quartz crystal, stood, and descended to the bottom stair above the lake. She dropped the stone into the lightening water and dove in after it, her naked body transforming to *ichthys* state in the air.

The stone bounced off jutting rocks along the lake's steep sides, descending in slow motion. Calandra turned to face the distorted visage of the goddess above the surface, the idol's colours washed out in the golden light of dawn. Opening her arms wide, she closed her eyes and hummed the final song into the lake waters as quickly as decency allowed, her voice resonating in her head.

Her duty complete, she opened her eyes and spun, intending to press for a surface afire with sunrise colours above her and take the quickest route back to her clothing.

Instead, she froze, her ascent arrested in mid-stroke.

Hanging in the water before her was Damon, his golden eyes piercing her with an accusing gaze.

"You have been away a long time, my little lark."

32

THE WATER SPIRIT

DAMON'S MOUTH MOVED AS HE said the words, but she heard them in her mind.

"Damon?" she said, or tried. Instead, an air bubble escaped her mouth and began an erratic journey to the surface.

How was it possible that Damon could be here? She hadn't dreamt of him since they'd left the palace, and she'd pushed aside thoughts of him whenever they'd occurred. She was happy with Osaze, and dreaded telling the possessive water spirit about her betrothal. She couldn't remember why, but she suspected he would not take it well. Besides, since Adonia had blanked the not-so-hidden aquamarine Atlantis stone they needed to find Calandra's family, she had no other reason to visit Atlantis.

Was it coincidence that he'd appeared to her almost the instant she'd discovered the Atlantis stone may not even be necessary?

She blinked. *Is he really here?*

"Yes, I am here before you, Calandra. Where are we?"

Calandra started. He could hear her?

"Yes, I can hear you." He looked annoyed. "Now answer my question."

Though he had demanded to know where they were twice, Calandra did not feel her normal compulsion to obey him without thought. She smiled.

However, she saw no reason not to answer him.

We are in Fire Lake, on Sirenia.

Damon nodded, then spun around, looking at the lovely bright-coloured sacred stones resting in the sand between the polished lake rocks on the steep wall next to them.

"We are at the shrine."

Calandra nodded.

He noticed the Tear around her neck, something she had never worn during their previous encounters.

"What is this?"

He reached up to touch it and she pulled away. He frowned.

"Is that any way to treat your consort-elect?"

His seductive smile didn't unsettle her like it usually did, though the longer he hovered before her, the more she could feel her body responding. His strange magnetism may not be as strong here, in the lake, with her awake, but he still possessed it.

"Now answer me. What is this?"

Calandra's resistance melted. *It is my mother's Tear. Adonia had it blanked before I could see my mother's whole message.*

Why had she blurted that out? Chains of Prometheus, she could be an idiot sometimes. Her thoughts fuzzed, softening as though she dreamed. She shook her head, struggling to maintain clarity.

How is it that you are here?

"You grow in power, my lark. You can now call me when you are awake."

Damon swam closer to her and the water around her swirled.

Her eyes widened. *In the name of the Mother! He really is here!*

"Yes, I am," he said, his voice in her head sounding amused. "Though my manifestation does have some limitations."

He caressed the side of her neck, and she shivered at his touch. However, when he tried to pick up the chain of her necklace between his fingers, it slipped through them as though he were a ghost.

"It is the same as when you come to visit me, except here, I am the apparition. But you are as stunning as ever, my dear."

He glanced over her naked form. His smile reminded her of a shark. Her hair covered much of her upper body in a floating blond cloud, but even still, she felt a rush of heat at his appraisal, as well as shame and anger. What right did he have to look at her that way, like she was an object that could be possessed? She crossed her arms over her chest.

Damon frowned. "Something is different. What is it?" He brushed a hand over her cheek and pushed some hair behind her ear.

Calandra cringed away.

He frowned and moved in closer, looking as though he might kiss her.

She backstroked away from him, putting a couple of lengths between them.

Damon retracted his hand, and his beautiful face darkened. "What has happened? Why do you recoil from me?"

Calandra shrugged. *Nothing has happened. I just don't want you to touch me like that anymore.*

"Why not? I thought you wanted to be together. You did agree to come free me and become my consort."

She'd agreed to become *his* consort?

He moved toward her, and she backed away further.

"Do you not remember? Dream communication can be so unreliable."

His golden irises swirled, and the memory of her promise came back to her.

She swallowed. "Things have changed."

In the corner of her awareness, she sensed a spike of alarm from Osaze—he must have awoken and noticed her missing. She closed her eyes and gathered calm to her, focusing on the sensation of the water through her gills and the rhythmic beating of her heart as it slowed. *I'm fine, my love. I will return soon.* She knew he couldn't hear her thoughts, but he'd sense her location and distress, and she didn't want him to feel anxious on her account and come looking. Not right now.

"To whom are you speaking?" Damon reached out and grabbed her wrist, pulling her toward him.

Reflexively, she lashed out with spirit, and he recoiled as though stung. *I said not to touch me.*

He looked at his hand in astonishment, realization dawning on his face.

"You have become much more powerful since we last met, which is excellent to see. However, that is not why you recoil from me, is it?" He ascended slightly in the water so he looked down at her. "You are in love."

She tensed.

"That's it, isn't it? Only infatuation with another could make you resistant to my charms. Ah, well, it shan't last. And you still need me."

Calandra frowned. *Why in the name of the Mother would I need you?*

Damon sneered. "Your all-knowing 'mother' is the reason you need me, isn't it? In her wisdom, she decreed the Heartstone could only be maintained by male and female powers working together. Powers, not merely life forces. It is not enough to have a consort—your human slaves are no good to you. And since there are no males of your kind left, if you ever want to have a hope of succeeding in your mission, you must free me."

"You're lying!"

Calandra's involuntary yell only released another air bubble. She clenched her fists.

That isn't true.

"Isn't it?" He raised an eyebrow. "You've told me yourself that in the last three millennia, no one has been able to repair the damage to your precious Heartstone. Is that not the same amount of time that your male birth rate has been nil?"

Calandra's mouth opened and closed several times. She knew she probably looked like a fish and shut it, feeling foolish.

If you have known this all along, why have you never said it before?

Damon sighed and crossed his arms.

"Because, in order to release the chains that hold me, you also need to work with male powers. It's quite the conundrum, isn't it? However, I think there is another way. That is why you must come to me—if you free me, then I can be the one to help you heal your precious Heartstone."

Calandra glanced up at the surface. Osaze was approaching. She hoped he didn't do something foolish and try to swim out to find her.

And what good would it do you for me to come to Atlantis? Do you know how to find the key to your prison, or even where the gate is?

"Yes to both. I believe the chains that hold me have weakened enough that you and I may be able to work together from opposite sides of it."

She didn't know why that made her feel so uneasy. She wrapped her arms around herself again.

What if you aren't the last one? I could still find my brother. And then why would I need you?

Damon looked amused.

"Oh, little one. You are so young and ignorant, you can't even comprehend all the ways you still need me."

He reached up to caress her face, caught her warning look, and dropped his hand.

"Can you find your brother before the solstice? If I were free, I could help you fulfill your duty to the Heartstone and you would then be able to go search the world for your absentee brother. Who knows how long that will take? The world is a very big place, and you are a very small girl."

Calandra narrowed her eyes at him. He was right—searching for her family without any clues would be like searching for a single krill in a swarm, and the Healing Ceremony was only two weeks away. However, she hoped she now *had* clues, that the Tear on her neck would reveal all, if she could ever go explore its contents.

He frowned at her stone. "What is on that Tear that you hope will provide you answers?"

She stiffened. *Nothing. It was blanked by my aunt, remember?*

"So this is the Tear your mother left you? The one that held the message?"

She nodded.

He pinned her with his golden eyes.

"And I suppose that between your slave-lover and a few words left by the mother who abandoned you, you think you can smother the void that blackens your soul."

Calandra froze, feeling as though the very water in her gills had stopped moving. Damon drew closer, sneering. The icy blackness of her nightmare ocean poured into her like ink from his gold-limned black pupils, pooling in her chest.

"Oh, yes, I know all about the fears that live at the core of you. I keep them and guard you from them. You think I cannot give them back?"

She blinked, unable to respond.

"And do you really think a human pet will be able to keep your nightmares away at night like I do? Having a lover who can never leave is not the same as having one who chooses to stay."

He's not *my pet. He is Unredeemed, but he* will *stay.*

She flicked her tail in frustration. Had she no control over herself at all?

"I see." Damon was directly before her now, and still she could not move. "So you have taken to letting your pets roam without a leash, and you still delude yourself that he will act like one who is tamed. Little one, you know so little. Why would he stay here, of all places?"

He loves me.

She hadn't meant to say it, it came of its own accord as though ripped from her.

Damon arched a brow and grabbed her hand. She tried to push him away, but her limbs remained locked. The creeping cold of the void slithered through her, making her fingers and toes go numb. She fought against the despair and fear.

"You only think he loves you. Easy to assume when you have all the power, isn't it? But if he were truly given a choice, would he still choose you? Even your mother chose your brother over you. If she left you, why wouldn't he?"

He laughed, and the cruel syllables echoed in the pit where her heart used to be.

"No, only I in my mercy could love a creature as pitiful as you. Without me, you will fail in your duty and go Mad. Everyone else is bound to leave you eventually. It is time to surrender completely, my dear. Stop this foolish rebellion."

Wrapping his hands around both her wrists, he crushed her lips in a suffocating kiss. The bruising pressure made her squirm, and she struggled to break free of his hold. She bit his lip, and he pulled away and laughed.

Get away from me, you monster!

"Oh, I think not. Our fates are entwined, my lark. I will not leave, and you cannot. You will come to Atlantis."

He said it with such calm assurance, such a confident curve to his lips, that Calandra immediately saw how much sense it made. Of course she would go to Atlantis and free him. What else would she—

What was happening? How was he doing this to her? She had to get him out of her head.

For the briefest of moments, the water around them flared with thousands of fine golden threads extending between them, bounding the inky black clouds that filled her vision. Calandra blinked, and the impression was gone.

Fighting with all her might, she bent her arms and placed them on his chest.

I told you . . .

She made a futile attempt to push. He leered back at her.

. . . not to . . .

Her eardrums felt as though they might explode from the strain.

. . . touch me!

With a final heave, she regained control of her limbs and pushed him away.

He blinked at her in surprise, then his expression twisted into something so dark she was afraid to look at him.

Without warning, he reached out and snatched the stone from around her neck, breaking the clasp.

She gasped, and he darted backward, the Tear in his fist. A smile of victory curved his lips.

She dove for him, and he swam away from her faster than she would have believed possible. As she pursued, his voice sounded in her head.

"The walls of my prison are weakening, little one. Soon, I may not need you after all. However, when I am free, you will wish you had helped me willingly. I expect to see you again soon, in Atlantis."

His laughter still echoed through her mind as he winked out of existence.

Her Tear was nowhere to be found.

*

NARCISSA watched from the trees, fuming that she was once again reduced to espionage to try to prove herself to her mother, as Calandra clambered out of the lake near the shrine and flung herself into her *doulos*'s arms. Her cousin—the girl who had stolen her throne—appeared to be quite upset, telling the bodyguard something in choppy, broken sentences.

Narcissa narrowed her eyes. Osaze was behaving . . . unusually. Stroking Calandra's hair, kissing her, wiping tears from her face.

A growing sense of delight came over Narcissa. She was so glad she had followed her curiosity when she saw Osaze sneak out of the villa alone. She had thought he might be up to something for Calandra, but this was even better than she'd hoped. There was only one reason a man would behave this way—Osaze was Unredeemed, and seemed as infatuated with Calandra as she obviously was with him.

Narcissa smiled. This was good news. Very good news indeed.

"Enjoy your hibiscus, *Opal Princess*, but don't get too comfortable with it," she snarled under her breath.

"Your highness?" came a woman's voice from behind her.

Narcissa whirled. Calandra's annoying maid stood on the path leading toward the villas, her head cocked in curiosity.

"What do you want?" Narcissa demanded.

"I was on my way to find my mistress. She had already left when I awoke. Have you seen her?"

Narcissa tamped down her irritation. So the brat didn't know what Narcissa had been doing.

"I saw her swim across the lake earlier. Now, if you'll excuse me, I have important things to do."

Judith bowed and pressed her bunched fingers to her forehead.

"Of course, your highness. Thank you. I will find her, I'm sure."

Her expression remained blank and conciliatory, but something in her tone seemed mildly accusing.

Narcissa gave a small snort and pushed past the girl, then stalked off toward her villa to wake up Mari and make plans.

Her lover was going to be thrilled with her news.

33

THE MESSENGER

May 19, 1799
Whydah, Kingdom of Dahomey, Benin

ZALE SAT IN THE CROW'S nest of the three-masted frigate and peered across the ocean toward the swampy African coastline—nearly a mile away—where he could see the *Atlanta's* pinnace launching. He leaned over the edge of the barrel and yelled toward the main deck.

"Pinnace, ho!"

"Pinnace, ho!" came the echoing cries as his message was relayed from mouth to mouth until it reached the captain.

On the quarterdeck, Captain Meredith stepped toward the rail with his hand extended to shield his eyes from the setting sun on their left, squinting toward the coast. He pulled a small brass looking glass from his pocket, pulled it out to its full length, and looked again. Having spotted his target, he collapsed the glass and cast a look of wonder up at Zale as he put it back in his pocket.

Zale grinned. He wanted to make good and sure the captain knew he was the best man for this job, and relished opportunities to do so.

He caught a glimpse of Berian on the poop deck. The reverend gave him that discomfiting, calculating gaze again, then turned to watch the progress of the pinnace. Zale squirmed. Not for the first time, he wished he knew what went on behind those hooded golden eyes.

The *Atlanta* had been sitting in the Bight of Benin off the coast of Whydah for over a month while the captain and supercargo had negotiated trade with the local slave merchants. Since they'd arrived and begun trading the cargo they'd brought for the human cargo that would make the Middle Passage with them, Zale was happier than ever that Captain

Meredith had seen fit to employ him as a lookout. Cramped legs were a small price to pay for the relative privacy and—now that they had loaded over two hundred Africans into the hold—fresh air afforded by his perch. Besides, he was used to spending prolonged periods watching the world from inside a tank—or a barrel, as the case may be.

A whiff of the result of so many human bodies confined to a space far too small and with only the most basic of basic amenities assaulted his nose. The odour rose on the evening air, carried by the barely-clothed men, women, and even a few children emerging from the hold to stretch and eat their victuals. Catching cat naps in the crow's nest might be less comfortable than a hammock below decks, but unlike the rest of the crew, Zale's olfactory senses never seemed to acclimate to the stench. He'd slept in pig barns that smelled sweeter than this stinking tub. And up here, he got some small relief from the tropical heat at night, whereas below decks, the heat never seemed to wane.

He glanced at Berian, who was mopping his brow with a soiled hand-kerchief, and a small shred of pity for the man pricked him. Cherub or not, this heat would be uncomfortable to anyone not used to it. Abela stood beside Reverend Berian in a freshly-laundered olive-coloured muslin dress and straw sun hat she had purchased, waving a Japanese-style paper fan at herself and alternately watching the advancing boat and the activities on the deck.

The slaves were coming abovedeck for their evening exercise and to eat supper—maize gruel and boiled yams prepared from the food stocks with which the steward had recently replenished the holds. The crewmen were on high alert, as they always were when the slaves were on deck, despite the fetters that bound the African men into pairs by the legs—a necessary precaution, Zale had been told, while in sight of the African coast. According to Kofi, meals were always the most likely time for the newly boarded Africans—especially the men—to do something stupid.

"Many Africans, dey t'ink that white men take dem on these strange floating houses to make dem fat, and then eat dem. Many o' dem would rather drown then die that way," Kofi had said with a wry smile not long after they had reached this accursed spot. Kofi had been crouched against the mizzenmast next to Zale while they watched another load of Africans being brought on board. "That's why I'm here. To tell dem dey's only to be worked to deat', not eaten."

He grinned sardonically, revealing perfect white teeth, then his smile faltered. Zale wondered if Kofi might be thinking of his family.

The whole time they had been on the coastline, Kofi had anxiously scanned the faces of each new load of slaves brought on board, but his shoulders had always slumped in disappointment at the end. Zale wished he knew how to help the man. He asked Abela about it once, whether the lumasi had the ability to find specific people that *weren't* being purposely hidden somehow.

"You said you had looked for my mother and me and couldn't find us because of some kind of magical shielding—"

"Not magic. It's science."

"All *right*. Anyway, can you usually find other people?"

She had hesitated before replying. "Yeees. Kind of. Every person has a frequency or a resonance that is unique to them. We—cherubim—can sense those frequencies in people around us, and we have devices called finders to look for people who are farther away. But we need to know what their frequency is first."

"Is that what Berian's pocket watch is? A finder?"

Abela looked startled. "I'm not sure. I haven't seen the face of it. What does it look like?"

"Like a red stone cat eye."

Abela's eyes widened slightly, but whatever had surprised her, she said nothing about it.

"Yes, that is a type of finder. Unfortunately, in regards to your friend Kofi's family, we have no idea who we are looking for, so I fear it would not be of much use."

Zale nodded, disappointed. "Well, thanks anyway."

Now, Kofi stood on the main deck, dishing out thick gruel from an enormous copper cauldron. Pairs of fettered men queued before the cauldron with little wooden tubs, waiting for Kofi to fill them before returning to the area of the main deck allotted for them and the rest of their messmates. The two servers distributed a salt cracker each to the other eight men in their circle, then squatted next to their fellow sufferers and dug into the gruel with small wooden spoons.

The women and children had it easier, not being restrained with anything. They had already been served and were eating on the quarterdeck. Some of them had finished and were walking about, stretching their legs. There were fewer women than men, and they were young, for the most part—Zale guessed some of them were even around his own age. There were five children under twelve amongst them, and despite their circumstances, the boys and girls made some attempt at play with a game that reminded Zale of Scotch-hoppers—except for one small boy, who hung listlessly on his mother's neck.

Zale wondered if the child were falling ill. Ever since Kofi had told him of the malaise, he'd wondered what he would do if someone else on board fell sick. Should he try to heal them as he had healed Kofi? Could he even do something like that again? He wasn't quite sure he understood what he had done the first time, nor how he might be able to affect different illnesses. He sent a small prayer heavenward that the child would remain healthy. He didn't want to have to test his ability in that regard again, especially on a small boy.

The pinnace had approached close enough for Zale to make out the faces of the *Atlanta's* supercargo, the two sailors who rowed it, and the passenger who sat in the midst of its bags and barrels. The gentleman wore a black jacket despite the sweltering heat, but his bright red hair was uncovered. The man kept peering anxiously at the decks of the *Atlanta*, scanning the people on board as though looking for someone.

It was Robert Cox.

What in the name of King George is he doing here?

Zale didn't have long to wait for an answer. No sooner had Robert climbed aboard and had a brief discussion with a flushed-looking Captain Meredith on the quarterdeck than the captain cupped a hand to his mouth and called toward the crow's nest.

"Mr. Teague! Get down here!"

Some of the slave men in the group nearest the stern—below the rail where the captain stood—cowered a bit until they realized that his shout was not directed at them. Cautiously, they resumed eating.

Zale swung his way down through the rigging as nimbly as though he had been doing it all his life—indeed, after four months, he'd had plenty of practise. With each minute that had passed since recognizing Robert, the pressure in his chest had mounted. What could have brought him so far? Had he found out the truth of Zale's crime against him at last and come to wreak his revenge?

On Zale's way to the quarterdeck, he passed Kofi. Finished serving for the evening, his friend had begun assisting the ship's surgeon in doing a nightly check of each of the Africans on deck. Mr. Wesley would inspect their mouths and skin for symptoms of disease or infirmity, and Kofi would administer a mouthful of lime juice to each person, which they would swish and spit overboard before being sent below decks again. Several of the men eyed the proceedings balefully as they waited their turn. As

Zale reached the top of the ladder to the quarterdeck, the little boy with his head on his mother's shoulder watched Zale without blinking, not even lifting his head. He looked unnaturally pale.

Abela and Reverend Berian had descended from the poop deck and come forward to stand with the captain and Robert.

Robert bowed, his speech jilted as he greeted them, particularly Abela. Mr. Crow also joined them, standing with his arms crossed.

Zale joined the group and bowed slightly. "Aye, sir?" he said to the captain.

"Mr. Cox," said Mr. Berian with a bow of his shoulders. "What has happened, sir? Why have you come so far to find us?"

"The direst of reasons, I'm afraid, sir." Robert glanced once more at Abela, his face reddening, and then turned toward Zale and clapped him on the arm. "You have no idea how good it is to find you hale and hearty, my good man."

Zale, once again caught off-guard by Robert's demeanour, smiled uncertainly.

"Why wouldn't I be?"

Robert gave him a look that said he was the bearer of ill news, then turned toward the captain.

"Captain Meredith, may we use your chambers for a private discussion, please?"

Crow scowled, but said nothing.

The captain merely nodded. "Of course, sir. Whatever you need. In fact, you may consider them your chambers for the remainder of the voyage. I shall move below decks."

"What? No, I'll not hear of it."

"But, sir, 'tis only proper."

Robert looked frustrated. "We shall speak of it later, Captain. First, I must speak with Mr. Teague." He turned to Zale and held out his arm toward the captain's cabin. "After you."

Berian stepped forward. "Mr. Cox, may we also attend?" He indicated himself and Abela, who waited beside him with the same question on her face. "The boy's welfare is of primary concern to us both."

"Oh. I see." Robert cleared his throat and glanced uncertainly at Zale. "'Tis up to you, Mr. Teague."

Zale looked at the two cherubim. He wished he could accept for Abela and not for Berian, but really, he had no reason to exclude the minister besides personal annoyance. He nodded. "Aye, they had best come, too."

Berian gave Zale a sharp nod of acknowledgement, a hint of a curl at the corner of his mouth as he moved past him and Robert to the captain's cabin door at the rear of the quarterdeck. Abela only looked worried as she followed the reverend. Robert ducked through the door of the cabin next.

Trepidation filling him, Zale followed, wondering what dire turn his life was about to take now.

34

WINDS OF FORTUNE

THE CAPTAIN'S CHAMBERS WERE TASTEFULLY appointed in light blue and cream accented with mahogany, with a bank of paned windows at the stern giving a view of the open sea. An elegantly carved wooden desk sat in front of them, and a matching four-poster bed rested along the port side. A walled-off privy along the starboard end of the room had been made available for Abela's use—the only lady on board, or the only free one, at any rate—so she would not have to use the heads at the bow, which the rest of the crew shared. A large table graced the centre of the airy space.

The group assembled at the captain's desk, Robert in the captain's chair, Zale and the others standing on the other side of it.

"There is no easy way to say this," Robert began, rubbing his hand over his face. His scars were puckered in worry and exhaustion, his red hair stuck out in wind-blown clumps, and the day's stubble prickled over his chin. He regarded Zale with hazel eyes.

Zale's gut stretched tight enough to snap. When he thought he could wait no longer, Robert continued.

"Zale, I fear you are in grave danger. It shames me to admit that my brother is involved."

Abela frowned in alarm. "What has Gryffyn done now?"

Robert's gaze snapped to her face, and her eyes widened.

"You forget yourself, Miss Bethel."

Her face reddened to a burnished copper colour.

"I mean *Mr. Cox.* My apologies." She dropped her gaze.

The corner of Robert's mouth twitched, and he turned back to Zale.

"After you left, I began making enquiries around Bristol about the gypsies I had seen and learned that they were involved with some very wealthy and influential people. Imagine my surprise when a note from a

Mr. Chapman turned up on my office doorstep the next day and, almost as soon as I'd given it to Gryffyn, he left in a hurry. Suspicious of his activities, I followed. What I found rocked me to my toes. By the next morning, I was on a carriage to London in order to board another ship departing for Whydah in such short order. I knew I had to find you."

"Why?" Zale squeaked. He realized he'd been holding his breath, and took a gulp of air.

Robert pressed his lips together, looking as though what he had to share pained him.

"I followed Gryffyn to a secret meeting in an empty storehouse by the river. My brother and the other people in attendance wore black hooded robes, as though they were some sort of druids or devil's enclave." Robert snorted in contempt. "At first, I thought they were all men, but there was a woman there. I think it was the gypsy woman."

"Josefine?"

Robert shook his head. "They did not give names. Though the gypsy man had said his name was Eric when I met him. Do you know him?"

Zale nodded. "Yes. Josefine Chapman is Eric's daughter. He rarely travels anywhere without her. Was Eric there?"

"Yes, I believe so. Perhaps the woman was this Josefine. At any rate, she is the one who summoned the—the spirit."

Zale exchanged glances with Abela and Berian.

Robert frowned. "Disbelieve me if you will, but I know what I saw."

"Sir, we believe you." Abela gave a gentle smile. "We know better than most the activities of spirits in this world."

Robert's eyes widened in surprise as he looked between them. Zale was reminded of the boy he used to play with in the orchard when they were young.

"You—you believe me?"

Zale nodded. After what he'd learned, it would be foolish to doubt that Robert could have seen Josefine summon a spirit. Besides, she'd had a reputation for being able to talk to spirits, often scrying for her customers with a crystal ball. She'd even done it for him once, though he'd later found out she'd been pretending—which was why he'd thought it was merely a way she'd used to separate gullible people from their money. That didn't mean she couldn't do it in truth.

"Indeed," Berian said. "Now tell us, please—what did you see?"

Robert's jaw tightened. "A beautiful being of light. She summoned it through some kind of black stone mirror. He did not come into the room, but he appeared in the mirror."

"Did he have a name?" asked Abela.

Robert shook his head.

"The others only referred to him as 'Master.'"

"What did he say?" Abela's tone was sharp, and fire flashed in her eyes.

Berian cast her a warning glance. Zale looked back and forth between them, then at Robert, who had gone pale behind his freckles, his scars contrasting starkly against his healthy skin.

"There was a great deal that was said, but the part I can make sense of is this—this spirit, whomever he is, has been communicating with my brother and these other people for some time. When they told him about your disappearance, he grew extremely angry. He frightened this Eric very badly. For that matter, he frightened me, and he did not even know I was there."

Zale was thunderstruck. "So Gryffyn knew where I was that whole time? He knew I was with the Roma?"

Robert cocked his eyebrow at the unusual word, then nodded, his Adam's apple bobbing. "So it would seem. It also appeared that he and these others had some purpose in mind for you."

"They want to use him to break the chains of their masters," said Abela.

"What?" asked Zale at the same time as Robert said, "Pardon?"

Berian glared at her, but she ignored him.

"This spirit, he is one of the Grigori, the spirits condemned to the Abyss thousands of years ago. If he can speak through a scrying stone, that means the bonds that bind him have weakened further than we realized. Our time grows short."

Robert gave Abela and Berian a sharp look.

"This is not the first spirit I have seen—or rather, not the first to enter my life. The last one gave me these"—he pointed at the scars on his face—"and blinded me before I could catch a glimpse of him. Those who told me of him now deny that he existed." He looked at Zale. "It was that day by Chyandour Brook. You were there. Do you remember seeing it?"

Zale shook his head, swallowing through a throat filled with cotton. "No. I didn't see any spirit."

He glanced at Abela. He'd tried not to lie, but then he realized even that was not strictly true. He hadn't known it at the time, but Talwyn had been a spirit.

Robert looked disappointed, then glanced at all three of them.

"You are the first people I have ever heard speak of spirits as openly as next week's dinner guests." He blinked at Abela and Berian in turn. "Who are you people? And what do you know about these spirits?"

Abela cast a glance at Zale, who squirmed uncomfortably, then back at Robert.

"I am sorry, Mr. Cox. There are some questions I will not answer now. Please trust that we are working on the side of the Light." She put a hand on Zale's arm. "We *must* find your mother before the Order does. And we must do everything we can to keep you hidden from them." She turned to Robert. "Why did you come? You did not sail for four months to tell us of a magic mirror."

"No, indeed, I did not. It was to tell you this—they know Zale took passage on this ship, and that he is going to Barbados. They intend to wait for him there, and I fear their purpose to be most nefarious. I was worried they might have overtaken you here, actually. And there is something else." He looked at Zale. "They have your mother."

Zale's chest tightened. "In Bristol?"

"No. In a place called Tartarus, though I know of no city by that name. How bad must a place be to name it after the Greek underworld?"

Abela paled and pressed her lips together. Berian's eyes widened, and he swallowed. It was the first time Zale had seen him taken aback.

"It is as I feared," the reverend rumbled. "Thank you, Mr. Cox. You have done us a great service, and we shall repay you somehow. But there is no need for you to come further on this journey with us. If you could convince the captain that we must set sail for Barbados post-haste as you leave, it would be much appreciated."

"Leave?" Robert gave a scoffing laugh. "This ship is still the shortest way home to England. I shan't be leaving. But I shall be happy to speak to the captain for you. I believe that was his intention, anyway, as he told me that the holds are full to bursting."

"Would you kindly do so now, please, sir?" Berian gave Robert a firm stare.

Robert hesitated, looking as though he were deciding whether or not he should be affronted at Berian's brusque manner, but then stood.

"Aye, sir, if it pleases you," he said graciously.

"It does. Thank you."

After Robert had stepped out to speak to the captain, Zale turned to face his and his mother's guardians.

"So we are still going to Barbados, then? Where is this Tartarus? Somewhere in the West Indies?"

Abela shook her head. When she spoke, her voice quivered. "If only it were someplace so droll. No, we are not going to a place named after Tartarus. We are going to the real Tartarus."

Zale gaped. "Say that again?"

The portly reverend, in a voice like the grave, said, "We are going to hell, son."

*

By the time Robert emerged onto the quarterdeck to stand at the rail with Captain Meredith, all but a few of the women slaves had been taken below, and sailors were already scurrying around the ship, preparing to make way. When Captain Meredith noticed Robert, his eyes widened in surprise.

"Is all well, Mr. Cox? You look quite done in. I shall have my things removed from your cabin immediately, so you may take your rest. Or will you be returning landward, after all?"

"No, no, captain. It is as I said, I will be staying at least as far as Barbados, and possibly all the way home. But I insist that I shall sleep below with the crew. You have much greater need of your quarters than I."

This time, the captain did not object.

"As long as you're certain. Thank you, Mr. Cox. I will have a space prepared immediately."

He turned and barked at a cabin boy, who hurried off to comply.

Robert paused to watch several sailors fitting iron fetters around the ankles of the barely-clothed slave women that remained on deck. He was glad he had convinced Gryffyn to allow for the slaves to be provided with a square of cloth each once they were brought on board. He knew many slaving vessels did not even provide that, and no African slave dealer ever sent their wares with a stitch of covering more than God had provided them. Seeing the women with so much flesh still exposed, he realized Gryffyn had gone with only the barest requirement of his promise.

"I say, is it quite necessary to shackle the women? Surely they pose no threat."

Captain Meredith followed Robert's gaze.

"Aye, but only until we are out to sea. It is when we first set sail that many of these Africans attempt to jump overboard, thinking they can at least die in sight of their own country. Our linguist, Smith, has tried to calm their fears, but we thought it best not to take chances."

Robert nodded, catching the eye of the only remaining woman there, who held a small boy in her arms while she waited for the irons to be secured around her ankles. The boy laid his head on his mother's shoulder, not unlike his nephew, Andrew, on the shoulder of his eldest brother's wife, Lady Alverton. The image was so picturesque and familiar, though in a different place and with skin a different colour, that Robert's conscience pricked him.

"I did all I could," he muttered to himself.

"Pardon me, sir?" said the captain.

"Never mind."

"Are you ready to make way, then? I want to be well out to sea before dark."

"Aye, captain. Make way."

Captain Meredith moved off and began barking orders, sending sailors scurrying to raise anchor and trim sails.

Robert watched the woman and her child as they were herded below decks, down to the special compartment he knew had been constructed for them on the orlop deck by means of a temporary bulkhead, which would separate the women and children from the men. He considered following her down to see the arrangement himself, but decided to wait. His stomach still dry-heaved on occasion from the smell that wafted up this far. He wondered how he would manage sleeping below, and prayed his constitution became accustomed to it soon.

Gryffyn, lured by the huge profit margins such commerce could bring, had insisted on trading in slaves on this voyage—no doubt prodded by his father-in-law, who had made his fortune in the trade. Robert had objected. He had been avidly following the work of the tireless abolitionist Thomas Clarkson, and had even once discussed the matter of abolition at length with House representative Mr. Wilberforce. Robert was persuaded that the trade, as a whole, was an affront to all of Christendom—but his objections were overruled. As usual, what Gryffyn wanted, Gryffyn got.

Now, standing on the vessel itself, he looked out over the bay at the silhouettes of masts representing countries all over the world, including the ship he'd arrived on only this morning. Even had he been able to persuade his brother not to join the slave trade, there would have been plenty of others willing to take their company's place. The fortunes to be made were simply too tempting.

In the end, he'd consoled himself with the idea that, with the money this cargo earned, he'd be able to do a great deal of good elsewhere. How many of Bristol's poor could be fed and clothed with the money gained from the sale of a single black slave in the New World?

Someone came to stand at the rail beside him. He turned, and started when he discovered Miss Bethel standing there, her golden eyes blazing, her dark cheeks and green dress haloed in gold by the setting sun. She studied him, and those fiery eyes cut right to his soul. He wondered again who she was—the mulatto daughter of a Jamaican planter, perhaps? He did not know many of the landholders on that island. But her next words cast doubt on the idea.

"Is the cost worth it, Mr. Cox?" she asked, somehow encompassing the harbour full of vessels, the fort on the hill over three miles away, and the hold full of Africans with a single flick of her eyes, cocking her head so that her soft corkscrew curls shifted to cover one of them.

He wanted to object, to defend himself. He wanted to reach out and push the hair back into place. But in the face of those piercing, bewitching eyes, he found himself tongue-tied and motionless as a statue.

She waited for only a moment before walking away, leaving him wondering how a single person could simultaneously provoke and intrigue him beyond reason. Who was this Miss Abela Bethel?

Suddenly, he was looking forward to the weeks of the Middle Passage. Sailing together with this divine creature on a small vessel would be the perfect time to find out.

35

JUDITH'S SECRET

Fire Lake
June 5, AD 1799/2 Didymoi 4155 EK
Calandra's 18th Birthday

ON THE TWO-HOUR WALK TO her family property, Calandra kept finding her hand fluttering near her throat, searching for what was no longer there. While the weight of her Tear was missing from her neck, the place inside her chest was an entire ocean of emptiness. Damon's words kept echoing through her mind. *You will fail in your duty and go Mad. Everyone is bound to leave you eventually.*

Judith walked through the forest ahead of her, and Osaze followed behind. Zoe, the siren who had accompanied her and Adonia on their walk the evening before, trailed at the rear, her dark brown braided ponytail swinging as she marched. Calandra tried not to begrudge her presence, though she would have preferred to have as little company as possible today. She was only thankful she had convinced her aunt that no further entourage was necessary for this day trip.

"It's up ahead," said Judith, pointing through the trees.

The path curved around a stand of scrubby pines, thick with undergrowth, into a clearing. When they rounded the corner, Calandra paused, overcome by the charm and beauty of the property that opened before her eyes. Elpida. *Hope.* Her mother's property. Her property.

Her hand reached for her throat again, and Osaze caught it in his. Judith and Zoe were already picking their way down the steep path ahead of them.

"Don't worry," he whispered, squeezing her fingers. "We'll get it back. Come on."

She smiled at him in gratitude. He returned the smile, then dropped her hand so she could walk ahead of him.

The path led down to a tidy yard with a stone stable, large stone warehouse, wine press, and several smaller outbuildings. At the far end, in the centre of a stunning garden, stood a grand whitewashed plastered-brick villa, with a red tile roof and a columned portico and wings extending along either side of a long U-shape swimming pool. In the centre of the pool was a statue of black stone portraying a naked human boy holding an amphora from which water streamed. He reminded Calandra of Osaze as a boy, though Osaze wouldn't have dreamed of posing naked in swimming pools. She didn't glance around at him, but she did smile to herself.

Surrounding the yard proper and sloping away below it, a patchwork system of small fields decorated the rolling mountainside, some with grapes on trellises, some with olives, cacao, or other fruit trees, and some pastureland where sheep and goats grazed contentedly. Chickens wandered around the yard, clucking softly and pecking at bugs. In the fields and yard, workers tended crops or mended tools. Calandra counted at least two dozen women, which seemed like a much higher number than a property such as this required for its maintenance. And why were there no men among the field workers? She frowned. She'd have to speak to the steward about this.

No sooner had the thought entered her mind than a fit, matronly woman in a lilac-coloured ankle-length tunic trimmed with beige embroidery came striding toward them from the house. When she reached Calandra, she bowed, pressing her bunched fingers to her forehead in salute. Her tanned face had very few lines, and the ones it did possess indicated an even temperament. Her green eyes glittered with their own light beneath sun-kissed caramel locks wrapped around her head in thick braids. She looked exactly as Calandra remembered.

"Steward Rhea," Calandra said, dipping her chin. "You look well. I am sorry to come with no notice, but it was not to be helped, I'm afraid."

"Princess Calandra, what an honour to welcome you here. You have changed a great deal since your last visit, I must say. And not to worry, we have been expecting you."

Calandra started. "You have? I did not know I was coming myself until this morning. Who alerted you and told you of my new title?"

"I did," said Judith, blushing. "I wanted them to be prepared for our coming."

"How did you manage it?" Calandra wondered, thinking of their hurried consultation with Adonia to request permission and their subsequent immediate departure.

Rhea smiled. "We have a communication stone that we keep in the house, m'lady."

"Ah, I see."

Despite the blackouts, Adonia had ensured that every town on the island had at least one active communication stone that was used for relaying messages, and which was available for public use for a fee. The fee would have been waived for an emissary of the royal party. Calandra thought she understood now, and felt a little embarrassed for not thinking of it herself.

She smiled at her lady's maid. "Well done, Judith. That was prudent of you."

Judith curtsied. "Thank you, your highness."

Calandra cleared her throat. She was still getting used to her new title and styling.

Rhea turned toward the lady's maid.

"Hello, Judith. Delightful to see you again."

Judith smiled and curtsied. "You, too, Auntie."

Auntie?

"You must be exhausted after your journey." Rhea gestured toward the villa. "Please, come into the house for some refreshment."

Calandra fell into place beside the steward and her party followed behind. She wondered what relationship existed between Judith and the staff here. Was Rhea her blood aunt, or had she only used that as a term of respect for someone she had known since childhood? Calandra would have to ask the girl later.

They made their way toward the welcoming garden oasis, and when Calandra stepped onto the dark flagstone pathway that bordered the pool, she felt she had been transported into paradise. The attention to detail in the garden was exquisite. The sizes and textures of each plant complimented, not competed, with the next, and not a single plant showed any sign of blight or damage.

"Who is the Head Gardener?" Calandra asked, admiring the white blooms of a plumeria tree as they passed, surprised it would grow at this elevation.

Rhea smiled. "I am."

Calandra glanced at her in surprise. "How do you have time to oversee the property and maintain such a delightful garden, also?"

Rhea touched a drooping purple orchid leaf as they passed and it sprang back to full vigour.

"I do not do it alone. My sister, Ignatia, assists me. She and I both studied plant healing with your mother, you know."

Calandra swallowed, preventing her hand from reaching for her absent Tear.

"No, I did not know that."

They reached the shaded portico and stepped through vaulted glass-paned doors into a cool interior of whitewashed stone, neutral colours, and pleasing textures accented with even more plants, the green fronds of fan palms and philodendrons accentuating the calm atmosphere. A dozen serving women in white tunics stood waiting in front of a stone fireplace to greet her, an even mix of human and undine, from what Calandra could see. They gave crisp bowed salutes in unison when she stepped through the door.

"Thank you all. You honour me."

Calandra noted again that there seemed to be far more servants than necessary for the upkeep of even such a villa as this—and again, no *douloi*. Did none of the women here have consorts? Did Rhea not employ even a few men to do heavy labour and provide children or companionship for any women who wished it? Calandra did not like the practice of sharing men, but she knew some noblewomen in the city ran their households that way. Sometimes, one did one's best with what income and availability allowed.

Rhea clapped at the servants. "You may return to your duties. If you will follow me, your highness?"

The servants dispersed, and Rhea led them toward the dining room beyond the wood-mantled fireplace. A long rustic dark-stained wooden table surrounded by straight-backed chairs awaited them, one end pre-pared with a light lunch and a place setting for one. Calandra gazed long-ingly at the cup of chilled white wine. Fruit, cheese, and cold cuts tempted her from a trencher within easy reach of the chair.

Zoe took up position near the table, as did Osaze, and Judith hung back. Several white-liveried servants appeared.

"Please, sit." Rhea indicated the table. "Your servants may follow Ster-gia into the kitchen for their refreshment."

She indicated a pleasantly plump young lady with dark brown eyes and a long blond braid who waited expectantly.

Calandra glanced at Osaze with regret. Even here, they would be subject to the watchful eyes of others. She nodded.

Osaze's expression tightened enough for her to know he didn't want to go, and their bond confirmed his protectiveness. He didn't know these people and hesitated to leave her alone. It had been the same everywhere they had gone on their journey. Fortunately, in most situations, he was permitted to remain with her.

The irony was not lost on her—three weeks ago, she'd never have guessed that a loyal freeman would be a much more dedicated bodyguard than a *doulos*. Now, she could hardly believe she'd ever thought otherwise.

Zoe stepped forward. "If I may speak, your highness, I would stay with you."

Calandra blinked in surprise. Of all her companions, she had the least desire to keep company with Zoe. She didn't have anything against the siren, but she felt least able to let down her guard around her. She wondered if, perhaps, Adonia had not thought one spy enough. Zoe could be present in situations where Judith may not.

"I would keep my consort-elect with me," Calandra heard herself say. "He may sit and take his refreshment here."

She softened any perceived slight Zoe may have felt by smiling at her.

"Thank you for your dedication, Singer kor'Dione. Please, take your leisure for the day. Explore the grounds or enjoy a swim. Osaze is capable of seeing to my protection on his own in this place. I doubt anyone here would see fit to harm me, regardless."

Zoe didn't look so sure, but she gave a crisp salute. "Yes, your highness."

The siren turned and followed Stergia and Judith out of the room. As soon as the two maids stepped through the tall swinging wooden door into the kitchen, a friendly conversation began between them, muffled as the door fell back into place. *They must know each other.*

Calandra wondered again at Judith's familiarity with the people here. When Judith said she knew the place and could guide them, Calandra had assumed it was only because of her connections within the community. In such a small place, everyone likely knew where everything was, and especially a local *latifundium*.

Then she realized she had her answer—in a community as small as Fire Lake, everyone also knew everyone else. For all Calandra knew, Judith and Stergia might have been childhood playmates.

Calandra smiled, glad that Judith would be at ease here. Then she harrumphed quietly to herself.

That girl would be at ease in the halls of Tartarus.

Calandra and Osaze sat—the bond reflecting Osaze's relief at

Calandra's decision—with Calandra at the head of the table. He placed his hand on the table as he sat. She casually brushed his fingers as though by accident while reaching for her water glass and felt a corresponding surge of warmth through the bond. She glanced at him from below her lashes, then back toward their hostess, who stood to the side.

"Is there anything else you need right now, your highness?"

Calandra smiled. "Yes. Please, sit and take this repast with us and tell me about this place. I have read the reports, but they did nothing to prepare me for what I have seen so far. It is stunning—both grander and more charming than I expected or remembered. It would please me to know the woman responsible for that."

Rhea's eyes widened slightly, and then her face crinkled in a delighted smile.

"It would be my pleasure, your highness. Thank you."

Place settings were laid for both Osaze and Rhea by two silent, efficient, pleasant-looking human women in white, and the diners began to sate their hunger and thirst. Rhea told Calandra about the bumper crop of wine grapes they were expecting, regaled her with a few tales from her school days with Delphine, and explained how they got their goods to market by a combination of wagons and a barge along the Fire River.

"But why are there so many workers? Surely they are not all needed."

Calandra grabbed another handful of luscious grapes from the trencher and popped one into her mouth.

"They are not all servants of the estate. Some of them are tenants who plow their own plots, rented with a small percentage of the harvest each year. It was a system your mother began as a way to help local farmwomen—especially human women, who may have difficulty finding employment in other ways."

Calandra nodded. "And what of the *douloi?* I haven't seen a single man except Osaze since we arrived. Nor did any *douloi* from Elpida come to the summons yesterday. Are there no men here at all?"

Rhea's eyes clouded and she glanced at Osaze, who kept up his mechanical, blank-faced eating motions.

"Your mother decided there were to be no . . . no *douloi* in Elpida. And there have not been, not for eighteen years."

Calandra stared at her in astonishment. "But what of companionship? Or heavy labour? Or even children? Do none of you desire those?"

Rhea looked like she was choosing her words very carefully.

"Of course we do. We are no different than anyone else. We—"

She cut off as the sound of lively conversation rang through the front hall, the speakers hidden by the massive stone fireplace. Rhea looked stricken as she stared toward the sound.

The voices were those of a woman and a man. They teased each other, breaking into laughter as they rounded the fireplace and came into view. The woman looked to be in her late forties, and she had the same sun-kissed chestnut-coloured hair as Rhea trailing down her back in a braid, with wisps creating a halo of curls around her face. The man looked Turkish or Lebanese, with good bone structure, curly black hair, and black eyes.

When the two of them saw the people seated at the table, the smiles disappeared from their faces and they froze in their tracks. The man's face went as blank as Osaze's, but it was far too late. Calandra knew the truth—the man was Unredeemed. She stared at the couple in astonishment.

"Rhea," the woman said, glancing uncertainly between the diners, "you never mentioned we were having company today."

Rhea stood, obviously shaken.

"The messenger must not have found you. Princess Calandra, may I introduce my sister, Ignatia. And this is her . . . husband, Jacob."

Calandra rose slowly, staring at the couple, who stared back, proper greeting etiquette completely forgotten.

Not consort. Husband.

A young boy of maybe four, with a head of thick dark curls and dark skin like Jacob's, burst into the room through the swinging wooden door from the kitchen.

"Mommy! You aren't going to believe who is here! Judy came, and I told her you would be so excited to see her. She's in the kitchen, Mommy."

He tugged at Ignatia's hand and then stopped, catching the mood in the room, and looked around at all the people who were staring at him. Osaze had risen, too, and he was glancing in wonder between Jacob and the child.

Calandra stepped toward the boy as though in a dream, then squatted before him. He stared back with a wide, unabashed gaze, his eyes the glimmering dark iridescent green of an undine's.

"What is your name?" she asked.

"Zeke. What's yours?"

"Calandra. Are you an undine?"

"'Course I am. Aren't you?"

The door from the kitchen crashed open and in ran Judith, yelling "Ezeki—"

Catching sight of their benumbed faces, she stopped short and looked uncertainly between them.

Calandra stood and looked at her lady's maid. "How do you know this boy, Judith? It's all right, you may speak freely to me."

Judith tensed, glancing between Rhea, Jacob, and Ignatia, then dropped her gaze and gave a small curtsy.

"He's my brother, your highness." She looked up at Ignatia and Jacob. "Hello, Mom. Hello, Dad."

36

HOUSE OF HOPE

THE KITCHEN DOOR SWUNG OPEN and Zoe strode into the room, stopping and taking in the tableau of stunned faces in a glance.

"What is happening here?" she demanded, hands on her hips.

Calandra became unfrozen at last. She squatted before Zeke once more.

He stared back at her, grabbing his father's index finger and leaning back against his legs. Jacob squeezed his son's shoulder protectively.

Calandra glanced up at Jacob, hoping to reassure him, then smiled at the child.

"Zeke, do you know how special you are?"

Zeke, having caught the gravity of the adults, replied with only a nod. He sucked in his lips, blew them out, and giggled with a mischievous grin.

Calandra laughed and stood, facing the group in the room. She looked at each person in turn, finishing with Zoe, who was staring at Zeke with narrowed eyes. Of all the people here, Zoe was the only one who might not understand what she was about to say. The siren's face reflected suspicion and confusion.

Calandra looked at the others. "Not long ago, I found out something that changed the way I viewed the world. I had always thought my mother had gone Mad, or was going there, and had abandoned me to prevent herself from inflicting the chaos that would ensue when she succumbed completely."

The women around her exchanged glances.

"Two weeks ago, I was able to access a message my mother had left for me. She said she thought she was pregnant with a boy, and that she was leaving to protect him. She intended to return when the time was right."

She looked at Jacob. "My father was on the message, and he was free,

Unredeemed. Like you."

She glanced at Osaze, her eyes and heart asking permission to expose his secret fully. He seemed less certain than she was, but he could not feel the fear in the hearts around him, the sense that their entire world was about to come crashing down around them—much as she'd felt every moment since she had Released him. She knew if there were anywhere on this island where their secret would be safe, it would be right here.

Except with Zoe. The siren's face had registered shock when Calandra had spoken, which now hardened into disbelief. She crossed the distance between herself and Jacob in a heartbeat, grabbing his arm and twisting it behind him. He pushed Zeke away from him toward Ignatia and twisted his body away, ready to defend himself. The other women exploded into action.

"No!" Ignatia shouted. She shoved Zeke behind her and whirled to attack Zoe. Rhea and Judith both jumped forward to defend their menfolk. Zeke began to cry.

Zoe started crooning, and soon Jacob and Osaze both had a sleepy, dull look in their eyes. Zoe grabbed Jacob's arms and twisted them behind him with an iron grip, but he was no longer resisting.

"Stop!" yelled Calandra. "Singer, stand down and be silent. Everyone, stay where you are."

Zoe stopped singing, but did not let go of Jacob's arms. The others froze, waiting to see what Calandra would say—except Zeke, who ran to his father and flung his arms around his legs. Jacob, alert once more, appeared to be on the edge of panic.

"This is standard protocol for an Unredeemed adult male," Zoe said. "The first step that must be taken is to incapacitate them. The best defence is a strong offence. He could have attacked you or any of these other women at any time."

"The only one to attack anyone here has been you. And you will stand down, as I told you. I take full responsibility for the consequences."

Zoe's eyes narrowed, and she looked like she may still disobey. But then she released Jacob's arms and stepped back. Her hand moved toward her travel half-*deiktis*, which was holstered on her back. At Calandra's warning look, she dropped her arm and contented herself with standing in a ready stance between Calandra and Jacob.

Jacob gave a proper bow and salute. "Thank you, your highness."

Ignatia also bowed and saluted, but said nothing. She scooped up the sniffling Zeke and held him on her hip, then shifted her body slightly between Jacob and Calandra, uncertainty and fear flowing from her like water from a spring.

"Do not fear," said Calandra.

She stepped away from Zoe and took Osaze's hand, weaving her fingers between his. He glanced at her in alarm and she smiled reassuringly.

"I, too, have a secret. I would like you all to meet Osaze bet'Urbi, my consort-elect and a freeman."

The release of emotion in the room nearly overwhelmed Calandra, but the intensity soon subsided. Rhea, Jacob, and Ignatia relaxed, breaking into smiles, then swarmed forward to greet Osaze and shake his hand. Zoe held back, staring around her in disbelief, glaring at Calandra. Zoe could be a problem. But she had already seen too much. Calandra would have to deal with her later.

Judith stepped toward Calandra, her face wreathed in smiles.

"I *knew* it! Well, I didn't really know it, but I'd hoped it. You were so careful, and you—" she turned toward Osaze, "you were so good at concealing your true state. How long have you been Free?" She placed a slight emphasis on the last word, as though it meant something more than it usually did.

Osaze smiled uncertainly. "Only two weeks."

Calandra watched him, beaming. Here was Osaze, *her* Osaze, talking to other people like any woman was free to do at all times. He was smiling, and she watched his tense shoulders relax, bit by bit, as the others made polite conversation.

Jacob clasped his forearm in greeting.

"I have been on this island for twenty-seven years, and have been Free for seventeen of those years—yet always in fear of the day when something like this would happen. How are you managing to live with it right in the palace? You must be on guard every second!"

Osaze nodded. "It has been difficult. At times, I thought I would be caught for sure, but Calandra has helped me. And there is a man in the palace who survived for forty-five years Unredeemed, until they caught him recently, so I know it can be done."

The conversation in the room went silent.

Rhea stared at Osaze. "Gerrick has been caught? What of Thea?"

"You know Gerrick and Thea?" Calandra's throat felt thick.

Rhea and Ignatia turned worried eyes toward her.

"Yes," said Rhea. "She had recently become headmistress when we were at the Academy. She . . . doesn't know about us. It took Ignatia and

I a while to come around to Delphine's ideas, and we did not know that it had been Thea and Gerrick who had inspired her research until long after our Academy days."

Thea inspired my mother?

Calandra glanced at Osaze. She hadn't had time to tell him what Adonia had declared about Thea's fate last night.

"Gerrick has been Redeemed by Adonia. Thea is in prison, and last night, Adonia told me that after Thea helps me heal the Heartstone, she is to be executed. I am to lead the Healing Ceremony at Summer Solstice, after Osaze and I are bonded."

Rhea covered her mouth, her green eyes wide. Ignatia pulled Zeke's head into her shoulder and nuzzled him, turning away, and Jacob laid a comforting hand on her back. Judith watched her mistress with sad eyes.

Calandra stared at the others, their emotions enlarging the hollow cavern inside her. *You will fail in your duty . . .*

Osaze hesitated, glancing around at the others' reactions, and then took Calandra's hand. She squeezed it gratefully.

"I am curious about one thing," said Rhea. "If you saw your mother's message and know that the bonds cause the Madness, then why did you not know about us?"

Calandra gaped. "What do you mean, 'the bonds cause the Madness?'"

The prickly bundle of threads that remained ever-present in the back of her mind moved squarely to the front. She shook her head at the sensation and pushed them away again.

Ignatia tilted her head.

"You don't know about that either?" She turned to Rhea. "How could she not know about that? Wouldn't Delphine have told her?"

Rhea shrugged. "Maybe she thought it was too dangerous to put in the message." She glanced at Calandra. "But why didn't she tell you to seek us out?"

"I only got to see part of the message before Adonia had the Tear blanked. By Thea. Only this morning, I discovered that Thea, while appearing to comply with Adonia's demands, actually left the bulk of the stone's contents intact and secure. But—"

Judith clapped. "I have been waiting for you to see it all. I have been watching, because I knew that when you'd seen the message, you would know why I had been sent to you. Have you seen it yet?"

Calandra shook her head. "How would I know about you from the message? You must have been no older than Zeke when my mother knew you."

Judith's green eyes went wide, her thick eyelashes making her look like a pretty, innocent doe. "Why, the quaternaria, of course."

She thrust her ankle forward so it protruded from her hem, tilting it so the small tattoo behind the anklebone was exposed. Calandra looked at it, and something that had been bothering her popped into focus—that symbol had surrounded her since she had arrived in Elpida. Each of the plantation's staff had had one somewhere on their body. She could see Rhea's behind her left ear, and even Jacob had one on his wrist.

Elizabeth had also had one—Calandra had seen it on her arm as they had dragged her corpse away. And Matthew had one on his ankle.

Calandra's eyes snapped up to Judith's as the pieces fell into place. She'd dismissed the frequent sightings of the symbol with Judith's prior explanation of being something common to Fire Lake. Now, she knew it meant so much more.

"Elizabeth and Matthew. They were a part of this, weren't they?"

Judith nodded, her eyes brimming with tears, and moisture blurred Calandra's vision, too. Osaze squeezed her hand and stepped closer to her.

"I used to play with Matthew in the barn over yonder," Judith said, pointing outside. "Elizabeth was one of the tenants. She was like another auntie to me."

Calandra looked around at faces now filled with silent grief.

"I am so sorry. What happened, it was not right. I didn't know what to do to stop it."

Rhea came and took Calandra's free hand with cool fingers.

"Judith told us what happened. You could not have prevented what Adonia did to Elizabeth. What you did for Matthew, healing him like that, it was a good thing. And now that you know about him, and us, you can Release him and send him home."

Calandra shook her head. "No, I can't. Adonia has given him to Narcissa. He is to be her consort."

Rhea went pale and put her fingers to her mouth again, then continued. "But for your own sake, you must Release him."

"Why?"

Ignatia took Jacob's hand. "Because no being should enslave the mind of another. And you will never be truly happy if you do."

Rhea wrinkled her nose at her sister. "But beyond the morals of it, it is one type of bond that can lead to the Madness. And, with the strength of your power, you are at particular risk."

Calandra gaped. "You mentioned that earlier, about the bonds. So you know what causes the Madness?"

"Of course. And if you've seen your mother's message, you should, too."

"That's just it. I haven't had a chance to watch the rest of it."

Rhea turned to the kitchen door, where Stergia stood quietly observing everything. Calandra hadn't even noticed her come in.

"Bring me a reader, please, Stergia."

The girl disappeared into the kitchen, and Rhea held out her hand to Calandra.

"Where is the datastone?"

Calandra swallowed, glancing from Rhea, to Osaze, and back to Rhea again. Her hand fluttered to her throat and landed on bare skin.

"It's gone."

Rhea's brow furrowed. "Where is it?"

Calandra still didn't know how to explain what had happened to her Tear. It had been difficult enough making Osaze understand.

"I lost it."

37

CONSEQUENCES

AFTER THE EARTH-SHATTERING REVELATIONS OF the morning, Calandra spent the afternoon touring the property, meeting the families that lived there, and learning about the legacy her mother had left behind for her.

She kept wanting to pinch herself. She found herself longing for Tanni or Thea to see this. Then she remembered that it was this resistance, this Free Will Society, as they called themselves, that had been responsible for the death of Tanni's mother, and her joy faded somewhat.

The compound housed twelve complete families, human or undine women with human husbands, all of whom were free and alert and involved in family life. There were also several single women and over two dozen children, some of them foster children, including about eight more undine boys—all under the age of twelve and with no manifested powers to speak of, which was a disappointment. She would not find someone to help her with her task here.

Still, Calandra gaped at the sight of the boys—something she would not have believed possible only two weeks earlier. Here was the proof her mother had been seeking, or part of it, at least. Women bonded to Unredeemed men could have boys. Something about the nature of the *sklavia* bond prevented male offspring from being conceived.

According to Rhea, Delphine had been convinced that the consort bond combined with Redemption was the primary precursor to the Madness—not childbirth, as had so long been believed. To create the consort bond with a man who had been Redeemed required so much more than withholding his will from him. It involved taking his life force and channelling it through your own, essentially cementing open the channel of spirit between two beings, but in only one direction. The undine's powers were enhanced by her consort's spirit, but at a price—a price paid most dearly by the most empathic healers.

"Delphine believed that the original purpose of the consort bond was to give, to share one's own strength with another," Rhea said as they toured the grounds, "and that when we take what has not been given to us, it causes resistance in our minds, like the harmonic dissonance of certain notes sung together."

"Except it's a cognitive dissonance," added Rhea's adult daughter, Xeni, who had joined them for the tour. Calandra had met Xeni's son, Jason, earlier.

They walked uphill alongside a stream that tumbled down the mountain toward the estate, feeding the pool and cistern and irrigating the crops. Jacob carried Zeke on his shoulders, playing games with him and answering the boy's frequent questions with good-natured patience.

Calandra kept glancing at the two of them in wonder. Zoe, who followed at the rear, did the same, but with noticeable tension between her shoulders.

Ignatia took up the explanation. "Over time, this resistance dulls our empathy and brings consequences. For most of us, they are not very noticeable—we become shorter-tempered, maybe, less compassionate to the plights of others, or have difficulty in finding pleasure in our lives while seeking it with ever-increasing abandon. But for those whose empathy is the source of great power, like powerful sirens and healers—"

"They go Mad," Calandra finished for her.

It all made sense. In fact, it made such perfect sense that she could not believe it had taken three thousand years for anyone to discover the truth. It explained why she'd been having such trouble Seeing since she'd started taking the bonds. Except Matthew. She shook her head, not wanting to think about him right now.

"Why has this not been seen before now?"

Ignatia exchanged glances with her sister. "Well, for one, panaceas and sirens of the strength that often succumb to the Madness are rare, usually coming along only once in a generation or so."

Calandra nodded. That made sense.

"Still, at one point this should have been obvious, especially soon after it began. It would have had to have happened when we started Redeeming men, and within a generation, it should have been seen that . . ." A puzzle piece clicked into place. "That's what happened to Nadia, isn't it? She Redeemed Alessandro and went Mad, destroying the whole island of Atlantis because of it."

Except now the spirit of Alessandro had been revived somehow and had stolen her Tear. She still didn't know how Damon had done that.

Rhea cleared her throat, looking uncomfortable with something.

"According to what Delphine discovered on Atlantis, that is partially true. Nadia *enslaved* him, imprisoned him, and once the Madness took her, destroyed the entire island to ensure that he would never escape."

From her position in front of Calandra, Judith spoke over her shoulder.

"We are unclear on why she believed that was necessary, because it is very extreme. But we believe the association between the *sklavia* bond, the lack of male births, and the Madness was never made because so few of our people survived, and those who did may have been in collusion to forget or suppress the ways of our people prior to that."

That also made a strange sort of sense. Calandra gave her petite lady's maid an appraising look. The girl—no, *woman*, she no longer seemed at all like a girl to Calandra—had been full of surprises today.

"And why did she Redeem him in the first place?" After Damon's recent behaviour, Calandra had her suspicions, but she wondered if there was an official record.

She looked around at the Elpida undines who walked with her. They *all* looked uncomfortable now. She didn't understand why. "What? What is the matter?"

Rhea glanced at Judith, who turned to Calandra.

"We are not sure why Nadia enslaved Alessandro—we haven't found the answer to that. But we don't use the term 'Redeemed' in that way. We prefer to call it what it rightly is—enslavement. To redeem someone means to free them, not to enslave them. Saying 'Redemption' obscures and distorts the truth, doesn't it?"

"But we do free them," said Zoe. "We free them from their base, violent instincts."

Rhea gave her a compassionate glance. "I once thought as you do, so believe me when I say I understand why you believe this to be true. But my husband is not a man of violence, and neither are any of the Free men of my acquaintance. We have been told a lie, and we've perpetuated it by terms that blur the truth."

Zoe clenched her jaw and said nothing.

Calandra stared at the women, thunderstruck. Judith was absolutely right, and her explanation solidified the whispering thoughts Calandra had been thinking for the last several weeks. But it had never occurred to her that a term like that may have been numbing her to the full, vile implications of what they did as a culture—a culture that prided itself on its values of equality and freedom and compassion. Even now, noticing the bundle of fibres in her head, she resisted thinking of the men as enslaved, though that was what they were.

She'd been transferring chains of enslavement, not bonds of Redemption. The realization drained the colour out of her beautiful surroundings.

"So you have all bonded your consorts without the *sklavia* bond? Does that mean the *syzagos* bond on its own is safe to use?"

Osaze looked at her, understanding registering in his eyes.

Ignatia glanced at Jacob, who was engaged with showing Zeke how to skip stones. She turned to Calandra and Osaze.

"Once the *syzagos* bond has been made, it's nigh impossible to unmake. And if it is made with an enslaved man, the structure is wrong, too unidirectional, and can't be changed. I have tried for years to undo what I did, but I have not yet found the solution." She glanced down. "He bears it well," she murmured.

"As does my husband, Hammad," Rhea said. "For those few here who married after finding the Cause, they used no bond at all beyond their oaths to each other. They chose partners they loved, and love is about freedom and giving, not using those we care about to gain power and control. So I'm sorry, we do not know the secret of the *syzagos* bond. Perhaps it was always meant as another form of exploitation. Or perhaps we simply haven't learned the proper way to make it. And as far as the Madness . . ." She paused, meeting Calandra's eyes. "I'm afraid none of us here are powerful enough to know."

Calandra nodded and squeezed Osaze's hand, keeping her thoughts to herself for the remainder of the walk.

Later, back at the dining room table with afternoon sunlight streaming through the windows, Calandra broached the topic that had been on her mind since the shock of meeting Zeke had worn off.

"What you have here," she said quietly, "is the proof that is needed to bring real change on this island. Zeke, Jason, and the other boys—if we could show them to Adonia, to the archons and citizens, and explain to them what you explained to me, we may be able to abolish Redemp—the use of the *sklavia* bond permanently."

Ignatia's eyes widened in alarm, and she grasped her husband's hand. "Would you have us sacrifice our husbands and children to that woman's madness? I won't follow in Elizabeth and Matthew's footsteps!"

"Peace, sister," Rhea said, raising a hand toward Ignatia. She turned to

Calandra. "You think we have not thought of that? But, as Ignatia pointed out, it is not that simple. We could be sending our loved ones into the siren's net, and ourselves to the guillotine."

"So what is your plan? Convert one woman every few years to your cause and hide here until—what? What are you waiting for? For the island to flock to you?"

Rhea sat back and sighed.

Judith glanced at her aunt, then at Calandra. "No. We were expecting your mother to come back. Since she did not, we were going ahead with her backup plan, which was to help you to do what she could not."

Calandra folded her hands tightly on the table before her.

"And how do you intend to help me? You have the proof, but you will not risk yourselves to expose it. Am I to bear the only risk?"

Osaze cleared his throat.

"And Osaze, of course."

"Tell them about Damon," he said. "And your Tear."

38

THE PLAN

THE PEOPLE AT THE TABLE turned confused expressions toward Calandra. She sighed, then told her new friends about Damon and her dreams. They peppered her with questions until she had explained his claim that she would need him or another male undine to heal the Heartstone.

"Perhaps that is where the tradition of only allowing bonded undines to participate in the Healing Ceremony came from. Because you need male and female powers," Jacob said.

Calandra blinked in surprise that he would know so much, then caught herself. Why wouldn't he? Her bias ran deeper than she realized. She glanced at Osaze guiltily. "Perhaps."

She finished with what had happened to her Tear, and Damon's taunt that if she wanted it back, she would need to retrieve it from him in Atlantis.

"Why does she even need it at all?" asked Judith. "I can't approve of this Damon fellow, but quite aside from concerns about him, Atlantis isn't safe. Is it worth the risk?"

"I want to know who he is," said Rhea. "He claims to be Alessandro, but if he were an undine, then he would be long dead by now."

"He claims that his body died, but his spirit cannot be killed," said Calandra.

Rhea's eyes widened. "And Nadia must have known that, because it is his spirit that's imprisoned, isn't it? Are you sure he is an undine?"

Calandra blinked. She hadn't thought of that before.

"He looks like one. Except . . ." She thought about it. "Except he is the only undine I have ever seen with golden eyes. Until today, I thought that it was because he was male. But now that I've seen Ezekiel and the others . . ."

Rhea looked thoughtful. "Golden eyes. That is odd." She turned to Ignatia. "Does that mean anything to you?"

Ignatia frowned and shook her head. "It is right odd, but I've never read anything that would explain it. We have so few stones left from before the Sinking." Her frustration was plain.

Calandra turned to Judith. "To answer your question, before Damon took the Tear from me this morning, I was able to do a rough scan of the stone using an, um, uncut crystal."

She decided not to mention that it had been a sacred stone. No sense offending anyone.

"That is how I know that the Tear still contains a great deal of information. I have no idea what my mother may have left for me, but I hope it will tell me where to find her and my father. And, I hope, my brother. Unless, of course, you know where Mother went?"

The others exchanged blank looks.

Rhea shook her head. "I'm sorry. We didn't know she was going until she had left, and she didn't give any hint about where she went. Your father was from Cornwall, so perhaps they went there?"

Calandra sighed. So much for that.

"Damon may be lying about needing both male and female powers to heal the Heartstone, but I don't think he is. And since none of the boys here would be able to help, I must either find my brother or find a way to free Damon if I am to complete my task. Since I don't have time for a manhunt around Cornwall right now, I need to go to Atlantis to get my Tear back from Damon."

"I don't want you to go," Osaze interjected, frowning.

Calandra turned to him in surprise.

He took her hand.

"We're talking about some kind of ancient spirit who can visit someone inside their head and somehow steal something from around their neck. How am I supposed to protect you from him?"

Through the bond, Calandra sensed the breaking of a barrier, like he'd been holding these questions in ever since she had stumbled naked out of the lake this morning and told him what had happened. She opened her mouth to answer, but Osaze continued, words spilling from him like water.

"Even if it turns out I can see him, how can I fight a spirit? If he can take your Tear to the spirit world, imagine what he might be able to do to you. Forgive me, but this is too much risk for you to take to find a family you don't know is even alive, let alone able to help you. There must be another way. Perhaps he is lying. Once we are bonded, that could be enough. Or perhaps we could wait until one of these boys is a little older. They might get powers, we don't know."

Ignatia and Jacob shifted uncomfortably at that, exchanging glances. They obviously weren't keen on that idea.

Calandra shook her head. "We haven't the time to wait for these boys to grow older. The Heartstone is not intact enough to last even one more year."

Shocked murmurs and gasps circled the room.

"Can it be true?" Ignatia put her hand in front of her mouth.

Calandra gave them a solemn nod of confirmation, then laid her hand on Osaze's arm.

"It's not only about the Heartstone. If this were your mother, wouldn't you do everything you could to find her?"

His gaze never wavered, but she knew she had convinced him.

"What should I do if something happens to you?" Osaze covered their clasped hands with his free one.

"Do whatever you can to get away and come back here. Judith or Tanni will help you. You can trust them."

He frowned. "That is not what I meant. I don't care what happens to me. I don't want to lose you."

Calandra swallowed, her throat thick. "And I don't want to lose you either. If something happens to me, I want to know you'll be safe. Promise me you'll try to stay free and come here. Okay?"

She didn't let go until Osaze nodded his assent, though he still didn't look happy about it.

"I think we can all agree that it seems unwise to free this Damon, even if you could figure out how," Rhea said to assenting murmurs and nods.

"Why can't you Redeem this guy and take your Tear back?" Zoe asked, producing a round of frowns from the Free Will Society members. "What? Are we never supposed to do it to anyone, even temporarily?"

Calandra frowned, hoping she wouldn't regret bringing Zoe into their secret. There was little choice but to trust her now, though. So far, she had said little, but had made no further threats. Perhaps she could be won over.

Rhea cleared her throat and spoke to the siren.

"We don't." She indicated the people of Elpida with a gesture. "We believe there is always another way."

Osaze rumbled deep in his throat. "As much as I detest this practise of enslavement, as a matter of self-defence, Calandra, I believe you should make an exception to this rule. I do not trust this water spirit, and you said yourself that he seems to hold some kind of ability to befuddle the mind. Best you not let him."

Rhea shook her head emphatically. "There must be another way. It would be better if our entire race forgot how to enslave the minds of anyone, though we are likely many years from that."

"Well, stun him, then," Judith replied. "That wears off eventually, and Calandra will be long gone before that happens. Stun him before he stuns her."

"He will not be able to communicate while stunned," Zoe said. "And neither will she. Stunning requires that the Song be continually sung. Though it is one of the few songs that can be used underwater, how can she protect herself with it and find out about the Tear at the same time? And if it takes her some time to search the Tear out, how will she defend herself against this spirit while she is distracted?"

Calandra frowned. "We don't even know for sure he'll be there."

"We don't know he won't be," Rhea said. "Didn't he bid you meet him there? This is the best chance we have to get that Tear back. I only wish we didn't need to send you in alone."

Rhea was right. Damon had told her to come, so he would be waiting. How she wished Tanni were here—her friend would have put herself at risk in a heartbeat for this mission, and for Calandra.

"She'll need protection," Osaze said. "I have only recently learned to swim, and I am still too slow and ungainly in the water. She needs an undine to go."

"I'll go with her," Judith said.

Osaze nodded, then looked squarely at Zoe. "You must go, too. While Judith's extra eyes will help, Calandra may need a soldier."

Zoe frowned, squirming under Osaze's direct gaze. When she spoke, it was to Calandra and the other women present, not him—nor Jacob or Rhea's husband Hammad, who had joined them at the table.

"I will go with you," she said. "If everything you have revealed today is true, I believe that the evidence will be in Atlantis in one form or another. I must see it with my own eyes."

Suddenly, the bundle of stinging nettles in Calandra's head flared red and began to burn. She hunched her back and shoulders, pressing her fingers to her temples. Osaze was at her side immediately.

"It's happening again," he said. "She had a seizure like this last night. Do you have any physics here?"

"I'm a physic." Xeni rushed over and laid a hand on Calandra's forehead.

The sensation of fingers against her skin was excruciating, but Calandra could manage no more than a pitiful moan.

Xeni dropped her hand. "Physically, there is nothing wrong with her. I have never seen anything like it."

"It's . . . the bonds," Calandra wheezed out between gritted teeth. "Of the men. They burn."

Xeni nodded, then put her palm on Calandra's forehead once again and hummed a soothing melody. A blissful sensation of coolness washed over her, and she drowsed.

When Calandra became alert again, the pain had subsided and the conversation had turned to Calandra's mission for Adonia to check the sklavia bonds, and what was to be done about it. Xeni had sat down beside her, but the physic's attention was on the others.

"If she only pretends to enslave them, she'll be caught," exclaimed Judith. "She'll do no good for our cause if she's imprisoned or dead, will she now?"

Ignatia nodded. "Judith is right. She must continue with her mission, and we will deal with the consequences later."

Rhea frowned. "Even though the *sklavia* bond does not have the same effect on the mind as the *syzagos* bond, we must remember that Calandra is extremely powerful. And with so many in her possession, it is apparent that she is already beginning to feel the effects. I cannot agree to this. We must find another way. She cannot be allowed to continue."

Anger flared red and hot in Calandra's veins and she pushed herself to standing. "How dare you?"

Every head in the room jerked in her direction.

"What do you mean, your highness?" Rhea said with implacable calm.

"You sit here and squabble over my life like a flock of gulls, as though I were not the Opal Princess and you were not my servants."

Their eyes went wide at her tone, but she continued.

"You talk about whether I can be *allowed* to continue to do a duty I have sworn to do. Now hear this. The decision about my mission is not yours, no more than any other part of my destiny. You are not the ones who will stand before the Heartstone in two weeks and be expected to heal that which no one has been able to heal. It will not fall on your shoulders if I fail."

She stared at each of them in turn.

"I do not like the bonds, and especially now that I know the truth of them, but I need them to fulfill my purpose. Especially since none of you will risk yourselves to help me prove that the key to its restoration—a male undine—could actually exist. And even if you did, no boy here could help me."

Ignatia and Xeni shifted uncomfortably and said nothing.

"So I *will* continue to gather bonds, and I *will* bond Osaze at our bonding ceremony, and I will do everything I must in order to fulfill my duty to Adonia and my people. And even if I did not need the bonds, none of you has the authority to release me from service to the queen. So stop. Your. Squawking."

When she had finished, her knees shook and she wanted to sink right back into the chair. She gritted her teeth and stared at the wide-eyed faces in the room, willing herself to remain standing. She'd been too sharp—she knew she had. But she wasn't sorry. Much like last night, her emotions dragged at her like a lead weight in her chest.

Osaze came and stood behind her, close enough that she could lean on him slightly for support without making it obvious.

Calandra took a deep breath. When she continued, it was in a much calmer tone.

"I thank you all for your concern. But even though the *sklavia* bonds bother me, I doubt they will send me over the brink of Madness in only a few weeks. And you have forgotten something important about Re-dempt—I mean, *sklavia* bonds. They can only be broken by the one who holds them."

It wasn't completely true, but she still didn't know how Tanni had done it. After she'd Released Osaze, she'd had no reason to pursue it any longer—not to mention, she'd been a little busy.

She looked around and watched the implications of her words sink in. Zoe regarded her thoughtfully. Judith smiled first, then Jacob and Ignatia and the others, and then Rhea nodded.

"When you have finished, you will hold the bonds of nearly half the men on the island," said Rhea. "Which means you could also Release that many at once."

"Not at once. I will still need to touch each man to Release him, which would require another island tour. But once the Heartstone has been healed, I will have no reason to continue to hold them, and Adonia will have no reason to require me to do so."

No longer afraid of appearing weak, she sank into her chair.

"The problem is, even were I to Release them all, there is nothing that would prevent any other undine from enslaving them again. So we need more than a wish and a hope if we want to change our people's future. We need a plan. I will *not* be the cause of another rebellion in which good people die."

She thought of Tanni and her heart pinched. These were good people. She couldn't hate them now that she knew why they had done what they'd done. They were soldiers in a war that had been going on for three millennia. *People die in war sometimes.* She wondered if Tanni's mother knew what she had been fighting against. Probably not. She would have been following orders, just as Calandra had always done.

Rhea smiled sadly. "None of us wants this to come to bloodshed. Our numbers are few enough as it is."

At the sorrow on the older woman's face, Calandra wondered whom she might have lost in the rebellion, or since. She thought of Matthew and Elizabeth and glanced down at the table.

"You are right, your highness. We do need a plan." Ignatia leaned forward. "And that is something I believe we can help with."

Calandra looked at Zoe. "And what about you, Singer kor'Dione? Will you also help us?"

Zoe sat erect, glancing at their expectant faces one by one. "I could be executed if I don't report what I've seen here."

Calandra's heart thumped in her ears. Zoe was one of Adonia's most loyal sirens, and might even be her spy. Had Calandra condemned them all by her foolish act of trust? She sensed the uncertainty in Zoe's heart. The siren was struggling—a struggle Calandra was familiar with. She met Zoe's troubled eyes.

"You're right, you could be," she said quietly. "But if you report us, we could all face that same fate. Are you certain that would be right?"

She indicated Osaze, Jacob, and Hammad, whose tension she could feel, even if it wasn't apparent. The men regarded Zoe, their faces perfect masks of calm.

Judith sat beside Zoe with Zeke on her lap. He leaned on his sister's chest with one hand wrapped in her braid and the other clutching her tunic, his eyelids heavy with sleep. Judith wrapped her arms a little closer around him and glanced at Zoe, moisture gathering in the corner of her eyes.

"After what you've learned today," Judith whispered, "do you not question our people's laws even a little?"

Zoe gave Zeke a lingering look and then stared hard at the men through narrowed eyes.

"There is much to consider." She clenched her jaw. "I don't know what to believe. So for now, I will not stand in your way, and I will omit certain . . . details about our visit here today from my report. At least until I can find the truth for myself."

The band around Calandra's chest relaxed. She would have to watch Zoe, but with careful handling, the siren could be another potential ally. She nodded and turned back to Ignatia, who was watching her children with an anxious expression.

Calandra folded her hands on the table in front of her. "So what did you have in mind?"

Ignatia tore her gaze from her son and glanced uncertainly at Zoe, then faced the room and explained her idea. The other women and men at the table joined in, and Zoe watched in silence. By the time Stergia and the others set the table for dinner, they had the outline of a plan in place.

For the meal, Calandra sat at the head of the table with Osaze on her left. But instead of only a few full seats, Calandra insisted that all who normally occupied it should eat there—Rhea and her husband and their three children, Ignatia and her family, and several others who oversaw various operations on the property. She laughed to herself. Adonia would be outraged to see her eating with the servants. But here, everyone seemed to be truly equal. Doing otherwise would have been unnatural.

All too soon, it was time to depart for Fire Lake. But Calandra was leaving with three things she had not had when she'd arrived—the truth, a plan, and hope.

As they prepared to leave, Ignatia pressed a blue quartz Tear into Calandra's palm. "When you get to Haven, give this message to Nicandra at the shipyard. She owns an underwater salvage business—and one of the few non-military submersibles still in use. You remember her, Judith, she's got that lazy eye she's always refused to have healed. She says it lets her see which way the wind is blowing."

Judith nodded, chuckling. "Good ol' Nick. It will be great to see her again."

"She'll help you. And Calandra, wherever you go, look for the quaternaria." She pointed to the small tattoo behind her ear. "There are not many of us Freewillers elsewhere on the island, but there are more than you might think." Ignatia grasped both of Calandra's hands in her own and squeezed. "Be careful. Your mother had to flee to protect our cause and prove the truth. I would hate to see you have to resort to the same fate."

*

THEY'D been on the trail back to Fire Lake for about half an hour when Osaze spoke up from behind her, loud enough for only her to hear it.

"Calandra, I would speak."

He put a hand on her arm, and she stopped and turned to face him, drinking in the sight of his handsome face by moonlight, noting the shallow ditch between his brows. He had never become entirely comfortable with the decisions that had been made that afternoon, but he had accepted them, or so she'd thought.

"We've gone over everything a hundred times, Osaze. This plan is the best option we have."

He frowned and clenched his jaw. "It is not about the plan."

Zoe's and Judith's footsteps crunched away ahead of them in the dark. Calandra shifted her feet, studying Osaze's bottomless eyes.

"What is the matter? Is it about what I said about bonding you at the ceremony?"

He came close enough for her to feel his breath on her forehead. He placed his hands on her arms, his spicy, sweaty scent enveloping her.

"No. But about that, I will say only this—for the sake of your duty, I would accept it. But for your sake, I do not think it wise. I would not have you risk the Madness when we think there is another way. Please consider my words."

She nodded. "Thank you. I will." She turned to continue, but when he didn't let her go, she looked up at him in confusion. "Is there more?"

"Yes." He kissed her forehead, then looked into her eyes. "Your eyesight is better than mine, and your burdens are heavier than mine. I know this. I also know you have many battles to fight against things I cannot see." He took her hands in his. "But I swear to you that I will forever be here to fight what battles I can."

Too overwhelmed to speak, she launched up on her tiptoes and wrapped her arms around his neck. Even as he spoke the promises she most wanted to hear, Damon's taunts echoed in her mind.

If he were truly given a choice, would he still choose me?

She kissed him with all the words she couldn't say. Then she turned and went on, hurrying to catch up to Judith and Zoe.

He would know what she meant.

39

CLOUDS

May 29, 1799
The Middle Passage, Atlantic Ocean

FROM HIS VANTAGE ON THE poop deck, Robert watched Miss Bethel help the slave women on the quarterdeck. She was feeding a toddler while the child's mother ate breakfast. He wondered whether it would be quite appropriate to ask her to take the air with him this morning, as usual—or whether he even wanted to.

The previous evening, she and Mr. Berian had been taking a stroll around the deck when Robert had worked up the nerve to pull her aside. Ever since they had first met, he had had a difficult time getting her out of his mind. She fascinated him and, despite how he knew Gryffyn and James, their eldest brother, would feel about him courting a coloured woman, he had increasingly realized that he did not care. Miss Bethel was beautiful, gracious, and mysterious, and inflamed a fire in his spirit he had never experienced before.

She had been cordial enough to him since he'd arrived on the *Atlanta*, conversing on many topics and willingly making rounds of the deck with him for exercise. But every time he'd tried to press his romantic interests with her, she had gently rebuffed him. Thinking that perhaps he hadn't been overt enough, the night before, he'd stated his case plainly.

"Miss Bethel, I have something I wish to say," he'd said as they walked upon the quarterdeck beneath the stars.

She turned to him, fanning herself, her wild curls framing her lovely face and up-slanted eyes with their unusual golden irises.

"What is it, Mr. Cox?"

He halted and fidgeted with the chain of his pocket watch.

"Miss Bethel, I find you captivating. Maddeningly so. I wish—" he broke off, glancing out to sea, then turned and met her uncertain frown. "I wish you and I could speak of matters of the heart."

Her fan clattered to the deck. He scrambled to pick it up for her, and when he handed it back, she accepted it with murmured thanks, her brow furrowed. She looked as though she were struggling to find words.

"Mr. Cox, I must confess that you have pleasantly surprised me several times since we became reacquaint—since we met in Bristol. And you do me honour by your intentions. But there are compelling reasons we could never speak of such things—reasons far out of our control."

He snatched up her hands, holding her brown fingers in his own pale, freckled ones. She glanced at their hands and swallowed.

"I don't care what other people say. I don't care what they think. I would be with you, even if you were from another realm."

She choked, and he released her hands so she could turn away and cough. Gathering herself, she turned sad eyes upon him.

"Unfortunately, some barriers are not so easy to cross." She gave him a small smile. "I am truly sorry, Mr. Cox. This cannot be. Now I must retire for the night. Good evening, sir."

He had stood dumbfounded as she'd curtsied and hurried away. He smarted anew at the memory.

This morning, the following wind played in Miss Bethel's sun-kissed curls as she handed the baby back to its mother and stood, slapping dust off her skirts. She caught Robert looking at her and met his gaze steadily, then looked away when another woman asked her a question in some African tongue that Robert could not understand. She seemed to speak the languages of all the slaves fluently.

Robert felt a presence beside him and turned. Crow stood there with his arms crossed, following Robert's gaze with a leering smile.

"She's quite the eyeful, ain't she? I've 'ad a mind t'bed 'er meself."

Robert's stomach clenched and he drew himself up. "Watch your mouth, sailor. That's a lady you are disrespecting."

Crow jerked a thumb at Abela. "You mean the 'alf-breed negress? Sorry, I didn't realize she was yer whore, sir. I'll not bother she again."

He sauntered away, whistling as though he hadn't a care in the world.

Robert stared after Crow, flabbergasted. Glancing down at the quarterdeck, he met Abela's disappointed eyes. Had she heard what Crow had said? Had she seen him do nothing to defend her?

"I . . ."

He could think of nothing to say. Swallowing, he turned and walked away, her sad, golden-eyed expression burned into his mind.

*

ZALE stood on the wires that ran beneath the main-topgallant yard with one hand on the mast and his other spread wide to the wind, whooping as the *Atlanta* dipped into yet another trough, then left his stomach there as the next swell pushed them back toward the sun. His loose hair whipped behind him, and the occasional spray of salt water cooled his skin. Other than his late night swims in the open sea, he'd never felt so alive.

"Zale, come down from there!" yelled Abela from the deck below, laughing. "You're not a bird."

"No, but this is as close as I'm likely to get," he shouted back in unabashed delight.

The ship had been making good time for the last ten days since leaving Whydah, thanks to the winds that Zale continually pushed into the sails. He'd chuckled when he'd overheard Captain Meredith exclaiming about it to Robert and Mr. Crow.

"Never seen anything like it," the captain had said. "At this rate, we'll make Barbados by the end of September."

Even Crow was perplexed, though he sounded more suspicious of such good fortune.

"We 'ave the devil's own luck, we do. As long as it don't attract the devil's attention, too."

Zale had only chuckled. *And I thought the Romani were superstitious.*

Abela shouted up at him again.

"Mr. Berian wants to speak with you."

Zale sighed. He took one last look at the horizon, with its gathering of clouds like sheep's wool, then called to the guardian. "Coming."

As he climbed down past the quarterdeck, he greeted the broad-shouldered sailor named Cogger who was manning the helm.

"Storm's a-comin', eh, Teague?" Cogger eyed the clouds on the horizon.

"Not if I can help it." Zale grinned.

Cogger gave him an odd look and then shook his head, going back to watching the sea.

Abela waited for him at the foot of the mast. As Zale reached her, Robert Cox passed by and tipped his hat. "Good afternoon, Miss Bethel. Mr. Teague."

His gaze stayed on Abela and he gave a tight-lipped smile.

Abela dropped a small curtsy. "Good afternoon, Mr. Cox. All is well?"

"Same as yesterday," he said, his voice oddly tight. Finally, he tore his gaze from Abela and looked at Zale. "I would speak with you at some point, Mr. Teague. Please come see me when you have some spare time."

"Aye, sir. Good day." Zale nodded, then followed Abela, who had already descended the ladder to the lower deck.

He nodded at Kofi and Cook on the way by the open galley where several other men were also preparing food for their messmates. Kofi stood stirring what smelled like a large pot of beans over a coal-powered brazier for the slaves' evening meal. He gave Zale a cheerful grin, but Cook didn't even look up from his work, simply muttered something under his breath as he seasoned a dish of crumbled hardtack and salted pork with intense concentration.

From the foot of the ladder toward the bow lay the crew's hammocks. They hung folded in half from single hooks like empty sacks now, except for those belonging to the few sailors who, like Zale, would be staying awake through the watches of the night. The deck's eighteen heavy cannon lined up on either side along the hull, with mess tables protruding from the walls between them, hanging from the ceiling by thick, knotted ropes on the outer end. Afternoon sunlight streamed through the gun doors, which were open to let in a bit of fresh air.

Abela led Zale astern toward the wardroom, which was lined with the officer's cabins—first mate and boatswain, surgeon and carpenter, steward and supercargo, as well as the chaplain's cabin, which was being shared by Mr. Cox and Mr. Berian, and the guest berth, which had been given to Abela.

"What's this about?" Zale asked Abela, nodding to some crew members who hailed him as they passed.

Abela turned to face him as they reached Berian's cabin door. "I'm not certain, but Berian sounded almost excited. Well, as excited as he ever sounds. I'm as intrigued as you are."

She rapped lightly on the door, and it opened immediately.

A flushed Berian answered, huffing as though he'd run a mile. "Come in, come in. Hurry, before Mr. Cox returns from his afternoon rounds."

He stepped back to allow them entry into the crowded space. The room's only furnishings included two narrow berths fixed to one wall, a chair that sat at the far end of the floor space, and above that, a small shelf and a few hooks on the wall. Berian offered Abela the chair, but she looked at it askance around his substantial midriff, which left little room to pass.

"I think I'll stand here, thank you."

"You will? Oh, yes. Fine, fine," he muttered, looking at the closed pocket watch he held in both hands.

Zale had never seen him so distracted. "Mr. Berian, what has happened?"

Berian looked at Zale, and one of his rare, magical smiles lit his face. It didn't exactly make him attractive, but he looked . . . less ugly.

"I have made a discovery. It is a thing I didn't know to be possible, but now that I have found it out, I should be able to use it to help find your mother. How marvellous!"

"Berian, you're not making any sense," Abela snapped. "Slow down. What have you found?"

Berian took a deep breath and opened the watch.

"I know how she hid you," he said to Zale.

Zale studied the watch face, fascinated. It had no markings, no hands, no impressions of any kind, only the same stone he had seen before—a circular, smooth surface with a red ring like an iris around the outside and a black slit in the middle, like an eye. It didn't move or seem in any way out of the ordinary beyond the fact that it was not a watch at all.

"How who hid Zale?" Abela put her hands on her hips. "Berian, you really have been Grounded for too long. Please start making sense immediately."

Berian seemed unaffected by Abela's rancour. He did a little hop-step jig on the spot.

"Oh, brilliant Delphine! I always knew she was clever, but this . . ."

The reverend snatched Zale's wrist, the one with the hemp bracelet his mother had made him.

"I had thought this was only a key to get past the barrier into Sirenia, which it is. I had also thought it was the Order who hid you from our finders all these years. You know what a finder is, boy?" He lifted his watch toward Zale's face, and Zale jerked his head back in surprise.

"Uh, yeah. Kind of. Abela mentioned them to me."

"Lumasi use finders to amplify our abilities and find people by their specific frequency, which is as distinct as your fingerprint or the shape of your snout."

"My . . . snout?" Zale touched his nose, wondering why Berian might call it that.

"Your nose! Your nose! I'm so excited, I can't even think of human words correctly."

Abela stepped forward and put a hand on Berian's arm.

"Perhaps you ought to sit down, Jowan. Take a moment to collect yourself."

Zale coughed. He hadn't even known Berian had another name, let alone that Abela would use it so casually.

Berian looked at her, and his expression went from wild to focused and calm. He nodded. "Thank you, young cub."

Abela smiled with a mixture of annoyance and affection. "You're welcome, old codger."

Berian sat on the chair and put his hands on his knees, the finder still clutched between the fingers of one hand. He looked at it, rubbing his thumb over the smooth surface.

"Delphine used to ask me many questions about the abilities of my kind, both those in the flesh and those out of it. She knew her children were the key to preserving the balance of the world, and as such, that they would be sought after by powers in all the planes. And so she found a way to hide you." He chuckled. "I couldn't figure out why I still couldn't Find you, not even when you were standing right beside me. Now I know."

Zale gulped. *Preserve the balance of the world?* Abela had once said he needed to help save his race. What were these two not telling him?

His gut churned, and an icy draft from beneath the door cooled the sweltering heat of the room. He took a breath. Things had been going so well—he didn't want to ruin it now. Even still, he patted his waistcoat and was reassured to feel the green bracelet beneath it in his pocket.

Berian pointed at Zale's hemp bracelet with its smooth brown stone.

"That stone is more than a key. It is a frequency dampener. Rather, it inverts your frequency so as to be unrecognizable as yours. Don't you see?" His small eyes lit up with uncharacteristic glee. "It wasn't the Order who hid you, it was your mother. And she wasn't hiding you from us—she was protecting you from *them*." He shook his head and chuckled, rubbing a meaty hand over his jowls. "I don't think anyone has ever managed such a thing before."

Zale shook his head. "If that's true, how did Eric find me in the first place, back when I was eleven? And how do they know we're on our way to Barbados now?"

Berian's gaze grew sharp. "It's a frequency inverter, boy, not a cloak of invisibility. There are other ways to get that information, and it was bad luck for you that they used them. But here is the good news—now that I see what she has done, and assuming she did something similar for herself, I can work backward to Find her."

"You can?" Abela cocked her head and crossed her arms, looking impressed. "Well, how about that?"

Zale looked back and forth between them. "I thought we knew where she was—in Tartarus."

Abela snapped her gaze to his. "You ever been to Tartarus? No? Thought not. It's a big place. As big as the Ground. It's not like we could simply show up, walk in, say, 'Delphine, there you are! We've been looking all over for you,' and walk out with her."

Berian frowned at Abela, his normal poise restored. "Have a care, Miss Bethel. Remember, he is much younger than you are."

Zale frowned, feeling about six years old. He didn't seem that much younger than Abela, and he wondered how old she was, really. Too old to be interested in someone like him? He wondered.

Abela sighed and turned back to Zale.

"He's right. I'm sorry, Zale. And Mr. Berian, thank you for sharing this delightful news. How soon do you think you can locate Mrs. Teague?"

"I'll begin looking immediately."

*

AFTER leaving Berian's room, Zale quick-stepped to walk beside Abela, stopping her before they left the wardroom.

"Hey, what did Berian mean back there about 'preserving the balance of the world'?"

Abela met his gaze, then glanced away.

"Nothing. Don't worry about it." She began walking again.

Zale put his hand on her arm to stop her and experienced the not-totally-unpleasant sensation of a rush of emotion. Her emotion. It had been happening with regularity since he'd healed Kofi, whenever he happened to touch someone. It had disturbed him a great deal the first few times it happened. Since then, he'd gotten into the habit of not touching anyone unless it was absolutely necessary.

Abela was feeling anxious. She looked at his hand on her arm, and he dropped it.

"You mentioned something to me once about needing to save my race. Now Berian is talking about the balance of the world. What is it you know that I don't? You must tell me."

Abela looked up at him and sighed. "Fine. There is something, but I'm not sure you're ready to hear it yet."

Zale's stomach clenched. He wasn't sure, either, but he also didn't want to be left to the tender mercies of his imagination on the subject.

"Tell me."

Abela shifted her feet, looking at the closed cabin doors as though she could see whether they contained any occupants. She chewed her lip as though weighing something in her head, then beckoned for him to follow her. She led him into her small cabin, which had only a single berth and was even tinier than the one they had just been in. After checking that no one had seen them enter, she closed the door and turned to face him.

"Remember how you once asked me if I would tell you why you were the last male of your kind?"

"Yes. Are you finally going to tell me?"

She gave him a sharp look. "Don't get impertinent, and I will. You might want to sit down, though."

Zale's heart leapt. The ship lurched as it went over a high swell, causing Abela to step back into the cabin door and Zale to stumble toward Abela. He caught himself with his hands on the door on either side of her head. From this close, he could breathe deeply of her unique scent—summer wildflowers and a roaming wind. He searched her gaze, which had an inviting vulnerability to it. Then it hardened, and she raised an eyebrow at him.

"Did you lose your sea-legs, merman?"

Zale flushed. "Sorry." He stepped back to the far end of the narrow walking space and braced himself with his hands against the berth. "Sea's getting rough, I guess. I should probably go check it out after this. I'll stand for now, though."

Abela smirked.

"Suit yourself." She pushed herself away from the door to stand upright. "I have told you how undines were created as guardians of the deep and the gateway to Tartarus."

Zale nodded, dimly recalling her telling him such a thing months before.

"Go on."

"Three thousand years ago, there was a great tragedy among your people. They subverted the natural order which Elyon had put into place for them, and as a consequence, have been unable to bear male children ever since. Instead, they have stolen and enslaved human men to father their daughters, and that is how they have survived."

Her face grew hard and her voice dropped.

"But they do not simply steal a man's body—they take his mind, as well. As evil as the chattel slavery you have seen here is, it is nothing compared to what the undines have inflicted on humans."

Zale recoiled, and the ship lurched again. This time, he only took one faltering step before he caught himself. Abela crouched slightly and swayed with the rocking motions as gracefully as a cat, the arms extended at her sides reminding him of the wings she somehow concealed inside this form, along with her feline characteristics. She frowned at the rocking deck, then at him, her gaze calculating.

"I think I've told you enough for one day. Let's go help Kofi serve supper."

She turned to open the door. He took two steps and placed his hand on hers on the latch. She jerked her head up to look at him.

"Please," he said, and closed his eyes.

He took a deep breath and released the tension in his gut. The floor still rocked, but without the severe pitch of the previous few minutes. Good.

He opened his eyes. "I want to know. How does all this affect me?"

She released the handle and tugged her hand out from beneath his, then turned to stare up at him. When she spoke, her voice was soft and gentle, like a velvet pillow.

"For three thousand years, your people have forgotten their purpose as guardians of the underworld and the spirits Elyon placed there, and now, the walls they were meant to maintain have weakened to the point that those spirits threaten to escape. If they do, the world as we know it may not survive."

Zale's chest tightened, but he kept his emotions in check.

"Is that what Berian was talking about? Some kind of end-of-days apocalypse? And how am I supposed to stop something like that?"

"When your mother fled Sirenia, she didn't know about any of this, she only had guesses. All she knew was that the way her society worked was not only wrong, it was a cancer that was killing them both morally and physically. But when Berian and I were assigned to guard your family, she found out the rest—that because there had been no males for so long, the gateway to the Abyss hadn't been maintained. Without male and female powers working together as Elyon planned, there had been no way to preserve it. *That* is why Berian has been pressuring you to learn to use your abilities. We may need them to enter Tartarus and save your mother.

But, more than that, we'll need them to ensure that we don't bring anyone but your mother back out with us. Because unless you and your sister, who is the most powerful undine healer since that tragedy three millennia ago—even stronger than your mother—unless you two can restore the barrier . . ."

Abela paused and tears welled in her eyes, the silence pregnant with all the horrors that flashed behind them.

Zale had a sudden yearning to kiss her, to assure her that it would all be alright, that he would do whatever was necessary to keep his mother and the world safe—but mostly to not have to see that expression on her face for another second. He inched closer to her, but she turned and yanked the hatch open and fled outside.

He watched her go, feeling suddenly cold, though the sensation was strictly an internal one this time—the deck rolled on a fairly even keel. She didn't need to finish her sentence. He knew the rest.

If he and his sister couldn't restore the barrier?

All hell would literally break loose.

*

When Zale exited the wardroom, Kofi stood on the other side, waiting. Behind him stood the slave woman Zale had noticed before and her small boy, his head on her shoulder, his lips cracked and dry, his cheeks sunken. He had obviously fallen ill, as Zale had feared. He knew Mr. Wesley had been seeing to the slaves a great deal more than usual lately, and now he could see why.

"*Obofo*, I need you to pray," Kofi said. "This child's life might depend on it."

Zale looked at the child doubtfully. The woman stared at him with round, fear-filled eyes.

"May I touch him?" Zale asked her in Twi.

Her eyes widened in surprise and she nodded.

He took the boy's hands and tentatively followed the path of emotion that opened inside him. The boy seemed to be taken with something much like what had taken Kofi, and he was very ill. Fire raged through his veins and inside Zale's head. Only a weak flicker of emotion signalled that the unconscious boy was present inside the fiery ocean of disease.

Did Zale dare risk putting this child through the process that had been required to purge Kofi? Couldn't that alone kill him? Zale almost turned Kofi down at the thought. He already had enough deaths on his conscience.

On the other hand, if he couldn't save this boy, how could he possibly save the world, as Abela and Berian seemed to believe he must?

He released the boy's hand.

"What is his name?"

"Sule," said his mother. "And I am Kisi."

Zale clenched his fist. He had to try.

"Okay, Kisi. I cannot promise anything. But I will pray for your son, and God will decide."

Kisi pressed her lips together. "God will decide."

Zale glanced around the gun deck at the sailors lounging or hurrying about their duties, some of whom were eyeing them in curiosity. "Let's go below."

Kofi nodded. "Yes, Zaleteague. That would be best. There may be others you can pray for, also."

Zale swallowed. He would not run away this time. Things were different now. He could control his powers, not like before.

Still, as he followed Kofi and Kisi down to the hold, the deck lurched once more, and he began praying in earnest.

Before he could contain hell, he might have to keep some souls from going there.

He hoped he was up to the task.

40

SEEKING ATLANTIS

CALANDRA STOOD NEXT TO OSAZE on the deck of the *Luz da Paz*, watching the water as the submersible plowed through the waves of the Atlantic Ocean northeast of Haven. Curls of white foam splashed backward into the sea alongside the bronze-coloured bow and then disappeared into the blue waves as though they had never existed.

Their tour guide for the day, Nicandra—a weathered, leathery woman with chin-length loose salt-and-pepper curls—stood at the helm in the glassed-in cabin behind them, Judith beside her. The passengers had been told in no uncertain terms that they were to refer to their skipper as Nick.

"A simple name's good enough for me," she had declared. "Saves time, too."

Calandra had never seen anyone who dressed like her. She wore no tunic, only a blue swimming bodice that was covered with a brown, fitted waistcoat, much like many human men wore when they were harvested, and a swimming belt with some extra metal rings and hooks, plus a few tools Calandra had never seen before, over a brightly coloured wrap-around sarong that could be discarded in an instant. This was a woman who obviously spent more time in the water than out of it.

Beside Calandra on the deck, Osaze's face was blank, but the bond revealed a sense of pleasure, contentment, and nervousness. He was not looking forward to their mission today. Or rather, he was not looking forward to Calandra being out of his reach. As much as he believed in the necessity of what she must attempt, he didn't like it.

Calandra glanced at him in affection. Even in his disapproval, he had been unwavering in his support. And this morning, he had proved once again why she had to do this—why she had to find the answers her mother wanted her to find and show her people why they could no longer continue treating men as the enemy.

He'd been laying on his cot in her chambers in the royal complex in Haven—a sprawling compound of whitewashed adobe and wood, with airy, spacious rooms—having just awoken. Calandra sat in front of a mirrored dresser next to the bed in the spacious room, with Judith brushing Calandra's hair.

Osaze propped himself up on his elbow to watch her. After a moment, he blurted, "If only the woman who holds a *sklavia* bond can Release a man, then how did Tanni Release me? Adonia held my bond, not her."

Calandra flicked her gaze at him, trying not to move her head. "What did you say?"

Judith listened to the conversation without comment, several hairpins wedged between her tight lips.

"When we were children. How did Tanni Release me?"

Calandra frowned. "To be honest, I've been asking myself that for five years. But did you say Adonia Redeemed—I mean, enslaved you? Right from when you were a boy? Why would she do that?"

Osaze swung his legs over the side of the cot. He wore only his loin wrap, and Calandra couldn't help but admire his physique in the mirror's reflection.

"I don't know. But she was the one who did it again afterwards, too."

Calandra frowned. "But I saw Thea do it. Didn't she transfer the bond to Mistress Margaret?"

Osaze squinted, remembering. "Is she the one who stayed in Fire Lake?"

Calandra nodded, and Judith made a sound of consternation between tight lips.

"Sorry." Calandra tightened her lips in apology and moved her head back into position for Judith, then glanced at Osaze in the mirror. "Yes, that's her. She was the palace Mistress of Bonds."

"Yes, Thea did transfer my bond to Margaret. And then *she* found Queen Adonia and transferred it to her at the earliest opportunity."

Calandra frowned, pondering his words. It made sense now. It had been Adonia who had Released Osaze on that horrible day in the Observation Chamber. She'd thought Adonia had merely been prepared for what she'd planned.

She studied a floral arrangement sitting on the dresser. "Mistress Margaret told me she hasn't held any bonds in the palace for years. Adonia didn't have me transfer any bonds from men in the city at all, only once we started touring. She has been reassigning all of Sireniapolis's bondmistresses to posts in the villages, as though she has no more need of them. Plus, she's been acting more and more unstable lately. You don't think . . . ?"

Judith took the last pin out of her mouth and stared at Calandra in the mirror. "How many bonds does Adonia hold?"

Osaze blinked as he put the pieces together. "And how long has she held them?"

Calandra arched her brows. "If what you said is any indication, a lot. Nearly as many as I have. And she's been holding them for a long, long time."

Her breath caught as it occurred to her that if Adonia hadn't betrothed her to Osaze and had her Redeem him, she wouldn't have been able to Release him until she had solved the mystery of Tanni's "mistake."

"As for your question, Tanni insists she doesn't remember how she did it. I've been trying to solve that puzzle for five years, but it's, um, been difficult to practise."

She met his eyes in the mirror, hers unexpectedly wet.

His gaze was soft. "I told you, I trust you. I know you were trying, Cali. I knew there were good reasons why it took so long."

Judith finished her final primp and stepped back, and Calandra turned to face him.

"Why are you so kind to me?"

He stood up and came over, lifting her chin with his hand. "Why aren't you kinder to yourself?"

She shrugged, dropping her gaze. "I can't afford to be."

"Well, you should be." He took Calandra's hand and drew her to her feet, then glanced between her and Judith. "It does make the plan more interesting, doesn't it?"

"What do you mean?" Judith asked.

"If Calandra can figure out how Tanni did it . . . if any undine could free any man, we could really do this." He grasped both his consort-elect's hands in his. "We could change the world."

Calandra nodded and met Judith's pleased look of comprehension. Total masculine emancipation was one of the goals of the FWS. But they still had the problem of showing the island's women why that was a good thing.

After they found out how to do it.

Calandra lifted Osaze's hands and kissed his knuckles.

"You are truly astounding, you know that? If only the women of this island all knew you, they would never doubt our message."

He smiled and bent to kiss her on the mouth.

Judith grinned and went to find something else to do for a while.

Zoe came up to the copper railing of the *Luz*, interrupting Calandra's line of thought. When Calandra turned to acknowledge her, the siren flicked her gaze toward Osaze's neutral face with a barely perceptible tightening around her eyes. Then she looked at Calandra.

"Nick says it's time to come in, we'll be submerging soon. And Narcissa wishes to see you," she said.

"Why?"

The siren gave Calandra a guilty look.

"You told her, didn't you? Despite your promise, you told Narcissa."

"I broke no promises, your highness. She knew something was up. She didn't believe this trip was merely for a pleasure cruise along the reef. And I thought there would be no harm in telling her that our true destination is Atlantis. You said yourself that we would tell her once we were out to sea."

"Is that all you told her? Nothing else?"

"No, nothing, your highness. Though I don't like this promise. It burdens me with secrets that should be shared. Now that the truth is known, why do you insist on keeping it to yourself?"

She cast a suspicious glance at Osaze, who maintained the pretence of Redemption. Calandra wasn't sure if Zoe's suspicion was because of the pretence, or because she knew him to be Free behind the mask of blankness. Perhaps her assessment that morning had been overly optimistic.

"Are *you* ready to accept a Sirenia full of Free men, Zoe?"

Zoe's gaze snapped back toward her. She shifted uncomfortably and didn't answer.

"And there is your answer. We will make the truth plain to everyone at the right time. For now, we must continue on as we have in the past. I must find my brother, and he must help me heal the Stone. That is all the proof we will need. Once Adonia sees that we need a male undine to maintain the barrier and protect our people, she will be forced to admit the truth. And then we can tell her how the rest of what we've been taught is a lie, too. Perhaps it will not be too late for her to reverse the effects of the lies on herself."

Zoe frowned. "What do you mean?"

"Never mind."

"But how are you going to find your brother in such a short time? And what if you can't?"

Calandra sighed. She did not like that the best-case scenario of this plan meant she had to somehow locate her brother and get him to Sirenia before she could both reveal the truth about Redemption to their people and heal the Heartstone. And the only way she could see to get him there was to first convince Adonia that it was necessary. Rhea had promised help from what resources they had, but those were few.

Worst-case, she and the others had decided she was to attempt to heal the Heartstone the traditional way, with the help of Thea and ten other stone healers in a Healing Circle after her bonding to Osaze. There was, after all, the possibility that Damon had been lying about needing a male undine. Perhaps he was only trying to convince her to free him.

None of them needed to say aloud what they were all thinking—that if he hadn't been lying, the Heartstone would likely fail before the autumnal equinox, leaving their island open to discovery by the hundreds of ships a year that passed their borders—all while Osaze and the other men of the society had to continue to pretend enslavement. That option was much less appealing, with more potential for violence.

"Then the Mother help us all. Now, let us go see what my cousin has to say."

Calandra followed Zoe down the ladder into the cabin, and Osaze followed her, closing the hatch tightly behind him.

"All in," Calandra called to Nick, who raised a closed fist in acknowledgement without even turning around.

Standing beside the skipper, Judith glanced back over her shoulder and met Calandra's eyes, giving a sharp nod of encouragement before facing forward again to look through the glass. Nick pushed a lever, and in moments, the increasing pressure that signalled descent popped in Calandra's ears.

"Zoe, please join Nick and Judith at the front."

Zoe frowned, but obeyed. Calandra was glad that, though the siren singer had made her opinions known, she had remained respectful and, so far, had remained true to her word that she would keep the secrets of Elpida. She couldn't say what the siren would do if their plan failed. Would Zoe continue to keep Osaze's secret day in and day out until they could prove their discoveries to the nation? Or, if their cause came to violence, would she be willing to fight her sisters to bring about an unknown future? Calandra wasn't sure that she was herself, let alone the siren, which is why she hoped to avoid a violent rebellion at all costs.

After their three days of bond-checking in Haven were complete,

Calandra had asked Adonia for this pleasure cruise under the pretence of a belated birthday gift for herself, never planning on Narcissa wanting to tag along. But as soon as her cousin had heard of it, she'd managed to wheedle Adonia into agreeing to let her and Mari go, too. She'd left Matthew behind to practise sparring with the sirens and their *douloi*—probably hoping he'd become a valuable training partner for her at some point.

Narcissa's arrogant smugness reached Calandra before she even entered the aft cabin, something Calandra had not sensed much of since Adonia had told her about Calandra being chosen as the new Opal Princess. Her cousin was definitely not going to make this easy.

Steeling herself, Calandra stepped into the restrictive but nicely appointed compartment, Osaze on her heels. Narcissa and Mari sat next to each other on a molded copper bench covered in a nubby padded red silk cushion. They were holding hands and whispering, and the heat between them confirmed what Calandra had suspected for years, especially once Osaze told her that in all the years he was in Narcissa's service, she had never become physically intimate with him. She had used him in other ways, ways he refused to speak of, but not in that one.

She smiled. That was one thing Narcissa hadn't managed to steal from her. And in two weeks, she and Osaze would get to experience it for the first time, together.

Even after learning that pregnancy would not bring on the Madness, they had decided they would wait until their bonding night to become intimate, lacking any sort of privacy while on the road. Catching a few snatches of private conversation or even a kiss had been difficult enough. Which is, so it appeared, the reason Narcissa and Mari had chosen to come along today. While physically intimate relationships between women were fairly common among their people, as the Opal Princess, Narcissa would have been expected to bond a male consort and provide an heir—so a same-sex relationship could not have been publicly advertised, even if it eventually became common knowledge.

Watching Narcissa snuggle closer to her lover, Calandra wondered if her cousin was even upset that she'd lost the title. Jealousy stabbed her. While Calandra's duties had gotten heavier, Narcissa had become virtually free. What would a life of freedom—to enjoy a life with Osaze at Elpida, away from the responsibilities of saving and then running a nation—be like?

She shook her head and pushed the vision away. No sense in coveting what could not be had.

Calandra watched Narcissa warily, her empathic and all other senses on high alert as she and Osaze sat. She felt as though she were a crab that had stumbled onto a sandbar full of cuttlefish, but couldn't see through their camouflage and had no idea where they were planning to attack.

Osaze's posture stiffened even more, if possible, and she could sense the same caution in him. He did not like Narcissa, but there was little he could do about her being here. He had stubbornly refused to let Calandra come on this journey without him, even though she'd given him the option once she knew Narcissa would be joining them.

"You'll need me more with that viper there, not less," he'd insisted.

"Zoe and Judith can protect me. And I can protect myself. I'll be fine."

He'd gently put his arms around her and drawn her to him.

"You probably would. But I would not. Bad enough that I must let you face this Damon alone. Narcissa I can handle. Watching your back around her is one of those things I can actually do." He patted his sword hilt and touched the knife tucked into the sheath on his baldric. "I know how she fights, remember?"

Calandra nodded uncertainly, her hands on his chest, and he pulled her close. She fought with herself, wanting to stiffen and pull away lest she be perceived as weak—a fear that ate at her more frequently all the time— but wanting more to melt into his strong arms. In the end, she'd relaxed and enjoyed his embrace. Moments in his arms were some of the few she ever felt completely loved and wanted, as though the fears that haunted her at night could never come to be—or they had been, before Damon's words had sunk into her heart like talons.

"So," said Narcissa, breaking into Calandra's thoughts, "the good girl has been tainted at last, has she?"

She let her eyes linger on Osaze for a long moment, smiling at a joke Calandra hadn't heard.

"Lying to Mother." Narcissa clucked her tongue. "She is not going to be happy when she hears about this, *your highness.*"

Calandra shifted uncomfortably.

"I intend to tell Aunt Adonia, but I have heard it is easier to get forgiveness than permission. Wouldn't you agree, dear cousin?"

She eyed Narcissa's sycophant, flicking her gaze to their conjoined hands meaningfully.

Mari simply shrugged and smiled. "Are you implying we need forgiveness? We have nothing to hide, especially not now. Whereas you . . ." She raised her eyebrows.

Narcissa leaned forward slightly. "So what do you intend? Are you on a treasure hunt? Is this some kind of thrill ride? That doesn't seem like you."

She eyed Osaze again. He pressed his fingers into his leg.

"No," Narcissa continued, "it must be something to do with that heat-blasted Tear and its message. Where is it, by the way? I've not seen you wear it for the last several days."

Calandra kept her hands firmly in her lap, resisting the urge to reach for her vacant décolletage.

"I have put it away for safekeeping. After losing it once"—she glared at Narcissa—"I wanted to ensure it would be secure."

If only she *had* done that, she might not be in this predicament.

"It is as you say, both things. After what was in my mother's message, it got me curious about what treasures might be hiding in Atlantis, waiting to be discovered. Have you never wondered, Narcissa?"

"Not particularly. But I'll not stand in the way of your little treasure hunt. Have fun. Don't die."

The last was delivered in such a tone that Calandra had no doubt as to her true feelings on the subject.

"Would you and Mari care to come? It might be educational."

The two young women exchanged glances.

"I don't think so," Narcissa said. "We'll be fine here. Won't we, Osaze?"

Osaze replied in the emotionless voice of the Redeemed. "Of course, your highness."

Narcissa waggled a finger at him. "Uh-uh. It's 'm'lady.' Your mistress has stolen my title from me, just as she once stole you. There are obviously so many things I must teach you while we get reacquainted over the next few hours."

Heat—and fear for Osaze—flared in Calandra's belly.

"Are you trying to make me look like an incompetent by having my *doulos* misstyle you in public? I don't know what you're playing at, Narcissa, but your *mother* named me Opal Princess. I had no choice, the same as you. And Osaze is my consort-elect as well as my *doulos*. He is mine, and knows which of your orders he is required to obey. If you lay one hand on him while I'm gone, you'll regret it."

Narcissa took this tirade with wide, innocent eyes.

"I have no idea what you're implying, dear cousin. I simply meant that Osaze would be here with me while you are off playing marine archaeologist in Atlantis. Is that not true? Or has he learned to swim and breathe underwater since he was in my service?"

Calandra narrowed her eyes at Narcissa, wondering if she knew more than she should. Had she found out the truth about Osaze? Had she discovered their secret swimming lessons or discovered that he was now Free?

She and Osaze had discussed him accompanying her with a breathing mask, but Calandra had been concerned about both his health and his ability as a swimmer at those depths. Humans were not designed to handle them like undines were and, though he'd learned quickly, he was still a very inexperienced swimmer. But when their unwanted companions had joined them, there had been no more argument. It would be riskier for Osaze to go and expose their secret than for Calandra to go without him.

Narcissa laughed. "Fine, if it makes you feel better, I promise not to lay a hand on your man. I have no interest in him anymore, anyway. I've got Mari and Matthew. What more could a girl who won't ever be queen want?"

She batted her eyelashes in mock innocence.

Calandra narrowed her eyes at Narcissa, who raised an eyebrow at her as though daring her to call her a liar. At last, Calandra nodded.

"Fine. Thank you."

Nick's voice vibrated thinly from the rock quartz communication stone on the wall between them. "Approaching Atlantis."

Calandra gave her cousin one last searching glare, and was met by the same smug smile Narcissa had worn since Calandra had come in.

Narcissa was definitely up to something. Calandra wished she knew what.

She rose and headed toward the fore cabin, Osaze behind her. She couldn't decide if the ice in her gut were because of the demon she was about to face, or the one she had just left.

41

DEMONS

THE SUBJECT OF WHAT CALANDRA would do if she actually succeeded in finding Damon had never been far from her mind for the past few days. He had not visited her in her dreams, despite her actively trying to call him, thinking of him until she fell asleep.

The plan was for Zoe to stun him if he became aggressive at all, and for Judith to help Calandra locate the Tear. However, Zoe had also warned her that the execution of any operation almost never went according to plan.

"If it all goes wrong, retreat back to the *Luz* as quickly as possible," Calandra had instructed her teammates. "We will find another way."

That was the best she could do.

Nick pointed through the window of the *Luz da Paz* at crumbling spires that nevertheless retained vestiges of intricate, carved details, much more elaborate than anything on Sirenia. Nick's small, four-pointed quaternaria tattoo looked like an odd black mole on the back of the webbed flesh between her thumb and forefinger.

"Thar she is, m'lady. Atlantis, the city of the goddess."

Calandra gaped, overwhelmed by its size. The buildings sprawled into the distance in every direction, and were taller than she would have thought possible to build, with floors upon floors of windows in each one. Assuming Damon were even here, how would she find him?

They glided through the empty channels that had once been streets. Sharks and other scavengers darted in and out of the abandoned buildings. Nick was practically salivating as she scanned the territory. She'd agreed to come as long as she could claim some treasures of her own to make the trip worth her while.

"You can have whatever you want," Calandra had said, "but any datastones belong to me."

Eventually, Nick set the submersible down on its landing pods beside the library, whose columns remained mostly intact. A tall tapered tower rose from the library's domed ceiling and elaborate stonework decorated the sides—tiny figures in multiple layers depicting scenes Calandra had never heard of in any book or history stone.

The efficient skipper adjusted some knobs and levers, and the slight hum of the engine lowered to a barely-there whisper.

"It's time," she said to Calandra, piercing her with her one good eye, the other appearing to look at Judith.

Calandra, Judith, Zoe, and Osaze assembled in the cramped water lock chamber below the main floor while Nick gathered her supplies above and waited her turn. One by one, the young women stripped down to their swimming gear and slipped into the water-filled hole in the floor—first Zoe, then Judith, until Calandra and Osaze were the only ones standing in the small cabin.

Osaze glanced at the hatch above them.

"Are Narcissa and Mari there?"

Calandra closed her eyes and checked. "No, they're in the back."

He slipped his arms around Calandra's bare midriff and gave her a firm kiss, one that left her tingling down to the tips of her toes. He pulled away, but let his hands rest on the swimming belt she wore on her hips.

"Come back to me, you hear?" he said softly.

She put on a brave smile, knowing full well he could feel her fear through the bond.

"He's only a spirit. It's probably no big deal."

Osaze stared at her reproachfully, and she nodded.

"I'll come back. Wild narwhals couldn't keep me away."

She laughed at her own joke, and he even smiled at that a bit.

"Don't let Narcissa get to you," she added, her hand on his chest. "If you're forced to defend yourself, it will be mighty difficult to explain."

He smiled. "Wild tuna couldn't convince me to spend time with her." He chuckled. "I'll be fine. I'll simply avoid her."

"Okay." She stood on her tiptoes and spoke into his ear. "I love you. I don't know how I ever survived without you."

Then, with a final peck on his cheek, she stepped down into the water, transforming to *ichthys* state as her head slipped below the surface.

*

THE three undine women swam between the broken marble columns of the interior of the Archive. At this depth, everything was shrouded in a murky green blanket, even though it was almost the middle of the day. Nick had supplied them with self-powered lightstones, which they had laced into the stone holsters on their bodices. The soft white light had little effect on the gloom, but Calandra was grateful for it, none-the-less.

They entered a large central chamber with vaulted ceilings and rows upon rows of stone cases, now toppled haphazardly onto each other like Chinese bone tiles that had been set on their edges in a row and tipped, their drawers open and datastones of all sizes strewn about. Calandra began gathering stones into the drawstring satchel she had clipped onto her swimming belt, as did Judith. Zoe kept exploring the perimeter of the room.

The communication stone on Calandra's wrist vibrated with Zoe's vocal code—the hummed melody that indicated she needed their attention. Calandra glanced up to see Zoe on the far side of the room, using her lightstone to signal *look at this* in diving pulse code, then shining it at the wall.

When Calandra and Judith joined her, Calandra recognized the mural on the wall. It was the mosaic of Hadad and Atargatis she'd often seen in her dreams when she'd encountered Damon, except with some curious differences. Instead of showing the god and goddess bestowing blessings on grateful undines, they were depicted bound in chains and being thrown into a pit.

Calandra frowned. What could that mean? Surely the First Mother and her consort hadn't been confined to the Abyss? Who could even do that to them? Couldn't be.

She scanned the area, double checking to see if there was another mural like the one she remembered, but finding none. Broken columns and stones lay in patterns that felt familiar to her. This was definitely one of the places where she had frequently encountered Damon. But he was nowhere to be seen.

Neither was her Tear.

She turned to her companions and used diving sign language to indicate they must keep looking. She pointed to a vaulted archway that led deeper into the structure toward the tower they had spotted from the outside.

Let's try in there, she signed.

The others nodded and indicated that she should lead the way.

Calandra entered a dark, spacious corridor with a person-sized door frame along one side, roughly where her spatial sense told her the base of the tower they'd spotted from outside should be. The wood of the door had long since rotted away, and the brass hinges were so corroded that when she touched one, pieces of it broke off and crumbled away. Beyond the opening was a hallway or tunnel that was completely shrouded in darkness.

There was something off about that place. Normally, darkness in the waking world was a comfort, a place to see without being seen. But the darkness in that tunnel pulsed and swirled, both calling and repelling her, like the void in her nightmare. She stared at, considering whether she should pass it by.

Judith touched her arm with a questioning look. Calandra shook her head and looked back at the door, but now the darkness was merely darkness. She frowned and signed to the others to be careful, then swam into the tunnel.

The tunnel was very short. Almost immediately, she came upon a heavy stone door. The brass knob crumbled when she tried to grab it. She reached into the hole that remained, grabbed hold as best as she could, and gave a heave.

Nothing happened.

She tried pushing and pulling, but it didn't move. The other two tried to help, but there was nothing for them to grab.

After several attempts, Calandra signed that they should back away. She turned back to the door and laid her open hand on it, then reached out with earth. In moments, it swung open on its stone pivot hinge.

What she saw on the other side left her dumbfounded.

Soft light danced across their faces as they swam into a circular chamber that rose many stories above them. Rock crystal tiles lining the walls caught what light filtered into the tower's open top from the surface far above and amplified it, refracting it back and forth so the entire column glowed. About two-thirds of the way up was a dark spherical stone suspended by golden spokes.

It looked exactly like the Heartstone except, instead of pulsing with the embers of life, this one was completely dead.

Calandra swam nearer to it, wary. As she drew close, she could see that it *was* like the Heartstone, but with a difference.

The sphere was not black because it was dead. It was an enormous black obsidian ball, polished to a sheen, and without a single crack or mar. The closer she got, the more she could feel its energy, pulsing through her like an angry heartbeat.

Several spans below it, she stopped, staring at her distorted reflection—and those of her two companions—in its glossy surface.

What is this thing? And where is Damon?

Calandra closed her eyes, reaching out with her emotions to see if she could sense other beings in the area.

Zoe's and Judith's emotions were strong—anxiety and anticipation and curiosity as sharp as her own. Beyond them, she felt many forms of sea life, discerned by their uncomplicated emotions of primal, base needs, and, as she reached further afield, she could sense Nick exploring in a building nearby. Narcissa's and Mari's emotional signatures were still on board the *Luz*, as expected.

Osaze, whom she could always feel through the bond, seemed fine, if somewhat anxious. She sent a burst of warm assurance through their bond to reassure him that she was safe.

She could not sense Damon anywhere, but she hadn't expected to. She'd never been able to sense his emotions before, and she didn't know why that would be different now. He'd said he only came to Atlantis when she called him.

Maybe that's what she needed to do.

She'd barely started to focus on him when his voice boomed through the tower.

"You came, little lark."

She gasped, and her eyelids flew open to find him staring back at her from the obsidian ball, larger than life. Instead of a distorted image stretched along the surface of the sphere, it was like looking through a window into a dark room, with his face filling the field of vision.

Around his neck, hanging by its silver chain, was her Tear.

The emotions of her companions remained unchanged, and they looked at her in curiosity.

"No," Damon said, "they cannot see me. Only you can. You and I, we have a special connection. Can you not feel it?"

Calandra could, or she thought she could. Something tugged at her, like a physical force, and she drew closer to the ball.

Was this his prison? Was this the actual Abyss, the place where Mad panaceas were sent?

I came, Damon. I'm here. What must I do to get my Tear back?

He smiled—the same sensual smile he'd always had, but now, instead of making her insides melt, she felt nothing but repugnance. He had gotten her here through fear and manipulation. She still didn't know why Nadia had gone to such extremes to imprison him here, but she was sure he'd deserved them.

"You must free me, of course."

Calandra shook her head, struggling to keep her thoughts clear.

Free you to do what? Rule at my side? I have a consort. That's not going to happen.

"Ah, yes, young love. How can I compete with that?" He made a face of mock unhappiness. "But what about your precious Heartstone? You need me to repair it, and I can't do that from in here."

She bit her lip. *But would you do it out there? How can I trust you?*

Judith and Zoe floated beside her, tense and ready, watching her face for a clue as to their next move. She held up a finger to tell them to wait.

"After all I have taught you, you still don't trust me?" He clucked his tongue. "I am disappointed in you, my dear."

Perhaps I'd be more trusting if you hadn't attacked me and stolen my Tear.

"Ah. Well, you have a point there." He cocked a dark eyebrow. "Tell you what, my dear. If I give it back to you, you must promise to help me leave this place. Are we agreed?"

His voice coated her in sugary desire, and her resistance to his will was crumbling. For an instant, as though it were a mere retina burn, she thought she saw thousands of tiny threads formed of golden light binding the two of them together, but then the image disappeared and she couldn't even remember why she was alarmed. But staring at the opal hanging from his muscular neck, her gut filled with desire and greed, and she did know she would do *anything* to get it back.

Fine. Agreed. Now how do I get my stone back?

"Simple. All you need to do is take it."

She blinked at him. How was she supposed to do that?

Judith put a hand on her arm, and when Calandra looked at her, her companion indicated they should leave.

Calandra shook her head and signed that she was talking to Damon.

Zoe and Judith exchanged looks, then looked up at the ball in confusion, which must have only appeared blank to them. Zoe pointed her harpoon at the sphere, but she swam around it and scanned the surface, seeing no target. Judith signalled again that they should go.

Damon's laughter filled Calandra's mind.

"Your friends can't see me, so they don't know what to do and think you should leave. But you see me. You know me. All I want is to touch you, my pretty lark. But this time, you must come to me."

Calandra's heart pounded. She looked into his golden eyes, mesmerized, wanting very badly to reach out and touch his face, feel his strong jaw, run her fingers through his dark hair—

"Nooo!" Zoe screamed beside her with a release of air, tugging at Calandra's arm, but it was too late.

Her hand had sunken right through the surface of the stone as though it were no more substantial than the skin of a soap bubble. She wrapped her fingers around the Tear on Damon's neck, but before she could yank it back, his expression changed from sensual desire to wicked satisfaction.

"Your friends were right, my dear."

He grabbed her wrist in both of his hands, jamming her palm against his heart.

A fiery flood of pain unlike anything Calandra had ever known surged through every part of her body. Energy rushed through her hand and into the creature on the other side of the obsidian globe's face. He laughed, and the sound sucked at her like the blackness of the abyss in her nightmares. Her sense of self began to dissolve.

Somewhere far away, Judith and Zoe tugged at her, but she could not move. Zoe began humming, but Damon was completely unaffected by the sirensong. The siren shot her harpoon at the sphere, but the bolt glanced off without even leaving a mark.

Still, Damon laughed.

The void closed in around her, filling her mind until the only thing she could see was Damon's golden-eyed face. Everywhere else was blackness. Only this time, instead of giving her light and hope, his golden eyes pulled light into them—drew her very being into them.

Calandra tried to thrash and yank her arm away, but she had no control over her body. He released her hand and it stayed in place, no longer obeying her.

"Why do you fight me, little one? Didn't I warn you this would happen? If you had only kept your promise to become my consort, we could have both ruled the seas together. But, one way or another, I will have my freedom, even if it means taking what you refused to give. Once your power is mine, then I will be able to break down my prison door from the inside."

Calandra watched everything from a corner inside her mind, unable to move, unable to scream, unable to even look away. Every moment, her power weakened, but she remained as rigid as someone caught in a lightning bolt.

Then the warm red darkness that was her constant companion surrounded and enveloped her in the corner of her mind where she remained, protecting her from the cold void that Damon poured into her. She didn't understand, but from behind the walls of its fortress, she held on to her sense of self with every fibre of her being as Damon's presence took control of her body.

She saw, but barely felt, when Zoe brought her sword down on Calandra's forearm several times. Distantly, she heard the sound of shattering bone. Blood trailed through the water as someone pulled her away from the stone from behind.

Sensation returned. Excruciating pain, followed by the comforting nothingness of sleep.

*

WHEN Calandra came to, she was lying on the floor of the central compartment of the *Luz*, staring up at the worried faces of Zoe and Judith.

Her arm throbbed. She held it in front of her face to see it. Blood-soaked bandages wrapped around a nub where her hand should have been. A tight tourniquet on her upper arm stanched the flow. A sob of gratitude that she was once again in control of her own body escaped her lips.

Nick stood dripping behind her friends, hurriedly unhooking her diving pouches from her belt.

"She's awake," said Judith.

Nick gave Calandra a perfunctory glance, slung her pouches over her shoulder, and started up the ladder.

"That's good. I'm going to quick-flip it out of here and get her to a physic so we can get that arm patched up."

Zoe looked a little relieved, and Judith seemed on the verge of tears. Calandra struggled to sit up.

"Don't even think of it," said Judith, pushing her down—not that it would have been necessary. Calandra collapsed almost as soon as she had gathered her strength. She felt like a vessel that had been completely drained of everything it held.

"Osaze," she croaked, or tried, and Judith held a glass of water to her lips. She drank a few sips to wet her parched throat. "Osaze," she said again, panic rising.

There was something wrong with him. She could sense him through the bond, but it was like he was asleep. No, worse than asleep—it was like all the warmth and vitality that should have been there were missing, leaving only a cold, dark, empty place in her mind.

It was like he'd been possessed by the void.

"Oh, I wouldn't worry about him." Narcissa appeared in Calandra's field of vision with a smug smile on her face. Mari was at her girlfriend's shoulder with a matching expression. "We looked after him while you were gone, and he's doing just fine."

Tight bands of fear constricted Calandra's chest.

"Where—where is he? What have you done to him?" Her voice sounded like it had been dragged over sandpaper.

"He's right here." Narcissa turned. "Osaze, come greet your consort-elect."

Osaze stepped into her field of view, staring straight ahead with the blank expression of the Redeemed.

"Hello, Calandra," he said in an emotionless voice. He didn't even glance down at her.

"Oh, that'll never do," said Narcissa. "You have my permission to kiss her."

Calandra watched in growing horror as Osaze knelt down and placed a wooden kiss on her lips, then stood again and turned to the princess.

"I have kissed her, your highness."

"Good boy." Narcissa patted his buttocks. "Go wait in the aft cabin."

Osaze left without even glancing down.

Calandra watched him go, and every shred of energy she had left drained from her. She didn't need to see Narcissa's smug, arrogant smile to understand what had happened. The empty eyes and heart of the man who had just kissed her and walked away told her all she needed to know.

Narcissa had discovered their ruse. While Calandra had been fighting with Damon, Narcissa had enslaved Osaze. And she and Calandra both knew there was nothing Calandra could do about it.

Narcissa squatted beside Calandra, audaciously smoothing a lock of hair out of her cousin's eyes.

"I kept my promise, by the way." She held up her index finger and laughed. "It only took one finger to Redeem him."

Calandra mustered the energy to lash at Narcissa with her good hand. Narcissa caught it by the wrist with ease, crushing it in her strong siren-trained grip.

"Tsk, tsk. How unbecoming for the Saviour of the Heartstone to strike at the Opal Princess. Yes, you heard me. Now, dear cousin, this is what is going to happen when we get back to Haven. You're going to tell Mother that you will not take the throne. You will also tell her you lost your hand to a shark while in pursuit of the information she told you not to search for in Atlantis, and I saved you. And you will say nothing about Mari and me to anyone."

Narcissa eyed the other two women.

"That goes for all of you. If you don't agree, I will tell her about our dear Osaze, and that you all knew about it. Understood?"

Judith and Zoe nodded, their faces tight.

Narcissa looked at Calandra again. "I'm fairly certain I can count on your loyalty from here on out. Am I right?"

Calandra stared and said nothing.

Narcissa smirked and stood. "Of course I can." She cocked her head. "You know, Mother was right about the *sklavia* bond. I do feel more powerful already."

With one final, malicious grin, the princess followed the love of Calandra's life into the back of the submersible, Mari in her wake.

While Judith and Zoe sat helplessly beside her, Calandra clutched her ruined arm, lay on the floor, and wept.

42

ANGEL OF MERCY AND DEATH

ZALE EMERGED FROM THE ORLOP deck, fire flowing through his veins.

In the last several days, he'd healed not only young Sule, but also over a dozen other slave men and women who had fallen ill to the flux, an illness to which they seemed particularly susceptible. So far, he'd manage to escape the notice of any of the crew, though he'd watched the increasing bewilderment of Mr. Wesley with amusement.

Fortunately, he'd also found a less-conspicuous way than a bolt of lightning to release the heat he drew from the sick people, which was to transfer it into the galley stove. Cook had barely noticed anything out of the ordinary. Well, except that one time when the extra heat had burned some scones he'd been making for the captain and Robert.

When Zale stepped off the ladder from the hold this time, however, there was a problem.

A large crowd of sailors stood between him and the galley, jeering and shouting about something happening in their midst. They were probably placing bets on a friendly boxing match again, which was no real concern—there was little else to entertain on the vessel in the men's few relaxing hours. What concerned Zale was that there would be no way to navigate between them without touching any of them, and he didn't dare risk losing control before he found a safe vessel for his fire. He didn't want to think about what might happen if he tried.

He cast about for another solution, and was about to ascend to the main deck to resort to his original action—releasing the energy far out to sea—when his brain finally pulled individual words and voices from the chaos.

That was no boxing match. A man was being flogged.

Zale squinted through the red haze clouding his vision.

Mr. Crow stood in the midst of the crowd with a cat o'nine tails, laying into a black man who was bound and stretched over the capstan. The man's back was a network of bloody welts. Abela and a slave woman stood near the front of the crowd. The slave woman looked terrified. Abela shouted at Crow to stop.

"That will teach you yer place, ye yellow-bellied dog." Crow let fly again, and the man flinched and grunted.

Zale stepped closer, straining to see who was receiving the lashes. The man's face came into view. Zale stopped short.

It was Kofi.

The heat that already rushed through Zale's body surged and boiled, and he pushed forward.

"Crow!" he yelled, at the same moment Robert burst from the wardroom door and yelled "Mr. Crow! Stop that at once!"

The young gentleman pushed through the crowd of watchers until he reached the front, surveying the scene. Zale paused outside the circle of people, panting like he'd run a mile.

Crow faltered in his rhythm, letting the tails fall behind him as he turned to face the ship's owner.

"Mr. Cox. This man attacked me. Ask anyone 'ere, they'll tell ye the same thing."

Robert's face darkened. He turned to Kofi, whose face was away from him.

"Mr. Smith, is that true?"

Kofi's face was contorted into sharp lines of agony. "Aye, sir. But—"

"Shut yer mouth, boy." The barrel-shaped sailor who stood over Kofi cuffed his face, leaving a bloody cut on Kofi's cheek.

Crow dropped his arm and put his hands on his hips, facing Robert.

"Ye kin see why the lashin' be necessary, sir?"

Robert closed his mouth, looking pained. Then he nodded and took a step back, clenching and unclenching his fists.

Abela stepped toward him.

"Rob—Mr. Cox, Mr. Crow was behaving most unbecomingly toward this woman. He was about to—to ravish her, sir. When I interfered, Mr. Crow turned his attentions to—"

Crow grabbed her arm and spun her around. "Shut up, ye draggle-tailed game pullet. Ye'll not speak of me so."

Robert pushed Crow away and inserted himself between Abela and her attacker. "Unhand her, sir. You will not behave that way toward a lady."

Crow snorted. "Lady?" He spit on the floor at Abela's feet. "She's no more a lady than this slave whore, no matter what she wears or what airs she puts on."

Robert's punch hit Crow squarely in the jaw, and the thin first mate stumbled backward. Robert shook out his fist, wincing.

"You will watch your tongue, or I will have you flogged instead." He turned to Abela. "I'm sorry you had to see that, Miss Bethel. Now, you were saying?"

Crow glared at Robert, rubbing his face where he'd been struck. His cronies stood dumbly around him, uncertain what to do.

Abela glanced around at them and caught Zale's eye at the back of the crowd. Her eyes widened. She had come to recognize when he'd done a healing and needed to vent. He was still maintaining control, but it was becoming increasingly difficult.

She turned back to Robert.

"Mr. Crow became . . . violent with me and threatened to bestow the same fate upon me that he'd been about to force on Binta. Mr. Smith came upon us just as Mr. Crow grabbed me, and he pushed Mr. Crow away by force. Things escalated rather quickly from there."

Zale's heartbeat thundered in his chest. He stood behind two men, and beyond them, Crow hunkered like a wounded animal. Zale ground his teeth, restraining himself from landing a blow on the first mate's other cheek.

He glanced at Kofi, whose eyes were scrunched closed, his cheek pressed hard against the head of the capstan. Zale wondered if his friend were praying.

Robert listened intently to Abela's statement, then turned to face Crow and the crowd of sailors.

"Mr. Cogger, Mr. Guppy, please remove Mr. Crow to his quarters and post guard. His behaviour cannot be tolerated. I will speak with Captain Meredith about what should be done with him."

He turned to face Kofi, who still panted against the capstan.

"Mr. Smith's behaviour, while unacceptable for a slave, could, perhaps, be excused as it was in your defence, Miss Bethel. At any rate, he has had punishment enough. Release him, please. And someone go fetch Mr. Wesley to see to him."

Abela, rather than looking pleased or relieved, had her brow furrowed in that way which Zale knew meant she'd been hoping for a different result.

Cogger and Guppy moved from their position in front of Zale to take

Crow's arms, but the first mate twisted away from them and lunged for Robert, a knife flashing in his hand.

Without thinking, Zale darted forward and grabbed Crow's arm, releasing the rage that flowed through him.

Crow arched his back, mouth stretched in a silent scream, eyes bulging out of his head. He stood like that, rigid and shaking, until Zale let go of him and he fell to the floor. A curl of smoke rose from his hair.

One look at his glassy eyes told the truth. Crow was dead.

Zale's throat closed. The red haze was gone, and all that remained was dread. He looked up at Robert, whose jaw hung open, and the sailors, many of whom looked between Crow and Zale in fear and confusion.

Mr. Wesley arrived and pushed his way through the men. He spotted Crow.

"What's all this?" He stooped and checked the man's pulse, then looked up in consternation. "Mr. Crow is dead. What has happened here?"

No one spoke. Zale dared a look at Abela, and the disappointment on her face pierced him.

He turned and fled up the ladder to the main deck, dimly aware of Robert calling for him to wait. He took three long strides to the rail and dove over the side, transforming to a merman as he hit the water, his breeches tearing as his lower body reformed itself.

Never mind what Crow had been about to do. Zale had killed him with only a touch. He was still a monster—not a guardian, as was his calling, but a demon of the underworld.

Save the world?

He couldn't even save himself.

*

"MAN overboard!" echoed along the main deck, and sailors raced to the rail to try to catch a glimpse of the boy who had flown past them into the waves.

Along the horizon, dark clouds gathered, coming toward them at alarming speed. The wind picked up and the rigging creaked from the billowing sails.

Robert leaned over the rail, his mind straining to believe what he had just seen.

Had Zale killed a man by touching him? No, surely not. But then, what *had* happened? And what of the charred footprints where Zale and

Crow had stood?

Robert could swear he had seen Zale change form as he'd thrown himself off the ship—and why would he do such a thing? It was madness, a sure death sentence. His jaw clenched. He told himself he'd imagined Zale's fish-like form—the form that fit almost exactly the description Jory had stammered out all those years ago of the demon that had blinded him.

But no—it was through the healing touch of Zale's mother that Robert's sight had been restored to him. And he'd heard a rumour from Mr. Wesley that the slaves regarded Zale as some kind of angel of mercy, that he had healed many of them by merely praying for them. They regarded him with a mixture of awe and fear when they came on deck, like he were some kind of deity. Mr. Wesley had no other explanation for the exceptional good health of the cargo, despite their conditions.

"We haven't lost a single one," he'd muttered in wonder.

Could life and death reside in the same person?

Robert clenched the rail, glancing over his shoulder. Mr. Wesley was speaking with Captain Meredith on the quarterdeck, their expressions grave. Miss Bethel and Mr. Berian conferred near the ship's boats in hushed tones and kept glancing at Robert and then out to sea where Zale had disappeared into the waves.

That's when Robert saw the truth in their eyes. They knew about Zale. They had known all along. That's what they meant about being familiar with the activities of spirits. Somehow, for some reason, they were working with Zale Teague—for what nefarious purpose, Robert did not know.

He strode over to them.

"Who the devil are you people? And why are you here? What have . . . ?" He faltered. "How could . . . ?"

A wave of nausea overwhelmed him. He clutched the rail of the main deck. Captain Meredith bellowed orders to the crew. They scurried over the ratlines trimming sails and dropping rigging in preparation for the oncoming storm.

A sudden gust of wind pushed the boom of the nearest sail around and the three of them ducked.

"Mr. Cox, Mr. Berian, and Miss Bethel, you'd best get below," shouted the captain from above them.

"Aye!" Robert yelled back. But when he turned to face his opponents again, only Berian remained. "Where is Miss Bethel?" he demanded, shouting to be heard over the wind.

"She is fine and safe. Come, Mr. Cox. Let us take refuge below."

Robert looked frantically around the deck for Miss Bethel, but she was nowhere to be seen. Deciding she must have already gone below, he allowed Berian to guide him toward the ladder.

The roaring wind was slightly quieter on the lower deck, but Miss Bethel was still absent. The crowd of sailors had dispersed, running this way and that to prepare for the squall. Kofi had been unlashed from the capstan, and the only evidence of the recent altercation were streaks of drying blood running down its sides and the charred footprints on the floor. Robert eyed them as he walked by on the way to the cabin he and Berian shared. Berian followed behind.

Once the door closed behind them, blocking out most of the noise, he whirled on his cabin mate.

"What the devil is happening around here? Is Zale some kind of demon?"

Berian sighed and pulled out his pocket watch, opening it to inspect its face.

"No. He's our only hope."

43

THE ONCOMING STORM

ZALE SWAM DEEP BENEATH THE waves until it became difficult to see, scattering schools of fish and avoiding pockets of kelp. His thoughts were as turbulent as the water around him.

He had thought he was doing better. He thought he could control himself now, and that he was finally doing something good to make up for the horrible mistakes of his past. And now he'd added one more casualty to his death toll. A person he hated, true—but who was Zale to decide who was worthy of life and who wasn't? It was far more responsibility than he wanted.

Eventually, his pumping blood slowed and he stopped, hanging in the darkening ocean. Far above him, a surface that should have been bright with daylight was dark and foreboding, and the water churned cloudy and grey. He pushed himself to the surface and looked around.

Dark clouds roiled in the sky. Rain fell in blinding sheets. Lightning flashed and thunder roared. He bobbed from the top of one dark swell into a trough between, and then to the top of the next. Powerful waves, higher than the mizzenmast of the *Atlanta*, stretched to every horizon. He could not see the ship, no matter which direction he looked. Fear gripped Zale in icy tentacles.

What have I done?

He tried to breathe, to calm himself, but that did nothing. If he couldn't get this storm under control, the people he cared about on the *Atlanta* would suffer even more consequences for his inherent evil, and their only mistake would have been to trust him. He closed his eyes and reached out with air and fire, trying to nullify the storm system that swirled around them.

Nothing happened.

In increasing desperation, he reached into the pocket of his waistcoat, which floated around him like a bladder. Tearing a hole in the lining, he dug out the stone bracelet and, with only a moment's thought, snapped it around his wrist.

Immediately, the world around him lost most of its colour, and his connection with the storm ceased. The storm itself, however, did not. He looked up at the clouds with their flares of lightning and shouted.

"God . . . Elyon, you must stop it! I cannot! Protect them all from me. Please!"

Abela appeared beside him in the ocean, her hair and dress plastered against her. She bobbed beneath the waves and he grabbed her arm, bringing her to the surface.

She spluttered, grabbed his arm with one hand, lifted her balled fist to her mouth, and blew into it.

*

In the next instant, the press of water around Zale's body had been replaced by air.

He sat on a sheltered ledge beneath the bay of windows at the stern of the *Atlanta*, Abela beside him. His tattered breeches hung loosely by the waist cord around his tail, and Abela's dress clung wetly to her skin. The ship still pitched on the waves, but they seemed to be lessening, and lightning no longer split the sky.

She noticed the green bracelet and put her hand on it. "You didn't need to do this."

He shook his head. "Yes, I did. And I know what else I must do. I must turn myself in."

He twisted his hand and clasped hers, willing her to understand.

She stared back at him from only inches away.

"I know." She squeezed his hand, and her eyes grew moist. "Tell them you caught the hull and climbed up here on your own. They already doubt what they saw as you changed. They'll be all too happy to forget it completely."

"And how did I do it? What do I tell them about that? How did I kill Crow?"

She cocked her head, pecked him on the cheek, then blew onto the chariot in her palm and disappeared. His hand where she'd held it felt cold.

He got her message.

What he told Captain Meredith and the others was up to him.

*

ROBERT stood with his arms crossed next to Captain Meredith's desk, regarding the bedraggled young man who stood between two sailors on the other side of it. Captain Meredith sat in the chair with his hands folded in the air in front of him, looking as flummoxed as Robert felt. Reverend Berian and Miss Bethel stood silently behind Zale, having been hushed by Captain Meredith already.

The captain pierced Zale with eyes the colour of an Arctic Sea, his face hard.

"So, you mean to tell me, boy, that you killed Mr. Crow?"

"Aye, sir."

Robert found himself staring at Zale, unable to look away from the young man's iridescent green eyes. He should have known eyes like that did not belong to any mortal soul. How had he not seen it before?

"And you did it by merely touching him?"

Zale swallowed. "Aye, sir."

Captain Meredith leaned back in his wooden chair. "How?"

"I can't tell you."

Robert ground his jaw.

Captain Meredith scowled. "Mr. Wesley has examined the body, and he can find no wound of any kind, no signs of poisoning or any traditional form of murder. The only thing he mentioned is that there is a small burn mark on Mr. Crow's arm. That, and his flesh has been cooked from within. You did this?"

The colour left Zale's face as the captain relayed the results of the autopsy, but he only nodded.

"And you can't tell me how? Or won't tell me."

Zale shuffled his feet and said nothing.

Captain Meredith leaned forward, staring at the lad. "Then tell me this—did you mean to kill him, boy?"

Zale dropped his gaze to the captain's bare desk. He shook his head. "No, I didn't. I was mighty upset with him, and wanted to stop him from hurting Mr. Cox, but I didn't mean to kill him."

Robert jerked his head up. "What did you say?"

Zale glanced at him, then looked away.

"I didn't mean to kill Mr. Crow, sir. It was an accident."

Robert shook his head and took a step forward. "No, about Crow threatening me. When did that happen?"

Zale looked up from beneath his wet brows. "After you confined him to quarters, sir. He lunged at you with a knife while your back was turned. I only meant to stop him before he could reach you."

Robert stepped backward, a numb sensation spreading out from his midriff. Zale had saved his life? Who was this boy? Demon or angel?

He strode around the desk and looked Zale in the eye. The lad's height was of a level with Robert's, but Zale's shoulders and head bowed with shame and made him appear shorter and much younger than he was. For a moment, Robert once again saw his childhood playmate, the one who had caught him with his brother's friends mistreating a girl and had stepped in to try to stop them, even though he was hopelessly outnumbered. The one Robert himself had watched the other boys torment, until a freak bolt of lightning had taken his eyesight.

"Look at me, Zale," he said quietly.

Zale hesitated, then met Robert's eyes.

Robert touched his scars.

"You didn't mean to do this either, did you? But it was you. All along, it was you."

Zale swallowed and nodded, then ducked his head again.

Even though he'd guessed the answer, Robert felt like he'd been kicked in the gut. He dropped his hand, muttered an "excuse me" to Captain Meredith, then stumbled out the door.

The storm had subsided, and the decks were busy with sailors mending sails, pushing water off the decks, and tidying up. Robert walked between them like a man drunk, barely paying attention to his route as he descended ladders and wandered the ship, until he found himself staring down into the orlop deck.

Robert hesitated at the top of the ladder. The aroma rising from the slave hold below assaulted his senses. His stomach heaved and he turned away, almost losing his nerve again. He'd been on the *Atlanta* for weeks, and he still had not gone to see the conditions in which the human cargo resided. He'd told himself many times that he would do it the next day, hiding on his pitching berth while the slaves took their morning exercise on decks, but there had always been a reason not to go.

Excuses. You always have excuses. You're pathetic.

Zale, the boy that had haunted his conscience for five years, had been the one who had blinded him. Zale, the boy who could pray and heal a slave. Zale, the boy who had killed a man to save his life.

Zale the merman. Robert knew what he'd seen, no matter what the others were willing to believe.

Robert had told himself that when he found the creature that had blinded him, he would have his revenge. But what revenge could be had on a boy he'd wronged, and who had then saved his life? For though the boy's powers terrified him, he could feel little sorrow for Crow's passing. The man had been a barnacle on the ship, one whom Gryffyn had insisted on hiring for some reason that was beyond Robert.

Suddenly, Gryffyn's interest in Zale made sense, and why he would never talk about what really happened that day in the woods. Robert had no idea what his brother intended, but he knew Gryffyn would have seen some financial gain to be had from someone with Zale's abilities. He shuddered to think what would happen if Gryffyn ever had Zale in his clutches. With powers like Zale possessed, would Gryffyn even live to regret it? Or would he somehow use Zale to do terrible damage?

Why did Gryffyn always get what he wanted?

Robert shook his head. He knew why. Robert let him.

No matter how much good he promised to do, no matter how he tried to protect those whom Gryffyn might harm, he never truly inconvenienced himself to do it. This ocean voyage was the riskiest thing he'd ever done, but even that was not because he'd wanted to help Zale—that had been merely an excuse.

The image of that burning dragon spirit still danced before his eyes in the dark of the night, and the memory of its chilling voice slithered along his spine until exhaustion finally gave him the gift of sleep. He'd been terrified, and he hadn't known what to do with the knowledge he'd accidentally discovered. If he were honest with himself, he wished he'd never gone looking for those answers. When he found them, he had to get as far away from what he'd seen as possible.

Miss Bethel's words from his first night on the *Atlanta* came back to him.

Is it worth it, Mr. Cox? she'd asked.

He stared into the darkness below and swallowed. No wonder she didn't think him brave enough to withstand the derision a union like theirs would invite. He could not even face his own brother, or the shame he knew awaited him in this very hold.

He turned away from the ladder.

I did all I could.

But had he? Had he truly done what he could to prevent any suffering from being accredited to his name? Or had he, once again, stood by indecisively while his brother did exactly as he wished, no matter the cost?

And how could he be angry with Zale for stepping in where Robert had been afraid to take a stand, even if the cost had been steep?

"Not this time," he said, turning back toward the ladder with resolve. He nodded at the seaman who had been posted as a guard, then began to descend.

With every step, the heat and stench thickened, so by the time he reached the lower deck, it was like standing in a cloud of pigswill. It was worse than the worst he'd ever smelled in a London slum, and hotter than the very depths of hell. He stood there and let his eyes adjust to the dim light that filtered down through the grate from the gun deck above.

He'd come down by the ladder nearest the bow, knowing this is where the men were held. Since they'd been out to sea, the women and children, which were held nearer the back, had been given free reign of the ship except at night, and he often saw them walking about the decks above. But not the men. Their movements were always highly regulated, and even when they were allowed abovedeck twice a day for meals and exercise, they were always fettered. They were also caked with filth, bringing the stench of this place with them.

Now Robert could see why.

The hold had been fitted with a false deck after off-loading the previous cargo in Africa—five-foot-wide shelves with less than three feet of space above and below. Into these spaces, the slaves were packed feet-first like sardines in a barrel. Human waste ran in rivulets over the floor, and human eyes stared up at him in numb misery.

Robert's stomach heaved, and he clapped a hand over his mouth to prevent himself from vomiting—or breathing.

He was responsible for this. He had allowed this to happen. How could doing this to even one person justify any good he might achieve from the profit? Never mind what others did in pursuit of Mammon, how could he ever stand before God with the weight of so much human suffering dragging at his soul?

Zale had accidentally harmed others while trying to do good. Robert had intentionally harmed others and salved his conscience with the good that would come of it. But no amount of balm could soothe him now.

With desperate stares flaying his back as violently as any cat o'nine, he fled up the ladder.

He didn't stop running until he reached the main deck and tossed the contents of his stomach into the forgiving sea.

44

HARD PLACE

Opal Palace, Sireniapolis
June 13, AD 1799/10 Didymoi 4155 EK

CALANDRA SAT AT HER DESK and flexed her hand, massaging the palm and side of her newly regrown appendage.

The treatments were not yet complete. There were still the last two joints of the fourth and fifth fingers to regrow, the nubs still covered in white linen. But after more than a week with her whole hand being in bandages, the relative freedom was refreshing.

Not exhilarating. The sight of her consort-elect's blank face beside her chamber door and even blanker connecting line of spirit were too sobering for that.

"Thank you, *daskala*," she said to Thea. She saluted the older woman with the bunched fingers of her good hand and ignoring the immediate frowns of the two siren guards who stood behind her mentor.

Thea shook her head and stood, then bowed and saluted Calandra in return. Calandra wished they were allowed to speak during the treatment sessions—but Adonia had strictly forbidden it.

"Not *daskala* now," Thea chided, then held her arms out to the sides so the guards could replace the feldspar bracelets that would dampen her powers.

"You'll always be my teacher," Calandra murmured as Thea was led out of the room.

When Thea had gone, Calandra looked at Osaze. He stood by the door at attention, holding his *deiktis* staff and staring blankly into the room.

Trying to ignore the gaping void his emotional absence left in her spirit, she turned her seat around to face the desk. The stoneworking project she'd been tinkering with before Thea had arrived for the treatment lay on the wooden desktop. Picking up a lump of granite and dipping it in water, she went back to carefully shaping a small piece of pale amber to fit inside an ear canal.

She almost wished she hadn't sent Judith down to the harbour to check on the dolphin pup. They had both known the errand was more of an excuse to be alone than because she needed to know. The baby was fine, well recovered from her injuries, and bonding well with the several undines assigned to care for her. But Calandra knew that Judith was frustrated at seeing her mistress like this, with so little she could do about it—and the constant strain of wondering when Narcissa would betray them all didn't help either.

A tear leaked down Calandra's cheek, and she fiercely wiped it away. She had no right to feel sorry for herself.

But for Osaze, and Judith, and Zoe?

She decided that tears of shame were justified, and let the next tear slide down to her chin and drip off onto her workbench unhindered.

Adonia had been furious that Calandra had gone to Atlantis after she'd been told not to. If Calandra hadn't lost a hand because of it, she could only imagine what her aunt would have done to her.

But when Calandra had refused to accept the role of heir, offering the truthful explanation that she was not worthy of such honour after her disobedience, Adonia had responded with a stony "We shall see about that."

Then she had sent Calandra and her retinue home to the Opal Palace to have her hand regrown by Thea, who was still the most skilful healer on the island, and had continued the tour with Narcissa checking and taking the bonds instead.

While Calandra had been relieved to not have to take any more *sklavia* bonds—the pain and guilt of the ones she already held were burdensome enough—the thought of what Narcissa would do with even a smidgen more power terrified her. She could only hope that Narcissa, with her mother's favour apparently bestowed upon her, would not feel the need to expose Judith and Zoe to the queen's mercy.

Not that Calandra could rouse herself to care about it much. As far as she could tell, her power had been undiminished by Damon's violation. It was her soul that throbbed with an aching hollowness she couldn't shake.

How short-sighted to leave Osaze alone with Narcissa and Mari, who had a great deal of talent with sirensong. It had taught her one thing—she would never be able to protect Osaze all the time. If only she'd insisted that

Osaze leave when he'd had the chance. She'd rather miss him knowing he was free somewhere in the world than miss him while he stood before her, presently absent. *If he truly had a choice . . .*

She twisted to look at him again.

"Osaze?"

"Yes, your highness?"

She winced at the honorific. She'd tried to get him to call her Calandra when in private, but he'd told her Narcissa had forbidden it. Of course.

"Please come here."

He stood before her. She took the staff from him and leaned it on the desk, then turned and wrapped her arms around him. His arms hung stiffly at his sides, his body erect and inflexible.

"I love you, Osaze," she said into his chest. "I'm so sorry."

He did nothing, said nothing in response. No order was given, so no response was required. She wondered if, somewhere inside his head, he could hear what she was saying to him.

She dropped her arms, feeling worse than before. She picked up his staff and handed it back to him without looking up.

"Resume your post, please."

"Yes, your highness." He walked back to the door and resumed his unfocused attentiveness.

Calandra turned back to her work.

She supposed she should be grateful that Narcissa had seen the necessity of having him obey her at all. The bondholder could always have the Redeemed do as she wished, of course. But even the princess had recognized that, as Calandra's bodyguard and consort-elect, Osaze would need to obey Calandra's commands. Calandra knew she probably *should* be grateful for that, but it was difficult. Not even Adonia had required women to give up their consort's Redemption bonds. She'd even had Calandra transfer Matthew's to Narcissa before sending Calandra home.

Calandra felt foolish. For all she knew, Osaze would report on everything she did when Narcissa returned to the palace. Best not to give him anything she could laugh about at Calandra's expense.

If only she could figure out how Tanni had Released Osaze when they were children—but no matter how she worried at that problem, she could not find a solution. She'd tried every variation she could imagine of the memory-loss Song from the old text stone that Tanni had brought her, with no result. She'd pored through the few Atlantis stones she'd kept, looking for a clue, but found nothing. She wondered if her mother had known how.

At the thought of her mother, her hands trembled and slipped. She paused, clenching them into tight fists to keep from reaching for the empty place on her throat where her Tear used to be.

She went back to her work, polishing the resin so hard with a piece of soft linen that a sharp aromatic pine scent surrounded her. From her wrist, the jingling of her panacea's triquetra bracelet mocked her.

"The most powerful healer on the island, but you're impotent," she muttered to herself.

I failed, Mother. I don't know how to find you. And I don't know how I'm going to heal the Heartstone. I'm going to be bonded to a man who is Redeemed, and I'm going to go Mad. Perhaps I should flee, as you did. That might be best. After all, if you couldn't succeed, how can I?

She clenched her jaw.

Tanni's presence drew nearer to her from the direction of the Royal Academy wing at a walking pace. Calandra wondered if her friend was speaking to her yet.

After her return in disgrace, Calandra had told Tanni about the Tear, and Damon, and the Free Will Society at Elpida at the first opportunity, as well as the Atlantis stones she'd sent back to them with Nick. Since things had gone so horribly awry at Atlantis, she'd wanted Tanni's help in planning what to do next, thinking Tanni would be thrilled about their plan to change the future of the island.

Instead, her friend had gotten angry. Calandra had never seen her so upset.

"There were not only human women in that rebellion, then," Tanni said, her voice hard. "Undines and men, too. And they're living at your family property. Did you find out which of them killed my mother? It could have been one of these new man friends of yours—did you ever think of that?"

"Well, yes, actually, I—"

"Was it Hammad? Or this Ignatia's consort, what was his name?" She didn't wait for a response. "Jacob. And they're breeding more. You know, maybe Adonia has the right idea. Men cause tears, they fight in wars, and they kill for pleasure. I can't believe you want to Release them all."

Tanni had avoided Calandra ever since, though her mother's old text stone had arrived by *doulos* the following morning.

But now, Tanni stood right outside the door. Maybe she was ready to talk at last. Calandra wasn't sure if she was glad or wanted to be left alone with her misery.

Calandra bade Osaze to admit Tanni without even looking up from her desk. Tanni came in and sat on the bed, staring at Calandra for a long moment in silence.

"How's the arm today?" she asked at last.

Calandra shrugged, holding up her bandage-wrapped fingers. "It hurts, but it's almost healed."

Thea had been regrowing her hand in stages, a process that was both painful and time-consuming. Unlike the bones in an undine's legs, which were made of a unique kind of fluid cartilage that reflexively rearranged and became rigid once more each time an undine changed state, their hands were made of flesh and bone similar to a human's, and regrowing them took time.

"You should be grateful, you know. If you were human, you may not be able to regrow a hand at all."

Calandra lay down her tools and sighed, then turned to face Tanni. Her friend was in a short sleeveless peach tunic—off-duty.

"I know. And I am. There is so little else to be grateful for right now, I'm holding on to the things I can."

"Here."

Tanni sheepishly handed Calandra a linen-wrapped package.

"What's this?" Calandra asked, examining the pretty purple string tied around the cloth.

"Just open it."

Calandra did, and pulled out a long diving knife whose bone sheath and handle were decorated with fine carvings of the Holy Triquetra motif surrounded by star, vine, and leaf designs.

"Did you make this?"

Tanni nodded. "Yeah. It was supposed to be your bonding gift, but after what happened with Narcissa and Osaze and . . . and us, I wanted to give it to you now instead."

Calandra admired the fine details. "It's exquisite. Thank you."

Tanni fidgeted with her own knife hilt. "You're welcome." She pressed her lips together, then drew a breath. "Look, I'm sorry for what I said. I wish I could have been there to meet Jacob and Hammad and the others. And I'm sorry for what happened to Osaze. I don't like seeing him like this either. And what Narcissa did was downright rotten."

She glanced at the big man, but he kept staring at some point beyond the wall.

"I didn't know my mother, but I'd like to think that, had she known what she was fighting against, her conscience would have prevented her from it." She leaned closer and lowered her voice. "Like mine has."

"Oh, Tanni."

Calandra threw her arms around her friend, and they embraced for a long moment. The icy vacuum inside her thawed a little. She sat back in her chair.

"You were right, though. Some men *are* violent and evil. Damon proved that." Calandra held up her bandaged hand for emphasis. "But so are some women. You should have seen Adonia's face when she killed that woman in Fire Lake. She had no compassion, no remorse. And look how Narcissa has been every day of her life. Her every thought is consumed with gaining power for power's sake, seemingly at any cost. No, violence is not limited by gender or race." She ran her fingers over the knife hilt, then tucked the sheath into her belt. "But neither is kindness or love. You should have seen how Jacob was with Ezekiel. And how Osaze was with me."

She glanced at her consort-elect and away, gritting her teeth and speaking for Tanni's ears alone.

"I know now why Thea risked so much for forty-five years to keep her husband free and safe. What we do to them, Tanni, it's not right. It's never been right. We have to make everyone see that."

Tanni twirled a lock of the thick black hair that fell loose over her shoulder around a finger as though they were talking about nothing of import, matching Calandra's tone.

"I agree with you. But how? You've obviously had no luck with the stone I sent you."

Calandra swallowed and spoke over her shoulder. "Osaze, please go wait in the hallway."

She hated that she had to do that, but it was best to be safe. This conversation was taking a dangerous turn.

"Yes, your highness." He left the room and closed the door as mechanically as he'd replied.

Calandra turned back to Tanni, but still kept her voice down.

"I'd hoped my Tear would help me find my family, and, since the Free-willers won't risk exposing themselves, that my brother would be the proof that the bonds cause androsterility. I also hoped he would have powers and could help me heal the Heartstone. The Solstice Healing Ceremony would have been too public to hide the truth, even if Adonia tried. But now, not only do I not know where to find my family, if I go ahead and create the *syzagos* bond with Osaze as Adonia wishes while he is under Redemption, I am almost certain to go Mad . . . and the Heartstone might be none the better off for it."

She punched her leg in frustration.

"Frankly, even if I did learn of my family's whereabouts, they could all be dead. And without having a male undine to help me, the consort bond is still my next-best option for healing the Stone, which I *must* do. If the Madness threatens . . . well, I know how to find the Abyss now."

Tanni frowned. "I hope it doesn't come to that."

Calandra thought of the void that took her hand, and the golden-eyed spirit imprisoned there who had been such a strange mentor for so long. Whatever his faults, she'd learned a great deal from him, and he'd seemed certain he could help her heal the Heartstone.

"Maybe I should go back to Atlantis and free Damon after all."

As she said it, she felt an inexplicable pull to do just that, to get up from her chair and swim back to him that instant.

What is wrong with me?

"No." Tanni shook her head emphatically, and the urge was broken. "Look what he's done to you. He can't be trusted. And Osaze wouldn't want that either." She frowned. "I thought you were going to use the consort bond on Osaze either way."

"He gave me permission, but he didn't want me to. He didn't think the risk of Madness was worth it, even when he was Free."

She wondered briefly if she could do what needed to be done while honouring his wishes. She hoped so.

"Tanni, I need to know something. You have always been there for me, and if your answer is no, you've earned the right to say it. But I want to make sure you weren't trying to escape a lousy situation or weren't afraid because of what happened to your mother . . ."

"Calandra, will you spit it out already?"

Calandra met her friend's gaze. Tanni's eyebrows had climbed nearly to her hairline.

"If you knew how to Release Osaze, you would tell me, right?"

Tanni's expression didn't change for several long seconds. Finally, she got up and walked over to the window, her face hidden behind her curly hair. Calandra worried that she had once again crossed the line.

"I was afraid for a long time that they wouldn't believe me. When Thea tested me for truth that first night, I panicked. Even though she *said* she believed me, I felt Adonia's eyes and ears on me for years afterwards. I didn't think she could possibly accept that a weaver's granddaughter from Haven could stumble over a secret no one even knew existed before. So I worked harder than anyone else to prove myself, and kept my reputation spotless. But nothing came of it. Maybe Adonia trusted Thea then. Or maybe Thea never told her what actually happened." She turned around, her brow puckered in hurt. "I always thought you believed me, too."

Calandra drew and breath and stood.

"I *did* believe you. I've always believed you. But I'm desperate, Tanni. You know a lot more now than you did then. I thought maybe, over the years, something could have tweaked a memory and you might have kept it to yourself. I wouldn't blame you. I wouldn't have wanted to see you die over this. Or for anything else." When had she started crying? "Tanni, I don't know what I'd do without you."

Tanni set her jaw and regarded Calandra for a long moment.

"I swear to you, Calandra kor'Delphine, I don't know what I did that night. And I have tried. Oh, I've tried. I knew how much your promise to Osaze meant to you."

Tanni was crying now, too.

Calandra clenched and unclenched her hands, staring at her best friend in amazement.

"You tried to do it again, even though you knew the consequences?"

Tanni's face bunched as though to say *you silly porpoise*. "Of course I did. I'd do anything for you."

The brave front Calandra had been putting up burst. All the tears she'd been holding in for as long as she could remember flooded from her in wracking sobs. She and Tanni met in the middle of the room in a tight embrace.

"I'd go to the ends of the earth for you," Tanni said into her hair. "No matter the cost."

"Me, too," Calandra said, still sniffling.

After their emotions had subsided, they parted and wiped their eyes.

"You know I feel the same way about Osaze, don't you?" Calandra asked.

Tanni made a face.

"You think I don't know that?" She touched her temple. "You're in here, remember? I knew you weren't going weak-kneed over me for the last three weeks."

Despite herself, Calandra laughed.

"Yeah, I suppose that might have been a little awkward from your side.

Sorry. But this is about more than Osaze. It's about every man on this island. And I *am* going to find the solution to this."

"I know." Tanni regarded Calandra with a level gaze. "Do you think this island is ready for a culture of Free men?"

Calandra looked out the window, which overlooked the entire Paradise Valley, beyond which was Fire Lake, then Haven, then Atlantis. Somewhere out there was where she had lost her hand, and where she'd asked Zoe almost that exact same question.

"I don't know. But I don't think it's up to me to make them ready for a change in a custom that should never have been created in the first place. I only need to figure out how to convince them that, once the men are Free, that's how things should remain."

"Mother help us," Tanni said, shaking her head. She glanced at Calandra. "If anyone can do it, I believe you can."

Calandra smiled, the first bit of pleasure she'd felt for days. "Thank you, Tanni."

Tanni looked thoughtful.

"You know, even without your brother, you could still use your bonding ceremony and the Summer Solstice Festival to spread the truth about the bonds. Bond Osaze to ensure no one can say you didn't do everything you could, and then go through with the Healing Ceremony. If you heal it, wonderful. But if you can't—if even you, the most powerful healer since Nadia kor'Hera, cannot restore the Heartstone—you can at least tell everyone why."

"And why would anyone believe me? When fear and prejudice have been part of a culture's beliefs for as long as our hatred of men, it takes more than someone's word that they are wrong. They have to see the truth for themselves. Like I did with Osaze. Or Thea did with Gerrick, or my mother with my father. They'd probably just think I'd gone Mad."

Her heart contracted as she thought of the request Osaze had made of her on that fateful night five years ago—right before he'd chosen to be enslaved rather than leave her. *Let me give you my heart without giving up my mind.*

He'd loved her even then. She knew that somewhere behind his blank eyes, his heart was still hers, but what did it matter when his mind belonged to another? If she could only change that, perhaps they could show the nation a new picture of who men were. Why should it matter that he was not an undine?

But unless they could find a way to free him, that didn't seem likely.

Tanni stood and held out her hand.

"Come on. I could use a swim, and I bet you could, too. Unless you can't get your bandages wet . . ."

Calandra looked at the two small linen strips. "No, I think I'm fine now. You can help me redress these after. And I would love a swim."

She led the way to the door and stopped when she saw her consort-elect's still form on the other side, pierced by a pang of sorrow that he would not be swimming with her. She could have him do it, but without the joy that it was meant to bring, what would be the point?

She glanced away, her throat thick.

"It's time to go, Osaze."

"Yes, your highness."

He bowed and saluted and waited for them to pass, his face and voice emotionless.

Calandra clenched her jaw, burning with determination to fix this, to free Osaze for good. Tanni squeezed her shoulder. Calandra led the way out of the bedchamber, then waited for her taller friend to match pace beside her and Osaze behind her.

"Tanni, can you do a favour for me?"

"Anything," Tanni said, moving with the confident strides of a rhapsodist. "What is it?"

"I need to speak to Thea alone. Perhaps she'll have an idea what to do. I know it's a lot to ask, but can you make that happen?"

Tanni gave Calandra a searching stare. Then she nodded and faced forward.

"Yup."

45

MEETINGS

WHEN THE TIME ARRIVED FOR Calandra's final treatment the next day, instead of two sirens arriving at Calandra's door with Thea between them, Meg arrived with a message. Since Calandra had come home, she hadn't seen Meg except across the dining hall at mealtimes. Now, the lissome girl's hand sparkled with a blue opal stone healer's ring, and a silver triquetra gleamed on her forehead, dangling from a chain laying in the part of her jet-black hair, just as Thea had always worn hers.

"What's going on?" Calandra asked.

"Rhapsodist kor'Zelia says you are to take your final treatment in the Garden of the Mother's Delight. She has Aunt Thea waiting there for you."

Calandra smiled.

Thank you, Tanni.

She cast a glance at Judith over her shoulder, who returned the look with hope-filled eyes. Smiling a *wish-me-luck* at her maid, Calandra fell into step behind Meg, Osaze trailing behind with crisp steps.

When they arrived at the Grotto, Meg leaned close to Calandra's ear.

"You must still be careful," she said, indicating the two siren guards who stood at the arched entrance between the colonnade and the garden. "There are more at each exit."

Calandra nodded and murmured her thanks, and Meg saluted and walked hurriedly down the colonnade toward the Great Hall.

Thea sat with her back toward Calandra on the bench facing the fountain of Atargatis in the centre. Calandra bade Osaze wait at the entrance with the singers on duty, ignoring the mental cringe like spiders walking on her brain as she did so, and stepped onto the flagstone pathway to the fountain. When she sat down beside Thea, the panacea spoke without looking away from the water.

335

"It's not outdoors, but I'm thankful for what little grace Tanni was able to provide," she said, rubbing her wrists where the feldspar bracelets had just been removed.

"I asked Tanni for this. I needed to speak with you."

Thea turned toward her. "I surmised as much."

Calandra glanced at her mentor's face, mourning that Thea's olive skin had lost its healthful glow and seeing lines that had never appeared there before. A siren by the archway to the terrace shifted and glanced at them in suspicion. Calandra offered her bandaged hand to Thea, keeping it low near the other healer's body, and pointed toward the guard.

Thea, following Calandra's signal with a glance, nodded her head and began unwrapping the bandages.

"How is the pain today?" the elder panacea asked with a physic's clinical interest.

"About the same." Calandra glanced over her shoulder, then leaned a little closer to her mentor and spoke in a hushed voice. "How I have missed you. There is so much to say and ask, but I'll need to be brief."

Thea kept calmly unwrapping the bandages and spoke in a normal tone.

"That bad still?" She flicked her gaze at Calandra in acknowledgement. "Perhaps I can suggest some extra herbs to manage it." She dropped her voice. "So do you care to tell me how you really lost this hand?"

Calandra nodded. "I visited Atlantis. A spirit who has been visiting me in my dreams for years appeared to me in Fire Lake and stole my Tear, right after I found the data you had left hidden on it but before I'd had a chance to read it."

Thea took this revelation in steady silence, appearing engrossed in her task, but Calandra could sense her surprise. When her mentor said nothing, she continued.

"I went after him to get it back. He somehow trapped my arm inside an obsidian globe in which he was trapped and began draining me of power. The others—Zoe and Judith—they couldn't see him. Zoe cut off my arm to free me."

Thea nodded. "These fingers are looking good," she said aloud. Then, quieter, "But why did you take such a risk?"

"Did my mother ever come up with a theory about why the Heartstone could not be healed?"

Thea shook her head and began rubbing some pain-numbing oil onto the nubs of Calandra's new fingers.

"Not that I know of. Have you learned your lesson about the ghosts of Atlantis?"

One of the sirens near the outer door cleared her throat. "Hey, no talking!"

Calandra glanced up and saw the guard frowning at them.

"It was nothing," she said. "Sorry."

She sat upright and lowered her chin, facing the plants behind them to hide her lips moving.

"Damon says that healing the Heartstone needs both male and female undine powers. If my mother indeed had a son—if I have a brother—he would be sixteen by now. Old enough for any powers to have manifested. If I am to heal the Heartstone, I need to find him. And that Tear is my only lead."

Thea whispered this time. "How did this spirit steal the Tear from you if he was only appearing in your mind? Are you certain he was even there in Atlantis, or was he only making it seem as though he were?"

Calandra shook her head. "Of course he was there. He stunned me somehow and had me put my arm inside that stone, and he wouldn't let me pull it out. How could he have done that if he weren't actually holding onto it?"

"He's obviously able to make you do things you don't wish to do, as though he were possessing your mind instead of simply stunning or Redeeming it. He could have shown you something that explained what you were seeing, but all the while you were only doing it yourself."

Calandra stared at Thea as pieces fell into place, feeling a little light-headed.

"The Tear," she croaked. "I . . . I saw him take it. I saw him disappear with it, and then in Atlantis, I saw it around his neck. But what if what I saw was not what really happened at all?"

Her gut tightened.

"What if . . . what if I pulled my Tear from my own neck and dropped it in the lake, all because Damon wanted me to see him stealing it and have me come to Atlantis so he could steal my power?"

Pain radiated from her new fingers, and she cried out.

Thea clucked. "I'm sorry. This process is nearly complete, but each growth treatment is as painful as the last. It is simply the way of it."

She massaged Calandra's fingers again, then clasped her foster daughter's hand in her own. "Brace yourself."

Calandra gritted her teeth.

"Adonia plans to execute you once you help me heal the Heartstone. But if Damon is telling the truth about what is needed, you and I won't be able to do that anyway, not even with every stone healer in Sireniapolis in the circle."

"And what makes you think he is telling the truth? He's already proven himself adept at deceit."

"True. He might be lying, and that would be better for us. But in case he is not, I have a plan. However, I need to know—do you know how to Release a man whose bond is held by another?"

Thea glanced up at her sharply. "You mean as Tanni did to Osaze?"

Calandra's heart quickened. "Do you?"

Thea bent to her work, but after a moment, spoke quietly again.

"After she did that, I worked on it for years. But you, the girl who healed the breathing stones when she was nine, I'm surprised you haven't worked it out on your own by now. Once I discovered how, the principle seemed so simple, I couldn't believe it had taken me so long."

The siren who had called to them before walked over to stand above them. "What are you two talking about?"

Calandra looked up at her. "Thea is instructing me how to heal this type of injury, in case I should ever encounter it. That is allowed, is it not?"

The woman narrowed her eyes at them, then nodded, but didn't leave. She spread her feet in a waiting posture and planted her *deiktis* staff in front of her with both hands. "Carry on, then."

Thea and Calandra stared at each other, Thea emphasizing the importance of what she said next with a meaningful tone.

"Now Calandra, if you must ever regrow bones this way, the important part is in how you use spirit. This is a little different than regrowing flesh. You cannot simply provide the energy by pulling it from the air or from water. You must stimulate the patient's own system to initiate the process. Basically, you have to make it remember itself."

Calandra nodded, glad Thea had kept to the cover story, though it was a lesson she had learned years ago. The wording was odd, though. She quirked her mouth to the side to show her confusion.

Thea raised her eyebrows at her pupil and tapped Calandra's upside-down palm with her finger using diving pulse code.

Osaze.

At last, Calandra understood.

Tanni had been trying to make Osaze forget them. Instead, she had made him remember himself. She'd created a door in the fortress of will that held him, and he'd been the one to walk out of it.

Tears welled up in Calandra's eyes.

"Thank you, *daskala*. I will remember."

Thea smiled and tapped *Gerrick*.

Calandra flicked her eyelids in acknowledgement. She couldn't tell her mentor that her plans involved so much more than freeing Osaze and Gerrick. But she poured her love and gratefulness through her hands into Thea's.

I'll free you, too, she thought. *I promise.*

*

CALANDRA could barely wait to get back to her chambers to tell Judith what she'd learned, Release Osaze, and get in touch with Rhea about the Tear. But as she was leaving the Grotto with her consort-elect in tow, flexing all five restored fingers of her new hand, she bumped into Urbi.

"Pardon me, your highness," the governess said, taking a step back, but her eyes were on her son. A wave of sorrow flowed from her before being shut off like water from a spigot.

Calandra stopped, Osaze halting behind her.

"Not at all. I wasn't watching where I was going. I'm sorry, did I injure your foot?"

Urbi shook her head. "No, your highness."

Calandra smiled and, unsure of what else to say, went to move past her.

Urbi put a hand on Calandra's upper arm. "Please, wait. I was looking for you."

Calandra turned back toward her. "Oh? What can I do for you?"

Urbi glanced up at Osaze, then back toward Calandra.

"I—I have a gift for you. A wedding gift, since you are soon to marry my son." She pulled out a long string of smooth red coral beads. "This is patterned after the necklace I wore when I married Osaze's father. The coral, it will bring a special blessing on your union. It is not much of a bride price, but it is the best I can do for you."

Calandra looked closely at the beads. Red coral did not grow near Sirenia and was difficult to come by.

"Where did you get this?"

"I made it. Some of my past charges helped me acquire the stone."

Urbi lifted the string, spread wide between both hands. Speechless, Calandra bowed her head so Urbi could lay the necklace onto her shoulders.

The woman wound it around Calandra's neck several times, then stepped back with a satisfied smile.

Calandra looked down and touched the beads, overwhelmed with gratitude and guilt. For the first time, she wondered what traditions accompanied a Yoruba marriage—and knew Osaze probably didn't even know the answer to that. How much of his own culture had her people taken from him?

"Thank you, Urbi. This is very . . . thank you."

She looked up to see Urbi smiling beatifically.

"When Osaze was young, when he was . . ."

"Free," Calandra finished for her.

Urbi's eyes widened, but she nodded. "Yes. He could speak only of you. I believe that, if he could choose, he would still want this union."

Tears pricked Calandra's eyes. There was no way Urbi could know that she had just answered the question that haunted Calandra.

She remembered how much Osaze had wanted to see his mother before they had left for their tour, but it had not happened. She also sensed from Urbi the undying devotion of a mother who would always do what was best for her son, no matter what the cost might be to herself. It had been a risk to speak to Calandra about this at all. Human women were expected to forget their ties to their sons after the boys had been Redeemed, yet here Urbi was. It struck Calandra that, if being separated from Osaze by Redemption had been difficult for her, it must have been pure torment for the woman who bore him.

Suddenly, Calandra knew she could trust Urbi. She also knew she could not keep the mother from her son for a single second longer. She smiled.

"Urbi, I need you to come to my bedchamber immediately. There is someone who wants to talk to you."

46

REDEMPTION

WHAT ARE YOU?

The question Gryffyn Cox had thrown at Zale on the bank of the Chyandour Brook five years ago was back, dancing around in his brain. When Abela had found him, he'd thought he'd found the answer.

Undine.

Guardian of the deep.

Someone who was needed to save his mother.

He'd had purpose. He'd dared to believe he wasn't a monster, or at least, not an irredeemable one.

And now this. He'd killed with a simple touch. Only a demon or a monster would have that kind of power.

He shifted position, his buttocks gone numb on the hard wood of the floor, his armpits aching from being stretched above his head and tied to a cannon on the gun deck for the last several hours.

The captain hadn't known what to do with him—the ship had no detention cell, but he feared letting Zale roam free. Zale couldn't blame him. Who would want a person who could kill with a touch wandering around a ship filled with hundreds of living beings?

Cogger walked by. He seemed to be in a hurry and avoided Zale's gaze.

"Hey!" Zale shouted. "Can someone bring me some water?"

Cogger kept walking as though he hadn't heard.

Zale kicked the floor with his heel in frustration, and the jostling made the stone bracelet clang against the cannon. He wondered where Abela was. Or Berian. Even Robert, though he didn't expect help or mercy from him.

In fact, he dreaded the next time they met. Now the truth was out, he wouldn't blame Robert if he insisted the captain had him walk the plank,

341

even if the punishment would not be quite as lethal as it was for most. He didn't relish swimming the rest of the way to Barbados, fending for himself in the ocean.

As though on cue, polished black shoes appeared in his line of sight. Zale raised his gaze to see Berian's jowly face above him, the reverend's golden eyes burning into Zale's. He held a ladle, dripping with water.

"Well, you've gone and done it now, young man," he said in that oddly mellifluous voice that seemed so ill-fitting against his unappealing appearance. He squatted and the lines of his jaw softened. He held the ladle up to Zale's mouth and helped him drink.

"Thank you," Zale said when he'd finished.

Berian dabbed the water off of Zale's chin with a linen kerchief, then let the ladle rest on his knees.

"How are you holding up?"

Zale shrugged, pulling the nonchalance he'd worn for five years in his tank around him like a protective shield.

Berian's gaze sharpened. "You can't fool me, lad. I've known you since you were born, remember? I wouldn't be surprised if right about now, you are wondering if you're cursed."

Zale frowned. "And what if I am? Cursed, I mean."

Berian settled on the floor beside Zale, his black-stockinged legs protruding comically from the legs of his trousers beneath his black waistcoat. He looked like a fat crow that had landed on its backside. He leaned against a wooden barrel and sighed.

"One thing all beings on this plane have in common is this—none of you get to choose the circumstances you begin with in life. You don't get to choose your looks, your race, your parents, your nation, or your class. You begin where you begin, and that's that, but it is not meant to be a curse. Elyon loves variety, and gives everyone different gifts and the choice about where to use them."

He gestured at his physique with a wave of his hand. "Not so for my kind. Well, that's not entirely true—to a certain degree, it *is* the same for us. But we are not of this plane, so when we come here, we have options the Born never receive."

He leaned forward, eyeing Zale intently with his hooded golden lizard eyes.

"Tell me, why do you think I chose to look like this?"

Zale blinked, uncertain as to what to say.

"Do not fret about offending me," Berian continued. "Look at me.

Take a good, long look, and tell me what you thought of me the first time you saw me."

Zale squirmed. "I—I thought you were ugly, and possibly not trustworthy. I thought you were a self-indulgent glutton because you are so fat. You rarely smile, so I felt uncomfortable around you." *Still do.*

Berian smiled now, and it changed his entire demeanour. He reached toward Zale, who flinched away.

The reverend hesitated, eyebrows raised.

"I don't bite."

Zale remembered Abela saying the same thing when they first met. He gave a brief nod.

Berian reached above Zale's head and laid three fingers on the exposed flesh of Zale's wrist. Immediately, Berian's form melted and shifted before his eyes until he looked like a tall handsome man in a flowing robe, with large black feathered wings on his back—every inch the angel Zale had always imagined. His entire form was composed of light. Zale squinted, awed at the creature's beauty.

"Would you think differently of me if you'd first seen me like this?" Berian asked in the same resonant voice, which fit this form perfectly.

His form shifted again, and he became an immense winged black bull with golden eyes, squeezed impossibly into the space between two cannons, his forehoof still touching Zale's flesh. The bull's hot breath snorted over Zale's face, and he lowered his head to stare at Zale.

Zale's pulse spiked in fear, even though he knew it was still Berian.

"Or this?" the bull said.

Berian changed again, once more coalescing into the familiar form of the homely minister. He dropped his hand into his lap and sat back on the floor, as unprepossessing and repulsive as he'd always been.

"Now you have seen me as my kind sees me. Tell me why I took this form for the Ground."

Zale panted and took a breath to calm himself. He hadn't really thought about it before, how the forms that Berian and Abela took were mere constructs, chosen with intentional purpose. While Abela had been beautiful in every form he'd seen her in, Berian could have chosen to be as handsome as Adonis, and yet, he'd chosen to be like this. What advantages would that have?

"Give up?" Berian asked.

"No," said Zale. "I know why. When you are like this, you are nearly invisible. People underestimate you and assume things about you that distracts them from your true purpose, allowing you to gain information you may not otherwise gain."

Berian smiled, nodding his head. "Canny boy. But you are only partly right. There is another reason. It is the same reason why Elyon does not give every person on the Ground the exact same advantages in life, and why this world can seem so terribly scary and unfair. It is the same reason you were given powers you must learn to control, while others are born with nothing, or wealth, or deformities, or extraordinary beauty."

Zale shook his head, completely confused.

"You cannot guess? I shall tell you. It's about love."

Berian smiled, revealing perfectly straight teeth. For a moment, Zale glimpsed the warmth of the being of light that hid somewhere behind the torpid flesh.

"I don't understand."

"When Elyon made this universe, he made it out of himself, out of love. His spirit is in everything that exists, giving order to disorder and life to all, from the smallest blade of grass to the suns that travel the skies. He made us, all of his children of every kind, to enjoy and populate the universe he made. We live because of his breath, his spirit that inhabits the planes."

Zale nodded, though he barely understood. "So you and me and Abela and this boat, and even blackguards like Crow, we're all connected by this mystical Power of Love? How could love be what connects us, when cruelty and hate are so prevalent?"

"Because," Berian continued, "we often make the same mistake Kesbeel did when he thought to circumvent the perfect order of Elyon's design because of his own limited understanding. He saw something he desired, and he took it. He thought his understanding was higher, so he did things his own way. And all of Creation has been locked in a war ever since. Sound like anyone you know?"

Zale frowned.

"Crow. Gryffyn." He thought of how he'd run away from home to avoid the consequences of what he'd done. "Me, sometimes."

Berian patted his knee. "When we work outside the order of love, a price must be paid. Love requires self-sacrifice, whereas pride and selfishness sacrifice others."

Zale swallowed, shame burning within his chest. It seemed all he ever did was sacrifice others, hurting people instead of helping them. Maybe he *was* cursed.

"What does this have to do with your looks or my powers?"

Berian shifted position on the hard floor.

"Because too often, the Born and the Made alike look only at the surface of things, but Elyon inhabits every part of his design. It is easy to love what is beautiful and see God in what pleases us, but it is difficult when we don't like what we see. When people see me, their reaction reveals their true character. It shows which side of the war of Creation they are currently on."

Zale's face grew hot as he realized he, too, had judged Berian only by what he saw, just like he had done with every person he'd seen through the walls of his tank for years. "I compared you to a pig and a lizard. I'm sorry."

Berian gave a chuckle, and Zale looked up in surprise.

"You're not angry?"

"I do look a little like those creatures, though I was going more for crow mixed with bulldog."

"I thought of those, too. Also a fish."

Berian laughed now, his face coming alive with joy as he chortled. "Truly?" He rubbed some moisture from his eye. "Brilliant, it really is." When he'd collected himself, he continued. "That simply goes to show that even an undine of the deep can get in the habit of looking only at the surface. But Elyon's essence is in unattractive creatures, such as pigs and lizards"—he gave another chuckle—"as well as beautiful ones, and his strength is made perfect in weakness."

He leaned forward and touched Zale's chest.

"A weakness like possessing a power so great you cannot control it on your own. Often, our weaknesses—or the weaknesses of others—present the greatest opportunities for us to learn how to love. They let us choose our side. For the greater we love, the stronger we truly become."

"I don't understand. How can power be weakness, or love be strength? None of this makes any sense."

In a graceful motion that belied his size, Berian shifted back to a squatting position so he could get close to Zale's face. He glanced around to make sure no one was near, then lowered his voice.

"You have a tremendous gift, Zale, one aspect of Elyon's being that he imbued uniquely into undines—the ability to see someone's heart and sense the order of the universe on the plane where Elyon inhabits it. That is how I could reveal my other forms to you just now without physically transforming—not because of my power, but because of yours. But your power did not come from you, and it is not yours to own. The strength you crave? It's in giving up your power completely."

Zale struggled to understand what Berian meant, but everything the reverend said contradicted itself. The man seemed to enjoy talking in riddles. The last part piqued his interest, though.

"Are you saying there's a way to give up my powers? Because I would do that in a heartbeat."

Berian eyed him, the light in his golden eyes swirling.

"Would you? Are you certain?"

"Of course."

Berian sighed. "That is between you and the Almighty. With him, all things are possible. But I was referring to something less drastic—instead of giving away your powers, give up your desire to bend them to your will and let Elyon be your guide."

"And how do I do that?"

"That's the simple part," Berian said gently. "You ask."

Zale's stomach tightened. "Ask? That's it? What's he going to do, take over my mind the way the undines take over the minds of others?"

Berian shook his head. "No, that is not his way. That is a distortion of your power's true purpose. Elyon never forces his way on anyone—it is always a choice." He stood, the ladle dangling from his fingers. "But if you truly want to know, why don't you simply try it? What have you got to lose?"

Zale stared at him and said nothing. Berian turned and walked away, returning the ladle to the hook on the galley stove beside a wooden water barrel as he passed, and climbed the ladder to the weather decks.

Just ask? That seemed far too simple. But what *did* he have to lose that he wasn't anxious to be rid of?

Still, despite Berian's assurances of the ways of Elyon, he couldn't help but wonder how the Creator would help him control his powers without removing them completely—and was that truly what he wanted?

Berian and Abela had said he would need his powers to rescue his mother. If he gave them up to Elyon, how would he ever save her from Tartarus?

And his powers weren't all bad. He'd *healed* people. He'd saved people's lives when nothing else could. He'd finally felt like he had a purpose for existing. Would a demon have healed the sick?

Then he saw his father's charred and broken body, Robbie's blistered face, and Crow falling to the floor, his clothes smoking.

He might not be a demon, but he was still a monster. Perhaps, if he gave up control, he could change that.

He sat there, torn and pondering, until the watch changed and the sky outside the gun door was splattered with stars. At last, he decided that if the Maker of the Universe had given him these powers, he probably knew better than Zale what to do with them, including how to use them to save his mother from the underworld.

Feeling awkward, he closed his eyes, but feeling too vulnerable, opened them again. He twisted and looked out at the sliver of sky he could see instead and, for the second time today, he prayed.

"Er, God? Elyon? It's me again. Earlier, I asked you something, to protect everyone on this ship from me, and you answered. No one was hurt because of the storm I made. Thank you."

He paused, his heart quickening.

"Now I need to ask for something else. I don't know if you can hear me, but Berian says you're everywhere, so I guess you probably can. I can't control these powers you gave me, not without this stupid bracelet. And that's not control, that's containment. But if you gave them to me, I guess you probably know what to do with them, too. So, if it's not too much trouble, I need your help with that. I need to give them to you."

He waited, but nothing happened. No answering voice came from the stars, and he didn't feel any different. He wondered if he should take off the bracelet, but how could he be sure if that would be wise? Not that he could without Berian's magic rod thing, anyway. He growled, letting his body go slack and his head hang toward the inner part of the deck.

A pair of bare feet stood before him. He looked up. It was Cogger.

"Captain Meredith sent for you, lad. Said he's made a decision. Come on wit' me."

Cogger untied the ropes around Zale's wrists—gingerly, arching his body over Zale's so as not to touch him—and when his arms had been released, Zale gratefully let them drop, massaging the ache out of his wrists and the back of his shoulders. He fingered the bracelet. Was this an answer? Should he ask Berian to take it off?

Cogger took a few steps back. "C'mon then."

The sound of a woman singing a lovely, wordless tune met his ears. Cogger's eyes unfocused and he stood staring straight ahead, but all Zale could think about was the song. It was otherworldly and woke every yearning he'd ever had, making him want to surrender to the bliss it promised.

"Thank you," he whispered, right before he gave up control completely.

*

Robert sat in the chair in his cabin, contemplating the knife in his hand. It had been easy to get it out of the open galley—Cook hadn't even noticed him take it. Now, its gleaming silver edge called to him with blissful absolution.

No matter what I do, suffering and death always results, always because of my weakness.

No amount of good gained from the profit on this voyage could ever absolve him of the cost in human suffering. The captain had commented that this was the first slaving voyage he'd ever heard of where they hadn't lost a single one of the cargo, and Robert knew who was responsible for that—not himself, with his so-called "humane treatment" demands. It had been Zale. Somehow Zale, like his mother, had been blessed with the ability to heal with a touch.

And to kill.

He touched his face, running his hands over the ridges of flesh. He felt adrift. He'd always been convinced that only a creature of pure evil could have called down lightning and taken his sight. But could he truly see Zale that way?

He stared at his reflection in the blade of the knife.

No, this *is what evil looks like.*

Every time he closed his eyes, he still saw that hold full of wretched people—the ones who were there because of his weakness. Even now, the stench surrounded him—he couldn't get away from it.

He'd wandered the ship for hours, pondering the slaves in the hold and wrestling with what he should do. He had not come up with any solution that pleased his conscience that did not also bring him and his family to complete financial ruin. He could not simply free them all. Cox Bros Shipping would never recover, and he could very well be outcast and cut off from his own family. As ill-welcomed as he'd always felt in the home of his father, Lord Alverton, at least he'd had one. He had a comfortable place in society, one where he didn't fear for where his next meal would be found.

At last, he'd had to face the monster in his own soul. His comfort had trumped the suffering of his fellow men. He was a fraud, a liar, and even God could not redeem the likes of him.

First Zale and Talwyn, now this. If I'm bound for hell, I may as well go there before I cause more misery and suffering.

He lifted the knife to his chest, wondering how to do it. It was a long knife, and could easily reach vital parts—but how does one go about killing oneself?

He had just decided that the best method would be to stab himself in the heart, up from under the sternum, like the Romans of old who would fall on their swords, when the door burst open and in walked Miss Bethel.

"Robbie! What are you doing?" she demanded. She strode over to him and grabbed the knife.

He struggled with her, not wanting to let go. Then, all resistance leaving him, he released it.

She threw it on the floor and kicked it away toward the door, then turned back to him. "Mr. Cox, what are you thinking? Have you gone mad?"

He stared at her, his mouth open but silent. He did not have words to explain it, how her lovely brown face served as a reminder of the ugliness in his soul.

The most enchanting singing he'd ever heard reached him, penetrating the hull of the ship from outside.

All is well, go to sleep, give to me your soul to keep, it seemed to say, though the song had no words.

Gratefully, he obeyed.

47

THE COURT OF THE REDEEMED

CALANDRA STOOD AT THE TOP of the broad steps of the Court of the Redeemed, relishing the cool evening breeze off the bay that pushed away the heat of the day and the odour generated by the hundreds of revellers below. Despite being three days past *panselinos*, the moon had already risen high enough above the black stone mountains that guarded the valley to obliterate the light of Atargatis's star, frosting the rooftops in a silvery mantle. On the ocean spreading out from the wharf at the foot of Court Street, small boats and swimmers alike could be identified by their dancing, twinkling lights.

It was the Redemption Moon, the last night before the Summer Solstice. Ordinarily, this festival was one of the highlights of Calandra's year. Strings of festive lights and lanterns criss-crossed the streets. Citizens in their finest and most colourful tunics crowded into the square, onto barges on the canal and bay, or frolicked in the water. Music floated over the city like a cloud of joy. Rickshaws and fishing boats were decorated with flower garlands and strings of shells and tiny self-powered lightstone beads, and royal entertainers tossed small coins into the canals for delighted children to dive for and find.

Tonight, Calandra found no pleasure in any of that—not with the net of anxiety binding her gut and the bundle of nettles flaming in her mind. She pressed her fingers to her temples, trying to keep the pain subdued, with marginal success. Tonight, for the first time, Calandra hated that this festival celebrated the annual harvest of human men, bringing in new human blood to bolster Sirenia's population by the shipload. Here she was, trying to figure out how to free their nation's men, and tonight, they were capturing more.

Then tomorrow, during the twenty-minute window when the sun

and its fire energy would be shining directly into the Mother's Heart, she would be expected to guide the circle of healers in the task she'd been raised to do. Worse, Tanni had left two days ago with the pods that would be bringing in their quarry, leaving her to face the newly returned Narcissa and Adonia alone.

Well, not alone. Osaze stood close enough behind her that she could feel his heat. She glanced up at him and smiled. He did not smile back, but the rush of warmth through their bond was all she needed to reassure her that he was there when she needed him.

In the past week, they had spent whatever time Calandra could spare alone together, relishing the fleeting moments of solitude and closeness. They had also found convenient reasons for Calandra to visit Urbi at least twice, and, on a completely legitimate errand to find a datastone among Thea's personal collection, Calandra had also Released Gerrick.

After the man's initial distress had passed, Calandra told him of all that had happened, and her plan to bring about change—and free Thea— during the Healing Ceremony. Then she gave him a pair of songstoppers, the new amber device she had invented based on an idea she'd found in an Atlantis stone. When tucked into the ear canal, they filtered sound and prevented the wearer from being affected by sirensong. It would not provide much protection against the *sklavia* bond, but the wearer would not be affected by simple stunning. Even Redemption would require someone with a great deal of power to enact, as she'd discovered when both she and Judith, who had a small talent with spirit after all, had tested Osaze's songstoppers with his blessing. Between the two of them, only she had successfully created the bond.

Glancing at Osaze's ears, she reassured herself that the small devices would be practically invisible unless you knew what you were looking for. She hoped it would be enough to protect him if he were discovered.

Calandra cast her gaze over the assembled crowd, illuminated by strings of paper lanterns, searching hopefully for a familiar face from Elpida, but still nothing. She caught sight of Judith standing on the far side of the bustling square from beside a street vendor's cart selling battered, fried prawns on a stick. Her maid's gaze was still roaming over the crowd, just as hers was. Apparently, her Tear had not yet arrived.

Narcissa approached between the columns of the portico, Mari at her side. Both of them looked stunning in heavily embroidered festival tunics. Narcissa's red one matched the hibiscus she wore in her hair.

As far as Calandra knew, Adonia had not formally declared Narcissa the Opal Princess, but she had not reprimanded her daughter for taking to wearing the hibiscus again either. And since the royal party had returned from their tour yesterday afternoon, Narcissa had taken every opportunity to remind Calandra of their arrangement—which both Osaze and Calandra had played along with out of necessity.

Narcissa hadn't noticed that Osaze was no longer tethered to her—but Calandra couldn't blame her for that. While testing the songstoppers, she'd also tested how much could be discerned about individual *sklavia* bonds by Redeeming Osaze and then having Judith Release him while she was in a separate room. After her experiments, she felt confident neither Narcissa nor Adonia would ever realize that a single bond in their collection had been severed.

"Well, if it isn't my favourite couple," Narcissa oozed as she stopped beside them. "Osaze, do you not have a kiss for your princess?"

"Yes, your highness," he said woodenly, and bent and gave her a peck on the cheek.

"Ah-ah. That's not a kiss," she said, gloating at Calandra. She crooked a finger at Osaze. "This time, on the lips."

Osaze's anger flashed through the bond, matching the boiling in Calandra's gut and the expression on Mari's face.

"That's enough, Narcissa," Calandra said. "You've made your point."

"Have I?" Narcissa laughed mockingly. "I'm not so sure."

She turned to Osaze and pointed to her lips. He bent to peck Narcissa on the mouth. She grabbed his head and kissed him deeply, then broke away, laughing.

"That's more like it, my pet. Can't let my cousin have all the fun. Though if that's what she has to look forward to, I almost pity her. I'm sure a fish would kiss with more passion." She gave an exaggerated sigh. "I suppose it is to be expected from the *Redeemed*. Come along, Mari."

A scowling Mari engaged Narcissa in quiet, urgent conversation as they turned away. Narcissa seemed as unconcerned about Mari's anger as she had been about Calandra's.

Calandra unclenched her fists, then turned to face her consort-elect, whose emotions said that standing blandly still was killing him.

"You may wipe your mouth, Osaze," she said aloud.

Gratefully, he did so.

"I'm sorry," he whispered from behind his hand.

"It's not your fault." She stretched up on tiptoes to wrap her arms around him and speak into his ear. "You could do nothing else. But tomorrow, all will be known and you will never need to pretend obeisance to her pettiness again."

"Hmm. Looking forward to that. And I can't wait to get you alone later and remind myself what a kiss is supposed to be like," he said into her hair.

She kissed his cheek as the clear, high-pitched call of a conch shell horn rang over the square. She turned to see Adonia standing at the centre of the top stair with Olympia, the Archaulos of Sireniapolis, on one side, her silver hair piled high and threaded with pearls, and Despoina Cleo in a royal-blue dress uniform on the other, quietly waiting for the crowd to calm. High Priestess Shinara stood holding the shell horn behind the queen, wearing an unusual long boxy white tunic, gold-threaded shawl, and turban Calandra thought must be inspired by her African ancestors. A bare-chested *doulos* beside her held a scroll on extended arms. High-ranking sirens, noblewomen, and members of the Royal Council stood at attention between the columns behind the queen's retinue, looking like a brightly coloured garden in their Festival finery, their *douloi* at their sides.

At the sound of the conch, the street musicians fell silent, and the entertainers halted their tricks. Soon, the whole crowd was staring at the queen. Torchlight from the columns behind Adonia set her red hair aflame. With her flowing cerulean gown, she looked like Atargatis herself, rising from the foam of the sea, and Shinara like the moon goddess Selene.

When all were silent, Adonia projected her voice over the square and the water of the bay. "Welcome, my people, to this year's Redemption Festival. We have just received word that the first ship was taken with *no* casualties."

Thunderous cheers met her announcement.

"In addition, there were nearly two hundred healthy men aboard." She beamed as she waited for the applause to run its course.

The *kyrias* in the crowd—those who made their living from buying and selling human men—looked elated. Several hundred years ago, when the humans had begun transporting slaves across the Atlantic in droves, the undines had begun targeting slave ships specifically as having the highest potential population gain. The influx of available males had led to a period of previously unknown population growth on the island.

Eventually, harvesting slave ships had become tradition. Even still, in the past, there had been times when a targeted ship had looked promising, but yielded barely more of a harvest than the crew that manned it, thanks to the barbaric and inhumane practises the humans used to transport their slaves.

"A marvellous number indeed," murmured a councillor near Calandra. "This is a promising night."

Calandra clapped half-heartedly as Adonia continued her speech. As soon as the submersibles full of people taken from the ships entered the harbour, she would be required to take on the bonds of all two hundred of those men while she helped Heo inspect and, if necessary, heal them.

Two hundred more stinging threads to add to the bundle that constantly throbbed in her mind—and that was only the first ship.

She'd been as disappointed as Narcissa when Adonia had declared that Calandra would be bondmistress for every man taken tonight, even if only temporarily until the Healing Ceremony was completed. Narcissa's bonds seemed not to bother her, and now that Calandra knew how to Release a man whose bonds she didn't hold, she no longer felt the need to take on as many as she possibly could.

Still, without a male undine available to help her with healing the Heartstone tomorrow, she could endure a few more stinging nettles. Calandra only hoped it would be enough.

Only for a little while longer, she told herself, and the men whose bonds she held, though she knew they couldn't hear her. *You will soon be Free.*

No sooner had she thought it than the airy call of a conch shell from down by the pier signalled the arrival of the first submersible. Shinara finished her dedication in a hurry.

With a heavy sigh, Calandra adjusted her panacea bracelet and glanced at her consort-elect, then descended the steps to cross the square to the Physic House. Might as well get this over with.

*

CALANDRA finished checking the human woman over, then pointed her toward the entrance of the Physic House, where a group of about another dozen women and their children were already gathering. Most of them had only a thin piece of indigo fabric wrapped around them for clothing and were infested with vermin, but other than that, were remarkably healthy. In fact, other than one African man who had obviously suffered a beating recently, she had hardly had to heal anyone at all.

"Go wait there, please," she said in Twi, the woman's language. "Barbara will soon return to escort you to the halfway house. There, you will be given a good meal and a place to wash up and sleep, and your options for your new life will be presented to you."

"Options?" The woman raised an eyebrow. "You mean, I am to choose?"

Calandra smiled. "Yes, Enohor. You are no longer a slave. Here, you will be able to choose your own destiny and make a life for yourself."

"May I return to my country?"

Calandra dropped her gaze.

"No, unfortunately. That is the one thing you cannot choose. No human who comes to this island ever leaves. But give it time. You may find you like it here. Work hard, and you will never want for food or for a place to sleep. You can provide for yourself and your children in peace." She touched the woman, projecting calm. "Do not fear. You are safe here."

Enohor, still not looking completely convinced, walked toward the area Calandra had indicated. Calandra watched her go. This woman had been destined for a life of slavery, to be used in either the cane or tobacco fields or the houses of humans, not permitted to have a normal family, not permitted to own anything, and not permitted to make her own choices. Here, she would become a functioning member of society, as would the others like her.

Most of them would, anyway, except the few who could not adjust to this life and would choose death instead. There were always some.

Calandra imagined how she would feel if she were ever forced to leave Sirenia and never allowed to return. Better life or no, she couldn't help feel that the undines were still robbing these women of something.

"Healer Calandra," called Healer Niobe from the far side of the dry bay, "you need to come see this."

Ordinarily, the middle-aged physic serviced clients on the far side of the city near her home, but she usually volunteered for the ingathering at Redemption Moon. A confused-looking siren stood beside her, staring toward the bed. The teenage boy who sat on it seemed to be the source of her consternation.

As soon as Calandra saw the young man—his tangled wheat-coloured hair tied back into a queue with a leather cord, his fine, high cheekbones and broad shoulders indicating good lineage—she knew he would be in high demand in the Court from the moment he entered. She wouldn't be surprised if he were the consort-elect of a noblewoman's daughter by night's end.

But there was something else, something she had never experienced with anyone before—a resonance between her spirit and his that grew stronger as she approached. As she drew nearer, Niobe and the siren stepped back, letting her stand in front of him.

And then he looked at her.

"His—his eyes," she said, pointing at them.

Though they were as unfocused as any of the other Redeemed men whose bonds she had taken from the capturing sirens, they had the iridescent green of an undine's. But that was impossible. Wasn't it?

She took a second look at his features. He looked to be sixteen or seventeen years old. With every detail she took in, her stomach knotted tighter and tighter.

Could it be?

"He's got this, which is odd," said the siren, lifting the young man's wrist and indicating a smooth shackle bracelet of green feldspar with gold links. Calandra touched it, then took the boy's hand.

An electric shock ran through her. Even under the *sklavia* bond and with the bracelet on, this boy's power was unmistakable. He was an undine. And not just any undine.

Without waiting for the siren to touch him, she laid a finger on his forehead and sang the notes that would Release him. He blinked, and his eyes began to focus.

"How did you do that?" asked the siren, frowning.

Calandra ignored her.

"Your mother," she said to the boy in Greek, not even thinking to check on his language first in her excitement. "What is her name?"

She held her breath as she waited for his answer.

He glanced up at her in comprehension and surprise, sweat trickling down his forehead.

"My—my mother? Delphine. Delphine Teague."

Calandra's heart slammed against her ribs. She'd been right.

"And what is yours?" she managed to get out.

"Zale," he said, taking in everything at once. He focused on her and frowned. "Who are you? And where am I?"

Calandra stared at him in wonder, feeling as though she were floating over a mile of clear blue sea.

"Zale," she said, relishing the sound of the word. "I am Calandra kor'Delphine. Your sister. And you are home."

48

THE MERMAN

Zale stared at the young blonde woman in astonishment. She looked like a porcelain doll he had once seen in a shop window combined with an angel. She appeared as surprised as he was, what with her hands covering her mouth and her eyes wide with shock—luminescent green eyes, exactly like his. And his mother's.

My sister?

The moment she'd said it, he'd known it for truth. She looked almost exactly like his mother.

"I've been so worried about how I would find you," she was saying. "All this time, looking for a clue, trying to find a way to get to you, and you came to me. Praise to the Mother!"

Beside her, the dark-skinned woman in brilliant blue cloth and leather armour had gone grey and clammy, and now turned and walked away as though she were being chased. The other woman, the one in a simple green flowing gown, kept staring at him, mouth slightly askew.

He latched onto a coherent thought at last.

"How did I get here?"

His sister—Calandra, he thought she'd said?—Calandra flushed pink. "We—we brought you here. You, and everyone else on your ship. Wait—are Mother or Father here?"

"What?"

He shook his head, still feeling like there was a great deal he did not understand. Behind Calandra, he watched several of the crew members and male slaves who'd been on the *Atlanta* walk by, their faces oddly blank. Dim memories floated to him—being loaded onto a strange bronze ship along with the others.

"No, Father died a long time ago, and I'm looking for Mother. She's in

Tartarus. Unless that's where I am. Am I?"

"Dead? Tartarus?" Calandra shook her head, biting her lip as her eyes filled with moisture. "No, this is Sirenia."

"Sirenia?" He stared at her, finally beginning to understand. "I made it?"

He looked around at the large stone room with fresh eyes. He could see many more people he recognized, men and women both, all of them being examined or possibly guarded by women of all heights and colours in strange clothes similar to Calandra's. From what he could see, they all had iridescent green eyes.

"Are you . . . are you all undines?"

Calandra gave a small slow smile, as though he'd made a joke. "Why, yes we are. Just like you."

Zale blinked around at the room.

"What's the matter?" she asked.

"Nothing, it's only that . . . I've been looking for somewhere to belong for so long. When Abela told me of this place, I thought I would find it. But now that I'm here, everything is completely strange." He stood up and glanced around, trying to spot his friend. "Where is she, anyway?"

*

Calandra held back tears, staring at her brother.

"I don't know who this Abela is, but we'll go find her soon. But did you say Mother is in *Tartarus*? Do you mean she's dead, too?"

Zale shook his head.

"No, not dead. She was taken there by some evil men who want to use her to free the Grigori. I'm going there with Berian and Abela to free her. Have you seen them? Berian's a minister, tall, fat, looks a bit like a bulldog crossed with a pig." He smirked. "Abela's about your height and looks like the sun turned into a person. She's an African English lady."

Calandra smiled at his descriptive prose.

"No, I haven't seen them yet. Perhaps they haven't been unloaded from the submersibles, though I thought I had already seen all the women from this ship. But what is a Grigori, and how could these men use Mother to accomplish their goals?"

That word *Grigori* was familiar, but Calandra couldn't place it.

Zale frowned. "I don't know, exactly. They needed me and either her or—or you. Berian knows the rest. We'll have to ask him."

Calandra frowned as she tried to fit all the pieces of the puzzle Zale presented together. The remarkably healthy people on this ship. The green feldspar bracelet. The men who needed Zale and either herself or their mother to work together. The power she could sense in—

"Zale, are you a healer?"

His gaze snapped to hers and he tensed. "What—what do you mean by that?"

"I mean, can you heal people in what some would consider a supernatural fashion, or have you been able to affect elements like water or"—she pointed at the brown stone he wore on his wrist, which had definitely been processed in some way—"or stones?"

Zale balled his hands into fists.

"Yes. Not water or stones. But I've healed people. And I can move wind and—and call fire. Can't . . . can't you all do that?"

"You can call fire?" Calandra gaped at him, then closed her mouth. "No. No, we can't. In fact, I'm one of the few who can work with air. And now I have another reason to thank the Mother. Zale, it has to be because of her that you are here, now, tonight. The timing could not have been any more perfect."

"What on earth are you talking about? Mother doesn't even know where I am. That's why I need to find her."

His shoulders slumped a little, and shame rolled off of him like a tidal wave.

She was about to answer and clear up his confusion when an imperious voice behind her made her stand up straight as a column.

"What is the meaning of this?" Adonia demanded.

Swallowing, Calandra turned slowly on her heel to face the queen. She was greeted by not only her aunt, but a whole entourage including councillors, noblewomen, the High Priestess, Tanni, Mari, and Narcissa. The women crowding into the bay blocked the path between her and Osaze, who stood by the door, but he betrayed no alarm through either his posture or emotions. In fact, despite their bond, she could barely sense him at all. She smiled—he was getting quite good with his emotional shield. And now was definitely the time to use it.

Heo hurried over from the patient she'd been working with, looking distinctly annoyed.

"What is happening here? With respect, your majesty, we don't have room for all these people, it will mess up our record-keeping. Could we take this outside?"

Adonia gave the Harbour Physic an irritated look, then a sharp nod.

"One moment, healer. Calandra, what is going on? Singer kor'Sonia said you Released this man without her even touching him. How did you do that? And why?"

Calandra swallowed, regretting her impetuous act.

"Your majesty, esteemed councillors, ladies of the court, I would like you to meet someone."

She stepped aside so the crowd could see behind her.

"This is my brother, Zale bet'Delphine. And he is going to help me heal the Heartstone."

*

AFTER a stunned few moments of silence, the room exploded with sound, everyone talking at once. Shock, fear, disbelief, confusion, and excitement sloshed over the women like water in a bathtub.

Calandra closed her eyes and took a deep breath, shielding herself from the flood of violent emotion. When she opened them, Adonia was staring hard at Calandra and Zale, and so was Narcissa. When Tanni recovered, she crossed her arms and smiled. Her emotions through the bond were nearly as jubilant as Calandra's.

After several minutes of chatter, Adonia turned and faced her court.

"Everyone, remove yourselves to the Court of the Redeemed. Singer kor'Sonia, Rhapsodist kor'Zelia, escort this young man to the Court. If he shows any signs of violence, use sirensong."

"What does that mean?" Zale whispered to Calandra.

She turned to him, struggling to figure out how to explain everything in only a moment.

"It means 'don't struggle, and everything will be fine.' Tanni kor'Zelia is my friend, and she's on our side. You'll be okay."

"What do you mean, *our* side? What is going on here?"

Calandra took his hand and projected calm into it. He wasn't terrified, only anxious, but elemental energy crackled through his veins. She suddenly understood why he wore the feldspar bracelet. He was powerful, but he had little control over what he could do. Her gut tightened. She hoped he would be skilled enough to help her with her task.

"I need you to trust me, Zale. There are many things I must explain to you, but now is not the time. Whatever happens, know I will always come for you to keep you safe."

"Someone else trying to keep me safe," he muttered. "Just what I needed."

Tanni and the other siren took his arms and urged him toward the now-cleared entrance of the Physic House. Zale frowned, then allowed them to guide him away. Calandra exchanged glances with Tanni before falling into place behind them, Osaze joining her as she passed through the doorway.

"Calandra," Osaze whispered from the side of his mouth. "You're going to tell Adonia now, right? About the bonds, and the Madness, and everything?"

She glanced up at her consort-elect, and the image of Matthew and Elizabeth in Fire Lake flashed through her mind. She faltered and tripped on a step, and Osaze reached out a hand to steady her.

"Calandra?" he repeated. "You should tell her now, okay?"

She swallowed the lump of fear in her throat and nodded, then turned her eyes forward.

Finally, she understood why Ignatia and the others had been so hesitant to risk confronting the queen. No matter how many men might be freed by coming forward, there was always the chance the one you loved could be taken away from you instead. And right then, the potential freedom of thousands of strangers seemed small in comparison to keeping her promise to the good man who stood beside her—a man she didn't know if she could live without.

I'll have to succeed then.

Her shaking knees laughed at her.

*

As they made the short trek across the square to the Court of the Redeemed, Calandra watched for the two people that Zale had described to her, but didn't see them anywhere. When they stepped into the well-lit hall, the Court was already full of people—revellers and businesswomen who had come to buy or simply to admire the new crop of genes being brought into the pool. Some considered it a good night's entertainment to merely gawk at each man as he was brought in, like they were goods on display—which, Calandra realized, they were. She touched her stomach, nauseous.

As Zale was led in and brought to stand before Adonia and her court in the middle of the open flagstone courtyard, all eyes followed their progress, and many crowded in closer. More curious people came in from the street until Zale, with the two sirens beside him, and Calandra, with Osaze beside her, stood in a clearing between hundreds of curious citizens on one side and Adonia, Narcissa, the councillors, and the rest of the court on the other. Behind the women, Matthew and Cain and a half-dozen other *douloi* stood at attention.

Adonia walked forward to stand before Zale, keeping a safe distance between them. She scrutinized him from head to toe, then looked into his eyes.

"Who are you? Where did you come from?"

"My name is Zale Teague, and I'm from Madron, Cornwall, in England," he said.

"And yet you speak perfect Greek. That is not common among the English."

"My mother, Delphine, taught me. She is an undine."

A hushed murmur ran through the crowd. Adonia glanced at Calandra, then back at him.

"You claim your mother was an undine, which means you are lying, which is to be expected. Undines cannot produce male children. It is a strange quirk of the Mother that she made us to require males to reproduce, yet withdrew the ability to birth our own."

Calandra stepped forward.

"With respect, your majesty, that is not true."

Adonia's gaze snapped toward her and she glared a warning, but Calandra continued, speaking loudly enough for all to hear.

"Before my mother, Delphine kor'Helena, fled this island seventeen years ago, along with my father, Kenver Teague"—another murmur ran through the crowd, and Adonia glared in warning—"she left me a message. In it, she claimed she was pregnant with a son. She had also discovered the reason for our partial infertility—it is the *sklavia* bond. Children conceived with Free men have as much chance to be boys as girls."

"Calandra! That is enough." Adonia shouted to be heard over the babbling crowd, seeming to grow larger. "You will speak of this no more. We have no proof this boy is who he says he is, and you have no proof that what you say is true."

"Yes, she does," came a voice from the crowd.

Everyone turned to the source, and Ignatia stepped forward carrying Zeke. Judith stood beside her.

Calandra's heart stuttered. *She came?*

Ignatia spun in a circle so the crowd could see her and Zeke as she spoke.

"This is my son, Ezekiel, conceived with a Free man. I have two nephews who were similarly conceived. Is that enough proof?"

Adonia's jaw worked. Then another gasp came from the crowd, and they began pointing and talking even more excitedly than before. Calandra turned to see Zale sitting on the floor in *ichthys* state, his breeches in tatters around his tail, looking up at Adonia defiantly.

"I *am* an undine," he declared.

"I see that," Adonia said dryly. "Get up, boy."

Zale changed back to *podia* state, his long shirt covering him to the knees over his ruined breeches as he stood.

"There is more that must be said," Calandra began.

Adonia cut her off with a raised hand. "You have said quite enough, niece."

Zale stared at Calandra. "Niece? To the queen?"

Why is there so much he does not know?

Calandra did not stop, but turned and spoke toward the crowd and the court.

"My mother did not go Mad. She was convinced that the Madness was caused by creating a consort bond with a Redeemed man, not by childbirth, as has so long been believed. Healer Thea kor'Aglaia is proof of this claim. She lived her entire married life with a Free man."

She raised her voice to be heard over the rising din.

"In addition, it is only through joined male and female powers that the Heartstone can be healed, which is why we have been unsuccessful for so long."

Chaos erupted in the Court, impossible to be heard over.

"Traitor!" Narcissa's voice cut through the noise and it calmed somewhat. She stepped forward, her face a mask of disapproval. "Calandra is merely trying to justify her own crimes."

Adonia arched a brow. "And what are those, daughter?"

"That of allowing her consort-elect and this boy to go Unredeemed."

Calandra tensed as all eyes turned toward her. She glared at Narcissa.

Narcissa took a few steps forward. "I witnessed it myself on the tour, at Fire Lake. What Osaze did to her is . . . well, is not fit to mention in the presence of children." She smirked and glanced at Zeke, as though she were only holding back the full gory details on his account. "I certainly never allowed such treatment when he was my doulos."

Calandra's hands were slick and her heart thundered in her ears.

"But she liked it," Narcissa said, crossing her arms with a victorious smile.

It took all of Calandra's control not to stuff a wad of solid air down Narcissa's throat. "That is a lie, Narcissa, and you know it."

Adonia's face contained an entire storm. She glared at her daughter. "Why have you said nothing about this?"

Narcissa blinked. "I—I took care of it myself. I'll show you. Osaze, come here."

Uncertainty filled the bond with Osaze. Calandra gave him a subtle shake of the head. It wasn't how she'd wanted to come clean, but the goddess had ordained otherwise.

"Osaze!" Narcissa screeched, jabbing a finger at the floor before her.

"He is not yours, Narcissa," Calandra said. "And neither is he mine. No man—or woman—should be owned or controlled by another. You were correct—Osaze *is* Free. And as long as I draw breath, I will do everything in my power to allow him to remain so. Him, and every other man on this island."

Osaze relaxed slightly, the mask of blankness dropping from his features as he zeroed in on Narcissa, whose eyes grew wide with horror.

"You are a terrible kisser, your highness," he said with a wicked grin.

"I have heard quite enough!" Adonia gave a signal.

Sirens surrounded and restrained Osaze, Calandra, Zale, Ignatia, and Judith, clasping feldspar shackles onto the undines' wrists. Ezekiel looked around at the fierce faces and nuzzled into his mother's neck before he was forcibly removed by a siren. He began crying, his arms outstretched toward Ignatia. She called assurances to him as she was bound and the siren took him from the room.

Adonia stepped forward and, with the efficiency borne of much practice, Redeemed Zale.

"No, Aunt Adonia!" Calandra cried, struggling against the arms that held her. "Have you heard nothing I've said? If we want to save our people, this is not the way!"

Adonia glared at her with eyes like emerald knives. "I believe you have overestimated your own agency, Calandra. I *am* saving our people. And I'm saving you from yourself."

Calandra struggled in vain against the strong arms that dragged her toward the steps, watching through her tears as Adonia Redeemed Osaze. Tanni had her hand on Judith's arm and let her slip into the crowd, but when she turned to find Calandra, there was too much distance and too many people between them. Then Tanni was also arrested.

Calandra's last image of the Court was of the confusion of the crowd, her supporters in chains, Narcissa's gloating smile, and beyond them, her brother and her consort-elect standing with blank faces behind her aunt.

The brooding thunderstorm on Adonia's face promised that the worst was yet to come.

49

THE ABYSS

Narcissa nursed her cup of coffee and stared through the window of the Observation Chamber at the dimly throbbing Heartstone, letting the voices of the archons ebb and flow around her. They had already gone around these same circles countless times since they'd convened after the excitement at the Court hours earlier. She took another sip of coffee, avoiding looking at Osaze in the line of *douloi* near the wall behind them. Even though he was now Redeemed, she couldn't forget the humiliation he'd put her through. He would pay for it.

She immediately took that thought back as beneath her—one did not take revenge on animals or *douloi*. As his mistress, Calandra had been the one responsible. And there were already so many reasons to make her cousin pay, this was merely another on the list.

Narcissa scowled and rested her mouth in her hand, her face turned from the table to hide her dark thoughts. While the others argued about Calandra's shocking revelations and whether or not she had been correct about the reasons behind their three thousand years of failure in healing the Heartstone, Narcissa had been puzzling about how Calandra had Released Osaze. She *knew* she had successfully Redeemed him on the *Luz*.

"Perhaps we should have the circle of stone healers try without her," Councillor Larissa was saying. "If she cannot be trusted and refuses to follow the old ways, then what choice do we have?"

"Councillor kor'Damiani is correct." Councillor Iris sounded as tired as Narcissa felt. Or maybe as weary of this conversation. "We are only hours away from sunrise and must come to a decision. If we miss this window, we will need to wait another year before we can try again—and I don't think we can afford to wait that long."

The other archons nodded at that, casting anxious looks toward the

Heartstone, which looked like a reverse full moon—a dark sphere against the luminous rock crystal column refracting its sister in the sky's silvery rays. The Stone had been fading more quickly every day.

"Why not let her try? This is what she's been trained for," said Councillor Hypatia. She wore grey robes, as always, and her thick black hair in the same plain bun, even for the Festival. "She's still the best candidate for the job. She isn't trying to skirt her duty, she's only been confused into thinking that—"

"What if she's telling the truth?" Narcissa muttered, surprising even herself.

Adonia, seated at the head of the table beside her, snapped her head toward her. "What did you say?"

Narcissa glanced at her mother, knowing the queen was still angry at her for the secret she'd sprung on her in public last night. She'd only wanted to shame Calandra—she hadn't thought how revealing her cousin's treachery and her handling of it in front of the entire Court would make both herself and her mother look bad. But it had been difficult to miss the whispers behind hands and the pointed looks the nobles and archons had given them as the royal family had exited the Court of the Redeemed.

She cleared her throat and spoke to the table.

"What if Calandra is right, and we do need both male and female powers to heal the Heartstone? Think about it. It's never been tried, and our best efforts have only been patches, at best, not a true restoration."

An angry murmur erupted in the room as archons threw comments both for and against that idea at her and at each other.

"It's what I've been saying!"

"I'll be chained before I let a freeman touch the Heartstone. Or any man."

"But how does he even exist?"

"It makes so much sense, doesn't it?"

"We've always managed just fine before, I don't know why we should change now."

"If we let her do it her way, what kind of a precedent will we be setting for the island?"

Adonia held up a hand and the archons fell silent. She turned to Narcissa.

"Speak, daughter. I would hear what you have to say."

Narcissa's throat tightened. It was rare for Adonia to let her give her opinion, and she almost choked. Then she straightened her neck and tossed her head to flip her braid behind her shoulder. If she were to rule, she needed to stop acting like an overjoyed guppy when asked for input.

"I am not saying we should let a freeman touch the Stone. I agree with Councillor Hypatia, that would be foolhardy beyond measure, not to mention implicitly condoning Calandra's blasphemous claims that men should remain Unredeemed to the Mother."

Several archons who had broached that idea as having merit based on history squirmed, but held their peace.

"What do you propose?" Adonia rolled her glass between her fingers—wine, not coffee—and regarded her daughter steadily.

"If all that is needed is both male and female powers, perhaps someone holding this boy's Redemption bond could channel his power. The bracelet implies he has some. You might be able to do it. Or me."

Adonia blew out a puff of air. "You still know so little about the bonds? The Redemption bond takes nothing from a man except his will and emotions. It makes him pliant. The added energy it gives to the keeper is not nothing, but it is small. Or have you suddenly gained levels of strength in the last two weeks, daughter? Should we apprentice you as a healer now?"

Narcissa's cheeks grew hot. She could sense the tethers of the hundreds of men she had Redeemed in her mind as though they were dim impressions, faint echoes of a sound or fleeting shadows in the corner of her eye. She could no more sense the emotions or elements—the Matrix of Creation, as she'd heard the healers call it—around her than she could fly.

"No, of course not. But I am only holding the bonds of humans. Wherever he came from, this Zale is undoubtedly an undine. You hold his bond. Have you noticed anything different about it?"

Adonia took a sip of wine, watching her daughter, then turned to the room.

"Yes, I have. His life force is strong, and so are his powers. I have had mine enhanced a great deal more than I expected. For instance, I've never been able to do this before."

She cupped her glass between her fingers and concentrated. In moments, the wine began to steam, then bubble, the glass flaring red around her fingers. The councillors murmured about using fire and some stood, straining to get a better look.

Adonia set it down, panting from the exertion. The bowl of the glass had slight impressions where her fingers had been.

"So perhaps you have a point," Adonia said to Narcissa. "But it would take someone more powerful than I to channel his power into the Stone,

I fear."

"What about if we used the *syzagos* bond?" Narcissa held her breath. "Does that not give you the other's power full force? Maybe that's all that's truly needed, the reason why we have only sent bonded women in to heal the Heartstone for all these millennia—we have simply lacked an undine consort to give the bond the proper strength. And I can't help but think that an undine would make a far better King Consort than a human."

Adonia leaned back, scorn on her face. "I see. And you presume the title is yours, do you?"

Narcissa tilted her chin up, refusing to wilt under her mother's glare. "Would you put a criminal on the throne, Mother?"

Adonia frowned and tapped her nails on the table. "One thing that Calandra said, I do believe—Zale is Delphine's son. Any of you who knew her cannot deny it."

A few of the archons murmured assent.

Adonia eyed her daughter, looking thoughtful. "Calandra cannot marry her brother—there is too great a chance of undesirable mutations in the offspring. And while a cousin is far enough removed to reduce the risk, you, sadly, lack the necessary control and skill to be of use in the Healing Circle."

Narcissa nodded, clenching her jaw. As always, her mother's logic was irrefutable—but that didn't make being overlooked again hurt less.

"That being said," Adonia continued, "Calandra has broken one of our most deeply ingrained laws. As such, she has earned the sentence of death. So what harm in her bonding her own brother if she will be dead before the marriage can even be consummated?"

"So he is to be Calandra's first, and then mine?"

Narcissa ground her teeth. Another castoff. How did Calandra always take the first cut and leave her with the scraps?

Still, she dared to hope. She had no interest in his pretty face. But from the moment she'd laid eyes on him, she'd known that with him by her side, she could use him to command something she'd always craved—respect. Castoff or no, she would be the first queen in millennia to rule with an undine consort. And her cousin would be dead.

Adonia smiled. "I don't see why not."

The archons' murmurs got louder.

Adonia glared at them all. "Silence!"

Iris wore an outraged expression. "You would execute our only two living panaceas?" she demanded.

"They have chosen their destinies." Adonia's eyes had no hint of softness or regret to them.

Narcissa didn't have any compassion to spare for her cousin. Her mother was right—Calandra had brought this on herself. And with her out of the way, Narcissa stood to gain everything she'd ever wanted. She squirmed in delight and glanced at Osaze, thinking of what Calandra would do once she found out. "Can we tell her now?"

"I think it best to surprise her," Adonia replied. "Don't you? She's been much too full of her own plans lately for my taste."

Narcissa smothered disappointment, then brightened as she realized her cousin's shame and surprise would be on public display at the bonding ceremony tomorrow, just as her own had been tonight.

"Calandra seems to have a deep infatuation for this *doulos*," Narcissa said, indicating Osaze with distaste. "And she also knows the Holy Sanctions against breeding full siblings. How are you going to make her comply?"

Adonia raised her eyebrows as though surprised that Narcissa had foreseen that complication.

"It's like you said, daughter—she cares for her consort-elect. And that gives us leverage." Adonia cast a pitying glance at Osaze, twirling her wine glass by the stem. "Poor Delphine. If only she could see how far her children have fallen."

She cocked her head and smiled at the Heartstone, seemingly lost in her own thoughts. The archons stared at their monarch with grim, shocked faces.

Narcissa could barely contain her excitement. She could not wait to see her cousin's face tomorrow when the plan was revealed.

No one noticed Osaze stiffen at the back of the room.

*

CALANDRA paced about the dungeon, trying to ignore the smell of mouldy straw, the scritching sounds of rats, and the small pellet-like objects her bare feet landed on. The moonlight coming in through the small window was enough to tell her what they were, but she didn't want to think about it.

She had failed. Utterly and completely. The Mother had answered her prayer and brought her brother to her, and she had messed it up. Not only had he been Redeemed, but Osaze—the man she had sworn she would never let be enslaved again—was once again a void inside her, while the burning threads of thousands of other men tried to sear all thoughts of him out of her head.

The pain flared red and hot. She collapsed to her knees on the straw, doubling over as it consumed her mind. Falling onto her side, she pressed her hands to her ears and started to sing quietly to herself—a lullaby she hadn't heard for many years.

"In the night, the Dragon waits to ravage in the dark, but Elyon will shield the ones who bear his watermark."

The pain began to fade as she concentrated on remembering the words.

"In the light, the em'rald-eyed protectors of the deep will, ever vigilant, defend the gates of Elyon's keep."

She breathed easier, and the notes became surer. "The dragons and the cherubim and undines all as one will love and celebrate the race to whom he sent his son."

It was one of those nonsense lullabies, with words that didn't make sense and whose meaning had been forgotten in the mists of time. As a child, she had wondered at the strange name Elyon, wondering who it could be referring to, but now it only made her think of the woman who had sung it to her. Her mother.

The pain in her head had faded to being bearable. But the pain in her heart broke open like a Panselinos popper, spraying all the pieces of her failure into the open.

Helpless to do anything about any of it, she lay there and sobbed.

50

THE PLAN

CALANDRA WOKE UP WITH A start and a gasp of stale air, her heart hammering against her ribcage, the image of Damon floating in her nightmare abyss burned on her retinas. It was still dark, but a small glimmer of firelight flickered through the bars on the heavy dungeon door.

She shifted on the mouldy straw and sat up. She had no idea how long she had been asleep—it didn't feel like it had been long. But the sky through the small window was lightening to soft green, so it had to be nearing dawn.

Now that she was calmer, she could sense Tanni in a cell nearby, along with two other presences she was certain were Ignatia and Thea. She could sense no other prisoners, only the purposeful boredom of the two sirens on duty, and dared to hope Judith had managed to escape, perhaps even to find little Zeke and get him to safety. She wondered what Adonia had done with Osaze and her brother, or what she intended to do.

Snippets of her nightmare floated through her mind, leaving her coated with the emotions of it—the loneliness, the sense of failure and abandonment, the helplessness, Damon's gloating boasts—

"He said *we*." Even her murmuring sounded harsh and loud in the darkness. "'When *we* finish with the Heartstone.' What did he mean by that?"

A shiver ran through her, and she fidgeted with her stone cuffs.

Two people approached in the hall outside, the lock rattled, and the door opened. In the dim light, she caught Zoe's silhouette holding the door open, letting Urbi—a small lamp in her hands—slip into the room. The cloying sweetness of burning ambergris came with her, masking the unpleasant odours of the cell.

"Ten minutes," Zoe said with a dip of her chin at Calandra, then closed the door.

Urbi set down the lamp and gave Calandra a firm, warm hug. The older woman pulled away and kneeled on the rough stone floor.

"You shouldn't have come," Calandra said, but felt warmed by it, none-the-less. "If Adonia finds out, your position and freedom could be in danger."

Urbi nodded. "There are some things worth risking our freedom for. Thea told me that once."

Calandra blinked. "She would know."

Urbi spoke in urgent tones. "After Adonia sent Osaze to his quarters for the night, he came to visit me and told me what happened."

"How could that be? He was enslaved. I saw it. I *felt* it."

She turned her attention to the bond she shared with her consort-elect and realized that, while the emotions she could sense were subdued, they were present. Had he been Free the whole time? She marvelled at his self-control, despite the distress it had caused her. Like Gerrick, her consort-elect had become skilled enough at shielding his emotions to survive even in the Opal Palace.

Urbi smiled. "He was only pretending. Your songstoppers worked."

Hope stirred in Calandra's heart for the first time since last night. If Osaze were Free, then he could escape. If she were to die, he could still have a full life without her.

Urbi continued. "The entire city is in an uproar because of what you did. You, and your brother, and my son." Urbi smiled proudly. "The queen and her council stayed in session until late into the night, and everywhere in the city, people are talking about the things you said."

The flickering lamplight danced in her black eyes as she leaned forward.

"Change has begun, your highness. Like the breeze that picks up sand before the storm, you have begun it."

Calandra dropped her gaze to her knees, fidgeting with the feldspar cuffs.

"But what a price has already been paid. Perhaps it would serve us right if the Heartstone fails and the barrier is lost. Then we would have to learn to get along with humans instead of kidnap and enslave them."

"What price? No one has lost their lives, but many likely would if your nation were known to the world. There is one thing your kind sees clearly about mine—humans have an irrepressible urge to control what they do not understand. Even if all you did was maintain your borders, a heavy price would indeed be paid. More than likely, many of you would become slaves. That is not progress."

Urbi put her hand on Calandra's arm.

"In my country, there is always fighting—squabbles about land, and power, and territory, and women. Small men fighting, taking lives and slaves to fill their own pockets and make themselves feel big. Pointless wars, for no reason but to bring luxury to a few and misery to everyone else. But this . . . this is something noble, m'lady. Change such as this does not come easily. If some of us must die so that the way of peace can carry on, we do so gladly. For if you succeed—*when* you succeed—this beautiful nation could truly become a paradise on Earth."

Her eyes grew moist.

"Your friends from Elpida who have come have all made their choices. They will be at your wedding tomorrow, waiting for the signal to rise into action."

"What? You mean more than Ignatia and Zeke came?"

Calandra shook her head. She'd been angry when they would not risk themselves, but now that they were here, she was terrified they would only meet the same fate as all who had tried before.

"Tell them to go home, and take Osaze and Judith with them. Tanni and Ignatia are already paying the price for my hopeful naiveté. If Adonia plans to execute Thea, it seems all too likely that the rest of us are also bound for the guillotine, especially me. I can't bear the thought of Osaze being enslaved again, of living out his life that way. Too many good people have already given up their lives for this cause by death or enslavement, and for what? I will not permit more to die for me, or for this. I will not have their deaths on my conscience."

Urbi laid her hand over Calandra's, wrapping her fingers around the younger woman's.

"A month ago, I watched you heal a dead plant. If you can do that, you can succeed at this, too."

Calandra snorted. "All I did was get that plant started. After that, it pretty much healed itself."

Urbi smiled triumphantly. "Exactly."

Calandra looked at her in surprise.

"Your highness, this movement is bigger than you. It is bigger, because it is right. All you did was get it started—but not even you. Your mother and Lady Thea and your Elpida friends before you, am I right? You are only taking up what they have begun. And any who may die fighting do so willingly. It is not your fault."

Tears pricked Calandra's sinuses. "I suppose . . ."

Urbi leaned forward. "Besides, I do not believe Osaze would abandon you while he has breath. You must know how much he loves you. More than I even realized. And the bonds of love are far stronger than any chains of enslavement could ever be."

Urbi's brow furrowed slightly, and Calandra wondered what conversation had passed between her consort-elect and his mother to cause it. She gave a small nod. Urbi was right. She knew she would never be able to make Osaze go, not even for the sake of his own freedom.

Urbi pulled her hand back. "There is more. Adonia plans to force you to wed your brother tomorrow so that you will be able to channel his power to heal the Heartstone."

"What?"

Calandra slapped her hands over her mouth at the involuntary shriek. She lowered her voice and whispered.

"That is disgusting! And it is not what I meant at all. I don't even think it will work. I am certain it is not enough to merely have a consort bond with a man. *He* must use his powers to heal." She thought about how Damon had tried taking her powers from her, obviously with some plan to escape his prison from the inside. "Or maybe channelling *would* be enough. But it's still wrong. My own brother?"

She got up and began pacing around the small cell.

"The consort bond must be initiated by me, so what makes her think I will comply?"

Urbi relayed what Osaze had overheard in the council chambers. As she spoke, Calandra's pace slowed, and she plopped herself on the cold stone.

"So I am to die regardless." She fidgeted with her healer's rings. "I had hoped for a different result, but if this is what the Mother has ordained, then so be it."

Urbi held up her finger, then reached into her pocket and pulled something out. When she turned her hand over, Calandra's breath caught.

"My Tear! They brought it."

"This was sent by Judith. Her mother gave it to her to give to you."

She handed Calandra the Tear, who clutched it tightly to her chest. Then Urbi reached back into her pocket and pulled out a small hexagonal clear quartz stone reader, which she handed to Calandra also.

"She says you must watch it immediately."

Her hands quivering in trepidation and excitement, Calandra placed the Tear on the reader and activated it. Thanks to what she'd done at Fire Lake, the contents were no longer encrypted, and the stone surface distorted into her mother's image.

This time, she let the message play to the end. Then she touched the stone and accessed the deeper information on the Tear, spending several minutes exploring the different topics her mother had included. She only had time to skim the surface, but each revelation left her chest tighter and her resolve stronger.

At last, she finally understood how big the Cause was. It went far beyond Osaze's or Zale's freedom, or even the fate of the human men on Sirenia. The words of her mother's lullaby came to her—she still didn't know who Elyon was, but at last, she knew where his keep lay.

When the message ended, Urbi turned earnest eyes toward her. "What are you going to do?"

"Wait, I'm thinking."

The lock rattled, and Zoe came back in. "Time's up."

"Zoe," Calandra said, "what is your duty during the bonding and Healing ceremonies tomorrow?"

"I believe I have been assigned as hall monitor," she said, wrinkling her nose in disgust. "Why?"

"Come here, please."

Zoe narrowed her eyes, but after sticking her head into the hallway, swung the door closed behind her and approached the other two women.

"What is it?"

"Do you know where Adonia is keeping my brother, the undine boy?"

"He is in the care of the priestesses at the temple."

Calandra nodded. That was unfortunate. She could think of no way to gain access to him before the ceremony tomorrow. She would have to find another way to get him out. But if she were going to save the world, she needed to know that Osaze, at least, was safe.

"Can you drive a submersible?"

Zoe shrugged. "Of course. Why?"

"And do you believe me that I need both Zale and myself if I am to heal the Heartstone, and Zale must be Free?"

Zoe gave her a long look. At last, she said, "I believe you."

"Will you help me make that happen?"

She nodded. "Yes."

"Good."

Calandra outlined her plan. When she got to the end, Urbi gave her a hard stare.

"Remember what I said, Calandra. We must all make our own choices."

Calandra scowled, annoyed.

"You told me yourself what Osaze would choose, but I can see in your eyes that you don't think his choice is the right one. It is not the choice he would make if he knew any other life. I only want to give back to him and to you a little of what we have taken. You, and the other humans on this island. This plan is about creating choices. But if you don't like it, speak now. There is still time to change your mind."

Urbi pressed her lips together, then shook her head. "It is a good plan. You are a true daughter of Yemaya, your highness. May the Orisha smile on you."

She pressed her fingers to her bowed forehead in salute.

Calandra had each woman repeat the plan back to her before they left. After that, she lay down on the straw to try to catch a few more hours of sleep. She would need whatever rest she could manage before the events to come.

For the first time, she dared to hope she could both keep her promise to Osaze and fulfill her duty to her nation. She didn't know which failure would be worse—failure to protect him, or failure to repair the Heartstone.

One thing she did know—she had to heal the Heartstone, no matter the cost.

The fate of the entire world hung in the void.

51

THE WEDDING

It felt as though Calandra had barely closed her eyes when the door squealed open and Despoina Cleo entered the cell.

"Come along, girl. It's your bonding day. Adonia would have you bonded and the Heartstone healed before she passes judgement on your crimes."

Calandra grunted and stood. She wondered if Cleo were lying to her, or if Adonia had lied to Cleo.

"What about my cuffs? I won't be able to do any of it with these on." She held out her arms in front of her.

Cleo looked at them skeptically.

"Cleo, you know how much I want to heal the Heartstone. I will not do anything foolish. Please, take them off."

"I wish I could, but Adonia gave instructions that they were not to be removed until absolutely necessary. I'm sorry."

She did look apologetic.

Calandra sighed. She left the cell and fell into step behind two sirens. Cleo walked beside her, and two more walked behind. She glanced over her shoulder at the entourage.

"Is this necessary?"

Cleo pressed her lips together. "It's orders."

When they reached her bedchamber, there was a whole group of women and *douloi* there, including Tailor Dorothea, a lady's maid Calandra didn't recognize, and Meg. A large copper bathtub sat in the corner filled almost to the brim with steaming water. A trencher of fresh fruit, soft white cheese, and fresh honeycakes sat on her desk. Calandra's stomach rumbled.

Meg stood near the door, moving to the side as Calandra entered, then turned to face Cleo.

"Thank you, *despoina*, I will take it from here."

Meg pressed her bunched fingers to her forehead in salute, and Cleo returned the gesture, then left with quick steps. Meg closed the door behind her.

Dorothea stood and examined Calandra with a critical eye, her hand under her chin. Calandra still wore her festival gown, which was rumpled and dirty, and she knew her hair was a mess.

"Well, the night in the dungeon didn't do you any favours, my dear," the tailor said. "But we'll have you fixed up soon enough."

Meg watched as the team washed and primped and preened Calandra into a glowing bride. Dorothea guided everything with a precise vision. Meg contributed where she could, but it was obvious she was only there to supervise the process—or Calandra, more like—giving guidance when Dorothea had a question.

After she'd finished her breakfast, Calandra sat quietly and allowed them to fuss over her, replaying the plan over and over in her mind until her nerves were wound tighter than a kithara string. She barely noticed the women and men as they worked.

Then Meg's *doulos* dropped a hair comb. As he fumbled to pick it up, a flash of hot embarrassment and fear radiated from him, and a similar spike of alarm blasted from Meg. He succeeded in collecting the comb and then handed it to the maid styling Calandra's hair, his emotions subsiding somewhat, though moisture pearled on his upper lip.

From that moment on, Calandra knew Meg's secret. She said nothing, but watched the man and Meg closely for the rest of the procedure, wondering how long Meg's *doulos* had been Free.

Then she realized, as she listened to the frantic beating of his heart, that he still was not. For how could any man who must live his life in fear be considered free? The breeze of change, as Urbi called it, may have been roused, but it was still a long way from the storm that would be required to bring true freedom.

The bundle of fibres in her head burned and she closed her eyes, using deep breathing to maintain control, then hummed the lullaby under her breath. How she wished she could go Release every single one of those men before they spent another second enslaved, and before she inched one step nearer Madness. But she supposed that, if Adonia were to execute her, both problems would take care of themselves. Then Adonia would have a whole new set of problems on her hands, as several thousand men around the island suddenly woke up from their slumber.

She wondered if that thought had occurred to her aunt. *Either I'll free them on purpose, or Adonia will do it by accident. Whatever chaos may ensue, at least my death won't be for nothing.*

"All finished, m'lady," Dorothea said, holding up a silvered hand mirror for Calandra to admire the results.

Calandra gaped. Her long white tunic was trimmed and girdled in scarlet fabric with teal and silver embroidery. Urbi's red coral bead string was looped around her neck multiple times to create a wide collar necklace. Her hair flowed in flaxen curls down her back beneath a braided crown with pearls, white plumeria blooms, and red hibiscus pinned into it. She reached up and gingerly touched the petals of one of the crimson flowers.

"Adonia will not be pleased by that. And neither will Narcissa."

"Well, it was not their decision," said Meg, and Dorothea nodded approval. "They put us in charge of getting you ready for the bonding ceremony. And, since Adonia has not yet formally declared an heir, this was our way of voting."

Dorothea cleared her throat.

"As the royal tailor and stylist, my politics are moot. But as a woman who would dearly love the chance to have a grandson or three . . ."

She let it hang in the air, shifting her substantial weight between her feet.

Calandra's vision blurred, and she wiped her eyes. "Thank you, all of you."

She looked directly at Meg's servant, and he gulped.

Calandra kept her eyes on his. "This cannot be done alone, and it will not be over until everyone on this island, regardless of race or gender, is free to determine their own destiny."

She smiled at him, and he hesitantly smiled back.

Calandra took in the half-dozen pairs of hopeful eyes that looked back at her, and realized that every man in this room was Free and every woman had joined her cause. Judith and Urbi must have been busy.

She swallowed the lump in her throat.

"Let's go change the world."

*

"Narcissa, quit fidgeting."

Adonia scowled and tapped Narcissa's hands with her folded silk fan, then spread it and went back to fanning herself while surveying the gathered crowd.

Narcissa surreptitiously rubbed her stinging hand against her thigh. From the chair on Narcissa's other side, Hebe giggled, then covered her mouth with her hands.

Narcissa scowled and made a face at her younger sister, releasing the loop of pearls hanging from her fuchsia silk girdle that she'd been fingering. She sat up straight and stared out at the crowd, aware of Mari's gaze on her neck from behind her. She cursed her fair complexion, knowing her neck would be as bright pink as it was hot.

She glanced back at the other girl, who looked radiant in a silver-embroidered amethyst gown, and Mari quirked her lips sideways in commiseration. Next to Mari, Matthew stood at attention in a grey dress tunic trimmed in fuchsia to match Narcissa's dress.

They were sitting under a white canopy that had been erected in the centre of the front courtyard of the Opal Palace to shelter the royal party, facing the bridal arbour that had been erected near the large carved double doors leading into the Great Hall. The courtyard was filled with noblewomen and their families, including the occasional consort, important city officials, House Heads, and archons from all over the island. The novices and apprentices from the Royal Academy sat out of Narcissa's view behind the canopy.

High Priestess Shinara stood under the arbour. A brilliant crimson turban covered her close-shorn black hair, and her tall, lean body was swathed in a matching boxy crimson tunic, her many rings and bracelets flashing from her clasped hands. She looked as impatient as everyone else for the ceremony to begin, though she was concealing it better. As the sun inched closer to its zenith, the amount of available time for completing the bonding ceremony and moving onto the healing ceremony was closing. Once the sun's direct rays left the Mother's Heart chamber, they would have to wait for another year before trying again.

Narcissa glanced past her mother and Cain, whom the queen had permitted to sit beside her, to the young undine man beyond. Zale had been bathed and styled and given a finely embroidered tunic and cloak to wear, but he sat as stiff and erect as Cain, staring at nothing. Narcissa could still hardly believe he was her cousin.

Oddly, she felt a twinge of sadness to see his blank, staring face, but quickly pushed the sentiment aside. Undine or not, he was male.

At last, there was movement from the doors, and the musicians positioned near the arbour began to play. The murmuring crowd quieted and sat up, straining to see what was happening.

Osaze, blank and passive, came through the doors and stood in front of the arbour wearing a fine silk agbada, a traditional African wedding suit—a rather rebellious touch by the tailor.

Narcissa smiled. She truly did not want Osaze, and never really had, but she couldn't help but feel secret delight that her cousin would not have him either.

She could hardly wait for Calandra to arrive to find that out.

*

CALANDRA stared at the assembled crowds through the tall windows at the front of the Great Hall, which was already filled with bustling servants setting the celebratory feast. She could see Osaze standing perfectly still near the arbour, maintaining his mask and his emotional shield, despite the heat. The barest trace of his anxiety trickled through the bond, but he betrayed none of it in his stance. Across the square, Zale had a matching posture in his chair beside Adonia, though she knew his blank face was not pretence.

Meg came up to her and began fussing with her hair and dress, smoothing and adjusting.

"It's a shame you can't wear your mother's Tear today. However, I'm sure she would approve of the use to which it will be put."

Calandra's gaze snapped to Meg's. Resolve and understanding filled the other woman's narrow green eyes. Meg pulled down the high neckline of her tunic, exposing the dark green opal Tear hanging around her neck before covering it again.

"Don't worry. I'll get the message out. For Aunt Thea and . . . Uncle Gerrick," Meg whispered.

Calandra nodded. Meg was the most skilled stone healer besides herself that the Academy had seen in many years. She knew Urbi had placed this part of the mission in capable and trustworthy hands.

"Are you ready?" Meg asked quietly.

Calandra was certain they must be able to hear her heart beating in the courtyard outside, but she squared her shoulders.

"Yes. Let's go."

She marched over to the double doors where Despoina Cleo waited with the keys to her cuffs. Calandra held out her arms, regarding the silver-haired woman with a level gaze as she deftly unlocked each one and handed them off to the rhapsodist beside her.

"Calandra, don't botch this," Cleo said. "Our people need you."

"Not only our people."

Calandra turned toward the doors, which two *douloi* pushed open wide, staring out at the people and the valley and the island she loved. She thought of Atargatis, who, as Inanna, had gone to the very depths of hell for her consort—a man who must have been Free for her to care so deeply. But thinking about what she must try to accomplish today, her knees quivered and her heart fluttered like a sacred koi's fins.

"May the Mother be with me," she whispered.

She went to stand beside Osaze before the priestess, who smiled at them. Then, both bride and groom turned to face the queen and offered the appropriate greetings. They both bowed and saluted her, and Calandra stepped forward to ask the required question, her heart pounding. The time for action was nearly upon her.

"Your majesty, Beloved of the Mother," she called over the square, aware of all eyes on her, "I request your permission and blessing to marry this man who has been Redeemed to the Mother . . ."

She paused. Since Osaze had been freed, she was quite possibly using the word *redeemed* accurately for the first time in her life. She repressed a smile and continued.

"And to whom I will offer my care and protection for as long as I shall live."

The spectators twisted in their seats to witness the queen's reply.

Adonia stood, a wide false smile on her face.

"I do not give it."

Gasps resounded around the courtyard, and Calandra's gut tensed even tighter.

"At one time," the queen continued, "I thought no Redemption harvest could offer a more fitting King Consort than Osaze. But last night, for the first time in three millennia, an undine male has presented himself— and not just any male. He bears the blood of queens all the way back to Nadia kor'Hera. There would be none more fitting to stand at the side of the future Queen of Sirenia than this man, Zale bet'Delphine. Zale, join your sister on the podium."

The crowd reacted with hushed, urgent whispers, pointing fingers, and aghast faces as Zale walked woodenly up the aisle toward Calandra.

Calandra swallowed and glanced at the royal platform to see Narcissa looking horrified and betrayed. The princess obviously hadn't expected Adonia to name Calandra heir while entrapping her niece. Even if Adonia planned to execute Calandra tonight, Narcissa would always look like second choice in the eyes of the nation.

Hebe looked remarkably unconcerned. She'd never wanted the throne and, as the younger daughter, never expected to get it.

Calandra's heart pinched. She had never wanted the throne, either, and knew she'd never truly have a chance to occupy it. She could only hope that Narcissa would gain some compassion and a sense of duty before she sat upon it. Even if Calandra succeeded in restoring the Heartstone today and proved her point about men, what freedom would the oppressed gender of this island find under her aunt's and cousin's misandristic rules?

She took a breath. One mountain at a time.

She straightened and called across the crowd. It would seem suspicious if she didn't react at all.

"You expect me to marry my own brother? And what of the man to whom I have been promised?"

She expected Adonia to send Osaze away into the palace to rejoin the ranks of the *tapeinos* guards, or possibly demote him to the position of her personal bodyguard, or even Zale's.

Adonia smiled, and Calandra was once again reminded of a shark.

"Excellent question, niece. Osaze, come here."

Calandra stifled alarm as Osaze glanced at her helplessly, then made his way up the aisle toward the queen, passing Zale on the way. When he got there, Adonia told Cain to stand behind her and patted his empty seat.

"Sit with me, *doulos*."

Calandra stared, the meaning of Adonia's actions—who tired of men as easily as she did gowns—horrifyingly clear.

She intended to make Osaze her next pet. But worse for them at the moment, he now sat in the most heavily-guarded area of the entire courtyard, with sirens surrounding the pavilion, as well as standing guard at all the entrances and exits to the square.

As soon as Osaze sat in the chair, Adonia took his hand—and a siren guard placed the tip of her knife to his throat.

"Just so you don't get any bright ideas, my dear," Adonia called to her niece sweetly. "Now let's proceed. The sun grows higher as we speak."

Sweat trickled down Calandra's back and the air crushed her like a mile of ocean water. She turned and faced Zale's blank green-eyed stare. That hadn't been part of the plan.

"Take his hands," Shinara said.

Calandra complied, her thoughts racing as Shinara began her dedication to Atargatis.

What do I do now? How will I get Osaze away from Adonia?

Then she spied a face in the crowd that gave her hope. Rhea sat near the queen's pavilion, and beside her, Xeni met Calandra's eyes and nodded. Calandra glanced surreptitiously around the square and noticed more familiar faces from Elpida, including Jacob and Hammad, who were camouflaged among the *douloi* lining the walls. Then she spied Judith near the Pool of Atargatis. When her maid saw Calandra looking, she flashed her the secret fingers-interlaced-between-their-palms praying gesture of the Free Will Society.

Calandra was far from alone.

She looked up at Zale, who looked right through her. It was a miracle that he even existed, let alone that he had shown up on the very eve of when she needed him most. She couldn't waste that divine intervention. If her mother could risk everything to show their people a better way, so could she.

Thank you, Mother. This time, I will not fail.

The next moment, her mother's voice rang over the square.

52

THE REBELLION

"Calandra, if you are seeing this before my return, it means that my plan has failed," came Delphine's tinny voice from everywhere at once. "I am sure you have many questions . . ."

Shinara stopped her recitations and looked around. "What is that?"

The rest of the crowd did much the same thing.

The ordinarily smooth surface of a falling water feature on the opposite side of the courtyard bubbled to life as though it were a quartz reader, Delphine's larger-than-life face on the display. *Good girl, Meg.*

"Everything I've done has been to help you and our people . . ." rang Delphine's voice from every soundstone around the courtyard, the ones Judith and the others had placed there in the night.

Adonia stood, staring in open-mouthed shock at the face on the water.

"Stop this. Whoever is back there, stop it at once!"

Shinara took several steps toward the waterfall, trying to get a better look. Calandra took advantage of the confusion by placing her finger on Zale's forehead and Releasing him. As he blinked at her, disoriented, she tucked a pair of songstoppers into his ears and tugged at his hand. No time to wait for him to get his bearings.

"Come on."

She pulled him toward the entrance of the Grotto near the Pool of Atargatis. The sirens guarding it were looking around in as much confusion as everyone else.

"What's going on?" Zale asked after a few steps, finally offering a little resistance to her urging.

They had nearly reached the encompassing walls of the Grotto. Calandra was trying to decide if she had enough fighting skill to take on the two sirens who guarded the entrance when a scuffle and shouts near the pavilion drew the guards' attention, and one of them ran that direction.

Calandra glanced over her shoulder to see *douloi* around the square blinking in confusion, the women of Elpida Releasing them as quickly as they could move and sing the notes. *Just like the plan.* More importantly, Osaze had overpowered and broken free from the sirens trying to stun him into submission, and Jacob, Hammad, and the others were covering his retreat. Calandra wished she'd had time to make more songstoppers, but was glad that at least her friends would be protected from the sirensong a few quick-reacting sirens had begun to croon.

She turned back to Zale. "Change. And you helped to bring it."

She turned to the siren, who shifted her feet wide to block their path.

"Pardon, your—your highness, but you are not permitted to leave."

"Tell them I didn't give you a choice," Calandra said with a gracious smile.

As the guard opened her mouth to reply, Calandra made a controlled jab for the bottom side of the woman's chin. The guard blocked it with crossed arms, thrusting Calandra away, then followed with a lightning-fast right hook. Calandra lunged beneath it and let the woman's momentum carry her past. She caught the guard's other wrist on the way by and twisted the siren's arm up behind her with one arm while placing her other hand on the woman's forehead and singing a few notes. The singer drooped, unconscious in her arms.

"Help me," Calandra grunted at Zale.

Her brother helped her gently lay the woman to the side of the path.

"How did you do that?" he asked.

"A physic's trick. Not what it was meant for, but handy at the moment. Now let's go."

She pushed him toward the archway into the atrium as Delphine's voice said, "Men are not our enemies, nor our servants. They were meant to be our partners . . ."

"Is that Mother's voice?" Zale asked, looking around.

"Yes, but she's not here. I'll explain later. Now, *go!*"

Osaze caught up to them, grabbed them both by the elbows, and urged them ahead of him into the building.

"Hello, Zale. Nice to meet you," he said as he released them, running behind them. "Sorry we didn't have time for introductions last night."

"Hi," Zale said. "Who are you?"

"Zale, this is my consort-elect, Osaze," said Calandra as she directed them along the flagstone pathways.

Zale nodded at Osaze, then tripped on the edge of a flagstone. Osaze reached out to steady him, but he easily righted himself and continued on without breaking pace.

"This place . . . is so . . . strange," he said, panting. "Why did the queen want me to marry you? That's just . . . gross. No offence," he added quickly.

Calandra laughed dryly, despite their hurry. "No, it is. It's a long story, one I'll have to explain later, when there's time."

"You've got a lot to explain later," he muttered.

"Yes, I do. Now come on."

Calandra led the way into the arched colonnade that ran the length of the covered garden, then turned in the opposite direction of the Great Hall. This route would mean going the long way to the Mother's Heart chamber, but it would also mean avoiding all the servants setting up the feast in the hall and the sirens near the courtyard.

It was also the fastest route to her secret cave beneath the palace. If she had her emotional bearings correct, the spot where Tanni waited far below them should be right outside the crystal cavern's door.

A siren on watch duty hailed them as they approached.

"Your highness, what is happening?"

Calandra slowed and ran toward her. "Someone has Released all the *douloi* at the ceremony. We are getting to safety. You'd best go help."

The siren turned to run toward the main courtyard. Calandra placed a hand on her forehead and Sang her to sleep. Osaze helped her tuck the woman's body against the wall.

When they reached the stairs, Calandra signalled them to stop, then leaned against the wall of the torch-lit stairwell with her hands on her legs, panting. The others followed suit.

"Zale, I am . . . sorry we have not had time to get to . . . know each other properly," she said between gasps. Collecting herself a little, she stood. "You've caught us at a rather bad time. You see, when I first heard of you, my reaction was nearly the same as all those women's you saw last night. You are the first—"

"—undine male to be born in three thousand years. Yeah, I know."

"You do?"

"Yeah, Abela told me."

Calandra frowned. "Who is this Abela person, and how would she know that? Is she an undine, too?"

She began to descend the narrow stairs, and the others followed, Zale first, then Osaze.

"No, she's one of the lumasi. So's Berian."

"Lumasi? But I thought they were all extinct."

Zale shrugged. "I guess not. From how they talked, they have a whole nation somewhere, though I'm not sure how to get there. Did you ever find them? You'll know them by their golden eyes."

Calandra stopped dead in her tracks and her brother bumped into her from behind. She turned to face him.

"Golden eyes?"

"Yeah. Why?"

She exchanged glances with Osaze.

"Do they have another form?" she asked Zale. "A non-human form, like we do?"

Zale nodded slowly.

"Yes, they do," he said carefully. "Abela is a lion-lamassu, and Berian is a bull-lamassu. They both have these massive sets of wings. It's pretty cool, actually."

Calandra nodded. She'd read that the lumasi were winged beings.

"You're sure they're not dragons?"

Zale's eyes widened. "I—I thought Abela was a dragon once, but she insisted she's not. She said she knows one, though."

Calandra began descending the stairs again, satisfied for now.

Osaze spoke up from the back. "Why would you even ask that about the dragons, Calandra?"

She explained as she ran. "It was something on my mother's Tear. About the purpose of the Voidstone."

"The Voidstone?"

"Yeah, that sphere I saw in Atlantis. That's what it's called." She glanced at Zale over her shoulder. "Anyway, I'm afraid that, even though we barely know each other, I must ask you for help. Remember those evil men who you said have Mother? I think I know what they wanted to use her for—to break the gates of Tartarus."

Zale nodded. "Yes, that sounds right."

"I need you to help me repair them."

They reached a landing and turned down another flight of stairs.

"What are you talking about, Calandra?" Osaze asked. "And where are we going?"

"Where we're going is a surprise. And I finally got to see the message on my mother's Tear last night, the one that's playing in the courtyard right now," she said, huffing. "There was so much more on there than I ever realized. For one, the Heartstone doesn't only power the barrier to the human realm. It powers the barrier to the Underworld, as well—the Voidstone in Atlantis."

"What?" Osaze asked incredulously.

"Abela said undines were created as guardians of the deep, but that they'd forgotten their purpose," Zale said, barely panting. "This Void-stone—what do we have to do?"

She stopped on the final landing and turned to face her brother. There were no torches here, only the dim lightstone on the wall casting a pale blue glow over them. Osaze stood on the steps behind Zale.

"I need you to help me repair the power source. I need you to take off your cuff and help me heal the Heartstone."

Zale's face went as pale as the marble walls.

"Abela told me about this. I know this is important. And I know it has to be me. But I—I don't think I can. When I use my powers, bad things happen. I—I kill people."

Calandra nearly wept at the guilt and shame that radiated from him as he spoke. "Why didn't Mother teach you to use your powers?"

The shame intensified.

"It's a long story," he mumbled.

She touched his arm, projecting calm and wondering what torment he'd had to endure because of who he was. After a moment, his fear subsided, but not the guilt. She could do nothing about that.

"I'll help you, okay? Just follow my lead."

"But what if I become too afraid? That's when I lose control."

She wrapped her hands around his, sensing the roiling currents within him.

Osaze chuckled and rubbed his chin. "Watch this."

She smiled at her consort-elect, a flush of shy pride blooming in her chest that he took delight in her ability. *What an odd, satisfying sensation.*

She flooded Zale with love and warmth. In moments, his heart resumed a normal tempo. He blinked at his hands as she released them.

"How did you do that?"

"It's one of my powers. Now, may I?" She held out her hand for the cuff.

He hesitated, then nodded and offered his wrist to her.

"I don't have a key. Berian used some magical device which I don't have to . . ."

Calandra held it, quickly manipulating the metal latch with her mind, and the bracelet clicked open. She handed it to him, and he took it, open-mouthed. She turned and dashed down the final, gloomy flight of stairs.

"Hey, I know where we are," Osaze said. "What are we doing here?"

When they reached the dark hallway at the bottom, she took Osaze's hand, then glanced at Zale.

"I assume you can see all right?"

He nodded.

She looked up at the man she loved and tugged his hand to get him moving. "Getting you to safety."

Osaze's eyebrows bunched and he pulled back on her arm.

"What do you mean? I'm not going anywhere without you, and you have a Heartstone to heal. We should be going there."

Zale peered down the hallway. "Hey, there are people down there."

"I know. I told them to meet us here."

The door at the far end of the hallway swung open, and gentle white light from the cavern beyond flooded the faces of Tanni, Thea, Gerrick, Urbi, and Zoe.

Thea still had her hand on the handle. She urged the others through, then peered down the hall.

"Hurry, you three," she stage-whispered.

Osaze pulled Calandra to a stop a few strides before they reached the door. "Calandra, wait."

Zale stopped, noticing they were no longer beside him. "All right?"

Calandra waved him ahead. "Go on. We'll be right there."

Zale nodded hesitantly, then went through the door. Thea followed, introducing herself and exclaiming her delight in meeting him.

Calandra faced Osaze, craning her neck to look up at him.

"What is it?"

"I need to know. Are you planning on abandoning your duty?"

She frowned. "Of course not. I couldn't do that. I *wouldn't* do that, especially not now. Osaze, there is so much I must tell you, but there isn't time."

"Then why are we not at the base of the Mother's Heart chamber as we speak?"

"I will be going there right after this. It's not far."

"Right after what?"

Calandra's heard sped up. She knew he wasn't going to like this, which was why she hadn't told him sooner.

Instead of answering, she tugged him into the amethyst-encrusted chamber. Inside, Zale was alternately answering the questions that Gerrick and Thea were peppering him with and gawking at the jewels lining the chamber. Tanni stood on the edge of the pool tying off the bow line of the *Luz da Paz*. Nick, the crusty tour guide from Haven, tied the stern line to a boulder on the shore of the pool, and Zoe greeted her with a polite salute. The other two submersibles still sat on their racks in the water a short distance beyond. Urbi stood at the edge of the pool gaping in awe at the surroundings, holding a satchel. She noticed them enter and started toward them.

Osaze took all this in and looked down at Calandra. "I don't understand. What are we all here for?"

Calandra took both his hands in her own.

"I had Nick come in this way to help us escape. As soon as Zale and I have finished healing the Stone, we'll come here and all go to a safe place together to plan our next steps. But for now, I want you and the others to go with Zoe in one of those submersibles so I know you are safe." She pointed at the racks.

Osaze shook his head, frowning. "No, Calandra. You need me to protect you. And you need the power of the consort bond to heal the Stone. I'm not going anywhere."

"I agree with Osaze," came Thea's throaty voice from behind Calandra.

She turned to see the others ringed around them, listening. Tanni's arms were crossed in disapproval, Urbi's in an I-told-you-so gesture, and Calandra's foster parents regarded her with both affection and consternation.

Thea folded her hands in front of her, as calm and assertive as ever, despite her tangled hair and soiled tunic.

"I have no intention of cowering in a grotto while you and your brother go risk your freedom. What do you take me for, child?"

"Don't you see, Thea? This is the only way I will know that you are safe. I'd send Zale, too, if I could, but unfortunately, he and I have a task to do."

Thea arched a brow. "You don't think I can handle myself?"

Calandra tilted her head. "Of course you can. But Gerrick needs you more than I do."

Gerrick's eyes were bright with life and restrained tears. "I have negotiated the dangers of this palace for forty-five years. I am certain I can do so a little longer. Especially for the sake of the two women I love most in the world."

He smiled at her, just as she imagined a father would smile at his daughter. A daughter he was very proud of.

Tears pricked at Calandra's sinuses. "I still haven't gotten used to seeing you like this. But I want the chance to do that. You, Osaze, Zale—you are all vulnerable in a way we women are not, even with the songstoppers. Please, Gerrick. Stay here and wait for us." She turned back to Osaze, whose hands she still held. "Please."

"And what of the consort bond?" Osaze said quietly. "Don't you need the power I could give you?"

Calandra held his hands to her face and kissed them. "You have already given me more than you could ever know. I wouldn't be who I am without you. But with Zale here, I don't need the power of the bond to heal the Stone. All I need to know is that you're safe and away from here."

"I'm not leaving until you do."

She'd been afraid it might come to this. She nodded reluctantly. "Will you at least wait here?"

He tilted his head, studying her. "Fine. I will wait here for fifteen minutes. If you haven't come back by then, I'm coming to find you."

She smiled. "Thank you. Now kiss me for luck."

Osaze bent his head to oblige. As his lips touched hers, she untangled the entwined spirit between them, severing the *pisti* bond. His head snapped up, and he frowned.

"What just happened? Something's wrong. I can't feel you anymore."

She nodded sadly. "I know. I wanted to give you a real chance at a new life without any ties to this one."

"*You* did it? You broke the bond?"

The hurt expression on his face would torment her nightmares. She gritted her teeth. This was the right thing to do—not because of Damon's torments. His words had dug deep because they were true. Real love meant letting go. Like Delphine had done for her.

"Osaze, your whole life has been here, living in fear, never knowing about your own people or getting to make your own choices. I couldn't bear the thought of you being Redeemed again, and the only way to make sure that doesn't happen is to redeem you for real. I am sending you and Urbi back to Africa, back to your home."

His face contorted with restrained emotion.

"*This* is my home. Calandra, I love you and I want to spend my life with you! Don't do this."

Tears flowing freely now, she reached up and cupped his cheek.

"I love you, too. That's why I have to do this."

She moved her palm to his forehead and sang the notes that would put him to sleep, and Zoe and Nick helped her catch the big man.

Urbi frowned, shaking her head emphatically. "This is not what he wants, your highness."

Calandra turned to face her. "Only because he doesn't know anything else. We talked about this. Don't you want to go home to see your family?"

Urbi hesitated. "Most of them are probably not even alive anymore." She stood erect. "But yes. Yes, I do."

Calandra moved to take off the coral necklace, and Urbi put her hands on Calandra's to stop her.

"Keep it. And thank you, your highness." She flung her arms around Calandra, who returned the hug.

Tanni stepped forward. "Calandra, we must go. We're out of time."

"We'll get the big guy into the sub," said Nick, indicating Osaze. She and Zoe were already moving into position to move him. "You go."

Calandra nodded and dashed over to a clump of deep purple crystals growing from the wall. She took hold of them, broke the bonds that held half a dozen or so to their roots, and ran back to Urbi, handing them to her. "Here, these should help you get started in your new life."

Urbi took them, murmuring thanks, and secured them in her pockets.

Calandra glanced down at the man on the floor.

"Take care of him for me," she said. "Help him find a good wife."

Urbi smiled. "I'm his mother. Of course I will."

Choking back tears, Calandra turned to Zale. "You have a choice, too. I will not make you do this if you don't want to. Would you like to go with Zoe, back to the human lands? Or do you want to stay here and help me?"

Zale gazed at her steadily, the emotions warring over his face a mere echo of the turmoil inside him. "If I stay, will you help me find Mother?"

"Of course."

"Then I say, let's do this. I will not run anymore."

Calandra gave her brother a nod of recognition, then beckoned for him to follow her and Tanni out into the hallway, Thea and Gerrick at her heels.

She jogged as fast as she could in her wedding clothes up the flight of stairs to the next landing, but then turned down a short hallway. The far end was flooded with luminous light bleeding from the Mother's Heart chamber beyond.

When they emerged into the access chamber, Thea turned to face them.

"Strip, now. The sun is already reaching the chamber."

Calandra glanced out the archway into the dazzling light beyond. It was time—the moment she'd been groomed for all her life. If she were to heal the Heartstone, it would be right now, today. She pushed aside the aching emptiness where her connection to Osaze used to be and began stripping off her clothes. Thea and Tanni helped her where they could.

"Are you going to get ready?" she asked Zale.

His eyes popped, then he nodded.

"Uh, yeah." He began stripping off his clothes. "I can't believe you did that back there," he said as he pulled his tunic off. "I don't think I could have done something like that."

She swallowed, her throat thick. "You'd be surprised what you can do for someone you love more than your own life. Zale, I must speak plainly with you. After we do this, I'm not sure what's going to happen to us. You'll probably be enslaved again. And I'll probably be killed. Aunt Adonia would never allow someone who flaunted the law as flagrantly as I have to live."

"Not if I have anything to say about it," said Tanni, deftly pulling pins and combs out of Calandra's hair. Flowers fell to the ground at her feet.

"I concur," said Thea, unbuckling Calandra's girdle.

Zale gawked. "Then why the blazes are we doing it?"

Gerrick took Zale's clothes as the boy tossed them aside and folded them into a neat pile as he listened.

"Because," Calandra said, letting her tunic fall to the floor. "If we don't—"

"All hell will be unleashed. Yeah, I actually knew that."

Calandra nodded. "Then you must also know that no matter what Adonia may or may not do, we're the only ones who can stop it."

"Yeah. I knew that, too." Zale sighed in resignation. "Do you ever wish you weren't so ever-loving special?"

Calandra smirked, sharing a glance of understanding with her brother. She dearly hoped she would get to hear his story someday.

"You have no idea."

At last, they both stood naked on the black triquetra in the centre of the stone floor. The sounds of shouting echoed down the stairwell behind them.

"Time to go," said Thea. "We'll hold them off."

Tanni was already moving into a defensive position near the entrance, brandishing the *deiktis* Zoe had given her.

"Calandra, I don't know what to do," Zale said, fear creeping back into his voice.

She took his hand and soothed his nerves.

"It's like healing people. You look for what is broken or out of place, and you repair it. Does that make sense?"

He looked anything but certain, but nodded. "Okay."

They turned to face the archway.

"Go with the Mother's blessing," said Thea.

"God be with us," Zale muttered.

Calandra drew in a deep breath, steadying her nerves. They had to succeed. After all that had happened, she could allow no other outcome.

"Now!"

With hands still clasped, they ran and dove off the ledge, transforming before they even hit the water.

53

THE DUEL

Narcissa arrived in the Observation Chamber at her mother's heels, bloody dagger in hand, and pressed her face up to the curved glass wall in time to see Calandra and Zale rise on a column of water to meet the blackened Heartstone. Her shoulder stung where a rogue *doulos* had struck her before she'd subdued and Redeemed him. Zale no longer wore his cuff.

"She's Mad," Narcissa whispered, fogging the glass. "They'll never do it, just the two of them."

Adonia slammed her fist on the glass, then dropped it, watching.

"She always had more determination than wisdom. Just like her mother." She paused. "*Their* mother."

The queen went to a small soundstone on the wall and placed her finger on it, opening a channel of communication into the tower beyond.

"Calandra. Zale."

Both of them spared a glance for the window, and the trepidation on Zale's face confirmed his Unredeemed state. *How does she keep doing that?*

Adonia touched the stone again.

"Don't do this, Calandra. Don't desecrate the Heartstone with the touch of a man, especially one Unredeemed to the Mother. You don't know what you're doing, what the consequences might be."

"Neither do you," Calandra shouted back, her voice carried into the Observation Chamber on the communication stone. "How can we expect our problem to be solved by applying the same solution that hasn't worked for thousands of years already?"

Adonia leaned toward the stone, her voice strained. "You think I haven't thought of this? When Delphine first came to me, you think I didn't want her ideas to be right? I *loved*—"

She cut off with a choking sob, putting her hand to her mouth as she struggled for control.

Narcissa tensed, watching her mother now, not the spectacle in the chamber beyond. Hebe slipped in through the door and came over to Narcissa. They stood in silent solidarity as their mother's steely exterior crumbled.

Calmer, Adonia continued.

"I loved Frederik. Thinking he would return my affection as Kenver did Delphine's, I Released him. But I was wrong."

Adonia's shoulders hunched in pain, the silk of her gown rustling with restrained sobs.

Narcissa wrapped her arms around herself. Should she go to her?

In the chamber, Zale and Calandra hovered on a column of water, watching through the glass.

Adonia put an arm on the glass to steady herself, head hanging as she took deep, rasping breaths.

"He hated me. He had a family already, somewhere else, and demanded that I return him to them. When I refused, he tried to escape. I was already pregnant by then, and my mother had recently been killed by an accident at sea. I would soon be queen, and I would *not* be the Queen Who Lost Her Consort. So I Redeemed him again."

Hebe went over and laid a hand on her mother's shoulder. Adonia stiffened, then turned to her younger daughter and wrapped an arm around her. Narcissa frowned. Her mother had always given Hebe, the red-headed girl who looked like a little mirror image of Adonia, more affection than herself, to whom she gave none at all. With a jolt, Narcissa realized why—she herself looked like her fair-haired father. The father who had rejected Adonia's affections and tried to leave her while Narcissa was still in the womb.

She clenched her fingers so hard that her nails bit into her upper arms as she scowled through the glass at her cousin.

"This is what you would bring upon us, Calandra," Adonia continued. "If you and this boy successfully heal the Heartstone, him of his own free will, then you will prove your point—and leave thousands of women who follow in your footsteps without consorts, servants, and workers. You will plunge this nation into chaos. Is that what you want?"

Calandra looked back sadly. "No, that is not what I want. But it is the price we may have to pay for our millennia of abuses. May the Mother forgive us."

With that, she and Zale turned away from the glass and looked at the sphere above them.

"No!" Adonia yelled, slamming her palm on the glass.

Her face contorted in rage as she focused on the two undines in the chamber beyond, her hand extended as though to grab them. Zale and Calandra started choking, clawing at their necks.

"Mother, no!" Hebe yelled, rushing over and pulling at Adonia's arm, but the queen thrust the girl away. Hebe crashed into a chair and landed on the floor, sobbing.

Narcissa rushed to her sister to comfort her. She looked up at her mother's face, not recognizing the woman who raised her behind the Madness in her eyes.

Calandra slowly turned, fighting against Adonia's power in order to face her aunt, extending her hand as though pushing through mud.

Calandra's friend Tanni ran through the door of the Observation Chamber and crashed into Adonia, bowling her to the ground. Tanni rolled away, then sprang to her feet to face the queen.

Adonia had barely landed when she writhed and turned, her face contorted in a grimace of rage. She jumped to her feet and lunged at Tanni with her bare hands. Tanni dodged. After several more dancing feints between the two of them, Adonia managed to grab the siren's arm.

Tanni's eyes rolled back in her head and she slumped to the ground, dead.

"No!" screamed Calandra over the soundstone. She stared at the scene through the glass as though her soul had been ripped from her chest.

"Mother, what are you doing?" Hebe screamed, staring at Tanni's lifeless form.

Adonia ignored her and turned back to the figures beyond the glass.

Calandra wailed again. Narcissa had never seen so much sorrow on a face before. The column of water faltered and the two undines in the chamber dropped below Narcissa's field of view. Adonia rushed toward the glass, her clawed hands outstretched to reach Calandra and Zale with her power even as they fell.

"Mother!" Narcissa yelled, afraid of the woman her mother had become. She'd never seen her so out of control. "Mother, please. Adonia!"

Adonia's gaze snapped toward her daughters, and she looked at them wildly, with no hint of recognition. She held out her hand toward them, and suddenly Narcissa was struggling for air. She gasped, trying to choke out a cry for help, but no sound escaped. Darkness intruded on her vision, and spots danced before her eyes.

"Adonia! Stop!"

Adonia's head jerked around to see who had called her. In the doorway, Thea stood like an avenging fury, her silver hair tangled and unrestrained, her tunic, though soiled from a month in the dungeon, seeming to shine and billow around her in a non-existent breeze.

Adonia dropped her arm and the pressure in Narcissa's throat stopped. She gratefully dragged in a rasping breath of air. Beside her, Hebe lay coughing on the ground.

Adonia turned to face the newcomer.

"Thea kor'Aglaia. I should have known that Calandra would free you. She did not come up with these seditious ideas on her own, after all."

"You know full well that her ideas and mine align because we saw them as truth, just as Delphine did. Why can you not admit the truth, also?"

"And why can you not simply die and leave me alone, old woman?"

Adonia swung her fist toward Thea from halfway across the room, and the panacea was flung backward into the wall on the far side of the hall as though she had been punched in the gut with a battering ram.

Adonia chased after her, screaming profanities Narcissa had never heard her use.

"What's going on, Narcissa?" Hebe said, sobbing. "Has Mother gone Mad?"

Narcissa looked at her younger sister in contempt for her tears. But in the face of Hebe's anguish, she realized this wasn't her sister's fault. She drew in a breath, giving her sister a look meant to comfort.

"I think she may have. Stay here. I'll see what I can do to help."

She checked her ceremonial diving knife, loosening the buckle on its jewelled sheath, then crept after the two duelling women.

She found them in the Grotto. Adonia kept flinging attacks at Thea, throwing weapons made of solid air, an element which Narcissa had only seen her mother use once before, at Fire Lake. Adonia's strongest element had always been spirit, and other than at Fire Lake and last night with the wine, Narcissa had never seen her use another. At one point, Adonia tried what she'd done on Calandra and Zale, but Thea put up her forearm and deflected the attack with ease.

Thea made no attacks, only defended herself with walls of water she pulled from the fountain. She stood in the water next to the statue of Atargatis, and every time Adonia flung her arm at her, Thea pulled up a sheet of water, solidifying it and blocking whatever had been hurled.

With every attack, Adonia advanced. Thea retreated until she reached the lip on the far edge of the basin, then stopped. Crouching down, she laid a hand on the marble edge and concentrated. The stone began to vibrate, and the vibrations spread, causing the floor to heave. Adonia stumbled and fell. With a resounding *crack*, the fountain basin split, and water poured from the seams onto the flagstones, trickling in crooked lines into the plant beds. Thea jumped out of the basin and ran into the trees beside one of the rivulets.

Adonia stood. "You think a few spindly lemon trees can hide you from me, hag?"

She carefully picked her way around the ferns and vines until she disappeared into the greenery.

Narcissa crept along the wall of the atrium on one of the stone paths, laying every step carefully with her bare feet so as to make no sound, crouching below the level of the thickest growth. Holding her heavily ornamented diving dagger at the ready, she stopped, listening.

Strange rustling sounds filled the air. She glanced around to discover the source, and noticed that the vines on the far side of the garden nearest the windows were moving, growing and thickening at an alarming rate. Her mother stood and regarded the wall of vines before her in consternation.

"Your majesty?" A siren singer came up the path behind the queen, holding her staff topped with a ceremonial brass trident at the ready. "Are you in danger?"

Adonia spun, her face contorted in rage. "No, you are."

With a quick lunge, she dove for the singer's sword, pulled it from its sheath, and cut off the singer's head before she could even react.

Narcissa gaped, frozen, as she watched her mother turn away without a second thought. Adonia started hacking at the vines with the long blade.

"You can't hide from me forever, witch," Adonia screamed.

The vines grew up again and began twining around Adonia's arms and legs. Shrieking, she hacked harder, sounding like a wild animal. Narcissa crept closer, unnoticed by both her mother and the healer.

Thea appeared in the gap left by the cut vines, a sad expression on her face.

"You had so much potential to be a good leader, Adonia. You really cared for your people and your duty. If only you hadn't let your hurt cloud your judgement and used it to justify hurting all those like the man who injured you—you took too many of the bonds, enough for even a mediocre siren like you to go Mad."

Narcissa blinked. How many bonds did her mother hold?

Adonia was completely incapacitated by the vines now. They wrapped around her arms and legs and body, holding her upright despite her struggle.

"Let me go, old woman! It wasn't fair. I'm the queen! I should have been the one to spend my life with someone who loved me, instead of only those who feared and served me. Why did you get to do it? Why? Why not me?"

Thea stepped closer and looked down into Adonia's eyes.

"You could have had that, too, if only you had recognized the gifts you already had. Unfortunately, the ties with which we seek to bind others often become our own undoing. Love is surrender, not control."

She reached toward Adonia's forehead with an open palm.

Just a little further. Narcissa tested the heft of her blade. If Thea would only step a little closer to her mother, and a bit to the side, she would have a clear shot at the woman.

Without warning, the siren's sword flew through the air and into Thea's gut. She cried out, hunched over the hilt. Adonia's hand, cut free of vines, still curled toward the weapon she had catapulted toward her opponent. The vines around the queen loosened, and she squirmed, working her way out of the green bindings.

"I did recognize what I had, you nasty old eel. I had a child who was next to the goddess in beauty"—Narcissa's heart leapt—"and power. And you and Delphine robbed me of her, too, polluting her mind with your blasphemous ideas of freemen and equality."

Narcissa's throat closed up.

Calandra. Her mother was talking about Calandra, not her.

Then it hit her. She would never be good enough—never smart enough or pretty enough or *powerful* enough to please her mother. No matter how many hours she spent sparring or studying or cleaning heat-blasted latrines, no matter how many *sklavia* bonds she held, her mother would only ever see her as the least desirable option.

Her blood rushed through her ears, and she tensed. She was very close now—the body of the siren lay on the path a pace away, the woman's ceremonial trident laying on the flagstones beside her.

Adonia stepped free of the vines and stalked over to stand above her fallen foe. Thea lay on the ground with her hands around the sword hilt, staring up at Adonia with a strangely calm expression. Adonia extended her hand as though she were clutching something, and Thea began to choke.

With one smooth movement, Narcissa leapt from the brush, scooped up the trident, and threw it with the accuracy she was known for. Adonia whirled at the sound, but the weapon hit its mark, tearing through the side of her mother's neck and through her jugular, becoming lodged with the tips protruding from the other side. The queen's mouth opened in wordless surprise, and she fell to the ground.

Narcissa sheathed her knife and stood over her mother, who gaped up at her daughter in gurgling shock.

"Yooou . . ." Blood foamed out of Adonia's mouth and pooled beneath her neck as she struggled to form words.

"I'm sorry, Mother. But you had to be stopped."

Adonia reached up and tried to pull the trident away, but her arm fell without even gripping it. Her eyes stared, unblinking, at nothing on the ground.

Thea, laying in a lake of her own blood, surveyed Narcissa with a pitying expression. "Be careful you do not become her, Narcissa."

Narcissa's retort died on her tongue as she looked back and forth between the two fallen women. Thea wheezed, staring up at the lemons hanging full on the branches above her. Narcissa felt a small twinge of compassion for the dying woman. Thea might have been insufferable, but she'd been one of the few to stand up to Adonia. She thought about going to find a healer to tend to her. But Thea had seen what Narcissa had done. Narcissa couldn't risk Thea telling someone else what had happened, and gut wounds were a long, slow way to die.

"Save your breath, healer. I'll be creating my own destiny from now on."

Narcissa pulled Adonia's dagger from its sheath and drove it up into the panacea's heart.

Thea gasped, her body going taut. "Gerrick," she sighed, then went flaccid with the release of death.

Narcissa turned and fled out the archway to the courtyard, where the fighting was dying down. About a dozen rebel women, including Meg and that maid of Calandra's, sat in a closely guarded group. Most of the men who had been in the courtyard were missing, and those who remained had been returned to their Redeemed state.

"The queen is dead! Thea has killed her!" Narcissa shouted, and Despoina Cleo, who had been scanning the area for any unmet dangers, dashed past her into the Grotto.

"Narcissa!" Mari called from the white pavilion in the centre of the courtyard. She and Cain were being protected by several sirens who still looked alert to potential attackers. Matthew was nowhere to be seen. Narcissa started toward her and Mari pushed past the guards to meet her halfway.

Just then, Cain drew his sword and simultaneously pulled another from the sheath of the nearest siren. Narcissa broke into a run. In a dance of death that lasted less than three seconds, he ran every guard on the platform through, then spun around, searching for an exit, blood dripping over his hands.

Mari opened her mouth to sing, but he stabbed her in the chest and pulled out the blade, then jumped down and bolted around the pavilion toward the gates of the courtyard.

The world slowed down as Narcissa watched Mari sink to her knees, her mouth agape and her hand outstretched. As Narcissa jumped onto the low platform, Mari collapsed onto the wood, blood blooming on her purple tunic and pooling beneath her.

"No!" Narcissa wailed. She fell to her knees at her love's side, shaking Mari and calling her name. "Don't die! We can have you healed if you don't die!"

But Mari's eyes were wide and unblinking, staring lifelessly at the canopy above them.

Narcissa collapsed on top of her lover's body, her entire world collapsing with her.

Then she raised her head, resolve flowing through her.

"Calandra did this," she said through gritted teeth.

She stood and, calling on several nearby sirens to join her, charged into the palace to find the girl who had ruined her life.

54

THE DRAGON

CALANDRA WAILED IN HORROR AS Tanni's body slumped to the ground inside the Observation Chamber, the void in her spirit confirming that Adonia had killed her. The water that held them lost its structure, and they plummeted into the pool below with a splash.

When they emerged, Thea called, "What happened?"

"Adonia killed Tanni," Zale called back.

All Calandra could manage were gasping sobs.

Thea's eyes widened. "She's gone Mad." She disappeared from the ledge above them.

"Calandra," Zale said, swimming over to her. "Calandra, I know Tanni was important to you, and I'm sorry. But look at the sun." He pointed above them, where the sun was already well past the halfway point. "We don't have time."

Swallowing tears, Calandra turned to her brother. She would grieve later. "Let us finish this. For Tanni. For Osaze."

"For Father and Mother," he added.

Taking a deep breath, she once again called the water from the deeps below and propelled them upward to within an arm's reach of the cracked surface of the Heartstone.

Far above them, the sun poured into the Chamber of the Mother's Heart, setting every refracting crystal on the wall alight. Unlike the last time Calandra had approached the Heartstone, this time, there was so little light in its heart that, against the dazzling fire around them, it appeared nearly as black as the Voidstone had been at the bottom of the ocean.

"I can feel the fire in it," Zale said. "But it's weak."

Calandra looked at him and nodded. It surprised her that there was fire in the stone, but it made sense. As far as she knew, no undine had been able to manipulate fire in any of the records she had seen. Perhaps the reason the stone required both male and female energies was that the elements favoured each gender differently. And the Heartstone needed all five elements to be made whole.

Calandra reached her free hand toward the stone, not touching it yet, though it called to her. Even from here, she could sense the same spark of life she had felt in it all those years ago, but it was dim.

"Reach toward it, like this," she told Zale.

He complied, reaching up with his free hand until he almost touched the Stone. He gaped at it in wonder.

"What can you feel?" she asked.

He closed his eyes, concentrating.

"It's big, much bigger than it looks. The storm at its heart is nearly quenched. It wants to be resparked."

Calandra smiled. "To me, it feels like a stagnant stream, wanting to be unblocked. All the elements inside are in the wrong order."

Zale frowned. "It's . . . sad."

Tears pricked at Calandra's eyes at the reminder of her own sorrow, and she blinked them away. "You can feel its sadness?"

He nodded. She gathered her thoughts, gazing into the dimly pulsing depths. She could feel the emotions the Stone contained, too—sadness, and so much more. Could this stone truly have a spirit of its own, as she had wondered all those years ago?

"Okay, Zale, before we touch the Heartstone, we need to share our spirit. It will be a temporary bond, but we need it so I can guide the healing. Close your eyes and picture the part of you that can heal others. This is different for everyone, usually something like a flower, a stone, or a bowl of water. Mine looks like a water lily." She paused as he closed his eyes. "Do you see it?"

"Yes." He opened his eyes in alarm. "It looks like a quiver of lightning, but that can't be right."

"Why not?" she said softly, hiding her own alarm that his healing power should take a symbol of such violence.

He dropped his gaze. "Because that's how I hurt people. The lightning is what blinded my friend, and—and killed . . . Mr. Crow, the first officer on the ship."

She thought he'd been about to say something else, but didn't press him.

"I suppose it makes sense. For every good our powers can do, there is an equal evil that could be accomplished. That is the balance of the universe. The object itself is not violent. It is only what we do with it."

She wondered if she were trying to convince him, or herself.

He bit his lip and looked like he was holding back tears, but nodded.

"When I begin singing, I want you to picture yourself holding out the quiver toward me. You will be extending a line of spirit, which I will be able to grasp and hold until we are finished. After the connection is established, I can guide what we do next. Do you understand?"

He looked at her dubiously. "That sounds like balderdash," he said in English.

She frowned and glanced up at the sun, which was growing ever closer to the far edge of the column.

"Just try, all right?"

He nodded, switching back to Greek. "Okay. I'll do my best."

She stared at him. He was still terrified, but she sensed his resolve.

"Now."

She began to sing the song of establishment. It took a second, but when she sensed his proffered line of spirit, it was thick and stable. She smiled, linking his spirit with her own.

She had guided a linked circle many times, but this was completely different. As soon as they linked, she could sense the elements that filled him—fire was the strongest, then air, with a little bit of earth and water. The power that surged through him was in almost complete chaos, barely held in check. No wonder this boy was so terrified of what he could do. It was a marvel he hadn't destroyed himself with it.

She stopped singing and took a moment to breathe, projecting calm into Zale and probing the shape of his spirit until she felt she understood it and could guide it. At last, she opened her eyes.

"Can you sense this?"

She pulled his power into her, tingling as it surged through her, at the same time as she shared her ability to shape earth and water. His eyes widened, and he nodded.

"At my signal, lay your hands on the Heartstone. I will guide the work. I want you to relax and watch what I am doing with your inner and outer eyes. Do you think you can do that?"

"Okay."

"Ready?"

He clenched his teeth and nodded, his hand above his head in readiness.

"Now."

As one, they laid their hands on the Heartstone.

*

THE moment Zale touched the Heartstone, he was flooded with a surge of images, like a river of memories roaring by so fast that he caught bare glimpses of them. There were undines and humans, cherubim and several other beings he didn't recognize. There was also something soothing, a welcoming presence he almost recognized.

Then he saw a man and a woman in a beautiful garden. In a tree, a red-gold serpent was wrapped around a branch, speaking words like honey to the woman. No, not a serpent—it had wings and claws, like a dragon. The woman, who looked like his sister, took a rosy red fruit from the dragon. Zale called to her, but she didn't hear him. She seemed entranced by the dragon. She took a bite of the fruit it had offered, then something shifted. She threw the fruit away. The dragon became angry, but she wouldn't listen. Then she turned and looked at Zale.

So did the dragon. It had golden eyes.

"Zale," it said in a hissing echo, and rushed at him with a billow of fire.

Zale screamed, but no sound escaped his lips. The dragon's mouth opened wide to swallow him and a red glow flared around him. He held up his hands in front of his face and recoiled, lightning blasting out from him in all directions.

When he opened his eyes, the dragon, and the Heartstone's warm red heart, were gone. He was staring once again at the surface of the charred Stone before him, surrounded by an electrical storm that filled the tower. The heart of the Stone beat weakly, and a deep fissure marred the surface. The sun had disappeared from above them. Lightning cracked and flashed around the chamber, water swirled around them in a torrent like they were at the point of an inverse whirlpool, wind blew his and Calandra's hair around . . .

Calandra drooped beside him, her eyes closed. The connection she'd established between them was gone.

The spire of water that held them aloft collapsed, and they fell to the depths once more. As they plunged into the salty water, he tried to sense her beautiful spirit, the one he'd loved from the start, through their clasped hands, but all he could feel was a vacuous emptiness.

His heart froze within him.

He'd killed his sister.

*

Calandra laid her hand on the Heartstone, and the Mother's Heart chamber disappeared.

She swam suspended in the too-familiar cold void, straining to see or feel anything. She had been doing something, but what? Whatever it was, she had failed, she was certain of it. All there was now was the abyss, stretching in every direction as far as she could see, for eternity. She was a consciousness without a body, trapped.

Fight.

The thought came at her instead of from her. Fight. But fight what? There was nothing to fight, not in this place. The fight had already been lost, and all she could do was give in and accept it. She would be here, alone, forever.

You must fight. You must heal the Heartstone.

She took a breath, water rushing through her gills—and with the sensation came the awareness that she had a form. She concentrated on her blood rushing through her ears, the press of water around her, her hand on something warm and smooth and sad . . .

She was not alone here. The warmth called to her, inviting her in, pulsing red like a slow heartbeat. She swam toward the feeling, and then stopped, shivering.

There was someone else here, too. She couldn't see him, but she could sense him.

Damon.

"I know what you are!"

He appeared before her, his powerful tail barely flicking to keep him upright, his dark hair floating in the dimly pulsing void. The space around her grew warmer.

"Hello, Calandra. I knew you'd come for me."

"I haven't come for you. I've come to ensure you can never bother me again."

He arched a black eyebrow. "Oh? I think not." He smiled, and it was predatory.

I'm not really here.

She focused on her body, feeling the touch of a warm palm against hers. *Zale.*

She glanced toward the source of the red fire, and emotion like a gentle whisper tugged at her, drawing her in. She glided closer to the spirit that called her, past Damon.

Suddenly, he was in front of her again, blocking her path.

"You won't succeed," he said.

She tried to push him aside, but he didn't budge.

He smiled.

"Such spirit, my lark." His golden eyes pierced hers, and her heart caught in her throat. "Have you forgotten me so soon? The one who has filled your emptiness, who has held your hand every step of the way?"

He cupped her chin in his warm hand, and she leaned into his touch. How had she ever feared him? Why had she pushed him away?

"You must accept me, Calandra. Then we can be together forever. Kiss me now, and we will be joined in spirit. I can finish what I began in Atlantis."

He bent toward her to kiss her, and she recoiled.

"Move aside, dragon," she growled, fighting to keep her wits sharp. Beyond him, the heart of the Stone throbbed, calling to her, beckoning her to surrender with that familiar tug . . .

He smiled in delight. "You *do* know who I am."

Before her eyes, his undine form shifted and melted and reformed until he appeared as a red-gold winged serpentine dragon, with four legs ending in sharply clawed feet, a horned head, and a barbed tail limned in the throbbing red light.

"Now you see me in my true, glorious form. Now you see who it is that calls you to rule the world together."

Calandra stared. Her mother's message had mentioned the dragons who had been imprisoned in Tartarus, but it was quite another thing to see one with her own eyes. He was magnificent, far more beautiful than any tale of old she'd ever heard, or any dim memory of dragons the humans had retained. He stared at her and his will pulled her away from the whispering warmth beyond . . . and she welcomed him.

"What do you want me to do?" she asked, ready to obey.

55

SURRENDER

"You must free me," the dragon hissed.

A manacle of fire appeared around his leg.

"Yes, *kyrios*," she said.

She laid her hand on the manacle. It didn't burn, as she thought it might. Not that it would have mattered. She would have set herself on fire for the dragon, whose will was the only thing that mattered. However, the manacle was weak, and only a small burst of power using all five elements would shatter it, releasing him to be with her forever.

She blinked. Why did she think she could use all five elements?

She had been doing something. Something important. Something to save the people she loved. Osaze. Tanni. Thea. Gerrick.

Her brother.

The red dark pulsed. Memory rushed in at her. She thought her heart would be crushed inside her chest. She pulled back, the trance broken. As though the light had shifted, thousands of fine golden threads appeared, wrapped around her, each of them beginning and ending in Damon's eyes. She thrashed and struggled, trying to break free of them, but no matter how she moved, they remained fast.

The dragon drew back in surprise.

"You can see your bonds, can't you? How is that possible?" He shook his head and frowned. "It doesn't matter. Come here. Free me now."

Calandra gritted her teeth, fighting the compulsion to obey his words even as she swam closer. "You never intended to help me, did you?"

The dragon laughed and her skin crawled.

"Of course I didn't, foolish girl. Why would I want to repair the lock on my own prison?"

"Why did you train me, then?"

She squirmed, but his hold on her was stronger than her will. She inched closer toward him, fighting her own hand as it extended toward his fiery manacle.

"You were my best chance at freedom. Despite the Heartstone's weakness, it is not quite so near to failure as you presumed. I knew that if I could gain your trust, I could use you to shatter my chains and set me free."

The truth of his words crashed in on her. How had she not seen it before? All this time, he had been grooming her to enhance her powers, to maximize her potential—but only so she would be strong enough to break the Heartstone, not heal it.

"So you only helped me so I could set you free?"

"Oh, I don't know about that. It was also pretty fun watching you use your powers to kill innocent animals, and then watch you torture yourself about it afterwards."

"You . . . you had me do that on *purpose*?"

"I thought it would grow on you. I didn't count on your blasted empathy and how it would keep pulling you back from my methods. It was so refreshing when your aunt finally had you start enslaving them."

"Why?" Calandra knew who he meant, but not how that had served his purpose.

"Because, my little lark, taking someone's will from them realigns you to the Spirit. Finally, you were able to *be water* and crush the elements, not coddle them."

Calandra stared at him in horror and disgust. He was right. When she was younger, she had never struggled with healing. It was only after she'd believed Damon's lies about the power she could have that she had begun flailing, insisting on learning his strong-arm methods. Instead, she'd killed the rabbit and further damaged the dolphin calf. It was only after Redeeming Osaze that she could control the elements as Damon wished—but instead of feeling rejuvenated afterward, as healers were supposed to feel, she'd been completely drained.

That's not how it had been when she'd healed Matthew. What had changed?

Her hand was nearly touching him now, the golden threads wrapping around her so tightly they cut into her flesh, manipulating her hand toward the manacle like a puppet on strings. But she would *not* let this monster use her to destroy everything.

She growled at him and pulled power into herself, preparing to blast him.

The dragon's smile widened and its laugh reverberated through the void like thunder.

"And what can you do against me, little one? By your own choice, you are mine. You carried me here from Atlantis, and you *will* break the Heartstone in pieces at last, releasing me and my kin from the prison that holds us."

"We shall see about that."

She tried to throw power at him, but nothing happened. She could feel the power, but she had no ability to damage her opponent with it. The threads around her burned, pulling her closer to the dragon. She could see their tiny chain links—they weren't threads at all, but very fine fetters. Her struggles only tightened the chains.

The dragon laughed.

"Still you fight, even now. But it is too late. The bonds you have given me to hold are too strong. You were so desperate for love and security, you gave me your will and soul. You are mine, Calandra, now and forevermore."

She stared at him, dumbfounded. *She* had permitted these bonds?

Her mind raced, and she remembered every choice she had made, every time she had agreed to do what Damon suggested instead of what her heart told her was right, every time she had accepted him a little more into her heart. He was telling the truth this time, and the cruel honesty of it galled her. She had allowed herself to be entangled in his lies. And now, no matter how she struggled, the threads only tightened around her. She fought and thrashed until she had no strength remaining, the chains choking her.

"That's better, my lark. Stop fighting. It is easier if you just accept this."

Yes, accept it. That's what she would do. She didn't have the strength to fight him, and accepting would be so much easier.

The red light around them pulsed, surrounding her with its familiar warmth, calling her to surrender to its guidance. It was familiar, the same call she'd heard every time she'd used her powers for years. She'd always resisted, thinking it called her toward darkness and weakness, choosing instead to force the elements to her will as Damon had instructed. Now, for the first time, she could see what it was.

All this time, she'd struggled for control in order to overcome this darkness—but the call to surrender hadn't been to the void, nor to Damon. It was the spirit of the Heartstone that had called her, inviting her to let it help her.

She inhaled in wonder and recognition. It had been the Heartstone spirit she had surrendered to in Fire Lake when she'd healed Matthew so effortlessly. And now the spirit of the Heartstone was calling her again. Not to take control, but to release it—to let her power be guided by the spirit that called. But unlike Damon's greedy demand to surrender, the call of the Heartstone was laden with promise, like a child eager to give a gift. There was nothing cloying or demanding, nothing selfish about this call. *Rest*, it said. *Let me strengthen you.*

It was the call of love.

She had never experienced anything so beautiful. It was far beyond what she'd shared with Tanni or Osaze. She wanted to accept, but she had clung to her fear and control for so long, she wasn't sure what to do. *How? Teach me.*

Give me your fear and heartbreak.

She closed her eyes, picturing the void that inhabited her whenever she thought of her mother, the sadness of losing Tanni, the fear of failing at her duty. The aching hollowness of it filled her and she began to weep. It had been her nightmare, but it had always been there. Could she really let it go?

But what did she have to gain by keeping it?

Here, take it. I don't want it anymore.

In moments, the void in her heart began to fill with the same red warmth that surrounded her. She had never felt this way before. Opening up her heart even more, she released the power she held, giving it up to the spirit that called her, releasing it into an ocean of love and acceptance. And from the dark, the reply pressed into her like a stone healer writing the pattern into her soul—*I will never leave you nor forsake you, daughter.*

She'd surrendered at last. With her eyes closed, she sensed every element that made up the Heartstone, and Zale, and the Chamber. She inhabited every interconnecting line of the matrix extending from her heart to the entire island and beyond. She had never felt so alive or at one with Creation. And she knew this was the gift of the Heartstone.

Now you know the truth. It is time to break free, it said.

With her eyes closed, she pulled in as much power as she could hold. Air, water, earth, fire, and spirit flowed into her along every line of the web and combined in a whirlpool of forces, swirling and growing in energy until she *became* the storm. The Heartstone responded, flaring with warm red light she could see even through her eyelids.

She opened her eyes to Damon's frantic expression. He was pulling wildly on the golden threads, but each one he grabbed tore away and faded.

"No!" he yelled, not to her, but to the light around them. "She's mine! You cannot have her!"

With each thread that faded, the light within her grew stronger. She held up her hands toward him, power flowing into them in readiness. "You . . . will not . . . enslave me!"

She released the storm with the fury of a hurricane, striking Damon full in the chest with a bolt of power. Lightning flashed around her.

He cried out and bowed against the onslaught, slashing at her with a clawed hand that fell just short of her flesh.

Power flowed from her extended hands in a stream of white light, and more and more of the golden threads snapped free. As they broke, so did her fear, her uncertainty, her need to control. In the dragon's eyes, she saw the same need to dominate that had bound her for so long. She wanted to blame Damon for her incessant drive for perfection, but she knew that would be avoiding the truth. Damon had only enhanced the fear she already had—fear of failure, fear of abandonment. He had used her own fear to manipulate her and, as a result, she'd nearly made all her worst nightmares come true.

She had sent Osaze away because she had feared losing him, thinking she was setting him free. Now she could see how her choice had only been one more way of controlling him, of treating him like a *doulos*. She still hadn't truly Released him, not even at the end. As a result, she'd lost the one man who had chosen to love her.

The dragon seemed to be weakening. His shape melted into an undine man—except the image kept blurring, as though he could no longer maintain the pretence. Or perhaps now that she knew the truth, she could see through the lie. His face contorted in rage, then, like a mask slipping into place, changed to the familiar seductive smile.

"Wait, my lark. You have no idea what you are giving up—the power, the esteem. With me, you could save not only Sirenia, but the world! You would be loved by everyone. Think of the good you and I could do together. Think of the lives we could save by curbing every violent bent of humanity. Isn't that what you want?"

She growled in rage and gathered her last reserves of energy, concentrating them in her chest, then paused. He had a point. Humanity seemed depraved beyond measure, and not likely to change. How much damage had they already done? How much more would they do if they were not stopped? If Osaze could become a good man while under the influence of the *sklavia* bond, what greater good could the undines do if they were actually trying to shape humanity into something better?

Then she thought of Jacob, and Hammad, and Kenver, and what they had risked for those they loved. She thought of Zale, of his fear of his own power, and how, when she had feared what she could do, she had only brought about destruction. She thought of Adonia, gone Mad with fear and power, and Tanni, who had given herself up to stop her. And she thought of Osaze and how, because she had surrendered to fear of what *could* happen, she had lost the love of her life.

Tanni. Osaze. The cost for her selfishness had already been too high. She had to end this now.

The Heartstone throbbed red with light and power, growing in strength, the warmth filling her until she thought she might explode with it. And suddenly, she knew how to defeat the monster before her.

She stared at Damon, letting her power melt out of her and into the Stone around them.

"Control is not the same as strength, and love has more power than fear."

The last of the golden threads faded away like wisps of smoke. Freedom, sweet as a freshwater spring, washed over her. She smiled.

"I don't want to control anything. I only want to be free of you."

His eyes widened in terror, and his appearance flickered back to being a dragon. Enraged, he growled with a resonance that had once frightened her, but no longer.

"I am Alessandro. I am Hadad. I am Semyaza. You cannot defy me!"

She stared back at him levelly, completely at peace, her heart filled with warmth.

"You're right. On my own, I probably couldn't. But I'm not on my own anymore."

Warm golden light flared, flowing outward from her heart, banishing the darkness. The water around her warmed as though she were suspended in the ocean near the surface on a summer's day with the sun on her fins. She could sense the pieces of the Heartstone bonding together, the opaline matrix renewing itself.

The dragon began to fade, becoming translucent, until she could see the red-gold light through his horned face.

"No!" he screamed.

Solidifying, he plunged his clawed hand into her heart.

Or rather, he tried. Instead, he rebounded from her as though repelled by an invisible force.

Calandra choked, jarred by the impact. The brimstone on his breath tasted bitter on Calandra's tongue.

He attacked again, mouth agape as though he intended to swallow her whole, but bounced off. Her ears rang like they had been boxed.

"No!" he roared again, then bowled into her, pushing her awareness partway out of the Stone.

Calandra gasped, winded and struggling to breathe, her vision fading. Damon retreated, making a sound between a snarl and a whimper. She became aware of Zale beside her inside the Chamber of the Mother's Heart, a strange double vision of both inside and outside the Heartstone. Damon's head snapped around and he stared at her brother.

"Zale," he hissed. Roaring, he beat his powerful wings and darted toward Zale as though he intended to drill right through him. Or into him.

Zale's face went slack in horror. He flung his arms over his head to protect himself.

"No!" She tried to gather the strength to shield her brother, but before she could react, Damon bounced off of Zale, just as he had Calandra.

Zale threw his hands out, and a blinding explosion of lightning filled the air. The sound of cracking stone echoed around her. The wounding of the Heartstone pierced her to her core, and the strength she'd been drawing on disappeared. She felt like the flotsam left behind at low tide.

Damon circled to attack Zale once again, talons extended toward his heart.

A storm raged in the chamber around Calandra, whipping her hair about her face and into her eyes. Every limb was being dragged to the depths with the weight of a sinking ship. Helplessly, unable to even lift her arms, she watched Damon strike at her brother once more.

Inexplicably, he bounced off. Roaring in frustration, Damon hissed at her, then flapped out of her line of sight.

All light snuffed out, and she fell into oblivion.

56

LONG LIVE THE QUEEN

NARCISSA POUNDED DOWN THE STAIRWELLS toward the antechamber of the Mother's Heart chamber, three sirens in her wake. Her thoughts were bent only on revenge against the one person responsible for all of her misery—Calandra.

She had reached the second-last landing when a rush of hot air came at her from up the stairs. A keening roar filled the column, and for a brief moment, she caught the barest flash of a strange creature's face rushing toward her. It passed into her, and she tasted ash and bitter stone. She whirled to see where it had gone, but saw nothing but the astonished faces of the sirens behind her.

"What is the matter, your highness?"

Narcissa narrowed her eyes. "The queen is dead at Thea's hand. I killed the panacea myself for her crime. Call me *your majesty*."

As she spoke, she was filled with a fire and a confidence she had never experienced before. These women would obey, because they should.

"But Adonia named Calandra heir . . ." the first one said.

"If it weren't for Calandra, Adonia would still be alive. She is a criminal and a traitor, and she must die. Do any of you deny it?"

All three of them stared at her, frozen.

"Your queen has spoken!" She glared, dagger held ready to strike.

"Yes, your majesty," they said almost in unison, then gave her deep bows and salutes.

"Good. Let's go take care of this."

She turned to descend the stairs and saw Zale running by below, heading down a hallway that led to some little-used rooms under the west wing of the palace.

"Where are you going in such a hurry, cousin?"

He stopped at her words. She descended several steps so she stood directly above where he craned to see her. He glowed slightly to her eyes, just like he had when she'd attacked him in the Heartstone. *Wait, what?*

"Narcissa, isn't it?" Zale fidgeted, backing away to stand at the far edge of the hall. He eyed her and the sirens with her, two of which continued down the stairs.

"It's *your majesty* now." She held up a hand to arrest the progress of her sirens, and they froze at the base of the stairs in uncertainty. "But you may call me Narcissa, since we're cousins, and soon to be more."

He frowned at that.

"Where is your sister?" she asked before he could speak.

His shoulders slumped. "She's dead. I killed her."

Narcissa, taken aback, reached out with spirit. *Since when have I been able to do that?* The thought faded away to nothing as soon as it had come.

"Yes, I can feel the truth of it in your heart. You have a strong, powerful spirit, Zale, yet you fear the darkness in you that gives you your strength. What you have done needed to be done. Your sister would have destroyed this kingdom, all in the name of trying to save it. She didn't know what she was doing."

"And you do?"

She descended the last several steps and slowly walked toward him. He backed into the wall and glanced down the hallway into the darkness behind him.

"Of course I do. I have been raised to take the throne." She smiled. "You need not fear me," she said. "I can help you learn to control your powers."

I can?

"You can?" He blinked at her. "That's what Calandra said, too, and now she's dead."

The doubt faded to certainty in a blink, as though there had never been a moment where she could not. She lifted her hand, palm-up, and a small ball of light appeared above it. It danced and twisted into the shape of an undine boy. He was swimming. Then the light show disappeared in a spray of glowing red sparks.

"I can. Trust me, you will not kill me so easily."

The sirens and Zale were all staring at her now. She smiled at him, curling her hand into a fist, then held her other hand out toward him.

He edged backward another step.

"How do I know you won't do that mind-slavery thingy to me?"

She cocked her head. "Never fear about that. The Age of Redemption has past. From now on, the Age of Revelation begins. And you can only learn what you need to know while your mind is free."

He still looked skeptical, and the glow that surrounded him brightened. Curse the Shield of Elyon he bore! She would have to use all her cunning to convince him to choose her way.

"Look, you can run down that hallway, but there is nothing down there but darkness and rats. It's not a good long-term solution. Or you can trust me and learn how to use powers that will let you rule the world at my side."

"I don't want to rule the world. I just want to stop killing people."

She smirked. "Okay, we'll start with that, if you insist."

"Will you help me find my mother, too?"

"Your mother is still alive? Where is she?"

"As far as I know, she is. I've been told she's in Tartarus."

Narcissa frowned. That was ironic, though she didn't know why.

"Absolutely. I'll help find Aunt Delphine, too."

He took a hesitant step forward, holding out his hand. She took it and smiled, attaching one tiny golden thread of spirit to his soul.

"See? I'm not so bad."

His eyes widened. "What's wrong with your eyes?"

"What do you mean?"

He squinted, then shook his head. "No, nothing. I thought they changed colour, but I was wrong."

She laughed. "The light down here can play tricks. Now, show me where you left Calandra."

Hand in hand, he led her back the way he'd come.

But when they reached the antechamber, it was empty.

*

CALANDRA pressed her mouth to Gerrick's, giving him another breath. They were so deep in the water of the Mother's Heart chamber, the light of the column above looked like a faraway window and her hair floated in the current of water flowing in from the ocean through the grates. She held him close to her, though the air she gave him tugged his body upward.

She'd woken up on the floor of the antechamber with Gerrick's worried face above her, his hand patting her cheek. She'd heard her cousin storming down the stairs and talking to Zale. She had tried to rise to protect him, but absolutely all of her power and energy had been drained from her.

She'd barely mustered the strength to grab Gerrick and roll them both back into the water, letting them sink like stones until they hit the bottom. She hoped they were deep enough that the water would obscure both their form and their spirits from those above.

It must have worked. Far above, she sensed Narcissa and the sirens leaving with Zale. As far as she could tell, he was unbonded, which was good. Perhaps Narcissa saw value in keeping him alive and free, despite the death wish she'd announced for Calandra herself.

When she was certain it was safe, she brought them to the surface. She changed state and they clambered out. Gerrick had to help her climb into the chamber, and then, as she lay on the cold stone floor, he draped her ceremonial tunic over her, working the belt beneath her to gather it to her body. He helped her to her feet, then draped her arm across his thin shoulders. Together, they limped toward the crystal cavern.

When they arrived, Nick rushed over to help Gerrick, her good eye roving the hall behind them.

"Where are the others?" Nick asked, assisting Calandra into the submersible.

"Tanni's dead," she said, choking on a sob. "Thea went to draw off Adonia."

"She's dead, too." The pain in Gerrick's voice cut Calandra to the soul. "I felt it the moment Thea died."

Calandra nodded, wondering what personal hell a consort bond severed by death would be, but the thought didn't diminish the vacuum in her own heart one iota. She was so empty and tired.

"We'll have to come back for Zale. I believe he will remain unharmed until we do. I haven't the strength to return for him now." She settled herself onto the red silk seat of the cabin.

"And the Heartstone?"

Calandra shrugged helplessly, and Gerrick gave Nick a look of uncertainty. She had broken Damon's hold on her, of that she was certain. But as far as the Heartstone—

"I don't even know."

Nick gave a terse nod. "We'll find out. We still have supporters in the palace."

She turned to leave the cabin so they could depart. They were to meet with Judith, Ignatia, and the others at a secret cavern the rebels had been using for years several miles up the coast.

"Nick?" Calandra called after her.

The skipper turned and acknowledged her with her good eye, waiting.

"Is it possible to—to hail Zoe and call her back?"

Nick cocked her eyebrow. "After all you went through to set that boy free, you're having second thoughts?"

Calandra swallowed. Yes, her method and her reasons for sending Osaze away might have been flawed. But with her plans in disarray, he would be far safer among humans than he was here with her. And he deserved a chance at a happy life, learning the ways of his own people. Her loss of Tanni and Thea didn't change that.

Shouldn't he get to decide that for himself?

She recognized the voice. Not Damon's, nor her controlling dark side. It was the Spirit of the Heartstone that spoke.

She turned to Nick. "Yes, I am. Please hail Zoe's sub. I have an apology to make."

Nick shrugged. "Suit yourself. I'll patch it back here."

She headed toward the cockpit.

Calandra and Gerrick waited together on the silk bench. The seconds dragged like hours. After what she had done to Osaze, he might not even want to talk to her, let alone come back.

After an eternity had passed, Nick's tinny voice came through the communication stone.

"I can't raise her. Maybe there's something wrong with the comms on that old tub they're in."

Calandra's throat closed. She couldn't let Osaze leave without telling him how sorry she was, and how wrong she had been. She had to see him again and beg for his forgiveness. And what if he weren't safe after all? Humans could still be dangerous creatures, and he'd never known what it was like to . . .

Unexpectedly, a sense of peace washed over her, calming her frantic heartbeat. The presence of the Spirit with whom she had so recently communed in the Heartstone settled on her heart. *I will never leave you . . .*

She closed her eyes and drew in a deep breath. She couldn't control this. She couldn't change it. She had to let it go. If she were ever going to see Osaze again, it would not be this day.

She opened her eyes. "Thank you for trying, Nick. We'd best be going."

"I'm good with that," said Nick. There was a click, and the stone ceased humming.

Gerrick gave her hand a squeeze and nodded in understanding, then put his arm around her shoulders and pulled her to him. Hugging him felt strange at first, but she soon relaxed. Why shouldn't Gerrick hug her? Human fathers probably hugged their children all the time. And he was the only father she'd ever known.

The motion and increased cabin pressure told Calandra that the vessel had submerged and was making its way through the underwater tunnels to open sea. She looked across at the empty seats, the ones she'd hoped would be filled with Thea, Tanni, and Zale.

"This isn't over yet. Somehow, I've got to make this right."

Gerrick nodded. "Yes, child. But first, rest." His voice trembled only a little.

She laid her head on his shoulder and grasped his hand. He laid his cheek on her hair. They comforted each other in silence, surrounded by the succor of a Spirit she could not see and did not yet understand—but trusted.

*

THE antique submersible rose to just below surface level, only the glass cockpit breaking the surface.

Osaze stood next to Zoe with his fists clenched so tightly on the edge of the console that his knuckles were white, staring at the sandy beach before them. Giant moss-covered boulders protruded out into the shallow, rough water, and the sand rolled up to grassy hills hosting stands of palm trees silhouetted against the setting sun. His mother stood behind them in hurt silence, stung by the words he'd just said.

He'd woken up only minutes before, and knew his reaction had been harsh. His mother had always been attached to the country of her birth, which was understandable. And, when he had been in her household, the importance of family and tribe had been emphasized over and over.

But Calandra was his family now, and Sirenia was his country. Why couldn't she see that?

And why hadn't Calandra seen it either?

"It looks different than I remember," Urbi said, breaking the silence. "I asked you to take us to Lagos. How far is that from here?"

Zoe twisted her hand on the navstone and the submersible rose another six inches, water streaming from the deck before them, then eased it up to some low boulders in the water about twenty paces from shore.

"About four thousand miles," she said, adjusting some controls.

"What?" Osaze snapped his gaze toward her, but her smirk had no hint of joking in it. "Where are we?"

Zoe cut the engine, powered down the console, and turned to face her passengers.

"Barbados. I don't care what Calandra wants, I'm not wasting the time and resources to return an Unredeemed man and human woman all the way to Africa. Did you seriously think we could go that far in only a few hours?"

Urbi's eyes widened. "Barbados! We can't stay here. Do you know what they do to our people here? I'd rather return to Sirenia."

Zoe pulled out an odd, gun-shaped weapon of copper with a red crystal at the business end and pointed it at them.

"Whoa!" Osaze put up his hands, and so did his mother. "What's going on, Zoe? What is that thing?"

Zoe glanced at the weapon.

"Oh, you like this? A little souvenir I picked up in Atlantis. Seems our ancestors weren't all about peace and books. And I've tested it. Trust me, you don't want me to have to give you a demonstration of what it can do. Now get up there."

She used the weapon to gesture up the hatch ladder.

Urbi began to ascend, her satchel over her shoulder, then stopped and turned her troubled gaze on Zoe.

"Why are you doing this? We have done nothing to you."

"Because Calandra has broken the cardinal rule that no human leaves Sirenia. Because no one on Barbados will believe you if you tell them of an island of 'merfolk' practically on their doorstep. And because the real threat to our island isn't inequality. It's the instability that her way of thinking would bring."

She pointed at Osaze, who had now reached the top of the ladder.

"Without you there to confuse and defend her, I have a feeling me and Ricardo here"—she tapped the weapon—"will have a much easier time taking her down."

"What? No!"

Osaze dropped down from the ladder, intending to snap the weapon from her hand and overpower her, but she fired. He landed on top of her in a paralyzed, quivering mass, every nerve in his body on fire, unable to control his own muscles. Somewhere above him, his mother screamed.

"Don't say I didn't warn you. Ricardo's got quite a bite."

Zoe rolled him off of her, then, keeping the weapon trained on him, she reached over with her other hand and pulled out his songstoppers.

"I'll take these."

She began to sing, and with nothing to block the effects, his mind soon slipped into soft, dreamy acceptance.

When he snapped out of it, he and his mother were clinging to a slippery boulder, watching the sub sink beneath the waves. A few minutes later, they waded onto the beach. On the crest of a distant hill surrounded by palms was a large, sprawling house. Osaze eyed it warily.

Urbi did, too, then turned to her son, covering her face with her hands.

"I am sorry, my son. I thought I was doing what was best for you. I never imagined that a daughter of Yemaya would betray us."

He scanned the darkening beach. The place inside him where he used to feel Calandra throbbed with a dull ache. He wasn't sure he could ever forgive her for sending him away, not like that.

"I know you meant well, Mother. But I think you have learned too much from your time among the undines."

He stalked toward her and regarded her through narrowed eyes, clenching his hands around her upper arms.

"Hear this. You are never to make a decision for me, ever again. I will no longer be *doulos* for anyone—not Adonia, not Narcissa, not Calandra, and not you. Is that clear?"

She stared at him with wide fearful eyes, then nodded.

"Yes, son."

He released her, then stalked away, barely caring if she followed.

He regretted his harsh words, though he'd meant what he said. His anger sprouted from the question that loomed before him now.

If he wasn't a *doulos*, a *tapeinos*, or a consort-elect—then what was he?

EPILOGUE

Voices roused Robert from unconsciousness. His head throbbed as though he had been trampled by a horse. He blinked to focus his vision, trying to remember where he was and how he got here.

I was on the Atlanta. *But I'm not now.*

The lack of pitching and rolling confirmed he was firmly on land, though he couldn't shake the sensation of movement—something that often happened to him after first returning to shore.

But what shore?

The babble of the voices solidified into coherent words, but they were speaking a language he did not understand. It sounded like Miss Bethel and Mr. Berian, but when he turned toward the source, what he saw made him gawk, then slam his eyes shut tight.

I did not see a lion and a bull talking. I couldn't have. No sane person sees such things.

No sane person tries to take their own life either. He saw the knife in a searing flash of memory. And the reason for it.

I am a failure and a fraud. Perhaps it would be better if I had gone insane.

"He's awake," said Miss Bethel.

Her cool hand touched his skin, and he cracked his eyes open. Gone was the frightening vision of animals, and in its stead were Miss Bethel and Mr. Berian, one as lovely as the other was repugnant.

He was in a small brick room with a thatch roof. A fresh ocean breeze and bright sunlight came in through the open window, and the squawks of sea birds and people going about their lives drifted in from outside. Next to him on a lashed-bamboo table sat his pocket watch, the one Gryffyn had given him.

"How are you feeling?" she asked.

"My head hurts," he said, propping himself up on his elbows. Pain rushed through his head and he put one hand on his forehead to steady it. "Where are we? How did we get here?"

"The ship was attacked, I'm afraid," said Berian. "The entire vessel and its cargo was taken. You were knocked unconscious in the fray. Miss Bethel and I were able to help you escape, and now we are in a hotel in Bridge-town, Barbados."

He slumped back against the soft pillows, his thoughts spinning. All those people. All that money, lost. More burdens to add to his load.

"And what of Mr. Teague?"

He looked back and forth between the two, the only people in the world he'd ever met who had golden eyes.

"He was also taken," Miss Bethel said. "Now that you are awake, we will help you find a ship back to England so we may go find him."

Robert shook his head. "No. I can't go back to England." Not like this. Not in shame, with his tail tucked between his legs. He saw his closed pocket watch on the nightstand and swallowed. "I'll help you search."

Miss Bethel seemed about to object, but Mr. Berian gestured her to the far side of the room. After a whispered consultation, they came back.

"As you wish, Mr. Cox," Berian said. "We would appreciate any help you can give, especially if you recognize any of your brother's . . . associates."

"Now rest." Miss Bethel smiled and gave his hand a squeeze. "We have much we can do from here while you recover."

Robert nodded, staring up at the palm thatch ceiling and beams.

"Rest. Quite."

He faded off to sleep.

*

ERIC knelt with his face to the floor. His black hood fell around his face and obscured his surroundings. Before him, Josefine's large polished black mirror sat propped against the wall of his and Josefine's room in Saint Michael's Inn. He had not overlooked the irony of the name. Beside him, Josefine cowered in similar obeisance, their knees pressed to the unfinished hardwood floor.

"What newssss have you for me?"

The sound of the slithery voice chased shivers up and down Eric's spine, as always. He dared another glance up at the Master in the mirror. Flickering flames lit the red-gold dragon face. One baleful red eye met

Eric's. He ducked his head again and spoke into the floorboards.

"The *Atlanta* has not yet arrived, but the finder reports that Mr. Robert Cox has. We have not yet discovered whether Zale—er, the undine lad—is with him, but we are keeping watch on the place."

"That isss the bessst you can do?"

The Master's presence seemed to fill the room with heat.

"N—no, Master. We have noticed two other people, a man and a woman, who frequently come and go from the place where Mr. Cox is staying—but they don't register on the finder at all."

There was a pause, and when Eric peeked up again, the Master looked thoughtful.

"Be ssssure not to let yoursself be ssseen by these two. Report back as soon as you find the boy. He cannot hide forever. Underssstood?"

"Yes, Master," Eric and Josefine said in unison.

The mirror returned to plain black obsidian stone, and he and Josefine sat up. Sweat trickled down Eric's temples, and it was not from the tropical heat.

Josefine flipped open a device that looked like a pocket watch and gazed into it. She shook her head.

"Still nothing. What should we do next?"

He stood and brushed off the knees of his breeches, admiring again the well-appointed room they had hired to lodge in.

Every time he had to submit before that creature, it rankled, but what the creature offered was far too tempting—and the cost of disobedience far too permanent—to do otherwise.

That didn't mean he didn't occasionally keep some information back. The Master offered eternal life. His other employer offered him comfort in this life—for him and his people.

"We write to Gryffyn Cox that we found the island he was looking for, and the barrier no longer holds. We found Sirenia."

Josefine smiled, snapping the Dragon's Eye closed.

DEAR READER,

Thank you so much for reading *The Undine's Tear.*

If you want more, I have good news—I have written a prequel novella about Zale called *The Waterboy*, which is available in stores in eBook or audiobook format or as a free eBook to members of my newsletter. If you would like to find out exactly how Zale came to be living with the Roma, sign up here: www.talenawinters.com/utfreebie. If you stick around, you'll get a monthly dose of Books & Inspiration as well as updates about upcoming releases and deals. Rise of the Grigori Book 2, *The Sphinx's Heart*, will be out in early 2021.

I got the idea for this world in 2010 while binge-watching a mermaid show. (Mermaids have been my favourite fantasy creatures since I was six.) Where are all the mermen? I wondered. That question gave me the seed of the idea for a book that I wanted to read—but to do that, I knew I'd have to write it. Which meant I'd have to learn to write fiction. Nine years, a long learning curve, a *lot* of research, and three novels later, I finally sent this idea out into the world. I hope you enjoyed it completely.

Can you do me a favour? If you read a free or pirated copy of this book and you enjoyed it, please consider purchasing a copy or, at the least, leaving a review. As an independent author, I pour vast amounts of time, love, and money into producing a quality product meant to bless and inspire my readers. The income I receive from this work allows me to help feed my family and produce even more work for you to enjoy. Thank you for being an important part of the free market for published works.

Word-of-mouth is an indie author's bread and butter, so please remember to review this book on the selling platform of your choice. (Just a single sentence makes a difference!)

Do you want to extend the story experience? There are bonuses meant to accompany *The Undine's Tear* on my website, including a curated soundtrack playlist inspired by the story. Check it out at www.talenawinters.com/undines-tear.

I love hearing from my readers! Drop me a note at www.talenawinters.com/contact. Also, find me on Instagram, Facebook, or Twitter. I'd love to get to know you!

Until next time,

Talena Winters

About The Waterboy

A Rise of the Grigori prequel story

Where can you hide from yourself?

Zale Teague grew up thinking he was an ordinary boy . . . until the day he called lightning from the skies and caused an explosion with horrific results. Now, at only eleven, he is on the run to protect his loved ones from disaster. But can he ever outrun the demon within?

Learn more and download the ebook for free when you join my newsletter community: www.talenawinters.com/utfreebie

About The Sphinx's Heart

Rise of the Grigori Book 2

Mistakes have consequences. This one could unleash hell on Earth.

As the most powerful undine healer in three thousand years, Calandra was supposed to be the saviour of her people. Instead, the malicious dragon spirit who haunted her dreams has been freed from the Abyss, her island has been exposed to the dangerous human world, and the peaceful society of Sirenia has been plunged into revolutionary chaos. Worse, though Calandra knows why she is going insane, she doesn't know how to stop it.

Zale thought he'd finally feel at home among the undines, but that was before he was imprisoned by them. Everyone expects him to help save the world—but how can he do that when he can barely control his own frightening powers? With his sister and sphinx guardian nowhere to be found, he doesn't know whom to trust. He knows one thing, though—he must rescue his mother from her prison in Tartarus, even if he has to do it alone.

Meanwhile, when new information about her people's past is discovered in Atlantis, the path to redemption leads Calandra through the very gates of hell. With the threat of Madness growing ever stronger, can Calandra find a way to undo a mistake that has plagued her people for millennia . . . before the entire world pays the price?

Learn more at www.talenawinters.com/sphinxs-heart.

GLOSSARY

Abela (uh-BAY-luh) - lumasi woman guarding Zale.

Abyss - a place of eternal confinement for undines and lumasi where their powers are negated.

Adonia (uh-DOE-nee-uh) - queen of Sirenia; Calandra's guardian.

Amelia Cox - Gryffyn Cox's wife, daughter of Mr. Albright, Mayor of Bristol, England.

archon (ARK-un) - a leader, either of a community or an elected councillor that represents a community in the Royal Council of Archons.

archpiper (ARK-pie-pur) - the third rank of siren officer. Usually oversees a city or several country precincts.

Atargatis (ah-ter-GAY-tis) - the goddess worshipped by the Sirenians; the first mermaid.

Atargasian (ah-ter-GAY-zhen) - an undine of the same race and form as Atargatis; undines that worship Atargatis as the First Mother.

Atlantis - an island in the Atlantic ocean destroyed by Nadia, queen of the Atargasian undines, when the Madness took her three thousand years ago; sister island to Sirenia.

Berian, Jowan (BEH-ree-in, JOW-in) - lumasi undercover as a Methodist minister.

bondmistress - a woman who holds the *sklavia* (Redemption) bond of at least one man. See also *kyria, Mistress of Bonds*.

Cain - a Redeemed man (*doulos*) and Adonia's lover.

Calandra (cuh-LAN-druh) - a panacea and the niece of Adonia, queen of Sirenia.

Captain William Meredith - captain of the ship *Atlanta*.

chariot - a lumasi gyroscope device used for teleportation.

Cleo - rank: Despoina. Head of the Atargasian military. Second in authority only to Queen Adonia and the Royal Council of Archons.

Crow - first mate of the *Atlanta*.

Damon - Atargasian undine male that appears to Calandra in her dreams.

daskala (DAH-skuh-luh) - teacher. Masculine: *daskalos*.

datastone - a crystal used to store information; must be created or modified by a stone healer; requires a special quartz reader to be accessed; usually shaped like a teardrop. Sometimes called a memory stone.

deiktis (DEEK-teez), plural *deiktes* (DEEK-tez) - the staff weapon used by siren soldiers; means "pointers".

Delphine kor'Helena (del-FEEN kohr hee-LEHN-uh) - Calandra's mother, Adonia's sister; fled Sirenia when Calandra was only one year old.

despoina (DEZ-pee-nah) - head of the military; answers only to the queen and Royal Council of Archons; highest rank of siren.

Domingo - Portuguese human bodyguard at the Opal Palace.

Dorothea - the royal tailor.

Doris - the physic of Fire Lake.

doulos (DOO-lohs), plural *douloi* (DOO-loy) - a man who has been Redeemed with the *sklavia* bond.

EK - the undine calendar, short for "*étos kataclysmos*", or "years since the deluge."

Elpida (AYL-pee-duh) - The name of Calandra's family property. Means "hope" in Greek.

Eric Chapman - Romani man who took Zale in as a child.

Ezekiel - Ignatia's son.

Gerrick - Thea's consort.

Haven - the town on the northeast tip of Sirenia that houses the trade academy; centre of arts and trades.

healer - an undine capable of working with one or more elements to repair stones, plants, and/or animals.

Heartstone (HART-stohn) - the quartz-encased fire opal that powers the barrier protecting Sirenia.

Holy Triquetra - a triquetra with a circle joining the three pisces shapes in an outer ring. Usually depicted with a single point on the top and two other points as the "feet". The undines use the symbol to represent Atargatis, the elements, their two states, the three spheres (land, sea, sky), and more.

Hypatia kor'Fotini (high-PAY-shee-uh kor foh-TEE-nee) - Royal

Council member for Trinity, a small fishing and mining community on Sirenia's northwest side.

ichthys **state** (IK-thiss) - the undine form that has a scaled, fish-like tail and gills.

Ignatia - (ig-NAY-shee-uh) - Rhea's sister. Resident of Elpida.

Iris - Royal Council member for Fire Lake.

Jacob - Ignatia's husband.

Josefine Chapman - Eric's adult daughter and right-hand woman.

Judith - Calandra's undine lady's maid.

Kenver Teague - Zale's and Calandra's father, Delphine kor'Helena's consort/husband.

kyrios (KEE-ree-ohs) - master.

kyria (KEE-ree-uh) - 1. mistress; 2. woman who owns or traffics human men. 3. a correct form of address from a *doulos* to his mistress. See also *bondmistress, Mistress of Bonds.*

Lida - head of the Siren House of the Royal Academy; in charge of student discipline.

lumasi (loo-MAH-see) - a race of spirits that can take the form of humans or winged animals; guardians of people and holy places.

lyrista (lee-REE-stuh) - the fourth rank of siren officer. In charge of a county. There are three lyristas on Sirenia.

Madness - the insanity that takes nearly all powerful healers eventually; the cause is unknown.

Margaret - for many years, the Opal Palace's Mistress of Bonds.

Mari kor'Ana (MAA-ree kor-AAN-uh) - siren cadet; Narcissa's friend.

Megara kor'Sibylle - stone healer acolyte; Thea's great-niece.

Melany - first-year novice at the Royal Academy.

Mistress of Bonds - 1. a woman in charge of holding the Redemption Bonds of unmarried men in a given community or organization. 2. A woman who deals in trafficking human men. See also *bondmistress, kyria.*

mindover - a lumasi medical device.

Nadia kor'Hera (NAH-dee-uh kohr HEE-ruh) - a queen of the Atargasians that ruled three thousand years ago; an extremely powerful healer, the first panacea to go insane, which resulted in the sinking of Atlantis.

Narcissa kor'Adonia (nar-SISS-uh) - princess of Sirenia, Adonia's oldest daughter.

Néa Selini - new moon. Marks the first day of the month.

Olympia - Archaulos of Sireniapolis.

Opal Palace - home of the government and royal family of Sirenia; also houses the Royal Academy. Located in Sireniapolis.

Osaze (ow-SAA-zeh) - Yoruba boy raised in the Opal Palace; Urbi's son.

panacea (PAH-nuh-SEE-uh) - a healer in all three disciplines of stone healing, plant healing, and physic.

panselinos (pan-SAY-lee-nohs) - full moon.

Panselinos (pan-SAY-lee-nohs) - the monthly festival celebrating the full moon.

Paradise Valley - the large, south-facing valley on Sirenia that is the location of Sireniapolis, the island's capital.

physic - an undine healer able to repair animal tissue.

piper - the second rank of siren officer. Usually in charge of a division of a city or one precinct. In villages, this my be the highest local military authority or law enforcer.

pisti **bond** (PEE-stee) - the loyalty bond; does not fade over time; creates an empathic connection between the parties involved.

plant healer - an undine healer able to repair and assist plant growth.

podia **state** (POH-dee-uh) - the undine form with human legs.

quaternaria (kwat-ur-NAHR-ee-uh) - the symbol formed at the centre of four overlapping circles (four conjoined pisces, or *ichthys* fish), joined by a fifth circle woven between the other lines.

rhapsodist - the lowest rank of siren officer. Usually oversees a group of twelve singers.

Rhea - the steward of Calandra's family property, Elpida.

Romea - siren singer, often on night watch at the Sireniapolis Harbour Physic House.

Royal Academy - the school for undines that show talent with Song and the elements. Entered at age six, specialized at age 12; usually graduated as a siren or a healer at age 17 or 18; located in the Opal Palace in Sireniapolis.

Royal Council of Archons - the civil council that serves as advisers to the queen, elected from among the people.

Shinara - High Priestess of Atargatis, serves in the temple in Sireniapolis.

singer - the lowest rank of undine soldier.

siren - an undine soldier, general name of the Sirenian military members; must be strong in the spirit element, but often has little ability with the other elements.

Sirenia - an island somewhere in the Bermuda Triangle; home of the Atargasian undines.

Sireniapolis - the capital city of Sirenia.

sirensong - the type of undine Song used to stun men to subdue them. The effect wears off as soon as the Song stops being sung.

***sklavia* bond** - the slave-bond known as "Redemption" which undine females are able to impose on any male.

stone healer - an undine healer able to repair and write datastones and crystals.

***syzagos* bond** - the consort bond.

Tanni kor'Zelia (TAH-nee kor ZEEL-yuh) - a siren, Calandra's best friend.

tapeinos (tah-pay-NOS) - the lowest rank of law enforcement, used for humans trained as guards. Slang term "*taps*".

Tasia - noble undine, friend of Adonia.

Tear - can be used to refer to any number of different types of stones and crystals used for storing data or communicating; shaped like a teardrop; often made from opal, aquamarine, or beryl.

The Grotto - the nickname for the Garden of the Mother's Delight, the garden housing the statue of Atargatis in the public-access portion of the Opal Palace.

The Mother's Heart - the chamber of the Royal Palace housing the Heartstone.

Thea kor'Aglaia (THEE-uh kor uh-GLIGH-uh) - head of the Healing House of the Royal Academy and also the academy's headmistress; Councillor; the only living panacea besides Calandra; Calandra's mentor and foster mother.

Tropos Hydor Zon (TROH-pos HEE-dor TZOHN) - the Way of Living Water, the name of the martial art practised by the undines. Sometimes shortened to *Tropos*.

tsiraki (tsee-RAH-kee) - student.

Trinity - a fishing and mining town on the northwest side of Sirenia.

triquetra (trigh-KET-ruh) - the symbol formed at the centre of three overlapping circles. The shape, if drawn with a single line, looks like three conjoined pisces, or *ichthys* fish. *See also HOLY TRIQUETRA.*

undine (UN-deen or un-DEEN) - an elemental water being, of which there are several races, such as Atargasians (merfolk), tritons, nixies, naiads, silkies, and more.

Urbi (UR-bee) - Yoruba governess at the Royal Palace of Sirenia; Osaze's mother.

Xeni - Rhea's adult daughter; a physic who lives at Elpida.

Zale Teague - merman raised in England.

Zoe kor'Dione (ZOH-ee kor dee-OH-nee) - a siren singer who goes to Fire Lake.

ACKNOWLEDGEMENTS

I would like to thank my Redeemer, Jesus Christ. He is the centre of my story.

Thank you also to my secret writing weapon, my husband, Jason. Your ability to triage story problems never ceases to amaze me and almost always gets me unstuck. Without you, this book may never have been completed.

Thank you to my sons for inspiring me, my mother for encouraging me (and for reading absolutely every version of this story), and my fans who have asked me to keep writing.

To my beta readers, thank you for helping me see the problems I couldn't, and for not letting me be a lazy writer: Virginia Janes, Jessica L. Jackson, Laurel Easton, Katrin Hilman, Melissa Keaster, Candace Marshall, Jabin Winters, and Jason Winters. Thank you to Lora Doncea for your contributions to the manuscript, and to Ceallaigh MacCath-Moran and Terry Leer for giving me quick research answers when I needed them.

Thank you to my editor, Ellen Michelle (ellenmichelle.com), for your gentle encouragement and constructive criticism. Thanks to sensitivity reader Viveca Shearin for your wonderful feedback, and to Denise Willson for reviewing the formatted manuscript. Thank you to my cover designer, Patrick Knowles, for the beautiful cover. And thank you to my son, Jude Winters, for drawing the wonderful map of Sirenia. (Can a fantasy book without a map even call itself a fantasy book?)

I'd also like to thank the many gracious, talented, and supportive authors whom I am privileged to call my friends. There are far too many to name, but without you, this indie author gig would be a much harder row to hoe.

And to you, dear reader. Thank you for entering into the magic with me.

Also by Talena Winters:

Rise of the Grigori Series:
The Waterboy (prequel)
The Sphinx's Heart

Romantic Suspense:
Finding Heaven

Inspirational Romance:
The Friday Night Date Dress

Short fiction:
Up in Smoke
All I Want for Christmas

Talena Winters is addicted to tea, chocolate, books, yarn, and silver linings. She writes page-turning fiction for teens and adults in multiple genres, has written several award-winning songs, designs knitting patterns under her label *My Secret Wish*, and is lead writer for *Move Up* magazine. She currently resides on an acreage in the Peace Country of northern Alberta, Canada, with her husband, three surviving boys, two dogs, and an assortment of farm cats. She would love to be a mermaid when she grows up.

You can find her on the web at www.talenawinters.com.